Praise for [...]
of Rob Thurman

Trick of the Light

"Rob Thurman's new series has all the great elements I've come to expect from this writer: an engaging protagonist, fast-paced adventure, a touch of sensuality, and a surprise twist that'll make you blink."
—*New York Times* bestselling author Charlaine Harris

"*Trick of the Light* is a beautiful wild ride, a story with tremendous heart. A must-read."
—*New York Times* bestselling author Marjorie M. Liu

"The Trickster series is another strong offering from the author of the Cal Leandros books. Thurman is adept at creating fresh characters, and snarky heroine Trixa's first-person exploits in Vegas have distinct details that leave a lasting impression. Fans and new readers will be clamoring for more." —*Romantic Times*

Deathwish

"Suspenseful.... Readers are assured of copious amounts of gut-wrenching action and creepy thrills."
—*Romantic Times*

"The action is fast-paced and exciting, and the plot twists are delicious." —Errant Dreams Reviews

"A solid addition to a suitably dark and gritty urban fantasy series." —Monsters and Critics

continued . . .

"Readers will feel the story line is moving at the speed of light as the Leandros brothers move from one escapade to another adventure without a respite. . . . They make a great team as they battle against overwhelming odds, leaving the audience to root for them to succeed and wait for their next misadventures."

—Alternative Worlds

Madhouse

"Thurman continues to deliver strong tales of dark urban fantasy. . . . Fans of street-level urban fantasy will enjoy this new novel greatly."   —SFRevu

"I think if you love the Winchester boys of *Supernatural*, there's a good chance you will love the Leandros brothers of Thurman's books. . . . One of *Madhouse*'s strengths is Cal's narrative voice, which is never anything less than sardonic. Another strength is the dialogue, which is just as sharp and, depending on your sense of humor, hysterical."   —Dear Author . . .

"A fast-paced and exciting novel . . . fans of urban fantasy will love this series."   —*Affaire de Coeur*

"If you enjoyed the first two wisecracking urban adventures, you won't be disappointed with this one; it has just enough action, angst, sarcasm, mystery, mayhem, and murder to keep you turning the pages to the very end."

—BookSpot Central

Moonshine

"[Cal and Niko] are back and better than ever . . . a fast-paced story full of action."   —SFRevu

"A strong second volume . . . Cal continues to be a wonderful narrator, and his perspective on the world is one of the highlights of this book. . . . The plotting is tight and fast-paced, and the world-building is top-notch."

—*Romantic Times*

Nightlife

"A roaring roller coaster of a read . . . [it'll] take your breath away. Supernatural highs and lows, and a hell of a lean over at the corners. Sharp and sardonic, mischievous and mysterious. . . . The truth is Out There, and it's not very pretty."

—Simon R. Green

"A strong first novel."

—SFRevu

"Cal's a sarcastic, sardonic narrator who pulls the reader into his world, both the good and the bad. Tightly plotted and fast-paced . . . full of twists and turns."

—*Romantic Times*

"A subtly warped world compellingly built by Thurman. . . . This book has an absolutely marvelous voice in Cal's first-person narrative. The combination of Chandleresque detective dialogue and a lyrically noir style of description are stunningly original."

—The Green Man Review

"A damn fine book, and excellent first effort."

—Rambles

"Gripping, fast-paced fantasy."

—Fresh Fiction

"Engaging . . . the characters are well drawn and memorable."

—Italics

ALSO BY ROB THURMAN

Roadkill

A Cal Leandros Novel

Rob Thurman

A ROC BOOK

ROC

Published by New American Library, a division of
Penguin Group (USA) Inc., 375 Hudson Street,
New York, New York 10014, USA
Penguin Group (Canada), 90 Eglinton Avenue East, Suite 700, Toronto,
Ontario M4P 2Y3, Canada (a division of Pearson Penguin Canada Inc.)
Penguin Books Ltd., 80 Strand, London WC2R 0RL, England
Penguin Ireland, 25 St. Stephen's Green, Dublin 2,
Ireland (a division of Penguin Books Ltd.)
Penguin Group (Australia), 250 Camberwell Road, Camberwell, Victoria 3124,
Australia (a division of Pearson Australia Group Pty. Ltd.)
Penguin Books India Pvt. Ltd., 11 Community Centre, Panchsheel Park,
New Delhi - 110 017, India
Penguin Group (NZ), 67 Apollo Drive, Rosedale, North Shore 0632,
New Zealand (a division of Pearson New Zealand Ltd.)
Penguin Books (South Africa) (Pty.) Ltd., 24 Sturdee Avenue,
Rosebank, Johannesburg 2196, South Africa

Penguin Books Ltd., Registered Offices:
80 Strand, London WC2R 0RL, England

First published by Roc, an imprint of New American Library,
a division of Penguin Group (USA) Inc.

First printing, March 2010
10 9 8 7 6 5 4 3 2 1

To my fans, amazing one and all.
And to Cal, Niko, Robin, and the gang. It's about damn
time you had a vacation. *Road trip!*

ACKNOWLEDGMENTS

To my mom, who suggested I give my old dream of writing a go. If I become a victim of artistic Darwinism, I blame her. Also to Lisa Powell, DVM, for her invaluable assistance in canine diseases versus lycanthrope diseases and for her wonderful treatment of my own pack all these years; to Shannon—best friend, designated driver for SDCC, and *undesignated* photographer of a night that would live in infamy . . . if I could remember it; to my patient editor, Anne Sowards; to the infallible Cam Dufty, whom I miss still; to Brian McKay (ninja of the dark craft of copywriting); to Agent Jeff Thurman of the FBI for the usual weapons advice; to the incomparable art and design team of Chris McGrath (an art *god*) and Ray Lundgren; Lucienne Diver, who astounds me in the best possible way at every turn; great and lasting friends Michael and Sara; and to Mara—keep those books coming. And last but never least, to Tasha—you made my life a living hell, and it was worth every minute of it. I will miss you always.

"The wolf also shall dwell with the lamb, and the leopard shall lie down with the kid; and the calf and the young lion and the fatted calf together; and a little child shall lead them."

—Isaiah 11:6

"Bullshit."

—The Wolf

1

Cal

I'd died six months ago.

Sounds dramatic, doesn't it? I'd died.

Only I hadn't, not really.

I'd lain spread-eagle in our apartment in a pool of blood that no amount of rug cleaner would get out. My eyes were dull and blank as they stared at the ceiling. My gun was still in my hand, but it hadn't done me much good, despite the dead monsters around me. I liked to think I'd taken a few with me.

I hadn't seen it, of course, any of it, but it was what I imagined . . . with a little help of the rug that Niko, my brother, had ripped to shreds with his knife and thrown outside into the hall. And I'd seen my share of dead people, so it helped with the details. Yeah, I pictured it in great if not necessarily accurate detail even though I hadn't actually seen it.

But Niko had.

Six months later and my brother still wouldn't tell me if I was on the money with my description. I think telling me would've made the memory of the hypnosis-induced illusion worse, sharper. I knew it had seemed completely real to him then, and even now, half a year later, I caught him once in a while looking at me as if he couldn't believe I was genuinely there, truly alive.

Too bad having little brothers with half monster genes didn't come with mental health coverage. Pretty goddamn unfair to Niko, all things considered. And with the life we'd lived, those "all things" would make horror movies look like kiddie cartoons. Demon-driven deductibles—they were a bitch.

But since I hadn't died in reality and Niko was faced every morning with half-dried toothpaste in the sink, wet towel on the floor, dirty dishes on the kitchen counters, and a trail of clothes from my bedroom to the bathroom, I think the memory faded bit by bit. And that must've been one helluva relief, because he didn't bitch about my über-slobbiness. He simply washed out the sink, hung up the towel, did the dishes, and tossed my clothes back in my room and closed the door. So a relief for him, but kind of a worry for me, because that wasn't Nik—not in any shape or form.

Niko had raised me from birth. And he'd been on my ass since birth as well. Okay, a bit of an exaggeration, but close enough. Pick up your clothes, do your homework, stop drawing cheat notes on your arm, eat your vegetables, quit trying to make out the porn through the scrambled gray zigzag lines. I was in my twenties now, so it was a little different. Run your five miles in the morning. Spar two hours in the afternoon. Study up on how to kill *F* through *H* in the *Mythological Creature Compendium*. Quit trying to make out the porn through the scrambled gray zigzag lines.

Well, some things never changed. And porn channels were expensive.

Niko had come a long way in those six months, although through all of them he would wake up in the middle of the night and stand in the doorway to my bedroom, making sure it wasn't a dream; making sure I was alive. Not that I'd caught him doing it. I didn't have to. I knew.

The illusion was my brother seeing me dead. The reality was that my brother would've torn the world apart if that illusion had been true.

So I wasn't surprised he stood there night after night. He'd raised me, been with me my entire life. I knew him all right; knew where I would've stood if the reverse had been true. And then one morning I woke up and knew that night he hadn't been in my doorway watching me sleep. How? The same way. I just knew.

And when I walked out into the hall, yawning and stretching to face his frown, that clinched it. "One:"— Niko held up a finger—"Pick up your clothes. I am not your maid. How do I know this? A maid cannot kill you with a tube sock. I can. Two:"—he raised yet another finger—"toothpaste, towel, dishes."

"All that under 'two'?" I muttered, bending to pick up a T-shirt off the floor.

"If I do them separately, we'll be here all day. Some of us have better things to do," he responded. "Three: I've disconnected the cable. You'll eventually get eyestrain, and fighting creatures of the night while wearing Coke-bottle lenses tends to cut down on your aim and agility."

"Not to mention my waves of sheer sexuality." I grinned as I hid my socks probably less casually than I thought under the T-shirt. The sock threat was a familiar one, but it didn't mean I wouldn't end up strangled with one someday.

"Four: Stop making me borderline nauseated with what you imagine to be witty repartee." He stood, dark blond hair pulled back tightly into a braid that hung several inches past his shoulders; it wasn't the waist-length one that he'd once had, but it was slowly getting there. His olive-skinned arms were folded across a gray

T-shirt—not a normal T-shirt of course, but one woven from the wool of the finest assassin-trained sheep, I was sure. Not that Nik was a wolf in sheep's clothing. He was a saber-toothed tiger in sheep's clothing; a T-rex without that whole if-I-don't-move-it-can't-see-me thing. I was half of a creature so malignantly murderous that the entire supernatural world had feared it; yet my brother, who was fully human, could kick my ass ten times out of ten.

All hail Sparta.

"So, no number five?" I asked as I retrieved a pair of wadded-up jeans from the floor.

His eyes, gray, the same color as mine—our whiskey-adoring mother had at least given us that in common—narrowed. "Number five: You've been an absolute pain in the ass for the past six months." The gray lightened and he gave that fleeting quirk of lips that passed for a Niko smile. "Thank you."

In the past, I would've thought to myself that he would've been better off actually mourning me those six months; better off if the illusion had been real, if I had died. But not now. My brutally homicidal relatives were extinct—hopefully—after a lifetime of my running from them. They were gone. No more running. No more fear they would kill everyone I cared for. No more possibility that they would take me from this world again to another and do things to me that would make death seem as bright and happy a prospect as a pony at your sixth birthday party.

The past was gone. Now I had pretty much everything I'd been sure I'd never get. I had two jobs: one working at a bar and one kicking supernatural ass for fun and profit. I had friends. Me. Crowned Mr. Antisocial for at least three-fourths of my life. I was even getting semi-regular sex. Life was as unshitty as it had ever been.

No, not unshitty. In fact, it was *good*. Life was good,

believe it or not. I was a changed man—man-monster hybrid. Whatever. Definitely changed. No longer morose and sullen. Not angry and cynical. No more Prozac Poster Child. That wasn't me anymore. I no longer thought the universe was out to get me. It was all good.

That had been this morning.

"Motherfucker." I kicked the revenant in the ribs. Yeah, it was dead. I kicked it again. And yeah, it was the equivalent of beating a dead horse. I didn't care, because it made me feel better. I couldn't have been more goddamn wrong—the universe *was* out to get me, same as always. I was late to my bar job, I was having to kick supernatural ass *without* getting paid, and I'd probably get heartworms from my werewolf friend with benefits, Delilah.

Speaking of wolves, I kept my Glock pointed at the Wolf on the left and the Desert Eagle at the one in front of me. I couldn't believe I was getting attacked in Central Park . . . even if it was night. That was boggle territory. Okay, revenants were stupid. They might look like humans on the decomposing side, nature's camouflage, and they were about as bright as fifth grade bullies, although as hard to kill as your average cockroach. They were tenacious little suckers. But they were smart enough to steer clear of the boggles. Revenants were a few rungs—hell, half the ladder—down the food chain when compared to boggles.

"Who came up with this bright idea?" I snarled. "Too ghoul for school down there?" I kicked the body again. Not that revenants, or ghouls for that matter, had ever been human despite what mythology said, but it was a good line and I used it. "Or one of you mutts, because I think the Kin would know better about me and my brother by now." As for boggles, a mutt couldn't take one, but he could outrun one.

The Kin were the werewolf version of the Mafia; just insert "butt sniffing" instead of "ring kissing." We'd had our run-ins with them once or twice. On the other hand, we'd hired a few for extra bodyguard help in the past. Then there was my dating one off and on, although that was not common knowledge. Some Alphas might keep the occasional succubus or incubus around for sex slaves, but no one was really good enough to actually date a werewolf, except another werewolf. They were Old Country orthodox that way and since I'd been born half sheep (human) and half Auphe (unclean nightmare from the beginning of time—try fitting that on a name tag), I didn't qualify either way. And as Wolves—again, no matter what the mythology told you—were born, not made, I never would be good enough.

"I mean, you crotch sniffers know who I am, right?" I waggled my Glock at the one on the left. "You. Speak. Arf arf. What the hell do you think you're doing?"

I wasn't vain enough to think every Wolf in the city had my picture with a big heart drawn around it up on his wall. Far from it. In the toilet bowl to piss on, maybe. But while every Wolf might not have known what I looked like, they all knew what I smelled like. Lucky them. It was the rare creature that could pick up the Auphe taint to my scent: dogs, werewolves, and trolls. There wasn't a Wolf in the city who wouldn't know who I was at first smell: the half-Auphe freak.

Humans told their kids about the bogeyman under the bed. It might grab your foot in the middle of the night and say boo. The supernatural told their rugrats about the Auphe. It might grab your foot in the middle of the night, drag you under the bed, disembowel you with one clawed hand, and pluck out your eyes with the other. I might look human, but to a Wolf I smelled like the darkness under the bed.

The bogeyman times a hundred; a monster to monsters.

So attacking me with one revenant and two Wolves? It was a good way to hump your last leg. Although no matter what they thought, that wasn't because of my Auphe genes. Good guns and a pissy attitude were enough for that. I wasn't the monster they smelled in me. Maybe I wasn't all human, but I wasn't a raving maniacal killer either.

Raving was a little too much work.

I tightened my finger on the trigger of the Glock. "I'm not hearing anything. I was in a good mood, too, one with the fucking universe, full of happiness and joy and all that crap, and now you've ruined it. Unless you want to find out how good my aim is by my neutering you, you'd better talk. Now."

He was a high-breed Wolf, no recessive traits at all from what I could spot. No furry ears, no lupine eyes or misshapen jaw with trash compactor teeth. To your average human (blind, deaf, and dumb) that's what he looked like . . . your average human—until he would turn. But he wasn't. He could go from man to beast in a helluva lot less than sixty seconds. It didn't make a difference to me. He could wear all the Abercrombie and Fitch he wanted, do the fake bed hair look, sport those retro preppy glasses. He could spray on a gallon of Axe. The commercials lied. He wasn't being tackled by a crowd of horny women, and I could still smell the Wolf under it.

The Wolf scent was better, trust me. My half-Auphe sense of smell was fairly close to being as good as a wolf's, Were or otherwise. This cologne was not my thing—so much so that as my finger was tightening on the Glock in a threat for info, my sneeze accidentally carried it through to a done deed.

Ouch.

"Goddamnit," I swore. "Sorry about that." Not sorry that I had to shoot him. He had attacked me—he had it coming. I was sorry that I'd shot him in the crotch, though. I had meant that as a bluff. I still would've shot him, but half monster or not, there were things even I wouldn't do if I didn't have to. Head, heart, sure—but in the block and tackle? You really had to work at earning a shot there. I winced in sympathy as he curled on his side, turned to a giant wolf in an instant, and howled his lungs out.

This meant, of course, I had to put his pal down with one to the brain. No partner—no *good* partner—is going to let that happen to his buddy and not do something about it.

He tried. He failed.

Great. Now I was stuck in the park with a dead revenant, a dead Wolf in human form missing a good chunk of his head, and another Wolf screaming for his mommy. That was if you were in the know. Nonhuman. Supernatural. Preternatural. Whatever you wanted to call it.

But for, say, your average cop who heard a screaming wolf and came into the depths of the park as opposed to patrolling the outer edges—to that cop, my little problem would look more like a half-rotted corpse, a freshly dead human, and a mutilated big-ass dog. That was a hat trick that would put me in the running for murderous nutjob perv of the year. Worse yet, the murderous nutjob perv of the year with two unlicensed guns equipped with illegal silencers, a matte black combat knife, three more knives, and a few other surprises hidden away.

One side of my heritage, the human Rom half, told me exactly what to do in a situation like this: run. My experience in the supernatural business world was of the same opinion—but one thing first. I knelt by the Wolf in a tangle of once purposely distressed clothing, now the real deal as claws had shredded it during the change. "I don't suppose you want to tell me why the three of you jumped me, ball-less wonder?"

Foam-flecked jaws and bared teeth were all the answer I needed. "Your choice." I shrugged. "You know they normally charge sixty bucks for neutering. I'm a bargain." I doubted I'd have been in a talking mood in his situation either. I thought of putting him out of his misery, but, hell, he'd brought it on himself. He tried to kill me. Him and that cologne.

What kind of Wolf wore cologne? It was a wonder he wasn't in the throes of a doggy asthma attack. Their sense of smell *was* better than my Auphe one. So why would he . . . shit. There was only one reason a Wolf would coat himself in something that strong. He was trying to cover up the scent of something—or some-*one* else—and hadn't taken the time or had the time to shower. I leaned back, out of the way of his snapping jaw, and took a deeper whiff.

Delilah.

My Wolf with benefits. She'd saved my life at least once in the past. I knew for a fact she'd saved my sanity by giving me that semiregular sex. Delilah was sterile. When you got to be the age of twenty-one, more or less, before you finally found someone you could sleep with and not run the risk of making babies even an Alien-Predator combo couldn't love . . . well, you knew what true friendship was. It didn't mean Delilah wasn't trouble, though. Not that she particularly cared one way or the other. Delilah was Delilah—exotic, erotic, and predatory to her bones. That meant one thing: Delilah looked out for Delilah. Period. And if you couldn't take care of yourself, then that was a damn shame.

For you.

Yeah, my furry fuck buddy. I'd never for a second thought I was her one and only hump day special. I was a lot of things, not all of them good, not all of them especially smart, but gullible? Ever have your mother spit at your feet when you were seven and tell you with drunken venom that there was a Hell, but you were an abomination so horrific that even it didn't want you?

No? Huh. Just me then.

Regardless, that cured gullible pretty damn fast. I knew there was no way Delilah was faithful and true and brimming with Hallmark's warm and fuzzy best: hugging bears and hearts and puffy silver balloons chock-full of Romeo and Juliet–style undying love. Why would she be? Friends with benefits tended to spread those benefits around. I knew if I weren't carrying around sperm potentially toxic to the concept of continued human existence, I might have had my eyes open for the occasional opportunity. But "Hey, great band and are you sterile?" isn't the best pickup line in the world.

So the cologne lover could've been just one of her other "friends." A jealous one—or if he'd found out about what I was, a bigoted one. She had a special spray of her own, lacking the sneeze quality, that covered up my Auphe-tainted scent, but nobody's perfect. She could've forgotten to hose down her den in the abandoned school once or twice. She didn't give a damn who knew about us outside the Kin, but within the Kin she was careful. Delilah had ambition, and screwing around, in all senses of the word, with a half-breed Auphe wouldn't help her at all.

And hanging around here wasn't going to help me either. I'd have the cops after me for grave robbing and murder, and PETA after me for animal abuse.

I'd take the cops any day.

Despite it all, if this did involve her, it didn't matter. I still liked her. Just . . . hell . . . liked her. Because she liked me. She wasn't disgusted by my Auphe half or afraid. To her I was just a guy . . . one with shoulder-length black hair, skin a shade paler than your average human, lots of guns, and a foul mouth—your average New Yorker, in other words. And her treating me that way definitely made her worth liking.

I holstered the guns and ran on into the darkness. I veered off my original path. I had been making up for missing my run this morning. If I didn't, Niko would make me run the five I'd missed, plus five more, and probably run backward ahead of me so he could mock my athletic failures to my face. Even though it wasn't conveniently located to our new SoHo apartment, I'd been running in Central Park as usual because it kept me on my toes.

Some people sparred in the gym boxing ring. Some of us ran through the habitat of a nest of mud-wallowing humanoid alligators on massive steroids. A workout is a workout. But this time I'd already had a different type of workout. And now I was late—later than usual—which was saying something. If I waited around to catch a bus or cab, I'd set a new record.

Bartending didn't pay much; the real money was in the supernatural ass kicking. At least usually, but this was the one bar where I could use the fire axe to take off the head of a drunk and rampaging homicidal lamia before dragging her body to the storage room, and no one would raise an eyebrow. Actually they'd probably be taking bets on who went down first, her or me, and although they knew better, they'd bet on her.

The bar patrons didn't much like me. They didn't like my human half, my pale-skinned Auphe half, or my sarcastic and heavily armed whole. Oddly enough, it didn't much bother me. Maybe it had some at first. But now if you didn't want to like me, I could not like you right back and with an enthusiasm you might not want to see. The job wasn't a bad job, and I wanted to keep it. So I took a shortcut—my shortcut.

There are shortcuts and there are shortcuts.

My kind came courtesy of my Auphe father . . . sperm

donor . . . sire. Whatever you call a thing that pays your mother to breed a bouncing baby interspecies bastard. I don't know if it—he—was disappointed I looked human, but in the end it didn't matter. I had enough Auphe on the inside, but I didn't let it control me— much. I used it.

I just hoped like hell my brother didn't find out.

Taking that shortcut consisted of ripping a hole in reality and stepping through. I called it traveling. Niko called them gates. Whatever you called them, you could cover miles in a split second—the entire country in the same—to another dimension that was the next best thing to Hell if you wanted.

Actually, radioactive Hell now, thanks to Niko, me, and a de rigueur secret society that had access to suit-case nukes instead of secret handshakes. And the Masons thought *they* were hot shit.

The gray light rippled before me in the night—gray, dirty, and wrong, but a tool, and a tool I could control and use. The sight of it even quieted the howling Wolf. "Hearing great things about prosthetics. Check it out," I told him, then stepped through.

Right behind my boss, Ishiah, in the bar's storage room. I don't know if he heard me, saw the light from the corner of his eye, or just sensed it. But his wings sprang out of invisibility into a banner of gold-barred white feathers as he turned and was already swinging a fire axe. We had one mounted in every room—less for fire; more for beheading.

"Whoa, boss. I'm not that late," I said with a grunt as I hit the floor hard to avoid a haircut that would've started about chest level.

"Do not do *that* in this establishment," he snarled. "Do you understand me?"

Ishiah was my boss and he was a good boss, which meant he paid me and hadn't killed me. But he had a temper like Moses seeing the Golden Calf and breaking the Ten Commandments. No, that was more like a temper tantrum. Okay, Ishiah had a temper like God taking out Sodom and Gomorrah for being the Vegas of biblical times and turning Lot's wife into a saltshaker just for wanting a look. Biblical references . . . Niko homeschooled me, and I knew a lot of obscure information when I bothered, which, according to everyone I knew, was rarely. But in this case it wasn't applicable. Ishiah wasn't an angel. There were no angels or demons, no Heaven or Hell. Fairy tales built on myths built on more myths, all built on the first caveman who refused to believe his kid, his brother, his mother, were gone for good. Who knew what the truth really was? Who wanted to know? Not me.

But here's what it wasn't. No angels. Ishiah was a peri, probably where the angel myth began . . . there and with all the Greek gods with wings. After all, the Auphe were where the elf myth had started and if you took away the hundreds of needle-fine metal teeth, the scarlet eyes, the black talons, shredding jaws, nearly transparent skin, and a raging desire to destroy humanity, then I guess you were close enough. The pointed ears were the same, right?

Thank God I hadn't gotten the pointed ears. Who wants to pass as a *Star Trek* or *Lord of the Rings* fan boy for the rest of their natural-born lives?

A slight increase in the weight of the axe on the back of my neck redirected my attention to where it belonged. Peris, per the mythology book that Niko had swatted my head with on regular occasion, were supposedly half angels/half demons or something midway between the two. In other words, I had no idea what Ishiah was. It didn't matter. Mythology was always wrong . . . like the whisper game. You started with one thing and by the time it was passed around the circle, it was something completely different. If you had even a seed of truth in mythology, you were doing damn good. Werewolves and vampires were born, not made, and were not all uncontrollable sex addicts, no matter what the local bookstore's fantasy section might tell you. Puck, Pan, Robin Goodfellow were all one trickster race; all looked exactly alike; were all male; and they *were* all uncontrollable sex addicts. Revenants and ghouls had never been human. I could've gone on, ticking them off in my mind, but the axe blade was getting uncomfortable.

"Got it. No traveling in the bar. I'll make a note." I didn't think he'd really chop my head off, but with Ishiah, you could never be sure. Can't say I blamed him, because you couldn't always be sure about me either . . . especially when I opened gates.

Why did I travel at all then? To avoid being late? Honestly? If it could bring out the worst in me and it wasn't to escape imminent, messy, ugly death, then why did I do it?

Good question.

And no good answer. No answer at all, only the excuse that it *hadn't* brought out the worst in me lately . . . not like before. So why not use it? I had control now, so it wasn't that big of a chance. Not anymore, although getting anyone else to believe it, especially Nik, wasn't something I looked forward to. But my brother wasn't the problem at the moment; it was my boss.

"Can I get up and sling some beer or are you going to cut my head off?" I asked Ish. "Either way, I really need to take a piss. It's been a long day."

He thought about it, then grunted and lifted the axe. "I'm docking you two hours."

It was better than having my head docked. I got to my feet and peeled off my jacket. It was summer in New York, which made it too hot for the leather jacket, but when you wore two guns in shoulder holsters, a cheerful smile wasn't quite camouflage enough—if I could even pull off cheerful, which was doubtful. I didn't need camouflage in the bar. Humans tended to avoid it like the plague—some instinct passed down from caveman ancestors who knew there were monsters in the world and a woolly mammoth wasn't the only thing that could squash you flat. The few random humans who did walk through the front doors were predators themselves— arrogant ones who ignored their instinct because they thought they were the shit and no one was more of a badass than them. Those humans usually didn't leave the bar . . . except in pieces. The bar didn't serve food, but that didn't mean it couldn't be found there once in a while.

I made my way to the bathroom, then out to the bar to toss the jacket under it and grab an apron. "Good crowd tonight," Sammy commented. Samyel was another peri, dark to Ishiah's light blond, with wings barred with gray. "Quiet."

Quiet was good. We didn't get it that often. I leaned on the bar and took in the small crowd. Vampires, lamias (kind of a combo between a vampire and a leech), three incubi, two *vyodanoi* (predatory, rubbery, man-shaped water creatures), but no Wolves. Not a one. While quiet was good, that was not . . . especially on top of what had happened in the park. There were always wolves in the bar.

I fished my cell phone out of my jeans pocket and called Delilah. Modern-day werewolves had modern-day accessories. I got her voice mail. I usually did. She had a busy life, between being a bouncer at a strip club and her Kin work, which could be anything from stealing to fighting rival Kin packs to things I might not want to know about. I had asked if she killed humans. She'd said no—she preferred real prey, real challenge, not bleating sheep. I thought she was telling the truth; she was all about the challenge. But I'd asked her that before I'd killed a few humans myself, so I wasn't sure I was in the position to judge. Mine had been bad men, but wasn't "bad" a matter of who was holding the gun and who was getting shot by it?

I left her a message that someone who smelled an awful lot like her had tried to kill me in the park and I hoped he wasn't a regular hookup, because he had nothing left to hook up with now. I also asked what was up with all the missing Wolves.

Ishiah, wings now gone, came out of the back room with a beer keg and scowled at my making personal calls on my first five minutes of company time. "Two and a half hours," he said.

Normally he would've made it three. I wasn't the only one getting sex. A fire axe to the neck and docking my pay were actually mellow for him. That was the good part. The bad part was he was getting it from a friend, the only one I trusted besides my brother, and this friend and frequent fellow monster killer liked nothing better than to threaten me with the details . . . and that was worse than any axe.

When Robin Goodfellow, a puck, threatened you with sexual details, you didn't need a porn channel and you didn't need *Hustler*; when he claimed to have cowritten the Kama Sutra, you believed his bragging ass. And the last thing I needed was to have my boss see me looking at him and trying damn hard not to picture wings and legs and other things in positions you'd need Silly Putty for bones to achieve. That would make him lose his mellow real fast. Goodfellow would like nothing better than to see his adventures on IMAX, but Ishiah was probably more private.

And my twitching at the mental picture wouldn't liven up the bar any.

I twitched anyway and turned my attention to wiping down the bar. It was clean, but it didn't matter—anything to keep my thoughts from going down that road. I'd done the same twitching when Nik's vampire girlfriend had once had some fun at my expense. There are some things about your family and friends you just don't want to know.

There are also things that *you* don't want *them* to know. Different things maybe, not that it mattered. Niko found out anyway. I didn't know why I tried. He always did. I discovered that this particular time twenty minutes later when my brother walked through the door . . . the only human who came and went at the Ninth Circle and lived not to tell the tale. I looked up the instant I smelled him . . . when I smelled the annoyance on him. More than annoyed, he was completely and totally pissed off. And it took some doing to get my brother pissed off. That didn't mean he'd hesitate in a fight to take the head off a boggle with his sword, but he wouldn't be angry when he did it. A job was a job. No need to bring emotion into that equation.

There was plenty of emotion now.

He walked to the bar, flipped open the phone in his hand, and put it down in front of me. The small screen was open to the GPS tracker connected to my cell. "I thought we had an agreement. You don't gate and I don't beat you within an inch of your life. Wasn't that it?" He leaned closer. "The *agreement*?"

"Shit." I looked down at the phone blinking accusingly.

"I had a friend of mine at the university program it to alarm every time your signal disappears and reappears approximately four seconds or less later." Which wouldn't pick up on the dead zone of the subway. Traveling was a helluva lot quicker than the subway. My brother was smart, probably the smartest guy I'd ever known, but just once couldn't he have taken a little more after me?

"Well? I'm listening. Were you in dire circumstances? Was it make a gate or die? I've always assumed if you escaped near death, you would give me a call afterward. Common courtesy." He leaned farther. My calm and cool-as-ice brother had a temper too. You had to dig for it, had to push him, but it was there and it could rival Ishiah's. Ice to fire, but when it was your butt in a sling, whether it was frozen or singed didn't much matter.

"There were two Wolves and a revenant." I reached over and snapped his phone shut, tired of the betraying beep. "They attacked me in the park. . . ."

"And?"

I wasn't going to lie to my brother. Don't get me wrong; if I could've skipped telling him some things I would've, both to save him the worry and to save me the ass kicking. But lie to his face? He was my brother. No way.

"And I handled it, was late, and traveled to the bar," I admitted.

His eyes narrowed. "Because lateness was life threatening?"

I could've half joked and said that with Ishiah it could be, but that would have been shitty of me. And while I had no problem being shitty with anyone else, I damn sure wasn't going to be shitty with Nik. He was the sole reason I was alive, the sole reason I was sane.

In the face of that, how could I be shitty? How could I lie? I couldn't, not to him. "No, but, hell, Nik, I need to stay in practice. How can I do that if I don't open a gate once in a while? How can I save our lives if I can't do it fast enough or if I start foaming at the mouth and become worse than what we're running from? How do we know if the meditation works if we don't test it?" I fingered the mala bracelet around my wrist as I asked. I'd gotten it from Nik—one of four that belonged to the Buddha-loving badass himself.

The bracelet was made of steel beads, each one a meditation mantra. It was supposed to keep me centered and in control of my nonhuman side, because in the past when I traveled, it wanted to come out and play. Meditation helped me push it back down. Control. It was all about control, because, believe it or not, they don't make a pill or a patch for wanting to tear people apart thanks to over a million years of genetic tendencies.

His gaze didn't shift a millimeter. "And that's what you were thinking when you *traveled* from the park to here? Practicing?"

Yeah, in a sling big-time. "Sit down. You'll need a good hour to ream me." I sighed. "Beer or tea?"

He didn't sit and he didn't speak. I went and brought back both. Brewing the tea took a few minutes, an opportunity for Niko to become a little less furious. I brought the tea that I kept for him under the bar, some mix that cost a ridiculous twenty dollars an ounce, but desperate times called for criminally overpriced tea. Kind of like throwing a virgin on some old god's altar in hopes he would cure that pesky leprosy. Probably wouldn't work, but didn't hurt to try.

I put down the tea. He looked at it, the beer, then me. "I can't decide which would be the more effective lesson: a bottle smashed over your head or hot tea thrown in your face."

Maybe it did hurt to try. I took the beer for myself. "I just . . . needed to. I feel like a hawk stuffed in a cage. I needed, I don't know, out."

"A hawk," he snorted. "A parakeet on your best day." But he sat down and wrapped his hands around the mug of tea. "You need to?"

"It's like a rubber band in me, stretched tight enough to snap. If I travel, I feel normal again."

Better than normal.

"And I haven't foamed at the mouth or tried to eat anyone even once, swear. I think with the Auphe all dead and losing the mental connection with them, I'm okay. Either that or the meditation is kicking in, but either way, I'm good. I am. And I've only done it twice in the past six months."

"Counting tonight?" he prodded.

"Three times," I corrected, and glumly drank more of the beer.

"I should've had the phone reprogrammed sooner. Meditation works, but not that quickly and not for one of your skill level . . . virtually nonexistent," he said darkly. "But we'll discuss this later. We're meeting a client here in a few minutes."

"Who?" It'd been three weeks since our last job. I'd been getting bored. Niko and I, and sometimes Promise and Robin, made up what Niko called Preternatural Investigations. I was convinced he called it that because I could barely pronounce preternatural. My nice, simple Ass-kickers, Inc. had been voted down. "Someone Promise recommended?" I asked. Promise, Niko's vampire girlfriend, sent the majority of our clients our way, although since they'd only recently reconciled, I didn't expect it to have come from her. They were taking things slowly from what I could tell, feeling their way carefully. With her daughter, Cherish, having almost killed or made mental slaves of all of us, it was for the best. And with Niko having bypassed the "almost" in killing when it came to Cherish, you'd want to make sure the foundation of the relationship was solid first.

"Actually, someone called my cell and asked for the meet." He decided drinking the tea instead of scalding me with it was the better plan and took a swallow. "He wouldn't say anything more."

That was weird. It wasn't as if we wrote our number on bathroom walls or paid for subway ads. Monster Maimers, Inc. Call 555-5555. Our work tended to come by word of mouth . . . from either Promise or Robin. "He, huh? Did he say what he wanted?"

"No. Think of it as a surprise."

It was a surprise. A helluva surprise.

One: It wasn't a man.

Two: She was human . . . in the Ninth Circle and not afraid.

Three: We knew her. And maybe she was human, but she was also one of the scariest humans I'd come across. A hundred if she was a day and a greedy, manipulative, borderline psychotic witch . . . and I didn't mean the *Wizard of Oz* kind. The only thing magical about her was the level of her pure vile nastiness. She liked me—I think because I'd been a little psychotic myself when I'd first met her.

Abelia-Roo.

Head of the Sarzo Clan. Rom. Toothless, wizened, maybe four foot ten, and didn't give a rat's ass who died as long as she got money out of it. She'd once sold us something we'd needed as ransom in a hostage situation and hadn't bothered to mention that activating it took the blood of a gypsy. That blood had turned out to be Niko's and that *I* definitely gave a rat's ass about—a giant rat's ass; big, furry, and pissed. It made me wonder how socially unacceptable it was to break the kneecaps of an old lady with her own intricately carved cane.

She leaned that cane against the bar, sat her tiny frame on the stool next to Niko, and arranged the red fringed shawl over her sacklike black dress. "Niko and Caliban Leandros of the Vayash Clan." Her black eyes glittered. "You enjoyed our hospitality once. I expect to be as well treated." She knotted her gnarled hands on the bar and rattled off something in Romany, which neither Niko nor I spoke. Sophia had never bothered to teach us the language. She had left her clan before we were born and when the clan had found out what she'd done to produce me . . . well, they hadn't exactly welcomed us with open arms.

Abelia-Roo grinned, showing her gums. "But I forget. You do not speak your own tongue. A disgrace. I will have a glass of your best wine. And if it is not your best, I shall know."

"I'll have to get a wineglass and scoop some water out of the toilet. Give me a sec," I growled, my eyes slits. "Or better yet, haul your wrinkled old ass back to Florida or wherever you've set up camp. And tell Branje hey." I'd threatened to slice off the nose of Abelia-Roo's main muscle man. Then again, when you had him on the ground, knee in his gut, the tip of your knife up a nostril and you fully intended to do it, I guessed it wasn't a threat.

The gums showed again, this time specifically in my direction. "Still a real man. It's difficult to believe the Vayash Clan ever produced one." The Vayash Clan also hadn't seen the need to spread around that they gave birth to a half-breed Auphe. The rest of the clans would've had serious words to say about that. She still didn't know about me then. "If I were ten years younger, my boy, I'd give you the ride of your life." She patted the white bun at the back of her head with a coy hand. It didn't do anything to cover up the pink-brown skin that peeked through the strands covering her scalp.

It was hard to stay pissed when you were trying not to spew all over yourself and the bar. I managed. I liked to think of pissed as number one in the repertoire that made up my general crapfest of moods. I was really, really good at it. Pulling in at the last of that emotional list would be forgiveness. "That'd still put you at nine hundred," I said with distaste. "No thanks. The only thing I want from you is to get the hell out of here. Thanks to your not telling us about the Calabassa, my brother almost died, you evil bitch."

Out of the corner of my eye I saw Samyel blink at my laying the b-word on what looked like a sweet old granny. But this sweet old granny would've drugged Samyel and sold his feathered butt to a chicken farmer. As a poor egg producer, he would end up an extra-crispy wing and thigh with a side of coleslaw before he even knew what happened.

"A man you may be, but worthless as a Rom," she scorned. "You buy an RV without looking at the engine and you come crying when it won't run because it doesn't have one? Pssssh."

"You—" I had my finger up and was ready to poke her in her bony chest.

Niko caught my hand and slapped it lightly down on the bar. "Pistol-whipping elderly women isn't precisely our mission statement, Cal."

I hadn't been going to pistol-whip her. Yell at her a little more, then pick her up and toss her out into the street. Some risk of a broken hip there, but that wasn't pistol-whipping . . . unless she tried to come back in. "You almost died because of her," I snapped, eyes still on her.

"Maybe I did not know," she said, the canny expression on her face replaced with all the innocence of the witch stuffing Hansel in the oven.

"Know what?" Niko asked pointedly.

"Whatever it is you think I knew," she answered promptly as she started pulling cloth bags out of the depths of her shawl—three of them and good sized. She placed them on the bar. "Now, I wish my wine and to discuss a business opportunity for you. Although, being that you are Vayash and half Vayash half *gadje*, I should spit at your feet." Niko was pure Vayash as far as we knew. The clan had passed through Greece generations ago and intermarried with the Northern Greeks before moving on, which is where the occasional blond one popped up. That and the darker complexion gave Niko Vayash cred. My black hair was Rom enough, but the pale skin—that would never pass.

She went on. "But, no, I am here to give you a chance to earn money, although I could've found much better to do the task. Remember that. But I am sentimental in my old age." She looked at me again and winked or had a ministroke; I wasn't sure which. "But not too old."

"Okay, Nik, you've got to let me pistol-whip her." I glared at her as I spoke. A *vodyanoi* stumping past in its oversized trenchcoat caught the edge of my molten expression, moaned, and headed for the back of the room—as far away from me as he could get. Abelia-Roo? Her, it didn't faze. Then again, I hadn't once killed quite a few of her kind with a sword and guns and one unfortunate margarita incident. *Vodyanoi* take to salt pretty much like a garden slug does—not too damn well.

"Cal."

"You almost *died*," I repeated, but with his tone I was in a losing argument. With Niko I usually was.

"But I didn't, and I'm curious." Niko tilted his gaze down by more than a foot to take her in. "You'd have to know, Abelia-Roo, that we'd have very little desire to deal with you after last time. You must be in quite a situation."

"A little trouble." She shrugged. "So tiny, it is too insignificant for one of my people to bother with." She took one of the bags and emptied it in a semicircle around her stool. It was salt. That would keep the next *vodyanoi* at a distance.

"Tiny." Niko didn't have to lift an eyebrow or use any of the tones he used on me. He only said the word and it may as well have been carved out of doubt.

"Perhaps very small would be a better term, but still quite simply solved." She clucked her tongue. "Strapping men and afraid of a little work. Your laziness puts all Rom to shame." Opening the next bag, she pulled out a tranquilizer pistol. I recognized it because I'd once had one used on me. Turning on the stool, she selected a vampire at a table by himself, hefted the pistol capably in her gnarled hand, and fired.

The vampire exploded.

Okay, maybe not literally, but close enough to get the job done. Every orifice, every pore, they all poured out blood so fast and furiously that within seconds he was a blood-covered limp body draped over the table. "Heparin," she said with wicked cheer. "*Gadje* magic." She gave the incubi an eye and went for the third bag. From that came a large pair of silver scissors that she snapped at the incubi with enthusiasm. They crossed their legs hurriedly and hissed, showing their snakelike, curved fangs. That along with the occasional glitter of pearly scale with their blue and black hair was the only thing that gave them away as not your everyday, average male hooker.

"Heparin?" I asked Nik.

"Blood thinner," he explained. "I didn't know it would have that effect on vampires."

"Is he dead?" I looked to see if he was breathing, because vampires did breathe, just like their hearts beat—although I wasn't too sure about this guy anymore. "Only staff are allowed to kill the customers. And then the boss likes us to have a good reason."

"He'll live," she said dismissively. "It was a light dose. He's lost only half his blood volume. He'll have to break into a blood bank when he wakes up. Those vitamins they take now won't help him, but that's not my concern. Keeping the *gunoi* in their rightful, fearful place is."

"These 'feces,' as you call them, are my patrons," Ishiah said from behind me. He spoke Rom and we didn't. Then again, he knew Robin Goodfellow from thousands of years back. You're going to pick up a few things along the way. Niko would know it himself; he knew a couple of languages, but Rom—he refused, with good reason.

"Do you think I don't have a bag for you too, little birdy?" she snorted. "Or stories of your kind to tell?"

How she knew he was a peri I didn't know. Both he and Samyel had their wings out of sight. Peris could do that. The wings came and went in a glitter of light. Where exactly they went, I didn't have a clue. I did know Ishiah wouldn't back down from a tiny withered woman. But it didn't come to that. Suddenly Abelia-Roo was done playing. "Shoo, little birdy. I'm ready to talk business with these two, words not for your ears. Fetch my wine and I'll be the sweetness and light of an angel itself." She spread her hands above her head. "See my pure gold halo? See the bright sparkle?"

Ishiah scowled, the long scar on his jaw stretching to a gleaming white, then bit off, "See that you are." He looked at me. "You owe me." He was gone before I could say I'd be just as happy if he tossed her out—happier, in fact.

"So . . . this business," Niko said, "that is too insignificant for you to be bothered with. What is it?"

"We have lost a thing." She lifted a hand and waved it as if it were nothing. "An iron box. Six feet long. Wide, like so. . . ." She held her hands apart, a little more than three feet.

"Funny, that's about the size of a coffin," I said. I took the glass of wine Samyel handed me and instead of passing it to her, I drank it myself—mainly to stick it to her, but also to see just how serious this "business" was. I was hoping she'd curse me and head for the door. But she didn't, and that meant this was serious all right. Serious, dangerous as hell no doubt, and our client would be Abelia-Roo. The first two I was used to . . . but the last. no way. "Nik, did you remember coffin retrieval on our resume? Because I don't."

"No, but rubbing warm, scented oil all over your favorite puck is. I wrote it in myself." Robin, our self-proclaimed favorite puck, draped an arm over Niko's shoulders and his other one over Abelia-Roo's narrow ones. I'd seen him come in the front, wavy brown hair windblown, green eyes bright with anticipation, and I didn't think it was at seeing us. He was looking for Ishiah. He did that daily now . . . more than daily. It was a wonder either one had the strength to stand upright.

Scary thoughts. Scary, scary thoughts.

"Who's your . . . ah . . . elderly friend . . . oh *gamiseme tora*." The puck pulled his arm away so quickly, it was a wonder he didn't yank it completely out of its socket. "The *skila* from the Sarzo piece of *skata* clan. Is this a nightmare? Zeus's wandering prick, let it be a nightmare." Goodfellow, as a puck, trickster, and used car salesman, had been put in charge of the previous bargaining with Abelia-Roo down in Florida. He claimed he was mentally scarred for life. I'd been there. I believed him.

"She wants us to find an iron coffin they seem to have 'misplaced,'" Niko said dryly. "Perhaps they left it at a rest stop."

"An iron coffin . . . an iron coffin? No. Suyolak? You've lost *Suyolak*? You have lost the Plague of the World?" Robin hissed. "You did not. You couldn't have. You have one responsibility: to guard the evil you spawned, and you've let him escape?"

I looked curiously at Niko. He might not speak Rom,

but if there was a monster, Rom or otherwise, he knew about it. He began speaking as casually as if he were telling a story about a well-known relative. The facts were at his fingertips and he did love to share those facts. "Suyolak, as legend goes, was a gypsy born almost a thousand years ago, one with a special gift. He had the knowledge of the cure for any illness, but he was chained to a rock. It was said should he break free, he would destroy the entire world. The Sarzo Clan wasn't mentioned."

"So he's a healer. Why would a healer destroy the world? Why lock him up?" Admittedly, however, the coffin was more practical than a big rock; you never knew where the next condos would be going up.

Robin's mouth curled with disgust. "The reason he has the knowledge of every cure is that he has the knowledge of every disease. Had, in his day, *caused* every disease. He's an antihealer. You do recall something called the Black Death, do you not? Fleas may have spread it, but he was ground zero for the outbreak."

Abelia-Roo's black eyes didn't blink as the truth came out. "It is so. He was a walking plague. Wherever he would go, people would sicken and die. He himself will not die; that cure he saves for himself. Age itself he tosses away."

"And I'll bet that was useful," I said with scorn. "Send him to a town, make a couple of people sick, then come and cure them . . . for a price. I'm thinking like a Sarzo now, hey, Nik? Maybe I'm not Vayash after all."

They still didn't blink—like black marbles, those eyes. "It is said Suyolak grew to prefer killing over money or loyalty to the clan. He cured no longer. So, while he slept, exhausted by several of the prettiest girls of that day and drunk beyond oblivion, he was locked away beyond iron and zinc that his powers could not pass through.

We carried him with us through the years, from country to country. He was our burden. All clans have one ... a duty ... a watch to carry out."

I wondered if that made me the Vayash's burden. Not that I was sure putting me in an iron box would do them any good. Healing was based on psychic talents, which were blocked by iron. Niko would be proud I remembered that. I didn't have any idea if my traveling was based in the psychic realm, but I did know trying to put me in any kind of box was only going to end in my seeing how many Rom I could stuff in there ... like clowns in a clown car—only with no way out.

"He is ours," she went on, tucking the defensive bags away back under her shawl, "and now after all these years, hundreds, more, of bearing our burden without complaint, someone has taken him. Men with guns. Sarzo died to protect our duty. And if those who have taken him turn him loose ... then Sara-la-Kali help us." Her eyes pinned us. "Now, you, who owe us for the help we gave you in the past, must return him to us."

Goodfellow protested immediately, his mobile face outraged, "We *paid* for that help and about ten times more than it was worth. I can't hold my head up among the other tricksters for that." Then, as inquisitive as he was angry, he asked, "How do you know he's not dead? He could be bones in there. You haven't opened it up to take a peek, have you?"

"And be struck blind, deaf, and dumb instantly, foolish puck? Or have my heart explode in my chest? No." For the first time she seemed unsettled. "We heard him now and again. Through the iron, we would hear his screams of fury. His sly whispers of rewards for his release. His singing. The old songs ... the ones for death. Dirges for any so suicidal as to try to look on his face."

Her dried face shriveled further, cheeks hollowing.

"Whoever took him, for whatever reason, it won't matter. Once they set him free, birds will plummet from the sky. Fish will turn belly up. Every creature whose path he crosses will fall to a crumpled corpse.

"He will devour the world."

2

Cal

"Why is it always the world?" I tossed at the wall one of the Nerf ninja stars I'd given Niko as a joke and watched it bounce. "Why is it never just half a block? Or Jersey? You know, something we could live without?" It was after work and almost four a.m., but I had a feeling I wasn't going to see my bed any time soon unless I gave in.

I wasn't giving in.

"Because life is a lesson to be learned, not recess for lazy-minded little boys." Niko snatched the star from midair and tossed it himself. This time the foam imitation of a weapon actually embedded itself in the moss green wall. Don't ask me how. I don't know. Niko not only defied belief, but physics too. "Have you heard back from Delilah regarding the park attack?"

"No. Either she's busy on a job or sniffing around"—I grinned—"so to speak. To see what's up."

"And you're sure they were Kin Wolves?" he persisted.

"Definitely. They brought a revenant." Only werewolves in the Kin would be hanging around with a revenant. They used them as pure dumb muscle—usually for things the Kin found too boring or disgusting to do themselves and because they considered them completely expendable. I had to agree with them there.

"Since Delilah's a wash for now," I went on, "what about this job . . . this job we are so not going to take, right?" I crossed my arms across my chest from where I was reclined on our apartment couch. The apartment was a nice loft in SoHo thanks to a big payday we hadn't expected . . . much nicer than anything we'd ever had. Up until then, we'd lived in anything from rat holes to trailers to not-quite-converted warehouses. But the sofa was the same one from our first days in New York almost three years ago. It was battle battered, repaired several times over, and perfectly hollowed out to the weight of my back and slothful ass. It took a long time to get furniture to fit the pickiest parts of my body.

"Plague of the World. A walking, talking, most likely extremely annoyed grim reaper out to destroy anything in his path. He also apparently lives forever. And you feel we should let this one pass?"

"You forgot he likes to sing," I grumbled. "Maybe he'll hit *American Idol* and that asshole Brit will humiliate him to death." I didn't watch reality TV. I was victimized by it. They turned it on in the bar. It was so hideous, you couldn't ignore it and if I shot the TV, it'd come out of my pay—like everything else.

Niko looked at me with as much disappointment as if I'd admitted to eating puppies for a late-night snack. "You watch—"

"*No*," I said, cutting him off. "I don't. And I don't work for Abelia-Roo either. She's a liar. She almost got you killed. And she's hornier than Robin, which scares the living shit out of me. Let her find someone else."

He considered it for a moment, slipped the sneaker off one of my feet dangling over the sofa's arm, and then beaned me in the forehead with it. "That, in case you

were curious," he said, "was social responsibility knocking at your door."

"Ow!" I glared at him and rubbed my forehead.
"Since when? We always looked out for ourselves and
nobody else." Except for Promise and Robin who had
managed to slide in when we weren't looking.

"Since the Auphe are gone and we're free. With freedom comes responsibility." He drummed his fingers on
the shoe still on my other foot.

"Well, in this case, responsibility can go fu—" The
second shoe hit me in exactly the same spot. "Will you
quit it, damn it!"

"That was civic duty," he said patiently. This time his
fingers were tapping on the TV remote on the end table.
"Would you care to discuss further the philosophy of
living in a civilized society?"

"Jesus, no thanks." I sat up hurriedly. "You know,
when I was a kid and didn't want to do something, you
made me s'mores and talked to me about it. You didn't
hit me with a shoe."

Making s'mores then had meant Nik begging a Her-
shey's bar off a neighbor in a neighborhood where no
kid should live, much less walk alone, melting it for
two seconds in our rickety microwave, and squashing
it between two saltine crackers. In reality they'd probably sucked. To a five-year-old who'd never had the real
thing, it was bliss. "You didn't throw shoes at me," I repeated with a grumble.

"You were five and good." He quirked his lips, but
his eyes said it wasn't with humor—nostalgia either.
Only regret. I knew what he was thinking: too good to
be five years old. Too quiet. Too careful. You had to be
around Sophia or you'd be sorry. Well, the days of quiet
and careful were long gone, but it turned out the s'mores
had stuck around. "Fine. I'll make you s'mores and we'll
discuss this like rational adults."

He was really going to make s'mores? This I had to see. It had been years . . . since I was thirteen maybe, and he'd been going away to college, after skipping a year of high school—no surprise. "And if I still don't want to do it?" I demanded.

"We'll see." He passed me on the way to the kitchen area, the TV remote still in his hand. Bargain, but have backup. It was a good rule to live by.

Ten minutes later I regarded the gluten-free crackers, soy chocolate, and a blob of tofu masquerading as marshmallow. "Just like the good old days," I said glumly, straddling the kitchen chair. "Not." Of course the good old days had also included fish sticks dipped in yogurt for tartar sauce.

Food had been a big part of our childhood. Getting it for one thing; it wasn't that easy. Nik had been born smarter than anyone had a right to be, honorable through and through although he thought—wrongly— taking care of me had something to do with that, but he'd also been born proud. Genetics are funny things, because he hadn't gotten any of that from Sophia . . . except the smarts. She'd been plenty damn smart when ripping off a mark, but damn stingy about sharing the money. I'd been in the third grade before I figured out Niko had had to go to the principal and tell him we needed free lunches. When I'd gone to first grade, they gave me free food, and I thought that's the way it was for everybody.

If it hadn't been for me, Niko would've gone without. Like I said, proud. He probably had gone without for his first four years of school or brought whatever could be scrounged in our mostly empty kitchen. Sophia wasn't much on grocery shopping, but everyone at the liquor store knew her by name. Some memories you didn't need a scrapbook for; a burning knot in the pit of your stomach got the job done.

She taught us one thing, though: When you didn't take food for granted, it could figure in all sorts of occasions—convincing, consoling, even celebrating. I'd grown up, technically anyway, but I hadn't forgotten what it felt like to know the only reason I wasn't hungry was because of my brother. And I hadn't forgotten to appreciate food.

But sometimes it was hard as hell to appreciate Niko's adult food. It didn't change the fact I picked up the s'more that would make even a hard-core vegan head for the nearest McDonald's and took a bite. It was every bit as god-awful as I knew it'd be. "Great." I chewed with the best imitation of enthusiasm I could whip up as I crunched cardboard, soy chocolate like muddy asphalt, and fake marshmallow that . . . Hell, I couldn't even think of anything to compare it to.

The taste might not have been anything like when I was a kid, but Niko was the same, keeping tradition alive. When the only ones you had were the ones you made up, they mattered. They mattered a helluva lot.

"Okay, convince me." I sighed. The first time I'd needed Niko's special brand of convincing was when I was five and I wanted my own bed. All grown up and wanting my own bed—same tiny bedroom, but different bed—because I hadn't known then . . . hadn't known there were monsters in the night. But Niko had known; he had seen it two years before and kept it a secret. Being in the same room wasn't enough for him after that. You never forget your first kiss, and you never forget your first leering package of death grinning at you through a kitchen window.

So, we had our version of s'mores back then and he'd said the one thing I couldn't say no to . . . not even as a little kid. "I'd be lonely," he'd told me, nine and solemn. "One more year, Cal. Okay? Just one more. When you're six and I'm ten and we're all grown up."

Five-year-old Cal never would deny his big brother anything. A twenty-one-year-old Cal wouldn't either, but I didn't have to make it as easy these days. This Cal would never be anything like that long-ago one. It was too bad; that had been a much better Cal. Ignorance was bliss and sometimes made for a much better person. But ignorance hadn't been an option for me for long. The few years I'd been lucky enough to be that way had been all due to Nik.

Once there had been an innocent, quiet, and good kid. Now there was me. I wasn't innocent; I wasn't good. I was quiet, but that was usually as I stood behind you a split second before I slit your throat. But that didn't mean I didn't remember. I did, and I remembered who'd kept me innocent as long as he could.

"Never mind with the convincing," I said around another mouthful. I might not have been the same, but Nik was. And I still couldn't tell him no. "I'll do it."

The absence of my usual stubbornness took my typically unflappable brother off guard for a split second. "That simple?"

I shrugged. "Next year, when 'we're all grown up,' I won't help save the world. How about that?"

"I think 'all grown up' won't hit you until your mid-eighties, but, yes, it's a deal." He handed me another s'more and, God help me, I took it.

"One thing, though," I said. "This time I get to negotiate with Abelia-Roo."

He paused in cleaning up, wiping the counter with typical Niko antiseptic zeal. "Robin certainly won't fight you for it, but why are you so eager to be cheated and molested to the point of post-traumatic stress disorder?"

Because Niko could have died because of her. Because I don't forget things like that . . . not ever. Because I wanted a little payback and I wasn't talking about the money.

For those she'd cheated in the past.

For those she'd cheat in the future.

For what she'd allowed to happen to my brother.

For good old-fashioned revenge.

I grinned with the same dark cheer Abelia-Roo had shown in the bar when bleeding the vampire half dead and added the last, equally valid, reason out loud.

"For fun."

Niko called Abelia-Roo to let her know we'd take the job and would be upstate that evening to talk terms. By the time Niko disconnected, her voice had gotten shrill enough I could hear it across the room. "In a hurry, huh?" I yawned.

"The entire devouring of the world, destruction of all living things, it seems to disturb her," he said dryly. "But obviously not you."

Destroy the world? I'd once nearly *unmade* the world. Not my fault . . . mostly . . . but it had rearranged my priorities some. Destruction of the world versus nap: Nap won. Since I couldn't get a full night's sleep thanks to the Kin and Abelia, a nap would have to do. Besides, as there was no way we'd catch whoever stole the gypsy grim reaper in a matter of hours, it didn't make much difference. I checked my watch. Five a.m. Groaning, I headed for the bedroom, losing a sock along the way, fell onto my bed, and instantly into dark, utterly empty sleep.

I woke up, who knew how many hours later, to that same lost sock stuffed halfway in my mouth. I spat it out and counted myself lucky it wasn't another of Nik's s'mores. I'd take the taste of a dirty sock over that any day. With cotton fuzz on my tongue, I flailed around for the alarm clock. It was eleven a.m. I'd had about six hours' sleep. Just about half of what I usually went for, but what could you do?

I rolled out of bed and gazed blearily at the piles of clothes on my floor, trying to remember which were clean, which were dirty, and which, just like Johnny Cash, walked the line. I took a sniff, made the determination, and grabbed a pair of jeans and a black T-shirt. I probably wouldn't hit up any wolves for info about last night's attack. . . . They might not all know about me and Delilah yet. It might have been just those two. But if the others did know, then that could get back to the Kin, which would be bad news for Delilah. Plus, all werewolves weren't Kin. Some were just living their lives: lawyers, waitresses, accountants, healers. . . .

Revenants, on the other hand, were a different story. I'd never met a revenant who didn't eat people. That's what they did. That's who they were. They were sharks, and people were walking, talking chum. And that meant there was no such thing as a revenant that wasn't better off dead . . . not in my book.

After the shower, I found a note in the kitchen from Nik. He'd taped it to the Lucky Charms cereal box so I wouldn't miss it. *Gone to work. Back for meet. Gate and I'll baptize you face-first in the toilet.* Short and to the point, my brother.

It was Tuesday, so that meant he was kicking ass, taking names, and being paid for the pleasure at the dojo on West Twenty-fifth. Most other days he taught as a TA at NYU. Mythology, history, fencing, all while supposedly pursuing his master's—or was it a doctorate? Hell, I could never remember. Never mind, the Auphe had put an end to his early college days quick. Robin Goodfellow had friends . . . philosophical friends from the good old days of orgies and gladiators . . . who still taught even today and pulled some strings to provide Nik with a degree from a Greek university.

Good for him. He more than deserved it. I, on the other hand, already knew more about the world than I cared to. The back of the cereal box was good enough for me—that and the weight of the guns in my holsters and my knives. Many knives . . . and then there was the occasional explosive round. I liked to think that made me easy to please, not paranoid and homicidal. You couldn't be paranoid if they were not only out to get you, but *had* gotten you. And homicidal? I took a bite of cereal and crunched. In my world even the beauty queens were homicidal. I just passed on the tiara.

I hit the street, checked my voice mail—still no Delilah—and decided which revenant hangout to hit. During the night they walked the streets, the human clothes and gloom enough camouflage against all but the closest looks. During the day, if they kept their sweatshirt hoods up and heads down, and slimy hands in their pockets, they could get by. But it was a risk. But just as peris had bars, so did revenants—if you took away the other customers, the bathrooms, and the whole sanitation issue. In other words, they drank alcohol in pools of their own filth.

Festive.

Revenants were sewer rats mainly. They were either too stupid or too lazy to get jobs unless it was for the Kin, and the only meal that really turned them on was human, so they would find a deserted place to take over and congregate. There were probably about twenty places like that scattered around the city. I'd been to only two in the past and that had been enough. No matter where they were, above or below, you could bet on one thing: They would be rank. Revenants were all about slaughter and nice, ripe gobbets of flesh, but hygiene? They weren't lining up for deodorant, that was for damn sure.

But this time I wasn't going down into the sewers. I'd had my share of those on a previous case and trying to track down revenants there by stench was a losing battle. Natural versus supernatural stink—I wasn't that good. I was still going to get wet, though, which is why when I knocked at Robin's door, I was surprised he was holding a cat carrier. I'd called him to see if he was up for a hunting trip and he'd been oddly enthusiastic. Now I saw why.

"Um . . . ," I said, hesitating as eyes made up of what looked like yellow candlelight peered at me through the metal bars. "Why? Cats don't like water. I don't think mummy cats would be much different." In addition to the eyes, there was a mouthful of fangs that showed when she grinned—and she always grinned.

Robin had managed to get the equivalent of "followed home" by a mummified cat during our last . . . "adventure" wasn't the right word. More like our last FUBAR. Whatever you called it, it didn't matter. What did matter was that shaking a mummy cat off your trail was a lot harder than shaking off a normal feline.

"Look, kid, I didn't say I'd go with you for this little interrogation/extermination project simply because the car lot offices are being painted. The Hair Club for Cats here needs some exercise. She's getting antsy and you remember what happened last time she got antsy. She arranged some playtime on her own."

She—Salome—had gotten out of Goodfellow's condo, killed a neighbor's old, senile Great Dane that was using the hall for exercise, and then left the carcass on Robin's pillow as a present like a good little mummified kitty. Mummy cats didn't eat, but they did like to play the same as live cats. And if no neighbors had any big-ass dogs left to play with, she might decide the neighbor himself would do just fine.

A hairless paw, with perfectly normal-looking claws that obviously weren't, came through the bars, followed by a dry-as-dust mrrrrp. "There, there. Who's a good kitty?" I said, taking a step back. I didn't pull a gun, though.

In my eyes that gave me balls of steel. In Salome's eyes, steel would just make them all the easier to roll across the condo floor.

"You love her, don't you, Goodfellow?" I said, taking another step back. "Admit it. She's your pookie bear."

"She's a boil on the cheek of my finely toned ass," he grumbled, but he let the paw hook around his finger. Robin, from what we knew, was hundreds of thousands of years old ... if not older. Friends came and went quickly from his perspective, especially human ones, but mummy cats—who knew how long they could live? Wahanket, the mummy who'd made her, was older than the pyramids. She could hang around for a long while. When friends were mayflies in comparison to you, a mummy cat wasn't necessarily a bad thing. "So, I'm in my casual clothes." By that he meant his non-Armani slacks, shirt, and long duster, which was good for concealing swords. It was when he concealed his sword without a duster that I started worrying. "Where are we going hunting?"

I grinned. "How do you feel about nature hikes? Wetlands? Save the yellow spotted leech?"

From the spitting of Greek curses an hour later as we splashed through the calf-high muddy water, surrounded by a cloud of mosquitoes, he thought about the same of it as I did. It sucked.

"Wet enough for you?" I commented, and ducked the water he kicked in my direction.

"*Ai pidiksou*," he spat, but continued after me.

We were at the Flushing Airport, abandoned since before I was born. Thanks to Robin's owning a car lot, we had access to whatever we needed ... including a Jeep ... if the subway and bus wouldn't get us where we needed to go. "This is what happens when you build an airport on a swamp," I grunted. Swamp was the non-fancy name for wetlands. Built in the twenties, closed in the eighties, and located on top of a damn swamp was the sum total of what I knew or cared to know about the place.

That and it was home sweet home to a bunch of revenants who worked for the Kin. This was actually a sort of reward situation for them. If they'd done good and not messed up for several months, a long stretch for a revenant's reasoning and willpower, you got hauled out in a party bus with several dead or mostly dead humans, twenty kegs or so, and left for a week or thereabouts to lie around, eat, drink, and do whatever revenants do to make little revenants. The last was yet another thing I didn't need or want to know.

There were two hangars and one smaller building. The blue sky reflected in the still water ahead of us and it was warm enough that I'd shed my jacket and left it in the Jeep. There was no one to see out here but revenants, and since I planned on their seeing my weapons up close and personal, there was no reason to hide them. Except for the mosquitoes, the mud in my shoes, and the stink of our prey, it was a nice day. Not that there weren't other opinions on that.

"Poseidon's barnacle-ridden testicles," Goodfellow snarled as he held the cat carrier up as I sloshed along. I sloshed. He moved through the water like a shark, soundless and with barely a wake. When you were possibly older than mankind itself, you were good at things like that. The temper hadn't seemed to have improved over the years, though. "Pick a building. I'm hot, I'm surrounded by water and mud . . . mud *without* naked women or men wrestling in it, mind you, and I'm not pleased. And why isn't Niko here? Surely he's not avoiding his duty?"

"Niko had to work, and the day it takes more than two of us to handle a bunch of drunk and passed-out revenants is the day we get a job stuffing teddy bears at the toy store. And speaking of naked mud-wrestling women, how is Ish handling your wild and woolly ways?" I grinned wickedly. "You talk him into the whole orgy scene?" Pucks loved a good orgy, or two, or a hundred. "Or do you just swing by his place afterward and cuddle?"

"Do not go there," he said with a grim set to his mouth.

I picked one of the hangars and headed for it. The other ramshackle wooden building was too small and the stench was everywhere, but a little stronger toward one of the hangars. "Don't get me wrong." I held up my hands. "I don't want details. I so don't want even a single detail. I don't even want to know that details exist. I'm just curious how it's working out since he's a little holier than thou and you're . . . well, unholier than pretty much the whole world and all alternate dimensions. In the sex area anyway."

"I said, *don't . . . go . . . there*," he gritted. "Or my sword will go someplace you think equally private. Are we clear?"

It was a big change from Robin's usual bragging ways. I'd once learned more in one hour from listening to him boast than I had from two solid years' worth of porn mags. He'd been the one to first get me laid. Not with him. Even if I were into guys, and I wasn't, but if I were . . . I'd once accidentally seen him naked. Walk softly and carry a big stick was one thing. Walk softly and carry the Washington Monument was another altogether.

"Okay. Okay." If Robin didn't want to be his normal bragging self, it was weird, bizarre, and probably a sign of the end of days, but it wasn't the time to yank his chain about it. It was time to slice and dice some revenants. And that, more than the sun and the blue sky, was what made this a nice day. As we approached the chosen hangar, I pulled my Desert Eagle, matte black, and my serrated combat knife, same color.

"You realize black really isn't very adroit camouflage in broad daylight," Robin drawled.

"Believe it or not, the Eagle doesn't come in sunshine yellow," I grunted before pausing at the partially askew huge metal doors. "Looks like a good place to turn her loose. You know they're waiting inside, right? She'll have to be quick."

"What? You think they heard the splashing of a tsunami crossed with a beached whale that is you walking through water? Surely you jest," he snorted.

"And I suppose you just walked *on* it in your day?" I snorted back as he opened the door to the cat carrier to let Salome bound out.

"Rumors. Lots and lots of wine and rumors. And the tide was extremely low."

Salome, finding herself in and surrounded by water, picked up a wet paw and looked at it, then back at Robin with woeful betrayal in those glowing eyes. Then her hairless ears perked as her head turned back, the whiskerless muzzle opened to scent the air, and she was gone—like a streak of lightning . . . wrinkled, bald, undead lightning. Okay, that wasn't exactly poetry, but she was fast as shit. I heard the ring of the hoop earrings in the tips of her ears and then I heard outraged screams. No way I was letting her have all the fun. I slipped through the crack of the two slightly agape doors and shot the revenant that immediately attacked me. I shot him in the face, which was good for killing a lot of creatures . . . and movie zombies . . . but for a revenant, it was just another hole in the head, literally. Granted, with a Desert Eagle .50, it was one almighty big hole, but it didn't take him down; it only slowed him down for half a second. Sometimes half a second was all you needed.

He staggered back from the force of the shot and I tackled him, taking him the rest of the way down, switching hands to saw through his neck and spinal column. It was the only way for revenants. Chop off an arm or a leg and they'd just grow it back in a month or two. Blow a hole in their brain—hell, they didn't use them that often anyway. Cut one in half at the torso—they'd die, but it would take weeks, and chain saws, props to Bruce Campbell, are goddamn heavy to carry around. Entertaining, yeah, but not very practical. Too bad.

Through the spinal column of the neck was the only way to put them down permanently and quickly. And fighting them is rather monotonous. You might have one trying to gnaw through your throat while another tries to beat you to death with the arm you just chopped off him. Or you might have one trying to break your neck while one beats you with the leg you just blew away. From what I could tell, the slimy shitheads never sat around strategizing a whole lot or watching old kung fu movies and taking notes.

Off to the left in a spill of light from a hole in the ceiling, I saw Robin swinging his sword and heads flying. Salome I didn't see, but from the howling from farther in the darkened recesses of the hangar, she sounded like she was having fun. I finished with my first revenant and turned to the next. "You," it hissed. "You dare come here. We know you. The Kin know you. You think you'll leave here without one of us tasting your defiled flesh?"

"Defiled? Big word for you. Big word for me too; I won't lie." He was smarter than most of his fellow flesh eaters. That made him the one I wanted to talk to. "Wait here, would you?" I tossed the knife into his chest just to distract him before pulling at the broad axe I had strapped to my back and swinging it one handed. Its head was three times the size of a normal axe . . . Viking stamp of approval all the way. I could use a sword and was good enough to get by, thanks to Nik's training, but I'd never be a sword person. And there was that heavy chain saw issue, but an axe ... If there wasn't anyone human around to see it, that didn't work too badly either.

I swung and cut him in half at the waist like a magician with his assistant, only there was no putting this one back together again. "Abra-fucking-cadabra." The milky white eyes widened, and mottled yellow and brown teeth, stained with blood and rot, bared in a silent scream as he separated and both halves tumbled into the shallow water. The lingering smell of a dead woman's perfume on his breath didn't make me too sympathetic. "Don't go anywhere." Then I gave him a savage smile. "What the hell, if you *can* go somewhere, give it your best shot."

Retrieving my knife and sheathing it, I moved on. I took on three more revenants with gun and axe, reloaded, and went after two more. I tried not to look at the floating body parts that drifted here and there, but I was used to seeing things like that and going on with the fight. It was what you did. Or you slipped up and you died, and I'd done a damn lot in my day not to die.

Then there were the times in my life I had wanted to die.

But that was then and this was now. Things were different—a world of different. The only way I planned on dying now was if I screwed up, and I wasn't planning to screw up. A weight tackled me from behind. I hit the water, rolled over onto my back, losing a few deep stripes of flesh on my shoulders to revenant claws trying to hold me down. Niko had taught me to break a hold like that and this revenant was no Niko. I dropped the axe, shoved the Eagle under his chin, and put two through the top of his bald head, the color of a toad's skin. The skull shattered, which staggered it slightly. It was when I put the muzzle of the automatic to its neck and emptied half the clip into it, destroying the spine, that it was blown backward, never to get back up.

I surged to my feet, taking the axe with me, and

headed toward about ten of them rushing Robin. Robin tended to have that effect on anyone who crossed his path. They either rushed him to molest him—I was sure that if it was for molesting, he was happy to have it—or to kill him. At least I knew he did have a problem with that last one.

"Why is it when I'm with you," he remarked calmly as he took two heads in one stroke, "I'm given the tour of New York's most odiferous locations? Never are your enemies running perfumeries or fine gourmet chocolate shops. No. Sewers, troll caverns, abandoned asylums full of decomposing corpses, your building's basement on your laundry day. I still debate to myself which has been the worst."

"Think of your cat. It's all for your cat," I said as I took a head of my own with the axe and finished the clip off on my Eagle into another revenant. I didn't take the spine out, but I did take both arms. If it wanted to kick me to death or take me out like the world's biggest snapping turtle, it could go right ahead. And naturally it did. I didn't have much respect for revenants, and compared to other predators in the city, they weren't quite as efficient in their murderous ways. But that didn't mean they weren't killers or weren't stubborn enough to come after you if all they were was a torso with one arm left to pull it along.

This time I passed the axe blade through his neck and his head flew into the darkness. All his stubbornness disappeared with it. I waited for more to come boiling out of the darkness in the rear of the hangar, but none did. But I heard something—hissing, groaning, and splashing, and quite a lot of all three. Followed by Robin, I headed into the dark. It was instinctual for people to stay out of the dark; that's where the bad things were. My human half had outgrown that core of self-preservation a long time ago. Now the dark was where the money was. With

the axe in one hand, I pulled my gun back out and used
the rest of the clip to fill the roof of the hangar with
holes. Daylight streamed in, letting us see better than
any flashlight. If it was something we wanted to see.

It wasn't.

It absolutely, completely was not.

Once . . . what was I thinking . . . a *thousand* times
when I was being homeschooled by Niko, he dragged me
to museums. If they didn't have weapons or dinosaurs,
I wasn't much interested. But sometimes things stuck
with me, like when your brother lectured you about fertility figures. The combination of horror and boredom
etched itself into your brain. One museum statue he'd
used had been a Venus. Not the good one, not the naked marble Venus with no arms, but nice breasts. No, he
chose a small figure that would fit in your hand. Found
in Germany or Austria or someplace with beer, it had a
head but no face, and enormous pendulous breasts that
hung over an equally enormous and pendulous stomach. The legs were tiny, the arms almost nonexistent. It
barely looked human. In fact, it looked like Jabba the
Hutt's girlfriend. It was enough to put off a seventeen-
year-old me from trying to get the newstand guy to sell
me nudie mags for a week or two.

That little piece of BC art bore one hell of a resem-
blance to what was squatting in the back of the warehouse . . . except she had three rows of those huge breasts.
She really was the size of Jabba, times two, and she was
expelling fully formed and grown revenants through her
giant—oh jeez. Okay, now I wasn't off nudie mags for a
week; I was off sex, and that was a much bigger loss.

I'd specifically not wondered where baby revenants
came from when we'd gotten out of the Jeep. And here I
was, finding out anyway. Ain't that life? Life and pained
eyeballs I suddenly didn't want anymore. The new revenants would slide out and land in the water, splash fee-

bly for a few seconds, then get to their hands and knees and crawl up the massive form that birthed it and, voilà, baby's first swallow. Breast feeding, it was a beautiful thing.

Mommy had no legs from what I could tell, and small arms ended in flippers that she flailed around as she hissed at us, then gurgled slowly, "I hunger. Mother hungers." The milky eyes were fixed on us, the mouth big enough to swallow one of us whole. "So very huuuuungry." All the new revenants turned toward us, including the one that just plopped out with gnashing teeth and swiping claws, and wet with more than water. Green and black, mucus or slime—whichever, it flew through the air. The smell that went with it was equally as appetizing.

"Yeah. Okay. The miracle of birth." I slammed a new clip home and tried not to gag. "You take care of this one, Goodfellow. I have some . . . ah. . . ." Another one came gushing out. Plop. Splash. That was it. Celibacy. The priesthood. That was for me. "Interrogation. I have some interrogation to do. Have fun."

"What?" Robin sputtered. "You bastard. You'd best not take a single step. . . ."

I'd taken thirty of them before he even said the word. Dashing past me in the opposite direction was Salome. Apparently she liked what she saw a lot more than I had, because I heard her loud and raucous purr all the way back at the front of the hangar where I'd left my Einstein revenant. I'd never heard a happier sound in my life. Damn, she really was a tiny patch of living hell in a rhinestone collar. And I thought *I* had monster cred.

The extra smart revenant wasn't where I'd left him. Brains and motivation. Too bad he hadn't gone to business school. He'd have a corner office by now. It still didn't take long to find him, though. You could only go so far when you were nothing but a torso and arms. He'd pulled his upper half into a patch of blackness, but I could still smell that distant hint of perfume. A woman had put that on one night, for her husband, her boyfriend, her girlfriend or just for herself, and probably thought for a moment that she was pretty and ready for the night. But it had been the night that had been ready for her.

I reached into the darkness for him, ignored the savage bite on my forearm, and yanked him into the dim light. Once I got him there, I used the barrel of my gun to pry his jaws open and remove my arm more or less intact. Blood probably stained the long-sleeved T-shirt, but that was the great thing about black. It didn't show blood and it was slimming—a must-own for pudgy serial killers everywhere.

I planted a mud-covered combat boot on the revenant's chest. "All right, Professor, I was in a damn good mood yesterday. Now tell me why two Kin Wolves and one of your kind cared to blow it to shit."

It snarled, a show of teeth now broken from the metal of the Desert Eagle, but said nothing. And really it had nothing to lose. It was dead. It might take weeks to get there but even a revenant couldn't regenerate an entire lower body. So nothing to lose . . . but something to gain. Pain. Nobody liked pain, not even revenants. Sometimes the threat was enough; other times it wasn't. I think the woman who'd died in her favorite perfume, the perfume on its breath, would understand that I didn't give a shit which way this bastard went in that regard. I unsheathed the combat knife, its serrated smile as unrelenting as my own. "Let's try this again. Who is fucking with my Zen?"

It was tough. I had to give it that, but in the end no one is tough enough. Everyone talks. Everyone. But sometimes the carrot worked better than the stick. I believed in equal opportunity. I used both. Weeks dying of starvation wasn't a good way to go. Neither were your fellow revenants or Mommy eating you alive. I promised it a quick death and I gave it a taste of what it'd be like not to have one. And when it talked, I gave it that quick death. Not because it deserved it . . . It didn't; not because I gave my word . . . A thing like it didn't merit my word. I did it because that's what exterminators did. Got rid of the nest of poisonous spiders in the closet. I didn't leave them half alive and waiting around for someone to stumble into.

"Did it talk?"

I turned my head as I wiped the blade against my jeans. "Yeah, it did," I said absently to Robin, who, as usual, had managed to do a nice tidy slaughter without getting one drop of blood on himself or messing up his hair. Only the wet bottom half of his pant legs was ruined. I, on the other hand, was soaked, muddy, bloody; the usual. If only there were lobster bibs big enough for monster hunting.

"Good. I'd hate to think I had to kill a kindergarten class of revenants and see a vagina large enough to drive a Volkswagen through for nothing." He used the back of my shirt to clean his sword. I didn't complain. I deserved it, leaving him as the world's most unlucky birthing coach. "Perhaps I should shove you up there. Expand your sexual horizons." Now that, nobody deserved. I stood and put away my blade.

An "I hunger" drifted mournfully from the back of the warehouse. He'd killed the revenants, but mom—which to be fair, you couldn't kill without a rocket launcher— was still good to go, which had me good to go as well.

"Well?" he said, beckoning for the information with impatient fingers. "What did it say?"

"It wanted to know where your cat got that rhinestone collar. Said it was tacky as hell." I headed for the opening to the outside, leaving our Venus out of sight, out of mind, and hopefully out of horribly disgusting dreams as well.

"It's rubies, not rhinestones, you fashion heathen, and I know you didn't drag me out here in New York City's version of the Everglades, ruin my shoes, my pants, my ability to function with anything female for the foreseeable future, and my entire morning to *not* tell me what you found out," he demanded.

"Pucks, you can't stand it when someone knows something you don't, can you?" I commented as I passed into the sun and headed for the Jeep. "Where's Salome?" Robin had picked up the carrier at the door, but it was empty.

He didn't answer me any more than I'd answered him. He did manage to call me every equivalent of jackass he could think of, keeping it all in English so a nonbilingual moron like me could understand each one. I nodded, snorted, and gave him the occasional "good job" when it was a really filthy one. When we got back to the Jeep, Robin still didn't have his answer, but I had mine. It turned out Salome had beaten us back to the Jeep. She was batting a revenant head around the floorboards with waning enthusiasm. To a cat, it was no fun when they didn't wriggle and squirm. She yawned when she saw us, her teeth suddenly much bigger with the gray furless lips peeled back, then went to her usual grin.

"No, no. Absolutely not," Goodfellow told her. "You are not taking that home and rolling it across my finely crafted floors. Do you realize how hard it is to remove blood from marble grouting? I thought not." He tossed the head into the water as he slid behind the wheel while holding the carrier. He picked up Salome whose Egyptian dusk eyes narrowed. "Yes, very fearful. You're the feline fatale. Take a nap." She was deftly popped in the carrier and it was placed on the backseat.

"Do dead cats nap?" I asked, although at the moment I wasn't particularly curious, but I was hoping to distract

Robin. I should've known there wasn't much chance of that, and there wasn't.

"So obviously you feel this is a need-to-know situation. I and my ruined wardrobe can both assure you that I need to know." He started the Jeep as I settled into the passenger seat.

"Oh, I know you need to know. Can't stand not knowing. Are flat-out dying to know." I closed my eyes and crossed my arms. I didn't know if dead cats napped or not, but I did. "But guess what? You're not getting to know." I ignored him as his cursing escalated and I closed my eyes tighter against the bright daylight.

Hell, I wished I didn't know.

But in the end I did tell him. He was right. He deserved to know. It was safer for him if he did. After I told him, the swearing stopped and he squeezed my shoulder sympathetically. "I am sorry, but I would be lying if I said I hadn't seen it coming."

I'd be lying to myself if I didn't admit the same thing. I'd learned in the past where lying to myself got me . . . in a world of hurt. Instead, this time I kept my eyes shut and did everything I could not to think about anything. No lies, no truth—nothing at all. As most things tended to do when you needed them the most . . .

It didn't work.

3

Cal

Abelia-Roo and her clan were at a campground in the Catskills. They would be tucked away in a less scenic and more private corner of the RV park where they could avoid any contact with outsiders, *gadje*. That wasn't to say they weren't running some cons, doing a little tarot or palm reading; Abelia-Roo wasn't the best role model or leader, but they'd be more likely to do that in the nearest town. Wouldn't want the natives having a map to the front door of your Batcave, or considering Abelia-Roo, to your volcano hideout complete with lasers for toasting the genitals of your luckless hero.

It was a two-and-a-half-hour trip late that same afternoon and Niko actually let me do the driving. We retrieved his car from where Robin let us park it at his lot, although in the back, far separated from the other cars like the old days of leper colonies. To give Goodfellow credit, it *did* look contagious: patches of different-colored paint, older than either Niko or me; no MP3 player; no disk player, cassette player; not even an eight track player. I wasn't exactly sure what that last was, but it would have to be better than the AM radio, which is all we managed to get. And with that luxury option, the big brown and maroon monstrosity was slightly better than his last car, which had bit the dust six months ago.

I was still surprised my brother let me drive his latest shitmobile. This one was a Cadillac Eldorado convertible back from the days when they were apparently made to double as tanks in case war broke out on the Jersey turnpike. He was possessive of each and every one of his massive, beat-up babies, although he'd yet to clue me in on why he kept his weapons, his clothes, his routine, his bedroom, his *life* immaculate, but the cars— they were the opposite. When I asked, he always said with a faint trace of condescension, "One day you'll understand, Grasshopper."

There were many *one day*s. I just chalked up the car one with the others and was grateful I actually made it in the big-boy seat. Granted, my window didn't roll down and the air conditioner . . . There was no air conditioner. I sat and sweltered in the heat, which had climbed since morning. "Jesus"—I mopped sweat from my face—"let me break the window. Come on, Nik, I'm begging you."

"And won't that be refreshing when January arrives?" He gave the rearview mirror an annoyed look at the bright red cubes that swung back and forth as I swatted them his way. "And what did I tell you about the fuzzy dice?"

"Hey, they're from Goodfellow. You'll take it up with him. Besides, if you drive a car that looks like fuzzy dice were in the option package, you're going to get fuzzy dice." I slammed the heel of my hand against the radio to shut it off. It stayed on. It always did. "Who the hell is Air Supply and why do they hate me so much?"

"Did you tell him what you learned from the revenant? And it's a band from the seventies."

Music before we were born and an evil that made revenants look like fuzzy puppies fighting over a chew toy. "How do you *know* that? You couldn't possibly listen to that crap."

"Because I know everything," he said as if it were the most simple of conclusions. And with Niko, yeah, it was. "And Robin?" he said, pushing.

"I told him. Better safe than sorry when dealing with the Kin." I trusted Robin with my life and he'd come through every time. That kind of trust was a huge step for me, and Goodfellow had never made me doubt he deserved it . . . at least not since the first time he'd saved Nik and me. Trust didn't have anything to do with why I almost hadn't told him, changing my mind only at the last minute. The reason was simple enough: I just hadn't wanted to talk about it. I had thinking to do. I also didn't want to do that. Not yet. My Zen, one-with-the-universe, happy-frigging-lucky mood had disappeared in that hangar—no getting it back, but it didn't mean I wanted to dwell on it.

It was hard to lose something that was almost impossible to find to begin with.

But I had told him all the same. The revenant had said the Kin had found out about Delilah and me, *all* of the Kin—not just her former screw du jour that I'd neutered in the park. "I didn't have to tell you though, did I?" I asked Nik.

And I hadn't. I'd walked into the apartment and he'd seen it, what I'd learned, behind my blank eyes and blanker face. He'd known, because he could read me like a book. He had asked what the revenant had said the Kin were going to do about it, though. But, that, the revenant hadn't known. It was easy enough to guess. They'd either kill Delilah or give Delilah the opportunity to redeem herself by killing me. Simple. To the point. The Kin weren't much on Machiavellian-style schemes. Hump it, eat it, or kill it—that was good enough for them.

Niko didn't dwell on it after the short discussion,

which was what I needed. He let me drive the car too, which I'd thought I'd needed, but now I was wishing for his side with the window that worked. Cooking in a sauna was a distraction, but not the most entertaining one. I'd switched to short sleeves and left the Eagle and Glock at home. This time I was carrying my SIG Sauer. I had to rotate my toys so they all got action. My jacket was in the backseat in case we were pulled over or had to stop at a public place and I needed to cover up the holster. The bandage taped over my forearm did the same for the revenant bite. I wouldn't have bothered hiding it behind a bandage after cleaning it; it had stopped bleeding early on, but people tended to notice what looked like a human bite mark on your arm. Oddly enough, that kind of thing didn't label me friendly, cheerful, and trustworthy to the world at large.

"It is unfortunate," he began, deciding the subject needed more discussing after all. "I'm only surprised it didn't happen sooner," he said, echoing Robin's earlier comment and my own thoughts. In sympathy, I guessed, he hit the radio with a much lighter tap of his hand and this time it immediately shut off. "When are you going to talk to Delilah about this?"

"You've had this car six months and you couldn't do that before now? And when I absolutely can't avoid it," I griped, annoyed at the months of horrific excuse for music I'd suffered through. I was scarred. My eardrums were scarred. From what I could tell, the seventies had been a time of singers whose balls hadn't dropped yet. Voices so high I couldn't believe they hadn't shattered every window in the *Titanic*'s rusty cousin we were cruising in. Although at the moment that would've been a good thing, since even with the top down the heat was god-awful. I mopped at the sweat again dripping along my hairline, thankful I'd pulled the now-damp strands back into a short ponytail.

"What fun would that be—not torturing my little brother?" He eased his seat back. "And avoiding it only makes the uncertainty last longer. This is something I would think you wouldn't want to be uncertain about." He closed his eyes, lecture over. "I'm going to meditate. If you see a Sasquatch looking for a ride on the side of the road, keep going. There's not enough legroom in the back."

I didn't bother asking if Bigfoot was real. I'd stopped asking questions like that when I was eighteen. Sooner or later you'd find out one way or the other. Why spoil the surprise? In other words, my brain couldn't begin to store all that was real, all that wasn't, and the rest no one had a clue about one way or the other. I left that to Nik. It was easier than getting a pocket encyclopedia entitled *When to Shoot, When Not to Shoot, and When to Run Away Like a Little Girl in Pigtails*. Not to say a little girl in pigtails couldn't be scary in her own right, especially if her teeth were pointed and her eyes glowed green in the dark. And you could bet your ass there were some out there like that. I might not have known the name or have seen one before, but the world was full of nightmares I hadn't seen yet. It didn't mean they didn't exist.

Diversity: It made the world go round.

"Meditate away, Cyrano." I tried to put my seat back. Naturally it was frozen completely upright and made for the comfort of the anal-retentive driver, stick up the ass a luxury option. "If I go through a drive-through, I'll ask for a bag full of grass and oats for you. Maybe a lactose-free, chemical-free, flavor-free shake to go with."

"You do that." He folded his hands across his stomach, linking fingers. "And don't think I've forgotten our discussion about gates. I'll give you a break for now, because of the unpleasant day you've had." The eyes, opened for a sideways gaze, steely and implacable, had me giving an internal wince. That was too bad, considering what I had planned for the rest of the day. It was too bad for me and too bad for my ass, which would receive a kicking requiring an organ donor with an Auphe/human-compatible gluteus maximus. And those were hard to come by.

"But sooner or later," he went on, "we *will* talk about it."

Sooner would be my bet, and those, unfortunately, were always the bets I won.

I drove on while Niko meditated. I didn't see Bigfoot, not until we arrived at the RV park, and then I saw them everywhere. Campers with their shirts off and backs hairier than any Sasquatch, Yeti, or woolly mammoth combined. My trigger finger twitched because, honestly, was someone with a carpet on his back, plaid shorts, socks and sandals, any less of a threat to the world—at least visually? But I drove past them and didn't shoot a single one. I wished for a Weedwacker or a little temporary blindness, but I didn't shoot, and that got chalked in the success column.

I followed Abelia-Roo's directions via Nik, who'd gotten them from her when he'd spoken with her on the phone. He'd written them down for me in his neat, precise handwriting. "Hey, we're here. Nap's over."

"Meditation isn't a nap and if you think it is, maybe once an hour isn't enough for you." Niko nodded toward a gravel road to the right.

Hourly was doable. Five, ten minutes and I zipped right through the mantras counted on my mala, but zipping through them probably wasn't the point. But flying through them or not, it was obviously working, or the meditation combined with the death of the Auphe was working. I'd made those three gates in the past six months without any of the Auphe side effects of the past. It was simple. I didn't lose myself to it or to something buried in me. I owned it now. It didn't own me. Only getting Niko to see that was going to be a trick, because he had seen the times it *had* owned me. And the memory of an Auphe-hissing brother, teeth stained with blood, and sanity on a temporary vacation, stuck with a person. It had stuck with Nik; that was for sure.

I just had to get him to see the light, and with his being equally as stubborn as I was, that was going to be a problem. When he was smarter than I was and capable of picking me up off the ground by my neck à la Darth Vader without the asthma—not that he would, but he could—that meant I rarely won an argument. At least I had the upper hand in knowing he wouldn't actually kill me—no matter how much I deserved it.

I stopped the car before a half circle of about thirty RVs. There wasn't a single person outside. That was different from the last time. They'd been wary, but I'd seen women, kids, and the not-so-shy-and-retiring muscle Branje who'd almost lost his nose to my temper. "How much do you think they have? The Sarzo Clan? Like down to the penny?"

"Fair-sized clan." He took in the condition of the RVs. "Their homes aren't too old, definitely not decrepit. Important enough to have several antiques lying about for sale." Like the Calabassa crown that had nearly been the cause of his death. "Liquid assets, probably a hundred thousand. Abelia-Roo is sharp in all ways. I doubt her money-making skills are any less effective."

"Okay then." I pulled the key from the ignition and tossed it to him. "In case you want to listen to the radio," I said, smirking.

His eyebrows went up. "You think I'm going to let you do the negotiating without me? You wanted to pistol-whip her last night. Both of us would provide a more balanced approach."

"Is that your tactful way of saying we play Good Ninja, Bad Monster?" I asked. I opened the door and climbed out of the oven. Draping over the top of the immovable window, I leaned down. "I need this, Nik. Because of her, you almost died. All she had to do was say a few words to warn us. Just a couple and she didn't. If it had been me instead of you, wouldn't you want to make her pay a little?"

That brought the brows down, the expression disappearing from his face. "I would want her to pay more than a little. I would want her to pay a great deal, which is why I don't think your being alone with her is a good idea."

"I won't lay a finger on her, swear," I promised.

He tilted his head, face still impassive.

"Or a knife or a gun," I added reluctantly. "Just talking, but I want to be mean and I want to be nasty. If you're there, I won't be able to be all that. Unfortunately, big brother, you bring out the best in me." And while the best wasn't much, it might be enough for me to see her—just for a second—as an ancient old lady, somebody's great-grandma, instead of the malicious piece of work she was, one who nearly lost me my only family.

"I want payback," I finished. "But I won't touch a hair on her balding, snapping turtle head to get it, okay?"

He sighed. "Ten minutes. I'll go ahead and start regretting my decision now and get that out of the way, but in ten minutes to the second I am coming in for you."

"Ten is all I'll need." That was big talk when our first bargaining encounter with the Sarzo had included Robin, who had ripped off anyone and everyone for the entirety of his long life, my knife up Branje's nose, and about five hours total of cursing, dickering, haggling, and the traditional imbibing of blackberry brandy. Maybe I should've been worried. I wasn't. I'd been pretending to be human then.

I wasn't now.

I closed the car door and headed straight for her RV.

I recognized it from last time. It was the only one with a cotton candy pink door. It's the baddest of witches that always have the best candy, isn't it? I didn't bother knocking. I wasn't a polite kind of guy. Opening the door, I walked in to find her waiting at the small kichenette table. "I don't see Hansel or Gretel. Did you eat them already?"

"You talk to your elders like that? Have you no shame?" she said sharply, the dark skin over her cheekbones faded to a dirty pale gray.

Well, well. Look who didn't like me anymore.

"Nope, not one tiny bit. And that's a real pity for you, Abelia-Roo." She was gray-faced, hands twisted in what looked like a painful knot before her on the table, the rank smell of fear floating around her like a cloud. Her eyes were looking at me, sliding away quickly, then looking again.

She knew all right—knew about me.

They all knew. That's why every single Sarzo was hiding in his camper, hiding from the monster, hiding from me. Once it would've eaten away at me. Once I would've despised the unnatural within. Now I just used it and, quite frankly, didn't care if these people thought I was worse than any story-tale demon—worse than a vampire, werewolf, boggle, troll, or revenant. The Rom knew what most people didn't. They knew what lurked in the shadow of the world. They knew all the creatures that lived secret lives and they knew the Auphe—first predator, first murderer, first monster. All that meant they thought they knew me.

And that was going to make negotiations so much easier. After all, it wasn't as if I hadn't planned on telling her myself, but this worked even better. Someone had done me a favor. She'd had a while to think about me and this meeting, and none of those thoughts would've been too pleasant. They really wanted that Suyolak guy back badly if they were willing to pay the devil times ten to do their dirty work.

Payback's a bitch, Abelia, I thought as I slid into the booth opposite her, just like you. So get ready to suck it up.

I looked around at the pink and green checkered couch with its small coffee table. There wasn't a crystal ball or pack of tarot cards in sight. Only ruffles, a flower-patterned rug under the table, and the fading smell of cinnamon from that morning's breakfast. All that was missing were big-eyed kitten teacups. "Damn, Abelia, you've gone all Martha Stewart on me. Where's the good stuff? The 'love spells,' the cards, the paste engagement rings, the hexes? How does all this Bible Belt country charm not dissolve you into a puff of smoke?"

That brought a glare out of her. "We do our work and we do it well. If the buyer is a fool, that is no fault of mine if they end up with less than they expected."

True enough. But I wasn't a fool and I'd still ended up with something I hadn't expected when she'd sold us the Calabassa—the near sacrifice of my brother.

I pulled out my knife and balanced it on its tip in the center of the table, then rotated it slowly with a lazy back-and-forth twist of my wrist. I'd told Nik that I wouldn't use it; I didn't say I wouldn't show it. "Against my better judgment," I said casually, "and, oh, despite our general loathing and hatred of you, my brother and I have decided to take the job. It'll cost you fifty thousand dollars."

She snorted, but it was a weak imitation of her usual snap. "Even a Vayash, even a *gadje* barters better than that—to start so impossibly high." Idly I noticed that matching candy pink curtains were drawn over the tiny window. Petal pink and this poisonous centipede of a woman; it would make you think twice about that old saying about stopping to smell the roses. There was no telling what would scuttle out and bite you when you did.

I smiled as the knife continued to turn . . . just as the gate began to turn behind me. I started it small, out of her sight hidden by my back, and let it grow until it was a full-sized mass of writhing gray light. "But I'm not *gadje*, at least not the kind of outsider you mean, am I?" I let my curved lips peel back to show my teeth. Some would've called it a grin, but only those like me—born in the world's shadow.

"Fifty thousand, take it or leave it." I turned my head slightly, letting my eyes slide toward the tarnished light. "Or you could go through there. Trade instead of money. Would you like to see what's on the other side, Abelia-Roo? Step through there and maybe we'll take care of your 'tiny' problem for free. You won't find a better deal than that." I showed more teeth. "Go on. Aren't you even curious?"

Her wattled neck convulsed as she swallowed, blackbird eyes surrounded by white. She managed to look anywhere but at the gate . . . or at me. "That . . . that is more than half of everything we have."

"You almost cost me my brother, who is the *whole* of everything I have. It seems more than fair to me." I stopped spinning the knife and slapped it flat on the table as the gate crept closer behind me. I could feel it. Eager but contained, and good; it felt damn good and nothing like before—no thirst for blood, no shredding of my control, no consuming hunger.

All right. Maybe a little hunger.

But mainly the feeling I could do anything; be anything; *was* everything. "You pay or we leave." I stood but braced my arms on the table. "I really don't give a shit either way. But when I do leave"—I looked at the gate again, thinking fondly what a good boy it was—"I'm leaving my friend behind."

I took my knife, slid it into its sheath, and headed for the RV door. "Enjoy. I opened it in the middle of a boggle nest. Have anything in your little bags for a boggle?" She didn't move, frozen—the mighty Abelia-Roo, who ruled with an iron fist and hadn't bothered to spare a word to save my brother's life, finally facing something she couldn't control, couldn't curse, and couldn't con.

"I didn't think so." I swung the door open. "Tell Mama Boggle you're a friend of mine when she comes through. She really loves me. I'm like the half-Auphe bastard son she never had."

I was letting the door swing shut behind me when she let out a strangled, "No, we'll pay."

Because she thought I'd actually do it, and it could be she was right. My brother brought out the best in me. People who messed with my brother brought out the very worst.

I caught the door. "Is that so? Damn. I'd been hoping you'd say no." I let the gate thin to nothing. I thought about it first, a long moment, but finally I did let it go before I motioned out the door to Nik. This time I did let it swing shut and went back to my former seat. "Who told you about me? Not that it matters. It's not a big secret these days. I'm just curious. And don't I rate any of that blackberry brandy?" She forked the evil eye at me. I forked my own economy version right back—just the one finger needed. "What do they say? The pot calling the kettle black?" I drawled.

"The Vayash told us," she said between disgusting puckered lips. "I called them after contacting you at the bar. I wanted to know if you were hard workers, would do well by us. Instead, they warned us and revealed to us what you are. Your clan revealed their shame to protect their fellow Rom. It is the kind of loyalty and honor our people share with one another, not that a creature like you could understand that."

"The same loyalty and honor you showed us at our last business arrangement?" Niko asked as he came through the door. "And if you think my brother is so lacking in it, why do you want to hire us?"

"Sometimes only evil can find evil, can detect its blackened wake." She looked as if she wanted to spit to cleanse her mouth of a bad taste, but that wouldn't have done her squeaky-clean linoleum any good.

"Takes a monster to catch a monster. Maybe I can get that on a T-shirt." I wedged myself in the corner to give Niko's longer legs some room, then promptly elbowed him for having the audacity to be a few inches taller than I was. Not my usual "on the job" behavior, but I wasn't looking to impress Abelia-Roo. She was impressed enough. Impress her any more and I might short out that shriveled black wad of phlegm she called a heart. While that might do the world a favor, it wouldn't get us fifty thousand dollars or save the world from a murderous, psychotic, and by now, claustrophobic, antihealer.

Niko did something under the table that cut off all feeling below my right knee. Catholic nuns had their rulers; Niko had his one hundred seventy-six ways of making you regret you had nerve endings. I winced and reluctantly tried for a more businesslike demeanor. "Nik, Abelia here, loving and generous granny that she is, is paying us fifty thousand dollars to find their lost jack-in-the-box, killer-in-the-box, whatever you want to call it. Where do we start?"

"Fifty-thousand? That is generous. Most generous indeed." The gaze Nik turned on me let me know I was lucky he didn't do something that didn't paralyze me from the neck down instead of the knee and then pound my head against the table. He didn't ask how I'd managed to get such a good deal—he knew. Big brothers could always look at their little brothers and not only know they'd been bad, but *how* they'd been bad. And brothers didn't come any sharper than mine.

I'd been aware of what I was going to do when I got out of the car and I'd been aware I'd have to pay the price, not from the gate itself, but from my brother. I'd done it anyway. If I had to pay a little for Abelia to pay a lot, then that was the way it had to be.

"Fifty thousand," I confirmed. "But no brandy. Although with your being pure Rom and human to boot, I'd think you'd rate."

"Forget the brandy." Niko turned back to Abelia-Roo, one more narrowed glance letting me know other things wouldn't be so easily forgotten. Those things were starting to add up at a fast and furious rate. I had four gates to pay for now. "When was Suyolak taken? Do you have a description of the men and the truck they transferred the coffin into? And were there any strangers around beforehand, asking questions about Rom culture or history?"

"A researcher, you mean. A professor and, yes, one did. We are Rom, not naïve sheep. Of course we know he was behind it. He came to talk of our legends. He brought up the legend of Suyolak over and over. Could he really heal any wound, any illness? We took his money, spun him nonsense tales, and sent him on his way. We'd planned on moving on the next day anyway, but the next day was not soon enough." She pounded her fist sharply against the table. "*Johai!* The card he gave us was false. The name equally false. He was a tall man, silver hair, dark eyes." Her hands fluttered about, then disappeared and reappeared with one of her infamous tiny bags. "That night they came, night before last. The truck had no license plate. The men wore jeans, black shirts, and ski masks. They shot five of our clan; shot them dead and carried Suyolak away."

Niko said, "He needs someone healed then." I nodded in agreement. Whoever it was hadn't been trying to hide that.

"It would seem." Abelia had spilled a small mound of gray powder on the table and was stirring it randomly with a sticklike finger. "We gathered the rest of our men and drove the roads searching for them, but found nothing. The Plague of the World was gone."

By now she'd drawn an elaborate figure in the powder, one piece of it pointed at me like a spear. I snorted and passed my hand over it, wiping it out and leaving a clean surface of powder. I drew a tic-tac-toe design in the middle. The letters to "screw you" fit perfectly—it even left a nice neat space between the two words.

"Unless that's anthrax and you've gotten Ebola-infected flying monkeys waiting outside for me, you're out of luck," I responded. "I know you fool the marks, but didn't your mommy tell you there was no such thing as magic?" The Calabassa she'd sold us had been a thing of technology made by a race long extinct. Iron and zinc were proven to block psychics . . . by science. I knew that because Nik had made me watch some long, boring documentary on it. And mummy cats? Wahanket infused them with a tiny portion of his own life force. . . . I absolutely did not want to know how.

But magic? Spells and fairy dust? Fall into the piranha pool at the local zoo and try tossing your magic powder at them. See what happens—beyond seasoning the human soup, doubtfully much. To believe in magic, you had to have faith. I saved my faith, what faith I had, for lead and steel, guns and blades. They worked. Even monsters laughed at the idea of magic.

She swept the powder back into the bag. "I and five of my best will follow you in your search. We will need to be there to escort the coffin back to the clan."

True. We'd need one of their RVs. People are going to give you a second look when you're driving down the interstate with a coffin strapped to the top of your car. Then again, I'd sooner ride on top of that coffin buck naked, eating nachos and waving a Yankees foam finger, than have Abelia-Roo tagging along.

"We can rent a truck," I said dismissively, "when we find it. Or just use the one we find it in."

"You will also need me to make sure the seals are intact on the coffin."

"We'll get a padlock. There are Home Depots everywhere." I nudged Niko with my shoulder to move the situation along. "Hand over the money. We'll call you when we have what's-his-name back."

Niko didn't cooperate. "She may be right. It might be a good idea to have along those who've been responsible for Suyolak for so long. They know more about him than we can find out in weeks of research. Weeks we don't have. If he gets free before we find him, they could be helpful. They are his people, after all."

"Who locked him in a box for hundreds of years," I pointed out. "The only help they could give us then is that they'd be the first people he'd go after." I thought about that for a moment. "You're right. It's a good idea."

Niko's lips twitched in a way that let me know I was both incorrigible, as he'd say, and on the money, as I'd say. "The money, Abelia-Roo, and we'll leave in the morning. By then I plan to have a direction, at least, to head toward."

She studied us both, although when she looked at me, it was with the revulsion of someone finding a black widow spider at her bare feet and no house shoe or book to smash it. Not that Abelia-Roo couldn't strike one dead with one second of her hemlock glare. She probably could and did at regular intervals, but it didn't work with me. I gave her a sunny smile with not one drop of venom to be seen. "The money," I repeated. The "I win" I didn't have to say. The price alone said it.

She twisted her features into one of those old dried apple doll faces you saw people selling by the road in Appalachia. It'd been a long time since we'd been that way . . . since I was eleven . . . but I remembered them. Most kids would've thought they were creepy, as if they'd come to life in the middle of the night and shove their apple heads down your throat to choke you before you had a chance to scream. But most kids didn't have a remote clue what creepy really was.

Creepy or not, Abelia would have those dolls winning beauty contests. She slid from behind the table and shook out her dusty crimson and dull black skirts. She definitely hadn't gone the Martha Stewart route in the clothing department. Abelia-Roo in a pink sweater tied around her narrow shoulders and matching slacks: It was enough to make your brain spasm at the improbability of it all, not to mention the added picture of her passing out holiday brownies . . . topped with cherries and just a hint of arsenic, of course.

And she was afraid of me. Didn't that put me in the big-boy category or what?

Rustling back toward the sleeping quarters of the RV, she passed through layers of scarves that hung from the ceiling, none of which were pink—Martha Stewart ended there—and disappeared into a gloom no stray ray of sunshine could penetrate. It took her a few minutes, which was not too good for me. Niko seemed to grow larger with each passing second until I felt about the size of that eleven-year-old boy who'd fed one of those apple dolls to a cow hanging her head over the fence by the road (she spit it out, by the way). Yeah, I was the salmon heading up the falls and Niko was the grizzly bear waiting for me at the top.

Finally we heard the sound of one of those cheap accordion doors closing and Abelia-Roo returned with a paper bag. She put it on the table before Niko, who opened it and counted it with quick and efficient fingers. He might be pissed at me, but that didn't distract him from the fact that trusting the old woman was a mistake only a fool would make; my brother was no fool. The fact that all fifty was there and not half now, half on delivery, told me something. If this Suyolak guy did get out, Abelia didn't see a future where money mattered.

"He is a monster," she said sharply to Niko, "this thing you call a brother, but perhaps you are worse. You are his keeper. We keep our monster under lock and key and you let yours run, free to kill and destroy as he sees fit. Everything he does, the responsibility is shared equally with you."

"Of everything he does, I'm proud to claim half." Niko rose to his feet. "We will see you in the morning." I followed him out the door and back to the car. I started to get back in the driver's seat, when a hand snagged the back of my shirt and jeans and helped me all the way through to the passenger side of the bench seat and halfway out the open window.

"I guess we're having that talk now?" I asked, looking down at the gravel beneath the car.

"Why not? Talking to this end of you"—his voice came from behind me, "behind" functioning in a dual sense here—"isn't any different than speaking with the other end and is about as effective."

I set my hands on the sun-hot door and pushed my way back in the car. Sliding back into the seat, I took the lap belt from the days when the highest quality of safety technicians thought that crushing your skull against the dashboard was just swell and wondered whether to fasten it or try to strangle myself with it. Asphyxiation would be less painful than one of Niko's "talks." This time, though, I knew I was right. All the other times, admittedly, I'd been wrong. I knew I was wrong and didn't bother to deny how very wrong I was. That made this unfamiliar territory.

He got behind the wheel and closed his door with a muffled click, carefully . . . quietly. It was Nik at his most annoyed. When you could do what my brother could, when you could kill as easily as most people could breathe, it paid to have control—the same kind of control he doubted I had. And to have that control in less than six months with what the gates had done to me before that, I didn't blame him for the doubt. I did have the gates in check, though, but getting Nik to believe— that was going to be a trick.

"I take it you have the payback you wanted."

His voice was as quiet and self-possessed as the rest of him as he stared straight ahead, although he hadn't started the car yet. I gave the bag of money he'd set in the floorboard a dismissive nudge with my shoe. It hadn't been about the money. It had been about making her feel at least a tenth as terrified as I'd felt when I thought my brother was gone. "I got some, yeah."

"I think you obtained more than 'some.' And there's only one way you could've frightened her that much." Now he looked at me, almost as though he didn't know me. That, oddly enough, scared me probably more than I had scared Abelia-Roo. "You did the very thing I told you not to do, and now here we are."

I opened my mouth, ready to defend myself—in a very real way, desperate to defend myself. Nik was my only family. I'd spent my whole life knowing without a doubt he was always there for me. If my ass needed saving, he would save it. If I was a screwup, which I was some of the time—hell, most of the time—he didn't care. He corrected me or accepted me. He was my brother. He knew me inside and out and that couldn't change. I might have control, but "Know thyself"? I didn't have a goddamn clue. From day to day, minute to minute, my opinion shifted. Man, monster, an ice-cream twist of the two? I didn't know. The bottom line was I didn't know who I was, but Nik did, and that was more than good enough for me.

"Nik . . . ," I started.

He shook his head, cutting me off. "You have control? You swear it?"

"Yes," I replied. I might not know who or what I was at my core, but the gates, that I was sure about. Absolutely positive.

"All right, then." He started the car.

"All right?" I frowned and smacked aside a fuzzy dice that swung and hit me in the face as the car backed up. "Just like that? No talk? No kicking my ass? No telling me I'm being a dangerous idiot?"

"I saw you born, Cal." He braked, cranked the steering wheel to turn the car around, and used the moment to give me the same look, but I saw it for what it was now. It wasn't that he didn't know me; it was that he was seeing something new. "I saw you grow up. Now I see the end product. I see the man, and you can't be a man if I don't let you be."

I exhaled and folded my arms across my chest in relief and a little disbelief. "I'm a man? Yeah? Do I get a bar mitzvah?"

"The bris comes first. Do you want to borrow my tanto? I sharpened it this past weekend."

This time it was my legs I folded and in a fairly unmanly fashion. "Funny. Funny stuff there." Home deliveries and a doctor/hospital-averse mother left me as nature made me and it was a little late to be changing that now. "I've been trying to cut back on do-it-yourself circumcisions."

He had driven us almost out of the park before he spoke again. "As a full-fledged adult, you will experience consequences to your actions, you realize."

"There have always been consequences." Bad ones usually.

"Yes, but in the past I was willing to let some of your idiocy slide. You are now wholly responsible for any and all of your decisions, no matter how catastrophic."

The sun was falling in the sky, spearing me directly in the eyes. I put on my sunglasses and groaned, "All of them? Is that even possible?" I meant it too. I might have made it to adulthood in Niko's eyes, but being an adult didn't mean I was a competent one. I was a gate-building architect extraordinaire and the Traveling King, but that didn't mean I still wasn't a screwup in a few other areas of my life. "Cyrano, can't we sort of ease into the responsibility part? One screwup at a time maybe?"

The Roman profile didn't shift from its serious set. "You're an adult, Cal. Embrace it. All little monster killers grow up. I saw it six months ago. I see it now. You can handle it. I have faith."

Niko's faith was different from my faith and a little less faith might be good. Killing, tending bar, trying to decide if I was more monster than human, and giving a shitload of bad attitude—that I was good at. Everything outside that was a different story, but if Nik thought I could handle the fallout of my occasionally wildly massive mistakes, then I'd give it my best shot. I'd make him proud—or do my best not to make him regret it.

"You're right. I'm old enough to kill for my country, die for my country, vote for president, and to be drunk while doing all three." I leaned back in the chair that worked, enjoying the air through the open window. Damn right I was ready.

"Yes, the very definition of responsibility," he commented dryly.

Maybe not, but considering my past record, it was a start.

*   *   *

When we made it back to the loft it was almost dark. Niko had already put his university contacts to work as we rode back to the city, starting the calls before we had made it out of the Rom camp. It seemed he had one contact in the anthropology department in whom he had special confidence. If anyone had a chance of knowing the foremost experts in Rom culture, this guy, Dr. Penjani, would know about it. Next was a tiny woman I'd met once who taught mythology. Her name was Sassafras Jones, Dr. Sassy Jones, and she was sassy too. Loud, big, fond of pink . . . lots and lots of pink, but it looked better on her than on Abelia-Roo. I was surprised there wasn't a tinge of pink to her wild halo of silver curls and in the icing on the horrible diet cardboard cookies she shoved on me. Not only did she know all the big mythology, anthropology, any-kind-of-ology experts in the country who'd have come across Suyolak in their studies, but she'd also be able to find out if any of them had terminally ill relatives. When it came to academia, Niko said, she was the equivalent of the neighborhood gossip . . . for the entire country.

"So what do we do when we find him?" I demanded, flopping on the couch and turning on the remote. Or rather pressing buttons in thin air as the remote disappeared from my hand more quickly than Houdini could've managed on his best day. Niko laid it on one end table. "Fine," I grumped. "No TV. Doesn't change the fact that if we find him and whoever took him has let him out, we're just a puddle of hemorrhagic fever goo on the ground. Or he might be nice and only explode our hearts or melt our brains, all before we get within a hundred feet of him. Even if I manage to shoot him before I go down or travel closer and break his neck, I still think he'll have time to take us all with him."

"Which is why we need a healer, and since we cannot reach Rafferty, we'll have to try our former client at Columbia, Dr. Nushi."

Who was in reality a Japanese healing entity called O-Kuni-Nushi. He was known to his less than observant human colleagues as Ken Nushi and worked as a doctor and special seminar instructor for the premed upper-classmen at Columbia University. With the only other healer we'd known, Rafferty Jeftichew, now missing for almost a year, Nushi was our only hope. You fought fire with fire; and you fought a hyped-up, homicidal, mega-lomaniac Rom Kevorkian with another healer—and not the kind healing warts for God and five bucks at a tent revival either. You needed the real deal.

Unfortunately, per his answering machine, Nushi had returned to his homeland two months ago—on a sabbatical—and was unreachable at this time. There was no forwarding number or address. Niko tried calling Promise, who in turn called in some favors from the non-human crowd—nothing. She even tried the other side of her life, the insanely rich—some of whom had buildings at Columbia named after them. Her luck wasn't any better there. Nushi liked his privacy. No one knew where he was or how to contact him. "Now what?" I checked my watch. It was almost nine, close to time for me to be heading to work. Until Niko's pals at the university finished burning the prime-time viewing oil, we didn't even have a direction to start driving.

"Go to work. I'll try Rafferty. It's bound to be point-less, but he's all we have left." Rafferty was a healer we'd met about three and a half years ago, maybe longer. If anyone could give Suyolak a run for his money, it would be him. Rafferty had kept me alive when I'd had a single drop of blood left in me. He'd also put me to sleep by merely *thinking* it and stopped my heart and restarted it without breaking a sweat. But he had a sick cousin and was, as far as we knew, traveling looking for a cure even he couldn't provide. We'd called a few times, but he hadn't felt much like communicating, because he hadn't answered a single call, had abandoned his house, and no one, not even Goodfellow with his network of fellow tricksters across the country, had seen hide of him nor hair of his cousin for more than a year.

Rafferty's cousin was a werewolf, same as Rafferty— a Wolf healer; weird, I know. They seemed made to savage, not heal, but, like people, Wolves were all different. But that was the only way they were like people. Werewolves were born, not made; they were a completely different species from humans, although the switching from one form to the other could understandably fool those in the past who had passed on the legends. Unfortunately, the cousin was stuck in wolf form. He was also slowly losing the human reasoning werewolves carried with them while wearing the fur. Rafferty was determined if he couldn't save his cousin, there had to be someone out there who could. He had his mission and he wasn't straying from it. I understood that. I understood family. But talk about bad timing.

"Go to work," Nik ordered, as he punched a number into his cell. "Watch out for the Kin—all of them." After what the revenant had told me, it wasn't something my brother had to tell me twice. Until I knew what the Kin's price would be, I'd be looking over my shoulder more than usual. I pushed up off the soft couch with regret at a lost nap, wished for once we'd catch an easy break, and was just grabbing my jacket when Niko said with a surprised tone I didn't often hear from him, "Rafferty? Is that you?"

Holy shit. Forget the break. Forget the lotto.

We'd just hit the jackpot.

4

Catcher

My name is Catcher.

My parents named me after *Catcher in the Rye*, the book on which they'd had to team up to do a class presentation. Until then, they hadn't been that interested in each other. But that book about teen angst and a loss of innocence had brought them together, and from then on they had been small-town high school sweethearts—depressing book; nice story.

But that's not the point.

My name is Catcher.

I thought that every morning when I woke up—every single one—to make sure I was okay; all there; in my right mind; not having an episode. I could picture the air quotes around that last word clear as a bell. "Episode"—what a stupid thing to call it. I snorted and opened my eyes to see the morning light streaming through the battered blinds. It was useless really. If I were in my wrong mind, I wouldn't know anyway. But the routine made me feel better, so I said it in my head. My name is Catcher.

My name is Catcher, and I'm hungry.

It wasn't *War and Peace*, but it was an accomplishment and a relief. I took it as such and lounged on the motel bed, its busted springs complaining under me while I waited for my cousin to bring back breakfast. They didn't like my kind in diners. They had their laws, their signs on the door: NOT ALLOWED. KEEP OUT. Pure prejudice. They had ramps for the physically challenged; parking spots for the same. For me they had nothing but the boot. The hell with them then. If I wasn't good enough for them, then I'd hang around and watch TV until my cousin came back with all the sausage and pancakes I could eat. It was better than dealing with cranky morning commuters trying to snatch some breakfast before work anyway.

Besides, any day I was myself was a good day, and I was determined to enjoy every good day to the fullest. My mom had always said I wasn't the glass-half-full type—I was more of an Olympic-sized-pool-overflowing kind. Moms, they always thought the best of you, but I had to admit she'd been right. If there was a bright side, I could see it. If there wasn't a party, I would start one. Life was a gift. I'd always known that—maybe for a reason. The universe was all about balance.

I yawned, and lazily smacked the remote bolted to the table. News. Smack. Morning show. Smack. Cartoons. Smack. Nature channel. Wolves of Alaska. Fighting wolves. Running wolves. Romping wolves. Mating wolves.

Hello.

The door opened and my cousin walked in with several Styrofoam containers stacked in his hands. He looked at the television and rolled his eyes. "Porn? This early in the morning?"

Like there was a bad time for it, but Rafferty wasn't a morning person, so I cut him some slack. I liked the morning myself, but I was easy to please. I grinned and yipped forcefully as I bounded off the bed.

"Yeah, yeah. I got your pancakes with apples and

whipped cream. Keep eating like this and you're going to be one fat son of a bitch." I pawed the air impatiently. "Don't get your tail in a wad," he grumped. "I have your two pounds of sausage and bacon too." He set the containers on the flimsy table by the window and began opening them up. I jumped up on one of the two chairs and dug into the pancakes. They'd always been my favorite since I was a kid. My mom fixed them every Sunday morning, the same Sunday mornings Rafferty would wander over. His mom, my mom's twin sister, had died a year after he was born, and his own dad wasn't much of a cook. Raff ate most of his meals with us.

We'd done most everything together. We were in the same grade. All the new kids would think we were brothers. When your mothers were twins, you tended to favor each other. We both had auburn hair, but mine was a shade darker, and neater than the I-don't-give-a-crap style Rafferty had had his whole life. My eyes had been the same russet of his—except when they were yellow.

They were yellow all the time now.

We'd grown up together, three houses apart. Gone to elementary school together, junior high, high school. Family stuck together. Wolves stuck together. When you were both, you really were glued at the hip. We'd even gone to the same college, although postgrad we'd gone different ways. He'd gone to one with a better med school, and I'd headed to one with a professor famous for his study of the rain forest. But we still e-mailed, called once in a while, spent the first year's spring break together chasing bikinis on beaches. Then the second year I'd chased my master's degree in biology to the Amazon.

Nine months later I'd come back and ruined my cousin's life.

I lifted my muzzle from the scraps of the pancakes. I looked back toward the blinds and the light. Years;

it had been years now. Five. Six. It was getting harder and harder to keep count, just like it was getting harder and harder to stay myself. I came and I went, more and more often now.

"You have whipped cream on your nose. Hard to mope with whipped cream on your nose," Rafferty grunted, pointing a piece of bacon at me. "We've got another chance. That guy in Wind River, Wyoming. The Arapaho healer. He's supposed to be good."

But not the best; Rafferty was the best. I knew it; Rafferty knew it too, but I wasn't going to push him on it. My cousin had done everything for me. I wasn't going to take away his . . . not hope. That was long gone. What he had left was denial. I wasn't going to take that away. It wasn't hope, but it was better than nothing.

And that nothing would come soon enough.

I ducked my head, licked the cream off my nose, then snatched the bacon out of his hand. Crunching it, I swallowed and gave him my best nonmoping grin. I looked back at the still-horny wolves on television, then at the food, and gave a low woo woo of inquiry.

"No. No good-looking waitresses. And stop with the I-need-to-get-laid thing. You know I'm a born asshole. A little sex isn't going to change that, and I have other things on my mind right now, okay?"

The born asshole who had just happened to give up years of his life for me. My family since I could remember. The only family . . . the only real family I had left now that our parents had died. They had gone too young, but I was almost glad they weren't here to see this. I sighed. Wolves do sigh, sometimes for the very same reasons people do. I picked out three pieces of bacon and dropped them in his container. It wasn't like he was afraid of germs. One: He was a healer. Two: He had plenty of Wolf germs of his own. His eyes flashed yellow and back to amber. "You're a pal." A born ass, a born sarcastic ass, but he meant it. Diamonds are a girl's best friend; meat is a werewolf's.

He ate them, but he was distracted—not *seemed* distracted. Not only could I read my cousin's face with the ease of long practice; I could smell him just as a person could smell a bakery. Humans could smell chocolate, vanilla, caramel, cinnamon, a thousand different things. But we Wolves could smell so many more things, and so much more intensely. Emotion was easy. A state of mind like distraction wasn't much harder.

I whuffed at him abruptly, jumped down from the chair, and moved over to the open laptop on the floor by the TV. Using my mouth, I picked up the pencil lying next to it, maneuvered it around, and tapped the mouse pad with it. I sat on my haunches as my settings loaded. Slow, slow. Give a wolf a break already, Dell. Finally, I pulled up Word and started typing. Still chewing bacon, Rafferty finally wandered over and bent slightly to read.

"Hey, 'Captain Jack-off' seems a little harsh, especially coming from someone who keeps forgetting to flush the john," he grumbled. He read further. "Damn it, I'm not keeping secrets. Yeah, yeah, you can pick the music today, but you play any country western and I'll kick your furry ass. Hell, no, it wasn't me stinking up the place last night. You were the one who ate all the White Castle sliders." He frowned at the next line. "You want to see the new Batman movie? The one that's in the theaters now? Catch, I don't know. Last time we almost got busted."

I growled. He snorted and echoed the growl perfectly. "Right. I'm terrified."

This time I growled and bared my teeth. When that didn't work any better than the other, I fell over onto my side and rolled onto my back, exposing my vulnerable stomach and neck. He groaned, "Goddamnit, fine.

We'll go tonight, but you'll have to take a bath, so no whining."

Sucker. I grinned around the pencil and sprang back up to type one last line with pithy punctuation. "*No*," he said with exasperation and a big fat lie, "no damn secrets, and if that emoticon of the guy doing the sheep is another subtle hint at my needing to get laid, cut it out."

I dropped the pencil, slammed the laptop lid down with a hard swat of my paw, and growled again. This time I meant it. The deep bass of it reverberated in the back of my throat before spilling out as my lips peeled back to show my teeth. Rafferty's eyes swirled between amber and yellow. "Shit." He straightened and rubbed a hand over his face. "Okay, it's Niko and Cal. Nik called on my cell last night when I was out getting us dinner." He never answered calls anymore. He hadn't since we hit the road more than a year ago. It was always someone wanting healing, and he didn't have time for that anymore. He was a man . . . well, werewolf . . . with a mission. Me. I came first—no more healings until I was healed.

Trouble was that I *was* healed.

My cousin, he was the best in the country—in the world. I didn't doubt it, but sometimes you did a thing so well, so right, that what you started out with was changed forever. I didn't blame him for this, for being stuck as a wolf with no ability to change back to human. How could I? It was this or death. Even if I'd died and hung around all wolf wings and wolf halo, I wouldn't have blamed him. Rafferty would've turned himself inside out, given up his own life for me if he could have. But sometimes your time was just your time. He knew that. He'd lost other patients. But I hadn't been just another patient.

We all made mistakes.

He gave me years I wouldn't have had. They weren't quite the way I would've wanted to spend them, not every minute of them at least, but I had them. That was something. It damn sure was. And if I lost part of myself with each passing year, nothing lasted forever. Not a thing—that was something Rafferty *didn't* know. And that was why we were covering the country state by state, rumor by rumor. It was for Raff, not for me.

"Stop it, Catcher. I mean it. Stop it right now," he snapped.

I realized I'd stopped growling and was feeling . . . melancholy, nostalgia, inevitability, resignation. Even in our human forms we kept our wolf sense of smell. I lifted a paw and he took it in his hand and squeezed hard. "It's not over. It's not. I'm getting you back, all of you. Got it?"

I twitched my ears. I got it. I did. Pulling my paw back, I poked my nose at the cell phone in his jeans pocket. "Yeah, Niko." He walked over and sat on the bed. I followed and jumped up to sit beside him. "I wouldn't have answered this time either. You come first, but I felt"—he shook his head—"something—something bad. There's a sickness to the east. I can't smell it or touch it, but I can feel it inside. It's like the worst bioengineered death germ a lab could come up with and it's about to crawl out of its petri dish and make a run for it. And I guess I felt like a shit for ignoring all the other calls and messages. The two of them, they're kind of like us—family. One of them not quite right in the head." He tried for the joke, resting his hand on my head and giving it a good shake. I blew out an outraged wet snort and reared up on my hind legs, waving my front ones in the air. I tried for a combination of roar and hiss, but it came out more a choked-on-my-Alpo gurgle.

Rafferty raised his eyebrows. "That's all you've got? That's the best Auphe imitation you've got?"

Disgruntled, I settled back down and turned my head away dismissively. Critics, they were all the same.

"Diva," he mocked. "And, sure, Cal's half Auphe, and I want to either eat him or piss on myself every time I smell the guy, but since New York City is still standing, he must be behaving himself. It's not as if we can blame him for who or what his father was." He turned his head . . . to the east, where he said he felt it, the sickness. "Anyway, they've run into a situation with an antihealer. Suyolak. Sickness doesn't come close to describing him." I looked back curiously with a never-heard-of-the-guy blink of my eyes.

"No, you wouldn't have," he responded. "Only the Rom and the trickster gossip network know about him. Well, they, and those who study mythology, and healers. All healers know about Suyolak, though. It's the first thing they teach you when you start healer training." And he wasn't talking about med school. That was only supplemental to being trained by a true healer. Rafferty at the age of thirteen had surpassed his healing teacher in six months. All healers had the same healing talent, but when it came to power—that was the difference between making a diabetic less prone to high blood sugars or flat-out curing him. Rafferty fell in the latter category. Most healers ran on double D batteries. Rafferty was a nuclear power plant. He was nothing like the healing community had seen.

He was unequaled—or at least I thought so until he started talking.

"Suyolak was a Rom healer. He's old. I don't know how old, but he almost took out Europe during the Black Death. He *was* the Black Death with the help of some fleas and rats. He was born a healer, but he became a killer." He lay back and stared at the ceiling. "They called him the Plague of the World. They always tell healers when we train: Do no harm. And not for the same reason they tell human doctors that. If we start to do harm, we could become like Suyolak; we might never stop. Destroying is easier than fixing. Don't go all Dark Side, in other words. Once Suyolak had a taste for killing, he couldn't stop—or didn't want to."

I turned three times, curled up, and rested my head on his chest as a "go on" nudge. "Somehow or another— I think poisoned alcohol and lots of naked women were involved—he was sealed up in an iron coffin. I imagine he was already waking up when that happened or they would've chopped his head off instead. His clan has spent the time since then hauling him around—apparently the bastard is *still* alive in there—until someone swiped him, coffin and all. Nik asked for our help, because if whoever stole him lets him out . . ."

The Plague of the World.

Rafferty could put people to sleep with a thought; he could stop their heart with a touch. My cousin was the best in the world, but it sounded as though Suyolak had been the best or the worst, depending on how you looked at it, in his own world. It would be a good bet that Suyolak would kill any nonhealer before his heart had time to move from one beat to the next. Niko and Cal needed the help and badly. It was one thing to put me first; another thing to put me first over the entire world.

I glared sideways at Rafferty. "I know," he said, giving in. "I'm an arrogant SOB, but on this, I know what I have to do." I curled my upper lip. "Okay, what we have to do. I'll call him back and let him know we'll meet him in a few days, after we hit Wyoming." I glared again. "Be as pissy as you want," he said, refusing to budge on that. "We're going to Wyoming first. We're getting you fixed there, and then we'll help them. It's the way it's going to be. Live with it. Now, go grab a bath if you want to see your movie." I lifted my head as he rolled out of bed to grab a suitcase. Digging through it, he pulled out a bright orange dog vest that read CANINE COMRADE in bold black letters. We'd discovered WOOFER WINGMAN didn't convince a lot of people. This one worked well enough most of the time and was my ticket into the movie theater.

"Same as usual? I have McKay-Stewart Spontaneous Colonic Hyper-spasm syndrome, and it's the dog for early flatulence detection or a bucket because there isn't an adult diaper big enough in the world."

I grinned in agreement and jumped down to trot to the bathroom and turn on the shower with my jaws. Two hours later I was lying in the aisle, watching a Batman movie. Given my size, I was actually blocking the aisle. A fire hazard, that was me. I knew Rafferty was watching me for any signs of an "episode," and I heard a few whispers about my size. How if I were a dog, then some guy would kiss my furry butt. I ignored it all as I buried my muzzle in a popcorn bag, extra butter, and for two and a half hours watched as some bad guys got their asses kicked, a hero fell from his pedestal, and an oddly sympathetic psycho villain took out people right and left, blowing them up; shooting them; catching them on fire; tossing them off buildings. But that was all right. It was just entertainment, not real life. For two and a half hours, I was able to escape knowing that that *was* real life for some. For two and a half hours, I was able to eat popcorn; I was able to sit with people, watch actors do their thing, and watch couples in the back make out.

I got to watch a brand-new movie. I got to hang out with my cousin in public.

I got to be normal.

It was absolutely a glass-half-full day.

5

Cal

That morning was Hell on Earth, which is my definition for every morning, but especially this one. Once again I was running on little sleep, about half what I'd gotten the night before. Three hours put my thinking skills at about the level of a highly inbred hamster or a former kiddie star turned pop singer, although that was insulting the hamster.

"Huh?" I said as I kept my eyes shut. Nik had said something, but honestly, right then, I didn't care what it was. I didn't care if he'd told me that alien space bimbos had landed in search of our seed and they all had six breasts, all double D. I only wanted to sleep.

"I said, we're here." A flick to my ear woke me up to the back of a taxi and a rising sun. "Why?" I groaned. "This damn early, why?"

Niko looked at me through opaque dark sunglasses. "We're on a mission from Buddha," he said matter-of-factly.

I snarled at him and fought the seat belt and door to get out. It seemed hamster brains and seat belts didn't mix. I considered sawing through it with my knife.

"All right," he modified in a humoring tone. "We're

running a day and a half behind and we're on a business transaction for a malicious old woman who'd happily see us dead, but that doesn't have quite the same ring. Besides, I think Buddha would believe we will gain good karma at saving lives from a deranged healer." He reached out with a single, somehow smug, finger and punched open my seat belt.

"Buddha can kiss my ass." I received a stinging swat on the back of the head as I dragged my two duffel bags behind me, one packed with clothes and one with weapons, onto the curb in front of Goodfellow's car lot in Brooklyn.

"And I know I'm heaped with good karma for putting up with your incessant bitching and moaning. If you didn't sleep, I wouldn't escape it at all." He placed his own bags beside mine and paid the cabdriver. "Forget the usual hundreds of reincarnated lives one usually must pass through. It's a wonder I didn't become enlightened and reached nirvana before you hit puberty for my righteousness in the face of incomprehensible suffering."

"Unh," I growled incoherently. "Asshole." There. That was a little more understandable.

"The first caveman grunting followed by foul language and the second a body that would've made Michelangelo's chisel salute north. The Leandros brothers have arrived," came Robin's voice. Unlike all other times, Niko's Eldorado was parked directly in front, convertible top down, paint proudly peeling, and two bare feet sticking up from the backseat and propped up on the side of the car.

"Tell me he's not naked," I groaned. "I'll pay you a hundred bucks to tell me he's not naked."

"I'm the one who makes chisels rise. *You* tell *me*." Niko took his bags to the trunk, opening it quickly enough to block his view.

The feet spread into a V, letting me see wildly tousled brown hair, overly bright eyes, a mostly empty bottle of wine cradled against his chest with several empty ones in the floorboards, and clothes. I might not be a God-fearing or believing man, but say hallelujah. There were clothes. I moved closer. It wasn't clothes after all, but pajamas. Silk, expensive like all Goodfellow's things were, and it looked like the shirt was on backward and inside out. There were also feathers in his hair—white and gold ones; Ishiah's feathers; my boss's feathers. And there was no unseeing that as much as I wanted to. "So, Goodfellow . . . ," I started.

"Tell Niko that I fixed his window. Free of charge." As he tilted the wine bottle back and finished it off, I looked at the driver's window. It was gone, and there was a mound of safety glass and a hammer on the asphalt beside the door.

"You're one helluva mechanic, I'll give you that." I tossed my bags over to Niko who was looking around the open trunk at the same pile of glass. I couldn't see the expression behind his sunglasses and that was for the best. I imagine it would've melted my face like a bad monster-movie special effect. "I take it you want to tag along on this job?"

"Tag along?" The puck frowned. "I do not tag along. I have led crowds of virgins to a mass fertility and deflowering rite. I accompanied the Argonauts because I thought I'd look amazing in golden fleece, and a threesome with Castor and Pollux was nothing to sneeze at. I told a drunken and toothless hedge wizard a ridiculous story about the Holy Grail and watched King Arthur's knights roam about the countryside forever, looking under every skirt and stone for the thing. I was with Columbus when he found the New World and at the Hawaiian barbecuing of Captain Cook, who, while a cranky bastard, was quite tasty." He pointed the empty

wine bottle at me and almost made it upright in indigna-
tion. "I create adventure. I live life as it has never been
lived before. I forge legends. I do not *tag* along."

"You're tagging along," I drawled.

"Yes," he sighed, falling back again. "I'm tagging
along."

"Why?" I asked. "You hated our last road trip. You
don't like fast food. You don't like gas stations full of
'the common people' . . . you know, anyone who isn't
you. You get bored about thirty seconds on the road and
start flashing ninety-year-old women drivers."

"Someone needs to verify they're taking their heart
medication," he mumbled, and sat up. "Ishiah suggested
it. He thinks I should go and test my resolve or more
realistically, he thinks, to give my resolve a rest."

"What the hell are you talking about?" It was way
too early to follow a puck's train of thought. They were
bullet trains at the very least. They would suck you into
their two-hundred-twenty-five-mile slipstream and it
would be all over for you.

He hesitated, groaned, then said, "Monogamy."

"Monogamous? You and Ish? You?" My mouth
opened, closed, and opened again as I heard Niko, infallible warrior born and bred with nerves of titanium
steel, fumble wildly at the M word and drop his bag.
"I mean . . . *you*?" Robin? The horniest puck in a race
that all but defined themselves by their level of horny.
Wouldn't other pucks rush to form an intervention?
Monogamous Anonymous? They'd tell him they'd have
him off his feet and onto his back again in no time. Or his
front. Or all fours—whichever he'd prefer. That Robin?
"Seriously?"

Robin glared silently. It was answer enough.

"How . . . Christ, how long?" I felt like the hammer
on the ground had levitated and smacked me in the
head. It was that unbelievable—inexplicable even. Only

brain damage could explain it—profound, massive brain damage.

"The whole six months." He dropped his head in his hands. "I haven't had it this bad since . . . Hades, since Pompeii when I was almost married. I mean, Zeus and all his conquests: Leda and Europa and Io and Callisto and so on and so on. How can this be?" He banged his forehead on the seat in front of him. "*Monogamy*. How can I support such a perverse lifestyle choice, especially when it involves *me*? How? Better yet, why? Why would I do something so horrifying and unnatural?"

Robin had once almost been married to a woman named Cyrilla. I remembered the name because it was one of the few times he'd said something about himself that had mattered, not the usual bragging and name-dropping. Cyrilla had mattered to him; she still did, although long gone, and I hadn't forgotten. Then was monogamy that out of the question? And he would've married her too, that had been clear, if she hadn't died with Pompeii. I knew that. He'd told me and I believed him. But that had been a long time ago and just the one time. Besides . . .

Robin Goodfellow?

"And Ishiah has a problem with this?" Niko closed the trunk, immediately giving a minute wince that meant he wished he could take the question back. The soap opera that was Robin's life could be time-consuming and we didn't have the time.

But . . . I was curious.

"Yeah, I thought he wanted you to be a little less . . . er . . . Goodfellow," I added. "You remember. . . . Less whoring around, less lying, stealing, and cheating." I'd thought that somewhat uptight. Robin was who he was. He was a puck, a trickster; he was born to do exactly what he did. Where did Ish get off saying he should be any different? "He's changed his mind?"

"It seems so." He kept his forehead pressed against the back of the seat. "It seems he's mellowed somewhat over the past millennium and feels he has been unfair to me; may have coerced me into fidelity. As if anyone could coerce me into anything I didn't want," he snorted, promptly forgetting his rampant fear of the one-on-one relationship he'd been raving about seconds ago. "So he thought a small separation of a week would put things in perspective for me. I would decide if I wanted to jump the first Hooters waitress I saw or stay noble and true for him. And—wrap your mind around this—he'll be all right with it either way. He's ready to accept me for good or bad . . . for nonpuck or for puck. He said he was wrong and he likes me the way I am, and the way I've always been. It just took him a while to become a little less judgmental and come to his senses."

"And this is bad how?" Niko asked as he swept a few stray bits of glass from the driver's seat and sat, shutting the door behind him. "This is the perfect Goodfellow situation. You can have your cake and eat it too." And we all knew how much Robin liked his cake. "I would think you'd be celebrating."

I went to the passenger side and was greeted by fangs shown in a cheerful greeting, jack-o-lantern eyes, and a ruby collar with gold ID tag around a hairless neck. I opened the door and Salome, who was sitting upright, regal, and ready for her ride, didn't move. I opened my jacket and showed her my gun. She opened her mouth and I watched her already-visible fangs slide farther out of her gray gums and double in size. I closed my jacket and got in the backseat with Robin.

"Celebrating what?" he asked mournfully. "That I've become something I'm not or that I'm afraid to become something new—if I even can become something new? And is new necessarily better?" This time he leaned against the backseat. "Perhaps peris and pucks cannot be. To do one justice, the other has to give up part of himself." He closed his eyes. "Bedtime. Wake me up at the first ninety-year-old lady in need of flashing."

"Or the first Waffle House waitress." There were times I thought that maybe a hundred thousand years of screwing anything and everything would get old after a while, even for a puck. Then I would go to the next logical thought: This was Robin we were talking about. Not to mention that pucks were born sex addicts. It was in their genes. I knew how hard it was to fight those, even if mine was only a half dose. I was glad it wasn't my problem to figure it out, but I had sympathy for Robin. When you were born to lie, cheat, steal, trick, and screw everything in sight—when that was your purpose designed by nature itself, that was a lot to fight against.

"When you've had sex with more than two people, you're allowed a comment." Goodfellow flicked a feather my way with an annoyed jerk of his hand. "Now? Not quite." Then he was instantly snoring and more feathers were wafting in the air.

"Great start. Yeah, couldn't have gone any better." I batted them away with annoyance. "Don't bother to wake me up in Canton, Nik, unless Suyolak is dropping every man, woman, child, and puppy in town. I don't have any desire to say hey to Abelia-Roo." I slid down, wedged into the corner, and got comfortable for the long haul. I planned on being nap bound as quickly as Goodfellow. I couldn't say I blamed Promise for not coming along. Our last road trip hadn't been enjoyable in any way, shape, or form ... multiple forms. Once bitten, twice likely to stay home in the lap of penthouse luxury.

We were following the old Lincoln Highway that ran across the country to California long before the addition of newer interstates. Niko thought, and it made sense, that whoever had taken Suyolak would know the Rom ... all the Rom in the country ... would be looking for his truck. They would stick to the interstates for maximum coverage and if the guy was smart, he wouldn't. And when Niko Googled last night an outbreak of ten meningitis cases, a higher number than your average outbreak, that were diagnosed the evening before in Canton, Ohio, along the Lincoln, it sealed the deal in his mind. He called Abelia to let her know where to meet us, and that Suyolak had either found some way of working through the coffin or there was one helluva coincidence in Canton. At least whoever had taken Suyolak apparently hadn't opened the coffin or else Canton would be a dead zone and surrounded by the army, fingers ready to pull the trigger on anything that looked like a sick chicken, sneezing pig, or a rabid monkey.

As for who had taken him, Niko's colleagues hadn't come through yet. He had given them the parameters: researchers or professors in the country who know the Rom the best, but had recently dropped out of sight—real life or virtual. All academics lived/breathed/worked on the Internet these days. And any hint of one with a sick relative would be ideal. Dr. Samuels, Niko's first call, wasn't having much luck, but Dr. Jones was positive she was close—she could smell it. I didn't doubt her. Wolves smelled everything; humans smelled gossip. But right now, that spelled nothing else for me to do except catch up on my sleep, which I was on the verge of doing when my cell phone rang. It was the missing-in-action Delilah. And Robin's problem wasn't mine to solve, but this one was.

"Pretty boy."

I'd never broken her of calling me that, especially with the large scar on my chest. Wolves did love their scars. "Delilah. Did you get my voice mail about unmanning, unwolfing, or whatever you want to call it, a friend of yours?"

"Yes. Grey. He hunts forever now," she said in what

sounded like an exotic accent, but was actually vocal cords stuck halfway between human and wolf. Delilah wasn't a high or fine breed, which should've put her below others in her particular Kin pack—or any Kin pack. But everything else she had going for her more than managed to overcome the social scorn that the recessive breeding sought by her minority Wolf sect, the All Wolf, brought out in the high breeds. "All wolf all the time" was their motto—no, more of a religion, I guessed. They were slowly trying to breed the human out of them to accomplish that. So far I hadn't seen much of a success story—just some really odd-looking humans with wolf teeth, eyes, and twisted jaws, though there could be more like Delilah, the differences internal and hidden.

"You don't sound too torn up about it." "Hunts forever" was the werewolf polite way of saying "He's passed on" rather than "He's deader than a rat in a university bio lab."

"He lost breeding equipment. Speaks not much of his fighting skills. Truth . . . to me, no difference before he had them than after. Have had better lovers." I could almost hear her shrug. "Not why I call. They know. Grey found out—you and me. He told Kin. . . . They know."

"Yeah, so I've heard." The revenant with the loose lips had turned out to be a reliable source. It was gratifying to know that I'd killed him for more than simply the practice and exercise. And I'd known there would be consequences for the Kin's knowing about Delilah and me. Kin were for Kin. Wolves were for Wolves. Having sex outside your species was damn near anathema for a Wolf. Sleeping with a human was bad enough, but sleeping with a half Auphe was an abomination not to be tolerated.

Someone would have to die for it; at least the Kin would think so. There was no way around it.

"We're leaving the city on a case, so I don't think I'll be

much help." Not that it mattered whether I was in town or out. While I was good, I wasn't good enough to take on the entire Kin. With thousands of criminal Wolves in NYC alone, who knew how many all over the country, there weren't enough pepper-spray-wielding mailmen in the entire world to take them all out. Delilah's brother, Flay, had come up on the bad side of the Kin sometime ago and he'd done the only thing a Wolf could do and survive that.

He ran.

"You going to run? Meet up with Flay?" I didn't love Delilah. Going with her and living another life on the run, again, wasn't an option. But if she was gone, I'd miss her sharp humor, her carelessness in the face of violence . . . because she knew she excelled in that field—Delilah with her masses of white-blond hair, her amber wolf eyes, her softer amber skin. I'd miss her intelligence and ambition, her fearlessness in the face of my Auphe blood, and her willingness to jump me anytime anywhere.

Hey, I was a guy. Grey might have lost his equipment, but I hadn't lost mine. The jumping part was going to figure into the equation somewhere. It didn't mean I wouldn't miss her for the other reasons too.

"No running," she replied, not sounding as worried as she should have. That was Delilah. There wasn't a situation she didn't think she could turn to her advantage or a creature she imagined capable of taking her down. And mostly she was right, but there was also a part of her that was crazy as hell.

"The Kin aren't going to let this go, Delilah," I said. She had to know that as well as I did.

She dismissed the grim warning. "I have friends. In many packs. This can be fixed, but good idea to get out of town for a while. Where do you go? I'll meet you. Help with job, for free even."

I paused, thinking, then answered, "Canton, Ohio. An IHOP on Cleveland Avenue. It's a little more than four hundred miles. We'll be there in hopefully less than seven hours, depending on Niko's excuse for a car. Call me when you get there."

"Seven hours," she laughed, sounding like rough velvet. "I'll have meal and five beers by time you come. Little boys riding tricycle." Still laughing, she disconnected.

I closed my eyes as I leaned my head back against the seat and folded up my phone, feeling Niko's gaze on me. "You're looking at me, aren't you?"

"I am." His voice was definitely not rough velvet, but unyielding granite.

"Is it a sympathetic look full of brotherly love? You know, the kind that says I have your back? Behind you all the way?" I asked without much optimism.

"No, it is not," he said evenly.

I kept my eyes shut. The sun-tinged pink-black was preferable to one of Niko's glacial glares. It wasn't as if I wasn't suspicious. I was damn suspicious. Delilah helping on a job for free? That would happen about the same time I caught the Easter Bunny hiding eggs in our loft, but . . . after all we'd been through, she deserved a chance to prove herself. "But I'm a man now," I said, "and able to deal with the consequences of my actions. You said so yourself."

"It appears I was wrong in that respect. Your bringing Kin business, especially this business, along on a job is not the wisest or most mature of moves. In fact, I can't offhand think of a more dangerous one. I revoke your pretend bar mitzvah. The bris is looking more likely, however." He started the car and we took off as if there were a jet engine under the hood instead of a thirty-year-old V-8. I felt the two thumps in rapid succession. One was the curb; one wasn't.

"The werewolf under the car?" I asked.

Robin would've seen the wolf slither under there, but would've known we would figure it out on our own and not bothered with a warning. I'd smelled it as soon as we'd gotten out of the taxi. Niko would've seen a stray strand of fur, a flicker of movement, or tracked a flight of birds across the sky and somehow read in their movements "potential roadkill below." With my brother, it didn't matter how. All you had to realize was that he would know.

"Yes, the Wolf under the car," he confirmed matter-of-factly, "and now you know why I drive big, old cars. A werewolf does very little damage to it when you run one down." I opened my eyes and turned to see what we'd left on the curb of Robin's car lot. The car might not have suffered any damage, but the Kin Wolf couldn't say the same.

The street sweeper was going to have a helluva time with that.

"More than a day for the coffin thief to make it to Canton from the Catskills." The evening before last the meningitis outbreak had taken place—bacterial meningitis, the bad kind; the kind that tended to kill teenagers in a day, maybe two. "That's not exactly making good time," I observed. It should've been about an eight-hour drive. "Maybe whoever hired the guys to steal Suyolak came along with them, dumped the muscle when he had the coffin in the truck, and is doing the driving alone." But still . . . eight hours a day? If it was as Niko and I had discussed and this guy was hoping to use Suyolak to heal a critically ill relative, he should be in more of a hurry than that.

"If Suyolak started ten or so cases of meningitis here, there's no telling what he's done to the men in the truck. They could have deserted. They might be in the hospital here. They might be in the morgue. This is not good news. He's not out of the coffin; if he were, a few cases of meningitis are the very least of what he could do. But in the coffin . . . he shouldn't be able to do anything at all," Niko said, parking in front of the Canton equivalent of IHOP. Not that Nik would normally ever consider eating at a genuine IHOP, but it was a good central location for Abelia and her own muscle, Delilah, and us all to meet.

"We need to have a chat with the Wicked Bitch of the East then, huh? See what's up with Suyolak." I got out of the car. "I'll go inside and get a paper while you call Abelia and find out where her wrinkled ass is. Call Delilah too, would you? She should've been here a long time ago." It was two. Niko had shaved an hour off the estimate. Maybe he'd been tinkering with the engine, because while the car looked like shit, the thing could move. I patted a growling stomach. It wasn't only a paper I was going to pick up.

"And when you return with your lard pancakes coated with diabetes-inducing syrup and chemically created whipped cream, perhaps I might give you a foot massage while you dine. We could see what kind of time *you* make chasing Suyolak on two broken feet," he offered in a tone so pleasant even the Dalai Lama couldn't have carried it off. When Niko was pleasant, it was a good idea to look for a safe place to ride out his irritation. . . . I wondered whether they still had bomb shelters.

Niko's opinion and mood over my inviting Delilah along or allowing her to invite herself had not improved, and that didn't look like it was going to change any time soon. He had every reason to be pissed. There wasn't any way this couldn't end in trouble no matter what Delilah said. But whether it was trouble in New York or trouble wherever we happened to be, it was the same. I wanted it over with. Keeping it hanging over my head only messed with my head. It was almost poetry there and true. I'd learned that lesson more than once.

"Yeah, okay. I'll call her," I grumped. "A foot massage would've been nice, though."

When I came back with a paper tucked under my arm and three bags, Robin was awake and Salome was following a homeless man around the parking lot. "Uh . . . Goodfellow?"

"She's just playing," he said dismissively. When he saw that didn't quite put my mind at ease, he added, "Not serious play. We won't have to stuff his body in the trunk or anything. What do you have against cats anyway?"

"Nothing . . . not against live ones that aren't feline-shaped velociraptors." I handed him a bag and put mine in the front seat—eminent domain, cat. Suck that up. Squatting rights were over. I also handed Niko a bag. "Plain yogurt, melon, and I bribed them to make you an egg white omelet. They cooked it in butter, but it was the best I could do. And you don't have to massage my feet."

"If only I could massage your brain into working," he muttered, then exhaled, reaching out a hand to rest on top of my head and give me a light, affectionate push. "I apologize. It's your decision, even if I think it's an idiotically foolish one." Nik did know how to make with the esteem boosters.

"Everyone deserves a chance." Or the few people I liked deserved a chance. The rest of the world . . . eh. "You taught me that by giving me about seven more than I deserved."

Before he could comment or give me any more ego-boosting brotherly compliments on my idiocy, a motorcycle rumbled behind me and came to a stop, going silent. "I'll make sure there's no problem," I went on to promise him quietly.

"You talk of me, pretty boy? I cause trouble? Never."

I'd smelled her over the motorcycle exhaust, but now I turned to see Delilah sitting on a pearl metallic white Harley. The paint almost exactly matched her hair, which was pulled back into a waist-length ponytail. She was wearing white riding leathers too, not to escape road rash. Wolves were too quick. If they crashed, they'd change in midair. If they did break a bone or two, they'd heal quickly in fur form. Delilah just liked to look good and she did look damn good in the leathers. Dark amber-tinted sunglasses hid equally amber eyes.

"I prefer the Godiva look, but it does have a certain superhero slickness to it," Robin offered as he investigated the contents of his bag.

"Superhero. No fun." She toed down the kickstand. "Supervillain." She smiled, her teeth bright against her dark gold skin. "Queen of Wolves. Queen of World."

"I guess that would make me one of your cabana boys," I said dryly.

She climbed off the bike in one smooth motion. "Work on stamina; then we see. And dirty talk." She shook her head with a disappointed clicking of her tongue. "Like Mormon with the dirty talk."

Goodfellow choked on a bite of waffle. "You?" he coughed. "You're bad at dirty talk? You said 'Goddamn it to fucking hell' in front of that Catholic priest and the two nuns in the restaurant the other day. And *you* are bad at dirty talk?"

There was a big difference between cursing like five shiploads of sailors and actual sexual dirty talk. "Just choke on the waffle and die already, okay?" I snapped.

"I mean, had I known you were so verbally impaired in the erotic area, I could've given you some pointers. Written a few hundred pages of my best lines down for you." He stabbed another bite of waffle, obviously too entertained to bitch about how beneath him the food was. "I had to help rid you of that crippling virginity of yours, and considering your charming personality and wide variety of fashion-unique T-shirts and jeans, black, black, and more black, don't think that didn't take some doing. And now to know I sent an unskilled and untalented worker into my field of expertise, I can barely live with myself." He pointed an accusing fork and waffle combo at Niko. "He's your brother. Isn't all this your responsibility?"

"Don't I suffer enough?" Niko retorted. "He can easily outshoot any policeman on the New York City Police Department, but he can't hit a target the size of a small watermelon from less than a foot away? Do you think yellow is actually a paint color I would choose for the bathroom wall behind the toilet if I had any other choice?" he asked with a resigned twitch of his lip.

This would've gone on for a while. It had in the past, but Abelia-Roo's RV rolled up beside us. She stepped out a minute later, which happened to be at the same time Salome, who must have found the homeless guy too boring a prey, jumped up on the trunk of the Eldorado. The old Rom's eyes, the spray of wrinkles around them deepening in disgust, flickered over us. "A traitor, an unholy half-breed, a goat, and a dog." She nodded toward Salome. "The dead cat could do better than the four of you combined, I have little doubt."

"Dog?" Delilah snarled with a genuine rumbling wolf growl. "Withered frog of old woman, will rip your arms and legs like sticks, tear your throat, piss in your foul mouth, then you know Wolf, not *dog*."

Abelia shook her dusty black skirt and toyed with the earrings cascading in silvery chandeliers from her drooping earlobes while she flashed toothless gums in a superior smirk. "I have the finest and most special of herbs for a flea bath. Best among all the Rom. I'll sell to you at the lowest price to be found. My word and my promise."

And just like that, we were on the verge of a Rom banquet for Delilah while the rest of us ate French toast and omelets—right in the middle of the IHOP parking lot. Not that I had a problem with Delilah eating Abelia-Roo; there were simply better places for it. Canton, Ohio, was not New York. The weird, strange, the out-of-place; it would get noticed here. And we were all three. I got between Delilah and the old woman while Niko ushered our beloved employer back into her Candy Land RV.

"If you want to come with us, you can't eat her," I told Delilah, "at least not until after the job is over. Then snacks all around for all I care."

She bared her teeth, but moved away back to her motorcycle and leaned against it as if Abelia wasn't worthy of being eaten. Stringy. Maybe spoiled and maggoty in the heat. That settled, I tossed the paper to Niko when he came back to the car. "All ten kids are dead," I said. Ten kids had been minding their own business. Then a truck drove by, and now those kids were headed six feet under—not to prom; not to homecoming; not to the science fair. They were gone for good. "Abelia tell you anything? How this could happen?"

Niko took his breakfast and started on it, although he didn't look too enthusiastic. As it turned out, it had less to do with the cooking than with what Abelia-Roo had reluctantly admitted when he'd backed her into a corner. "It seems that our employer will admit the seals she spoke of earlier may be weakening through, of course, no fault of hers—of course," he repeated, and Niko was not much on repeating himself. "It could only be that the zinc and iron powder she was sold was contaminated. How can she be held responsible for *gadje* selling chemicals that are inferior, less than pure?" The bite he took of his omelet was smooth and controlled, but if he'd let himself, he would've stabbed at the egg angrily. But that wasn't my brother.

"Suyolak was able to do this shit just because one of Abelia's subpar seals has the coffin leaking like a rusty hazardous waste barrel?" I asked, not particularly surprised—by Abelia or our luck.

"Now think what he can do if he gets out of the coffin," Niko offered as he continued carving off pieces of his eggs with careful, controlled motions. "Nearly a thousand years of rage simmered to the sharpest of storming insanity. Damage so catastrophic that the Black Death will look like a forty-eight-hour flu."

"So stocking up on cough medicine isn't going to do us any good." I'd reclaimed my seat before Salome could. Not that I got sick; I had an Auphe souped-up immune system, but I had the feeling that this Suyolak guy could take my immune system and tear through it like tissue paper. He might forget disease altogether and go for stopping my heart, burst vessels in my brain, or if that was too mundane, he could instead tie my intestines in a bow. I was sure he'd had a long time to think of a whole mass of party tricks.

"Not a good deal, no," my brother responded dryly, "which is why we'll need Rafferty. We'll also need to know if the truck is still on the Lincoln or not."

"The waitress didn't happen to mention a truck and a coffin, did she? A man weeping into his pancakes over his dying relative or just weeping fluids in general, green and puslike, perhaps?" Robin finished off his waffles, unfazed by his self-painted image. "And did she happen to be hot? Stunning? Worthy of a shred of my attention?"

"Believe it or not, no, she didn't see anything. No big black trucks that anyone saw. And, yeah, she was hot . . . in that I-never-saw-a-sheet-cake-I-didn't-like kind of way. I'd never seen knuckle hair on a woman before. Go for it. I'm sure Ishiah would understand your leap off the monogamy diving board into that pool."

I opened my bag and had my French toast, cream cheese, blueberry deluxe down in three minutes flat. "So what now? Keep following the Lincoln?" And keep checking the Internet via Niko's BlackBerry for disease outbreaks. Those were about our only choices. Canton wasn't New York, but it was still far too big a city to stop at every gas station to ask questions.

"Go west, young man," Robin confirmed with a yawn as he balled up the trash, tossed it at me, and took advantage of the free backseat to stretch out again.

Salome eyed me in the passenger seat, her grin less cheerful than usual, but she settled down on Robin's stomach. And that had me wondering. . . . I looked around the parking lot, double-checking, and groaned, "Oh damn," at the sight of a limp body hanging over the edge of a Dumpster. "You psycho cat from Hell, you didn't. . . ." The legs at the Dumpster kicked and the homeless guy came back out with a prize of several bags of leftovers.

"Calm down," Robin said dismissively. "She doesn't kill humans."

"How do you know for sure?" Niko asked pointedly.

"Because I spray her with a water bottle if she does. Very effective."

Delilah, back on her Harley, pulled up on my side of the car. "Ride with me?" She patted the seat behind her with a coy smile. "Vibration can be interesting. *Very* interesting."

I would bet it could. Delilah and I cruising down the highway, with me sitting in the politically incorrect "bitch seat" . . . There'd be some serious vibrations all right, but I just couldn't do it. If she didn't kill me, Nik would for giving her the opportunity. "Sorry," I said. "I'm not sure I'm that secure in my masculinity."

She gave a snort down her elegant nose. "True. Why would you be?" Then she roared off while I continued to sit in a pimpmobile with fuzzy dice, feeling an odd kinship with the soft and easily squashed dual fluff balls hanging from the mirror. "You know," I exhaled, "I've had better times on a job."

Niko started the car. "When?"

I thought about it, then gave up. He was right. They all sucked in their own unique way, although with the Kin trouble, I expected this one to stand out. "Why don't you drive already?" I growled.

He raised an eyebrow, punishingly turned the radio on to something that made even Salome howl in terror, and we were off on the Leandros Road Trip to Hell.

Meditation led to control—sometimes. Other times, meditation led to naps in the warm sun that streamed over the convertible. Take it a little further and naps led to dreams. And when the dreams turned into a nightmare, I wasn't much surprised. With my life? Get real.

But there was a difference between this nightmare and my usual ones. It was startlingly clear. Normally I have only flashes of claws and teeth, darkness, and the sensation of falling, pain, and screaming. Fun. Flashes were all I wanted of that. I was into abstract dreaming. If you could frame one, you could sell it as art . . . extremely deranged, horrific art. This one, though—this one was crystal clear, painted not with a brush but with the sharp edges of a knife.

The day was gone. It was night with a moon so huge and brilliant that the horse cast shadows on the dried mud road. There were reins wrapped around my hand, and I knew if I turned my head, I'd see a gypsy wagon painted in red, yellow, and green, although the colors would be muted and faded even under this moon. A harvest moon—I had no idea what that meant, but

I knew that's what hung pregnant and heavy in the sky.

"It's a time for the *gadje* to celebrate what they scrabbled in the dirt for. Their plump and juicy vegetables, which later on we'll barter for, stealing those muddy farmers blind in the process. Then we'll make a nice stew and drink wine to toast their stupidity. With full bellies, we'll sleep with our wives or the willing wanton. The good old days." The man was straddling the broad rump of the horse and facing me. He had hair to his shoulders. It was black like mine, but with a slight wave to it. He also had dusky skin, dark eyes, and a sly and cheerful smile. He was dressed in black pants and a rough, woven shirt. Cream or white, I couldn't tell. Over that was an embroidered vest, his best festival gear. His feet were bare and dirty—roguish. He was a good-looking guy, Rom through and through. The women probably loved him, *gadje* and gypsy both. Robin would've jumped him in a heartbeat.

And that's what made it disturbing when that smile widened. "And when we leave that farm, Mama, Papa, and their three little ones will be dead. Cholera. In minutes they'll be rolling on the floor, clawing at their throats while bucketfuls of vomit gush from their mouths. Masses of it until they choke on it. I'll let their dog live, though. I like dogs. Not that they like me." He swayed with the horse and rested his hands on his knees. "They don't like you either, eh, my friend? Because they know who you are, what you are, just as *I* know what you are." The horse stopped and the man leaned slightly toward me. "I can cure you."

That's when he changed. The shoulder-length hair, its waves turned to tangled clumps, fell to his corpse-raddled feet. The clothes were rags and the body beneath them a skin-covered skeleton. The face was the same: a skull with skin; dingy teeth framed by shriveled lips. The hands that had been resting on his knees were now resting on mine. His nails were at least a foot long—thickened and yellow. They were twisted and corkscrewed, a graveyard party favor. The eyes were blank white orbs. There was nothing to see in a pitch-black coffin, was there? He'd kept himself alive ... barely ... all these years, devouring himself, but there was no point in wasting energy in keeping your vision if there was nothing to see.

"Suyolak." I jammed a hand against his bony sternum and pushed him away from me. The horse was a skeleton now too, one covered with a dusty hide and a slow swish of a matted tail.

The living skull grinned. "The Plague of the World"—one perverted spiral of a nail touched my own chest—"meets the Unmaker of the World. What good Rom doesn't like a little competition?" The nail was touching my chest, but I *felt* it in my head. "I could remake the Unmaker, Caliban. I could kill those worthless parts of you and let the better take over. You could be whole. For the first time in your life. One. Complete."

There was an ache in my brain that sharpened to a stabbing pain. "You can't make me human," I gritted. "No one can."

"Human?" The skull flew back and the laughter spiked the pain in my head to the nearly unbearable. "No, *bar*. No, my brother. I said cure, not castrate." The white eyes glowed like the moon. "I'll make you what you were meant to be all along. Auphe." The nail flicked up as the palm of the desiccated hand moved to take its place on my chest. "So easy it would be, brother. You're human on the outside only. Let me put you right. Let me *cure* you."

For a second I saw myself as if I were separate from my body. I saw albino skin, jaggedly sharp angled joints, pointed chin, a legion of metal teeth, an acid rainfall of pallid hair, and eyes that were a blazing red inferno that would eat you alive.

If you didn't already live there.

If it weren't already home.

I woke up on the living room couch, trying to back my way through it. I'd already pulled my gun from its holster and was a millimeter of force away from shooting our front door. With my other hand I was feeling desperately at my face. It was all I could do not to try to rip it off. But it was the same as it had always been. Human. No matter what that bastard said, I was at least half human. It didn't seem like much, but it was. I wasn't an Auphe in a cheap polyester human Halloween costume. No fucking way. I put the Eagle back in the holster, grip sweaty and tight, and drew in ragged lungfuls of air. Human—human enough. That was all that mattered— never mind how I ended up on the couch; never mind the pure-Auphe trick.

My cell phone rang. Not a big surprise. You went to sleep in a car somewhere in Ohio and woke up in your loft back in New York and that was going to make anyone's sphincter pucker, even Niko's. I ran a quick hand over my face again, just to make sure, and answered it. "It's not my fault," I said as soon as I flipped the phone open.

"Somehow I doubt that," Niko said grimly. "Where are you?"

"Back at the loft. I had"—Jesus, how humiliating—"a bad dream. Either that or Suyolak paid me a visit. If I get to pick, I think I'll take the dream."

There was a pause. It was either Niko thinking, un-puckering, or both. Finally he said, "We can't rule out that he did speak to you. Healers 'talk' to your body while they mend it. They tell the blood when to clot or when to thin, tumors to shrink. It's a combination of te-lepathy, telekinesis, and skills as yet uncategorized. Your brain is part of your body. He well could have spoken to you while you slept and your conscious defenses were down. But as fascinating as I find all my own lectures to be, I'm more concerned with *your building gates in your sleep*." I heard him take a deep breath and go on more evenly. "And how you're going to get back here."

It couldn't have been the most entertaining event to be driving down the highway and without any warning see your sleeping brother glow gray, then pop out of existence—the same brother he'd thought dead months ago. It was enough to strain even Niko's legendary calm. "Do you think you could pull over into the emergency lane?" I asked.

"Do you imagine I'm still driving down the road looking for a new third to chip in on gas money?" he snapped. "I've already pulled off and backed up to where you disappeared."

Definitely strained. I closed my eyes and felt for the car. It was like following a path in my mind, gray and winding . . . cold . . . silver and mist. "Can you find us?" Niko's voice echoed distantly in my ear. He knew I couldn't travel to a place I hadn't been to before at some time in the past. I had to know the way. I'd never left a moving car before though, but . . .

"I know the way," I said confidently. And because I knew the opportunistic bitch had made her move, I added, "Toss Salome in the back and I'm there." I built the gate around me instead of in front of me—didn't want to dissolve the dashboard, and then, as I'd told Nik . . .

I was there.

6

Cal

Suyolak's leaving mental landmines for us, which meant he knew or felt us following him, or Niko's smacking the back of my head; I didn't know which was responsible for the headache, but it didn't matter. What did was that I needed some Tylenol. Suyolak in our heads, using that mixture of telepathy, telekinesis, and whatever else Niko had said—okay, I was going with that as the cause of my aching head. Niko's swats I was used to.

We'd pulled into a gas station at the first exit after I traveled back to the car. We needed to fill up the tank anyway, and getting about a gallon of coffee to keep ancient Rom antihealers from paying any of us another visit wasn't a bad idea either. I could also raid the first aid kit we kept in the trunk. It didn't fit in the glove compartment. If we needed first aid, we needed a hospital in a box—but besides morphine, codeine, staples and stitches, occlusive pressure bandages, and other advanced medical supplies, it also had your run-of-the-mill Tylenol.

I downed two with the coffee, although other than the headache, I didn't feel bad. I wasn't that wild about Suyolak poking around in my dreams . . . Mengele/

Freddy Krueger—not a good mix. But aside from that and an annoyed, worried brother, I kind of felt good— revved up, as if I'd already drunk that gallon of coffee. It seemed clear now that Suyolak couldn't have my Auphe half gobble up the human part. If that were true, the last time I'd seen our healer Rafferty, when he'd repaired a near-fatal stab wound to my abdomen, he would've done the opposite. He would've gotten rid of my Auphe genes, and he wouldn't have waited for me to ask either.

Suyolak was like most power-hungry monsters: He liked to mess with your mind, because to someone like him—*something* like him—fear was as tasty a meal as that stew he'd talked about. He was full of shit and as long as we met up with Rafferty before we came across Suyolak in the dehydrated flesh, we'd be fine—except for some nightmares.

I deftly dodged the third or so swat Niko aimed at the back of my head, as if he could behavior modify me into controlling my subconscious to not let me travel, and asked, "Heard from Dr. Sassafras or that boring guy yet?"

He took revenge by reversing the motion of his hand and flicking me briskly in the forehead. "Yes, while you were in the gas station stocking up on sugar, trans fat, and various other undigestibles, I called them both. Dr. Penjani has yet to find out anything, and he's not boring; simply evolved beyond the Homo Pornographus that is you. Dr. Jones, however, has had better luck. There are two anthropology professors, one in Seattle, one in San Diego. Both have family members who are critically ill; both fit Abelia's description of older men with gray hair. One has a wife with a brain tumor who has a week to live, perhaps two at best, and one has a son who was in a car accident. Multiple injuries, brain damage. Both are too unstable to be moved, which is why our thief didn't take the easier route of bringing Mohammed to the mountain, instead of vice versa. The professor in San Diego tends to concentrate on Australian aborigines. The one in Seattle obtained his PhD twenty years ago in the varying levels of Rom assimilation from country to country. I would say he is our better possibility."

"Which one is he? The one with the sick son or the wife?" I asked, tapping my fingers on my leg. This music on the radio; maybe it wasn't as bad as I'd thought. The not being able to tell if the singer was a man or a woman was like a mythological time before testosterone was introduced into the gene pool.

"Does it matter?" Niko asked.

"No, guess not. Depressing either way." Although I didn't feel depressed or empathetic or any other of those big words Niko half believed he'd never genuinely pounded them into my head. I should have—I mean, dying wife . . . dying kid. Jesus. That was sad, right? They had support groups for that sort of thing, so it must be sad. But I didn't particularly feel that way. That up feeling was still with me. What the hell—I'd feel bad for them later.

I turned the radio up a little and opened a bag of Cheetos. I offered one to Niko. He refused, of course, with a look of distaste for the food and disgust for my hopeless eating habits. I then turned to offer the bag to Robin in the backseat. "You know, for what it's worth, this whole monogamy thing with Ish? I think you should give it a try. In your lifetime you've screwed your way through half the world population, if not more. Not to mention Ishiah can take your shit. And believe me, that's a lot of shit to take. A *lot*," I emphasized. "Give it a chance. Listen to the radio. There wouldn't be a twenty-four-hour love song station if there wasn't some truth behind that whole hearts and flowers crap, right?" I patted his shoulder with a dusty orange hand. And why not? Ish was a good guy, a good boss—trying to chop my head off with an axe wasn't that far out of line. Forgive and forget. And Goodfellow had been a better friend than I deserved. If he could find happiness, why not?

God, I sounded like such a girl. I'd grown some ovaries without noticing. The breasts couldn't be far behind. Yet that didn't particularly bother me either.

Robin carefully removed my hand from his shoulder and leaned back out of reach. "I'm not sure which of the three is more frightening: that Suyolak can go high-def in your head, therefore I'm assuming *our* heads, for sport; that if we get too close he could give us a venereal disease that would turn us into giant, walking pus boils—also merely for his entertainment; or your new mood."

"Me?" I asked, distracted by the taste of the Cheetos. I'd always liked them. You didn't have to cook them, they were readily available at any store in the country, and they had no nutritional value whatsoever, but kept you alive anyway. They were the Great American Food. We should've been shipping them to Third World countries. It would solve all their problems—well, foodwise.

"Yes, you. You and your bizarrely altered mood." He dusted every orange particle off his shoulder with exquisite care.

"What's wrong with my mood?" I protested.

"It's good." Salome jumped on his now-clean shoulder and they both studied me with identical, unblinking stares. "I expected an improvement over your usual gloom, doom, despair, and suicidal moaning and groaning when you killed the last of the Auphe, but this?" He waved a hand at me. "And *now*? The Kin know about you and Delilah. That's if not almost certain death, then certainly a huge inconvenience and probable loss of furry booty. Then Suyolak played with your mind as if it were a Rubik's Cube—before your time, I know, not to mention a thousand times more complex than your mind, but the analogy stands." He shook his head. "And

I can't imagine what horrific things a creature such as he could whisper in your ear."

"That he'd turn me into an Auphe. Full Auphe." I finished the bag and dusted my hands free of orange. "Strain my human bits out like seeds from freshly squeezed orange juice. Can't buy that off an infomercial."

Now he did blink. "And you're taking that quite well. You're as happy as those Mormons Delilah compared you to. You could even say you're cheerful. Caliban Leandros, *cheerful*. It's not only wrong; it's unimaginable. Inconceivable. Confess. Have you gotten religion? Drugs? A lobotomy? Because this is not you, not remotely."

"He feels good after he gates," Niko said. "Don't you, Cal?" While Robin had leaned away, Nik leaned in close to take me in—every breath, every beat of my pulse at my carotid artery, a scrutiny closer than any microscope.

"I noticed last time," he went on, "but this time . . . This time it's more pronounced. Isn't that right? You said you needed to fly. Back at the bar, that's what you compared it to. Being let out of a cage. Being free."

"Maybe it is the traveling, but so what? If it makes me feel good, it's no different than your getting that adrenaline high after running, which, by the way, *I've* never gotten. Just a desire to puke. I think I'm due. You get it from running. I get it from traveling, and that's only if you assume I'm never in a good mood." I looked between the two of them. "So? Is that what you guys really think? That I'm never in a good mood?"

Niko said, "Goodfellow, hold his head. I'll check his pupils."

I guess that answered that.

"You've got to be kidding me. Hey, cut it out," I protested as I tried to duck, but when Niko was serious, there was no avoiding him. His hand secured my chin tightly as he stared into my eyes as the overhead lights of the gas station canopy flickered to life when the dusk swallowed the sun.

"They're not dilated or pinpoint." He frowned. His hand was on my neck. "Your pulse is elevated, but only mildly."

"So you mean normal, right?" I demanded, my good mood—which I was allowed for once in my life, damn it—disappearing.

"I can't imagine normal being applied to you in any way—hygiene, diet, exercise habits, literary or video preferences," he replied immediately. "But you don't seem drugged." His frown deepened. "Let me do a reflex test."

I was more than willing to prove my reflexes were fine by grabbing Salome by her tail and beating my brother over the head with her hairless, bony body, but Delilah interrupted all that. She pulled up on her motorcycle and said sharply, "Stop silly games. Found something. Up the road. Come." She didn't wait, roaring off. We were ten miles from Dyer, Indiana, where there had been, per the almighty Google, another meningitis outbreak—more dead, cold and still in the hospital morgue. Suyolak was still definitely on the Lincoln, and we were on his diseased trail.

Indiana was a big change from New York. Corn, corn, cows just for a change, and then more corn. It was old times all over again. Traveling from town to town with Sophia, draining the marks there dry, then moving on. Then after the Auphe took me and I came back, there was running for our lives instead of simply being pulled along in Sophia's wake as she searched for new marks. I wasn't sure how I felt about this road trip. In some ways it had me looking over my shoulder for creatures that didn't exist anymore. But in another way . . . it felt right. Comfortable. We might not be accepted by the Rom, but we *were* Rom, born to hit the ground running.

While Niko followed Delilah's taillights past the exit

on-ramp and Abelia-Roo's RV followed us, I used his BlackBerry to scan for disease outbreaks ahead of Dyer. There weren't any, at least nothing reported yet, but I didn't doubt they'd pop up. Leaks only got bigger, not smaller. Those seals weren't going to repair themselves. Goddamn Abelia. It was her responsibility and she'd fucked up. Contaminated ingredients, my ass. It was pure ego. Abelia thought she was better than anyone and everyone, full concentration and effort not needed, but Suyolak was looking to prove her wrong.

Ahead of us, Delilah had pulled over a few miles from the gas station after turning onto a gravel road. "You do realize this could be a trap," Goodfellow pointed out. "It's back to nature. A city Wolf might enjoy killing you out here, Cal. An exotic back-to-her-roots vacation with your murder as a cherry on the top. If she is going to kill you, I'd have to commend her for choosing this spot and thinking outside the box. The Kin aren't usually very good at that."

"Thanks for that. You're a true friend. Be sure to take pictures. I'd hate for you to forget any juicy details," I growled. Although it was as Robin said . . . back to nature, but I thought if or when Delilah made a run at me, it wouldn't be within sword reach of my brother. She was smarter than that. No, I thought that was something else entirely—but still about death; just not mine.

The interstate noise was gone. There was nothing but crickets and the distant low of a cow. Delilah took off her sunglasses—the moon would be more than bright enough for a Wolf—as we pulled up beside her. She shot a challenging glance toward me. "Yeah, it's a graveyard," I said. "I can smell it." No matter how old they were, I could always smell them. "So what?"

She rolled her eyes as she undid the tie from her hair,

setting it loose down her back—a cascade of moonlight. "Like teaching cub. Smell again."

I did, sampling the air. "Shit, it's closer."

"Graveyards, as a rule, don't move around on their own," Niko observed, turning the ignition off and stepping out of the car to draw his katana from the sheath strapped to his back and hidden by a lightweight duster. We all suffered in the summer when it came to concealing our weapons. "Cal, are you up for this?"

"Do you mean am I in a pissy mood again? Am I not going to hug whatever creepy-ass putrefying thing comes our way? Yeah, I am completely up for this," I answered, irritated. If I got a little happy in my life, everyone assumed I was an alien pod person. How fair was that? "It's not revenants," I added. "Whatever it is isn't alive. This is genuine decomposition on the move." That was something we hadn't run into yet, not in our lifetimes. But I was assuming if you were decomposing and still moving, a gun wouldn't do much in the way of slowing you down. I went to the trunk and dug through my bag until I found a machete and then a second one.

"It is the mullo." Abelia-Roo's voice came from behind me. She and her five best had disembarked the pink pleasure palace on wheels, which had been tailing us mile for mile since the IHOP. I ignored Branje, her second, as he wasn't worth my time, and he looked anywhere but at me. Since I'd almost cut his nose off the last time we'd met, that was the best social interaction we could hope for. And he'd thought I was human then. Now . . . he probably woke up every morning checking the bathroom mirror for that nose, praying that half-breed Auphe bastard hadn't crawled in and cut it off during the night. If Branje hadn't been such a dick last time, I might have felt sorry for him.

Nah.

"Mullo? Could you be more specific? Rom legend

is rather divided on that subject." As Niko was direct-
ing the question to Abelia, Delilah was stripping off
her leathers to reveal nothing but skin. I wasn't sure if
wolves didn't have the same sense of modesty as humans or if it was just Delilah. It didn't matter. I simply
enjoyed the sight.

"Don't want leathers stained. New and pretty. Like to
keep them that way." Then she was on all fours, covered
in white fur, and twice the size of any wolf in the wild.
Her amber eyes were bright and her tongue lolled happily. The hunt . . . All wolves lived for the hunt, even the
non-Kin ones.

"Mullo are the dead. Suyolak must have raised them.
He is getting stronger at the hope of freedom or the seals
are getting weaker . . . through no fault of mine." She
turned and pushed at the men. "Go. Back in the RV. This
is why we pay their kind. To take care of this problem
for us. This one and many potential others." She smirked
at us as she headed back with her men.

Other problems on top of the walking dead. Great. A
man couldn't enjoy his Cheetos without getting slapped
in the face with dead raised by Suyolak and the hint that
Suyolak could do more than that little trick and then
some.

"Yes, be that as it may," Niko said coldly to Abelia as
she shuffled away, her skirts swinging, "*our* kind would
appreciate a little more information. Do they suck blood
as legend says?"

"You wish," Robin complained as he climbed out of
the car behind us. Salome stretched out to take the space
he'd freed up, not interested in playing this time. "That
would be the dhampir you are thinking of. The mullo
and the dhampir have become two legends when they
are but one reality. The mullo are the dead, reanimated
flesh, raised by a highly annoyed healer. I'd say Suyolak
is the only reason the mullo ever existed to begin with

as he is the only evil healer—an antihealer, I suppose—that I know of powerful enough to do it." He had his sword out now as well. "The dhampir are said to be the offspring of a mullo and a human, born as a large pile of flesh as slick as mucus. How decorative. Just what one wants around the apartment. In actuality, the mullo and the dhampir are one and the same—a raised corpse, the decomposing flesh of which slides off its bones. It then becomes a giant predatory and quite smelly amoeba. It covers its victim's faces, smothers them, and then, I assume that with its task complete, goes back to rotting while Suyolak has a nice laugh."

"Oh, you have got to be shitting me," I said in disbelief. I'd done sewers and revenants, insane asylums and mummies, mud pits and boggles, caves and trolls. Hell, I'd even done butterfly-winged spiders that filled you full of acid and sucked out your liquified organs. But an entire graveyard full of giant decomposing amoebas that wanted to suffocate me? "At least tell me they creep along the ground at the same pace as zombies in the old movies."

Abelia's lips curled in a smile both satisfied and malignant. "We paid your price. Now let us see you dance for that shiny penny." She closed the door behind her as she went into the RV.

I guessed that would be a no. Decomposing *and* fast; what a combo. I slammed the trunk shut. "We should've brought the flamethrower."

"Be realistic," Niko reasoned. "How often do we honestly need a flamethrower?"

"Two," I said blackly. "This would make two. Two makes it a regular habit from now on. At least on road trips." I looked down the gravel road dimly lit by the car lights. "How many dead people with flesh still on them could be there anyway? There have to be other graveyards. This can't be the only one." That had to cut down on bodies Suyolak could use.

Niko was already moving down the road. "Dyer, Indiana, has a population of just over thirteen thousand. I can't imagine there are more than three cemeteries or so." Nik and his damn memory; he couldn't pass a sign with some mildly pertinent knowledge without committing it to a brain cell. "I wouldn't think they have a high daily, weekly, or even monthly death toll, except for today when Suyolak went past and those corpses won't be buried yet. As for bodies still moist and gelatinous enough to slither about in this cemetery, I suppose it all depends on how skilled the embalmer was."

"Thanks for that," I said, following behind him. "That didn't make me want to barf at all." Delilah loped ahead of us, tired of our careful pace. The path was lined with old trees, pines, looming enough to dim the car headlights further. The smell was sharp and fresh in the air.

"I'm sorry." He wasn't. "Does your work of fighting the rotting dead conflict with stuffing an entire bag of orange puffy chemicals down your throat in less than a minute?"

Before I had a comeback in defense of what I'd formerly believed to be the perfect food, I watched the ground erupt to one side of us. It was a man, a dead one, clawing himself out of his own grave. It was like a monster movie come to life, almost as if we were watching late-night television rather than something true and real directly before us. He kept digging until he was all the way out and swaying, his eyes and mouth stitched shut, his best Sunday suit covered with large stains of decay and rot.

Abelia had insinuated they were fast, but this one wasn't. We could've cut him down before he managed to make it out all the way into open air, but ... damn ... this was our first semizombie. Of course, it wasn't a zombie at all, not actually, but it was something you didn't see every day, in our dark world included, and sometimes

you had to let your curiosity get the best of you. This was
B-movie legend. I'd seen this a hundred times on TV
and in the occasional video game when I was younger.
I'd enjoyed watching a good zombie throw down then—
who didn't? I wasn't enjoying this one, but neither was
I as wary or prepared as I should've been. What happened next showed me that.

The thing stood for a moment, wavering, and then the
flesh literally fell off its bones, which did nothing good
for its already compromised suit and did even less for
my stomach. The rotting flesh continued to pool around
the feet, wave after wave, before finally extruding hungry, mottled-green feelers in the air. Okay, *that* . . . that
was not right. The skeleton, along with some stringy
ligaments and cartilage left behind, abruptly collapsed
with the suit, and I lost my taste for zombie movies just
like that. A shambling zombie was one thing; a running
zombie was not bad either, but zombie Jell-O I could do
without.

And when a mass of putrid flesh dropped from the
nearest tree to race across the ground on hundreds of
tendrils, wrap around me, and climb to cover my head,
neck, and shoulders while we were distracted watching the other show, that cinched the no-zombie thing
for good. It happened in about two seconds. Abelia
was right. It was so incredibly quick that I barely saw
it; I only got a flash of what it looked like. It must've
been only fairly fresh. It was still mainly flesh colored,
spotted here and there with dull green and moist gray.
One closed eye slid across it as it moved. How it sensed
me, I didn't know or much have the time to care. It still
smelled strongly of chemicals—embalming fluid—not
that it covered the stink of rot. Rot against my nose, my
mouth—everywhere; it wouldn't have to suffocate me.
I'd choke on the stench first as it pressed closer against
my face, wrapping even more tightly around my head.

I dropped the machetes. It wasn't as if I could chop my own head off to get rid of this thing. I ripped at it with my hands. If Niko was calling my name, I didn't hear as moist pulp filled my ears. He could've been under attack as well. I didn't know. I continued to rip at the hood of skin and meat over my head. My fingers slid through it with a sickening lack of leverage. How do you fight putrescent pudding from Hell? You can claw and claw and never catch hold.

It wasn't coming off. Jesus, it wasn't coming off. I couldn't breathe. I couldn't get it off and I couldn't breathe.

But I could leave.

I pushed out blindly, because if he could be there, he would be there. I pushed once and hit nothing; twice and struck a hard form. Niko. I knew he'd be doing what he could if he could shake off any attackers of his own. I shoved again and let myself fall backward away from him at the same time to give myself space and not take part of him. I didn't want to take a Nik fingertip, thumb, or entire hand through with me when I went. That wouldn't be good—not good at all. As I fell, I made the gate around me, something that clung to my skin this time that I welcomed.

And then I was back in the car with small pieces of corpse in my hair and one or two sliding down my face. I vaulted back out, wiping them off with a hurried hand, and ran back up the road, promising myself a chance to yak up Cheetos—the perfect food no more—far and wide when this was over. I saw Niko ahead chopping my personal graveyard amoebas to smaller and more-manageable pieces. There was no martial arts skill required there; only butchery. The mullo was fast, but it—or Suyolak—had been taken off guard by my disappearing act. It slithered back and forth in confusion, still trying to find me. Niko wasn't one to let an opportunity to fillet an opponent get away. "Are you all right?" he asked as he stamped his boot on one wriggling piece to hold it in place while he finished a damn fine filleting job on the rest of it.

"Except for smelling like Romero, the latest in zombie cologne, I'm fucking great." And I was—I meant it. Fan-fucking-tastic. The smell still bothered me, but as for the rest? Vampire, troll, revenant, boggle, mounds of racing blobs of decomposing bodies: It was all the same—one damn good time. Bring it on. So what if it ruined Chee-tos for me? There were a thousand other snack foods to take their place. I scooped up my machetes as I passed Niko and tackled another mullo that was about to take Robin from behind as he held off another one in front of him. This one had either been in the ground longer or had been a customer of an extremely crappy funeral home, because as it hit the ground with me on top of it, it virtually disintegrated. There was only a large puddle of extremely foul-smelling goo under me. The tendrils that surrounded its "body" fluttered, then melted as well.

I looked to one side to see Delilah laying into an-other mullo as if it were a pork-scented chew toy. But as quick as she was, it was quicker. It managed to wrap around her lower body, taking out her hind legs. She snarled as she went down—no yelping for her. When the mullo moved up toward her head, I was there to drop my machetes and grab it. This one must've been put in the ground only a few days ago, because I was able to hang on to it and rip it off before it could cover the snapping wolf head. It didn't matter what the Kin had in store for her or what she had in store for me. I couldn't let her go without giving her a chance. What she did with that chance was up to her.

But as I pulled it off her, I lost my grip as it thrashed muscularly under my hands. In the moonlight I could see it was covered with lines and curves that made up nothing recognizable now, but had probably once been a wealth of tattoos before death. He or she had been in good shape before hitting the slab, because it had more fight in it than all the others combined—a gym rat maybe putting dead muscle to strong use. Its attention turned from Delilah to me, it lunged, tendrils grasping eagerly at the air.

And that is all it got—nothing but air.

I reappeared behind it and Delilah. When it had gone for me, she had gone for it and rode it down to the ground, her muzzle buried in muscle and meat, ripping chunks of it away. I retrieved my machetes and joined in. It wasn't long before it was a stretch of quivering pieces spread far and wide on the grass and gravel. I stood still, both blades ready, and listened, although if anyone was going to be the first to hear something, it would be Delilah. I kept my eyes on the triangular white ears that pointed forward, then back, then forward again before she yawned and began energetically rubbing her muzzle back and forth on the grass. No more mullos.

"I suppose that embalming fluid isn't the tastiest additive to spice up your meal," Goodfellow commented, disgust dripping from the words as he came up to us. For once, he hadn't escaped the multisplatter that had gotten the rest of us.

Not that she'd actually eaten any of the mullo. Delilah had made it very clear in the past that she didn't eat roadkill—which in her eyes was the dead or pathetically slow humans. The first was degrading and the second wasn't nearly challenging enough. Robin held out his arms and grimaced at what he saw and smelled. "Don't start," I warned before he could complain. I was covered nearly head to toe in graveyard goop from taking down the mullo that had almost had him from behind.

"No one is getting in my car like this," Niko said. His

hand fisted a handful of my jacket. "And how did you say you were feeling again?"

Yet another good mood was washed away in the cemetery's ornamental pond. We were attacked again, this time by two ill-tempered swans. The one time I wished Salome had come along for the fun and she couldn't be bothered. I asked Robin if skinny-dipping with the big white birds could be considered cheating on Ishiah. If I'd had any positive feeling left at all from my traveling that Niko hadn't managed to drown, they were finished off by Goodfellow trying to strangle me while a swan pecked irately at my head.

Then it was back on the Lincoln. With both our candidates for coffin thief living on the West Coast, there was no reason for the truck or us to leave it . . . and then there was the trail of disease that had led us here so far. The driver probably didn't know we were behind him. Suyolak knew, though. If he was appearing in my dreams, he knew we were coming. No doubt he knew Abelia and her men were behind as well. Clan ties, blood ties. I hope he gave them worse dreams than he'd given me. But although he obviously did sense us behind him, I thought he was confident he could slow us down long enough until he was out of the coffin. He'd definitely oozed confidence in my dream. And with Abelia's crappy, carelessly complacent seal application, he might be right to feel that way.

"When do we meet Rafferty? Better yet, when do we make a motel stop?" I asked Nik as the night air rushed into the car to dry our clothes on our bodies. Only Goodfellow had felt the need for nudity in the swan pond. Delilah had kept her fur on while splashing among the water lilies and swan feathers. While that water had been an improvement over the rancid slime we'd been wearing, soap and a motel shower would be better. It was a given that Abelia wasn't letting us all pile into her RV to clean up.

"I think we'll be able to combine the two events," he answered. Robin was already snoring in the backseat. "I meant it when I asked, you know. How *are* you feeling?"

"You're not going to let it go, are you?" I groaned. "For once I finally got something good out of the Auphe package. I think I'm due."

"You're more than due," he said. "No one in your life knows that more than I do, but it seems too good to be true. And anything that seems too good to be true often is. There's usually a price to be paid. If there is one, I want to know what it is."

You couldn't hold it against your family for caring too much about you. You might want to, but you couldn't. "Is my being in a good mood that scary?" I complained halfheartedly.

"Terrifying," he said. The word rang with sincerity. "Absolutely terrifying."

By the time we reached Monroe County, Illinois, I was behind the wheel. Niko had caught a few hours' sleep and Robin had yet to wake up from our graveyard festivities. He wasn't a big believer in sharing the load. The fact that he'd changed on the road and hadn't been fighting mullos in his pajamas from the car lot was a lucky break for us—and for the mullos, if the dead could be scarred mentally. It was a little past eleven at night when I pulled into the parking lot of the motel with the best rooms money could buy. Thirty-six bucks a night. How could you go wrong?

"We check in, shower, and keep going?" I asked. It wasn't a problem with Niko's and my being able to switch off driving. Delilah had a werewolf's stamina; I knew from personal experience. Although with the

Kin's finding out about us, it was unlikely I was going to keep experiencing that too often in the future—one way or the other. I had to wonder, though, if even Delilah, fearless as she was, wanted to face my brother if she tried and actually succeeded in killing me. Delilah was Delilah, though. She believed she had no equal and in some respects she was right. But Niko . . . She thought she knew him, but she couldn't, despite seeing what he'd done six months ago when he'd thought I was dead. She'd seen it, been there, but because she *was* Delilah, she couldn't let herself believe it.

Niko was out of her league. Niko, when he wanted to be or had to be, was out of anyone's league—except for Suyolak's, who was a whole different ball game. One I wasn't sure we could play. Killing with a thought: What the hell kind of game was that?

"No, we'll spend the night. Rafferty is going to meet us here in the morning." Niko flipped his phone closed after talking with the healer. Being that his side of the conversation had been *yes, I see,* and *yes* again, I hadn't gotten much out of it, besides hoping Rafferty knew how to play Suyolak's game and win. "He's leaving his motel now. He also said it's on the news: Three men were found eighty miles west of Dyer, Indiana, dead of an almost unheard-of cholera outbreak." He tapped my forearm with the cell. "Their ID is out of state. The authorities are trying to determine now if they'd traveled outside the country and caught it there."

"But we know better," I said grimly. I'd given Niko all the details of my dream about Suyolak. "Three strangers with out-of-state ID. You think our thief just lost his muscle." And lost his relief drivers, which would slow him down. "I still don't get it. Suyolak knows what's going on, at least enough to be messing with dreams. The slower whoever snatched him goes, the worse for him. He might think he'll get out before we catch up, but his chances would be better if there were more guys for the drive."

"Killing is Suyolak's nature. He might not be able to help himself. Knowing what's wisest and being able to do it are two widely different things." He tapped my arm again with the phone.

"Yeah, that last one was subtle. Not aimed at me at all," I retorted.

When he checked us in and came back with one key, that was about me, too. Delilah had parked her Harley and was lounging against it. At the sight of the key, she narrowed her eyes at him, but before she could head to the office for another room—our room—Niko told her, "If the Kin find you, they find my brother. I would prefer we showed a united front in that case."

Robin woke up at that—part of him anyway. A puck mind could sense this type of opportunity at any level of consciousness. "A foursome should be united front enough," he mumbled. He was climbing out of the car and his eyes hadn't quite opened yet, but he was unbuttoning his shirt. "Prepare for the pucking of your life."

"Ishiah," I said. "And I can't believe you actually consider that a pickup line."

His eyes opened to peer through wind-tangled strands of light brown hair and his fingers paused at the third button. "You couldn't have let me stay asleep, could you? If I'm unconscious, it can't be cheating." He buttoned his shirt, tucked Salome under his arm, and headed for the back of the car. "Even if I were conscious," he muttered as he opened the trunk to retrieve his bags, "sex with the magnificence of me would at worst be considered a heroic act of community service. Ishiah would no doubt give me a medal for benefiting humanity. And that line has worked more times than you've drawn breath."

He plucked the key from Niko's fingers, scanned the squat building, and started for the far end as he grumbled on. "Cheating isn't even a word in my language. Just as the old saying that the Eskimos have many words for snow, we have many words for sex—a thousand and three, I think, but not a single one for infidelity. Doesn't that say something? Doesn't that mean something?" He vanished behind the motel door, still talking to himself; still questioning himself. But Robin was the only one who could come up with those answers.

As for the issue of Delilah and me, I already had my mind made up: "Nik, I think we can handle a united front if we're in the next room," I pointed out.

He folded his arms and stared at me. I stared back, telling him silently that I could take care of myself. Aloud, I said, "It's the Kin, Cyrano. I can handle the Kin. I've kicked furry ass in the past. Now is no different."

"I think it's considerably different, and you know it. There're Kin and then there're Kin," he returned—not particularly cryptic to anyone, but I didn't think he meant it to be. He let it go, though, and went for his own bags. "With Suyolak capable of toying with our dreams, I would sleep in shifts." He slammed the trunk shut, tossing me my own bag. "If you sleep at all," he added dryly.

I didn't.

I wasn't sure if Niko had either. Robin might be living the puck ultimate terror of monogamy, but Niko was a big fan of the "Trust no one" philosophy. He had his exceptions. He trusted me, and he trusted Robin as well. He trusted him to watch his back in a fight and to step up whenever we needed help. He trusted him in any situation that could go south fast. But he'd also been chased ruthlessly by Robin before the puck's reconnection, in all senses of the word, with Ishiah. Niko had an infallibly long memory and an extremely sharp sense of survival. Whether it was a sudden catastrophic monogamy failure and things going south in an entirely different way than how the phrase was normally used, Niko would be prepared for any eventuality.

That was why I wasn't surprised to see him in the parking lot just after dawn when I opened the door, leaving a gloriously nude Delilah stretching and yawning in bed. With an exotic and fiercely intelligent woman, is there any other kind of nude? "Go. I sleep. Will catch up." I didn't hesitate. She would catch up, like she said; I had no doubt about that, just as I had no doubt about what she'd told me last night in the nest of sheets with the lullaby rush of cars passing by on the interstate. "The Kin cannot control me," she'd said, her eyes reflecting the faint light coming through the blinds in a way a human's never would. "I will survive."

"I know you will," I'd replied, and I believed her.

"I will do what I must do."

"I know you will," I'd repeated, and that I had believed, too—completely. If she had to kill me to get back in the good graces of the Kin, she would. If she could do the same without killing me, she would do that. Until the actual moment came, I had no idea what she would do. That was life.

Possibly death too.

I closed the door behind me and spotted Nik over at his car, having breakfast while sitting in the lotus position on the hood. He wasn't alone. There was a man with shaggy auburn hair sitting beside him, but with legs hanging over the grille and a large reddish wolf at his feet: Rafferty and Catcher—finally. "Rafferty, you son of a bitch. Where the hell have you been?" I said as I walked toward them.

He turned his head and frowned at me. I didn't take it personally. For a healer, his bedside manner was all but nonexistent. He was the guy who would tell you that you deserved the heart attack and why not eat some more pork and cheese while you were at it, you fat bas-

tard. Try blocking up another artery. Not a great lover
of his patients in general—of anybody in fact, outside
of Catcher.

"None of your business," he grunted. He had angular
features and hadn't bothered to shave in a day or two.
A nod to the June humidity, he was wearing a T-shirt in
the same faded condition as the one I was wearing that
said GUNS DON'T KILL PEOPLE, BUT GOOD AIM WILL EVERY
TIME. He was also wearing a pair of equally faded jeans,
and they weren't fashionably faded. They had Goodwill
written all over them. Rafferty didn't give a damn how
he looked or whether people liked what he said or how
he said it. He couldn't give a flying shit. I liked that about
him. It reminded me of myself, minus my new discov-
ery about traveling's effect on me. Thanks to Niko, the
happy-go-lucky, high-as-a-kite happiness didn't last anyway. He didn't think it was natural. He might be right,
but I wasn't sure I cared. To have my Auphe blood benefit me instead of curse me for once . . . I'd take that.

As for that Auphe in me . . .

When we first met Rafferty and Catcher a few years
ago, I'd smelled the difference in them . . . werewolves . . .
and they'd smelled the difference in me. Rafferty hadn't
known what the difference was at the time, or so I'd
thought, because then I didn't genuinely know what the
Auphe were. Now I knew that Rafferty had known all
along but hadn't said anything. Either he didn't want to
be involved with an Auphe half-breed—couldn't blame
him there—or figured it was none of his business. I wasn't
foaming at the mouth or eating the pigeons and squir-
rels running around. That was good enough for him.

We'd met only in passing the first time in Central
Park. Rafferty was tossing a Frisbee and Catcher
was bounding into the air for it. Even then he'd been
stuck in wolf form, with Rafferty, his cousin, doing his
damnedest to get him back to a werewolf's changeabil-

ity. After an exchange of wary sniffs, Rafferty fished around in the pocket of his baggy cargo pants, then passed over a rumpled card. It had the letters RJ on it—for Rafferty Jeftichew—as well as that snake and staff sign doctors had plastered around and a phone number. "Here," he'd grunted, handing it to Niko. "You might need a healer someday." Then he looked over at me, his straight slash of eyebrows lowered. "In fact, I can guarantee it. And this one can't go to a doctor or, hell, worse yet, a hospital, or it'll probably be alien autopsy for you."

Niko and he had talked some more. I thought they related. One with a sick cousin and one with a brother who might be considered a little worse than sick. Catcher and I went off and played more Frisbee. That had been three years ago. Rafferty had been right. We'd ended up needing a healer. He'd saved my life, but he wasn't any closer to his goal.

Now Catcher gave me the second sign he was still sick. He lifted his upper lip to reveal an impressive show of large white teeth and growled. The look in his yellow eyes, many shades lighter than Delilah's, was feral and suspicious. Catcher had been frozen a long time as a wolf. Maybe that wouldn't have been so bad, but little by little he was losing the human intelligence werewolves kept when they shifted from skin to fur. One day he'd be wolf and nothing but wolf. I had no idea how that felt to him. No idea what it was like to be only wolf . . . like he was wolf now as he growled at me.

Rafferty rested a battered sneaker on top of Catcher's head and rubbed. "It's okay, Catch," he said gruffly. "It's just Cal. Half-Auphe. Possessed. So annoying his own brother stabbed him. No big deal."

Confusion clouded the wolf's eyes for a moment. Then they cleared and he snorted a spray of fine white mist—the leftover of a vanilla shake, from the smell of it. Just like that, the intelligence was back—human intelligence bright and sharp in wolf eyes. He yawned, recognition and dismissal all in one, and rolled onto his back for a furry nap. I knew what it was to lose myself. I hoped it was less painful for him . . . if not for Rafferty.

I leaned against the car. "You survived the night," I said to Nik.

"Barely." He continued eating a sandwich of sprouts, sprouts, sprouts, and some liquid slop to keep them on the bread—well, slop and a tangibly foul mood. "Robin and Ishiah had phone sex last night . . . until I cut the line. Then Goodfellow used his cell phone. I broke it, quite, *quite* thoroughly. When he finally went to bed, in less than five minutes he was asleep and having what I guessed from the moaning to be a dream of the nocturnal emissions kind. I slept in the bathtub with a knife wedging the bathroom door closed."

"Gotta walk it off, Nik." I grinned. "It's a dangerous world." I bit my tongue at his glare and didn't go any further with it, not having much of a desire to be wearing that sprout sandwich.

"Ass," he said without any surprise at the fact. He finished the sandwich and studied me with a look unreadable to anyone but me, commenting, "You survived as well."

"Barely," I echoed smugly. My stomach began to growl as Rafferty finished a bear claw. "Get me one, Jeftichew?"

"Yeah, I hauled ass from Wyoming, driving all night drinking bad coffee, to bring you a damn doughnut." He wiped his hands on a napkin. "Doing your job and keeping the world from being wiped out by a psychotic Marcus Welby from Hell isn't enough. What was I thinking?"

I scowled. "You might've saved my life, Rafferty, but

that doesn't mean I won't kick your ass, furry or not."
Now that was the normal me.

"Yeah, I smell you're into walking on the Wolf side
now." His eyes, reddish brown, went a much paler amber. "Don't think that means you can give me shit. Going wolf is the least I could do to you. Want to piss pure
liquid fire for the rest of your life? Better yet, want to
piss your pants right now?"

"Because you can do what Suyolak can do. Like
when you once stopped Cal's heart," Niko said quietly,
not particularly concerned about my urinary tract from
what I could tell.

"I can." He finished wiping his hands. "But I don't.
Usually. I have to have one damn good reason or I
wouldn't be a healer. I'd be nothing but an executioner
with a hard-on for genocide like Suyolak. Healers have
that code precisely because of him. Do no harm." His
eyes paled further to Catcher yellow. "Unless you can't
avoid it. When you're a healer and a Wolf, there are
caveats."

I, not wanting to have a urinary tract infection for the
rest of my life or to piss my pants in a cheap motel parking lot, eased up. Rafferty and I were two of a kind: asses.
Except that he healed and I killed. He was also having
a helluva bad time with his cousin. He had shit enough
in his life. He didn't need more from me. "Speaking of
Suyolak. He paid me a visit in one of my dreams. Said he
could make me all Auphe. He can't do that." I hesitated,
shifting against the metal of the car. "Right?"

He looked down at Catcher who was already kicking
a back leg in his sleep. When he looked back, his eyes
had reverted to their normal color. "If the Auphe were
shapechangers like wolves, then, yeah, maybe. But they
weren't, so, no. He can't make you Auphe, and I can't
make you human." He shifted his shoulders uncomfortably. "Sorry."

"Eh, I'm over it."

His eyebrows shot skyward at my offhand dismissal. Niko wasn't so quick to give up on the subject, although he approached it from a different angle—sneaky bastard. "So why can't you change Catcher back if he's a shapechanger?" he asked. "You say you can't change Cal. I understand that, but what of Catcher? If that's true, from what you told us, that doesn't make sense. You should be able to cure him."

Rafferty threw the wadded paper napkin as far across the parking lot as it would go. It was impressively far. "I'd tell you again it's none of your business, but hell." He rubbed at bloodshot, tired eyes. "I did cure him. Five years ago Catcher was off at some damn college retreat in the Amazon. He loved crap like that. Save the planet. Whatever. He's Wolf and wolf—Were and not; guess he comes by it naturally. He'd been gone almost a year. Long time." He leaned down and rubbed Catcher's stomach. "We're the only family left, except for some Kin uncle." He curled his lip. "Thieves and murderers."

"Catcher?" Niko prodded.

Rafferty exhaled and pushed the hair from his eyes. He was long overdue for a haircut. I don't think he noticed. I know he didn't care. "He came back with leukemia. ALL: acute lymphoblastic leukemia. We Wolves heal fast and we rarely get sick, but we *do* get sick. Once in a blue moon." The grim joke flashed across his lean face and was gone. "By the time he got home and was just starting to show symptoms, it was too late. He'd had it for at least eight months. You know what the average survival rate is even with treatment? Not good. I thought he'd have a better chance of being healed in wolf form. We're stronger then. But as good as I am, and I'm fucking good, don't you ever doubt it," he said matter-of-factly, "it wasn't enough. He was slipping away and—shit. He's my cousin, my only damn family. I couldn't let him go.

So I went deeper . . . to the genetic level . . . where heal-ers aren't meant to go."

"And?" I said when he went quiet.

"And that's where I fucked up," he responded flatly. "I healed him. I healed him like no other werewolf has ever been healed. Did you think we were like vampires—a pasty anemic branch that split off from the human race? Did you think we were extra-hairy humans and along the way developed a mutation that allowed us to change to wolves?" He shook his head. "We were wolves first. We started that way. We evolved as wolves and along the way a mutation did occur. We did split from the primary race . . . but that primary race was wolf."

"Then you're not werewolves; you're were*people*?" I asked with a healthy dose of skepticism.

He rotated his head and massaged the back of his neck. "Why do you think some werewolves want to get back to wolf, and nothing but wolf? It's how we began, fifty, sixty million years ago. I did cure Catcher of the leu-kemia by mucking around with his DNA. Only trouble is I cured him too well. I cured the mutation. I can't cure him now because he's not sick. He's how we were meant to be. And I can't go the Suyolak way. I can't force him to mutate. I might get a werewolf back, but it wouldn't be Catcher. His brain would be altered—his personality. I don't think he'd ever be fully human again when he changed. I'm good. Goddamnit, I'm the fucking best, but I did too good a job the first time and there's no undoing it now. I've looked everywhere. Talked to everyone. No fucking undoing it. At least that's what they say. I don't have the power. I need more." He propped an elbow on his knee and rested his forehead in his hand. "Somehow I have to prove them wrong," he muttered so low that I barely caught the words.

Catcher slept on and for once I managed to keep my mouth shut. Rafferty had to know that no one could restore Catcher if he couldn't, but he wasn't able to admit it. He'd traveled the country, looking for a nonexistent cure and watching every day as bit by bit his cousin slipped away. One day he would look into the passenger seat and see nothing but wolf eyes looking back; no human intelligence; no memories of their past. Still, they were family. That they would never lose, but his cousin would be gone and an instinct-driven animal left in his place—an animal that thought, but certainly not in the same way humans thought.

He'd never remember the ski trip.

I'd never known Catcher as anything but wolf, but I'd seen a picture in their house of Raff and him on the ski slope. He looked like a good guy. A prankster. I'd bet Rafferty's skis had disconnected from his boots halfway down one of the difficult slopes—Black Diamond all the way. I'd seen that glitter in Catcher's eye in the photo. He was someone I might have liked . . . a rare finding; someone I might've trusted . . . especially rare. But I wouldn't know now, and that was one damn shame.

"You." It was breathed in a tangle of worship and disbelief, distracting me from my thoughts of skis, snow, and a guy who was already on his way to being half gone. "You are true. You are *right*. You are *Wolf*."

Delilah came across the asphalt, wrapped in an orange and green polyester bedspread that did nothing to distract from her tumble of pale hair and warm glow of skin or the tattoo of Celtic knots, curves, and wolf eyes that circled her neck. It was art. She was art. But none of that was aimed in my direction. She crouched beside Catcher and began to sniff the fur on Catcher's chest, neck, and behind his ears. Then she was nuzzling deeply. Catcher's eyes had opened, luckily human in their awareness. They rolled up to his cousin in question. You could all but see the *Uh, hello?* Then again, they were wolves. Maybe it was more like *Mmm, nice, but you need to get her to move a little farther down.*

"This." Delilah looked up, her eyes brighter and more intense than the rising sun. "This is what we want. This is what we were. What we want to be again. I didn't think it could be done. I thought the All Wolf hopeless. But it can be done. We can. How? How does this happen? Tell me!"

"By accident, and it's not going to happen again," Rafferty snapped. "You and the other Jurassic wannabes can look somewhere else for somebody to rip your intelligence out by the roots, because I am not doing that shit. Not again."

"Actually, it was the Pleistocene era, not Jurassic, but point taken," Niko said, spreading knowledge far and wide. My brother, he simply could not help it. He *was* more helpful when he snagged Delilah's makeshift toga and pulled her up and off Catcher. Catcher shook himself, stood, shook again, and sat down at his cousin's feet. Then he gave Delilah a wolf grin. I recognized that grin. Human, wolf, puck. "Hey, baby" transcended all languages and all species.

"'Jurassic' sounds better and, hell, no." Rafferty knocked on the top of Catcher's furry head. "Don't you even think about it, Cuz."

There was a throaty mixed rumble and snarl from Catcher. I added, "Especially not in front of me, fuzzbutt. I might not be good enough to officially date a Kin and she's her own Wolf, but it doesn't mean the pride wouldn't take a hit seeing you two go at it in front of me."

Niko gave Delilah a push back toward her room. "Not to mention in a parking lot that's overlooked by the interstate. Jeftichew, why don't you get Catcher in the car. He'll look slightly more inconspicuous." With the top on the convertible already down, Catcher gave the *rrrowrr rrowrr* that was a wolf's complaint and jumped in without waiting for Rafferty to speak up, demonstrating in his good moments he knew exactly what was going on. The baring of the teeth said, "Don't talk about me like I'm a damn Labrador." The humiliation of being all there and other times completely gone—lost in the wilderness of his own unpredictable brain—had to suck.

"I apologize, Catcher," Niko said, bowing his head in realization of how the Wolf felt. Catcher sighed and lay down on the backseat, averting his eyes from all of us. Anything else we could've said would've only made it worse.

Several parking spaces away, the Rom's RV pink door popped open and Abelia-Roo peered around the edge, smacking toothless gums in disgust. "Two more dogs. I am underwhelmed with confidence. Useless *gadje*. Worthless as humans, worthless as monsters. If we are to save the world, we do not do it by forming a circus train, collecting a flea-bitten zoo." The door slammed behind her as she turned and went back inside. *"Gunoi grast!"* That made it through the door without trouble and I might not know Rom, but once again, some things transcend. Filthy language is one of these things and a personal favorite.

Delilah disappeared with another door slam at the same time Robin weaved out of his and Niko's room, Salome winding through his legs causing the half stumble. "And who do we have here?" He smiled . . . yeah, that same "Hey, baby" smile . . . at Rafferty. Then the smile disappeared. "Oh Zeus, it's *you*. The Hippocratic ass."

"You still hanging around, Curly?" Rafferty drawled. Robin had been there when Rafferty had healed my stab wound and hadn't gotten far with him then either.

"Some appreciate my grandeur and glory, you spite-

ful bastard." He straightened his already immaculate
silk shirt with one hand and carefully tousled his hair
with the other. "And it's Robin Goodfellow. Pan. Puck.
Goblin of the Hob. Your superior by name and mea-
surement of any other kind."

"Is that what you think, you horny goat?" Rafferty
snorted. "How would you like my foot up your grand
and glorious . . . holy hell, what is that?"

That was Salome jumping up on the trunk of the car.

Then it was Salome and Catcher trying to eat each
other in the back of Niko's car. Catcher might fool some
nosy human into thinking he was a harmless, good-
natured husky mix when he was grinning and pawing
the air for a treat—he had to hate the mortification of
that—but in full fight: he was wolf, all wolf, and you
couldn't fool anyone into thinking anything else.

I checked my holster. "I'll hold off the office from
calling the cops." Hopefully the cars passing on the interstate would be moving too fast for a good look below
at a wolf-cat fight.

"Don't shoot the desk clerk," Niko warned as he,
Rafferty, and Robin moved to break it up.

I growled a little myself. "If you'd seen what was living in the closet of the room they gave us, you might let
me." I looked back behind me as I moved. "Five bucks
on the dead cat." I'd seen Salome in action. That was
one safe bet.

floor around him. There was so much that only part of it had dried. It was mucus. Under the secretions his face was bluish purple from lack of oxygen. He'd drowned in his own mucus and pardon me if I didn't whip out my PocketMD to run down that symptom. I coughed and felt a rattle in the base of my lungs.

Oh shit.

I grabbed at my cell phone and got Niko. "Put Rafferty on, Nik. Put him on *now*."

I didn't read much. That wasn't news to anyone who knew me. Old detective novels with big-breasted hookers with hearts of gold. Old Westerns with big-breasted saloon girls with hearts of gold. Old science fiction books with four-breasted alien brood queens with hearts of gold-plated titanium. That was good enough for me. But once . . . out of sheer stupidity . . . I'd read a different kind of book. I'd been sixteen. We'd been at the local library of whatever town we were hiding in then. Niko had started homeschooling me a few months before and it was book report time. If boobs weren't on the cover, I didn't care what I read. So I'd just walked down an aisle, closed my eyes, picked a book at random, and what do you know. I'd lucked into Stephen King's *The Stand*.

At first the weight of it alone was pure terror. Twenty-five pounds if it was an ounce, but Niko was right there, an amused glint in his eye, and there was no backing out. And then it managed, unbelievably, to get worse.

There was no way anyone could've convinced me the flu could scare me almost as badly as the Auphe. Swollen blackened necks, people gasping for their last breath as their eyes started from their sockets, choking and gasping for help through the gurgles of slime blocking their airway. Oh, and God and Satan, separating the good and the bad like naughty schoolchildren by killing off most of the population. Gotta break some eggs to make that omelet. It made me glad I didn't believe in God.

I believed in Rafferty, though. As soon as I heard his voice, I said, "Owner's dead. It was . . ."

"Suyolak," Rafferty finished for me. "It's viral pneumonia. It's nasty and he's made it about a thousand times more contagious and aggressive than it should be. If I hadn't been thinking about other things"—like Catcher—"I'd have known when I pulled into the parking lot. Hell, I would've known twenty miles down the road."

At least it wasn't the legendary fictional, fucking badass flu of all time. I rubbed my chest. It was beginning to ache. "Contagious. Great. There's probably some floating your way from when I opened the door."

"I know," he said quietly. "And it already has you. Do you feel it?"

I coughed again. I was feeling it all right—the increasing rattle and with it a heaviness at the base of my lungs. "Yeah, and not a bottle of cough medicine in sight."

"Sit down, back against the wall or the desk. Whatever you do, don't lie down, got it?" he ordered. "You lie down and you'll drown."

Didn't get much clearer than that.

"Got it. And whatever *you* do," I said, echoing him, only more sharply, "don't let Nik come with you. He'd drop dead an inch past the door." If he made it to the door. This was taking me down and doing it fast. Like I'd thought, Suyolak had ripped through my Auphe immune system as if it were tissue paper. Our barbecue-loving friend had probably died in seconds. I sat down hard, back against the desk while Santa's bowlful-of-plague-ridden-jelly twin lay to the side, keeping me company. His conversation was for shit. He wasn't exactly fragrant either.

I watched through the door as Rafferty spoke to my brother and roughly from the looks of the finger he jammed in Niko's chest. He then pointed the same fin-

ger at a still cat-battling Catcher who promptly fell over
asleep in the backseat, ending the fight. Salome preened
and made herself comfortable on the furry new heap of
a bed. Robin grabbed Niko's arm when he started after
Rafferty as the healer began running toward the office.
Niko yanked and Robin refused to let go. Niko could've
gotten away, but he knew coming to my side only to die
before I did wouldn't do me much good. Not exactly as
festive as a Get Well Soon balloon.

My cell rang. "Nik," I answered, "stay put and don't
worry. Hell, Rafferty rewrote Catcher's frigging DNA.
All I have is pneumonia." I coughed yet again and began to shake as the temperature of the room felt as if it
had plummeted thirty degrees in a single moment. "It
reminds me, though." My teeth chattered as I glanced at
my office mate again. What's blue and purple and dead
all over? Hell, you had to be philosophical there. The
pork clogging his arteries would've gotten him before
too much longer anyway. "You know that goddamn Stephen King killed off my favorite character? Did I put
that in the book report?" I smothered another cough.
It was the last. Suddenly there was barely enough air to
use to cough and the rattle had become a rising tide of
thick mud.

And I was sleepy. I was sitting next to a deceased motel clerk—at least I wouldn't have to worry about paying for the headboard that Delilah had ripped off the
bed—and I was sleepy. That didn't seem quite right.

"Stephen King . . . ? I remember. It was a good book,
though, Cal, wasn't it?" His voice was solid and firm,
something to hold on to as the waves of tiredness crept
over me. "And nearly a hundred times longer than any
other book you've read—before or since." His voice began to drag toward the end, the words crawling into my
ear.

Fast, I thought again. The disease moving through me

so damn fast—while everything around me was getting slower and slower.

"I'll never go to Vegas. The devil lives in Vegas," I slurred. "Think the Elvises would've kicked his ass." I stopped for a few seconds to drag in air. I wasn't too successful. "Or is it Elvi? Sounds better ... like that. More ... snooty. More . . . scientific." Niko would like that. He liked science. He liked anything boring and academic—like the dead guy. I focused on him. He was pretty academic now—ancient history and uninteresting.

My gaze drifted back toward the door. Rafferty looked as if he were running in slow motion, and around him the air began to spark red. Pinpoint explosions of light. Viruses biting the big one. By the time he reached the door, he was surrounded by a massive halo of scarlet light flashing brighter and brighter. I closed my eyes. It didn't help. I tried to block the light with my arm across my eyes. I lost my balance when I did, sliding down the desk and falling onto my side. The oxygen fought its way through the swamp sludge that had filled my lungs in a matter of seconds. "Cal?" The cell phone had fallen from my other hand to the floor next to my ear. "Cal? The book, it was a good one, wasn't it? Tell me. *Cal*, tell me."

Trying to keep me there, keep me with him. "Scared ... shit ... out ... of ... me. Me ... the ... monster."

"You're not a monster. You're an annoying, messy, kid brother who might be twenty-one, might be an adult finally." I didn't think it was delirium that made me think he emphasized "finally" so strongly. "But you still don't listen to those who are smarter than you. Now sit up, you son of a bitch. I can see you lying down on the job from here. Sit up *now*."

Easier said than done. But I did try ... for my brother, who always made me try whether I wanted to or not. I took my arm from my eyes and I did. I did try.

I failed miserably, which wasn't usual for me. Ordinarily I failed spectacularly with explosions, splattered body parts, holes ripped in time and space, and other equally entertaining things. This time I just failed in a typically ordinary way. I slid back down, this time flat on my face. With an effort so huge it was ridiculous in its pathetic result, I turned my head . . . but I only managed enough to see the door.

It was the same door that opened as the entire room disappeared in a shock wave of crimson so bright I thought the world was on fire. The earth had hit the sun or vice versa and there was not one damn Elvis around when you needed one.

"Suyolak, you bastard." There was respect there— loathing and disgust, but respect too. If Rafferty thought someone was close to half as good as he was, that was bad news. If Rafferty actually had enough regard for Suyolak's talents to curse him for it, then we were fucked as they came. I twitched my fingers at the healer in the best attempt at a wave I could pull off. I could see the blue tinge to them as the red faded from the air. Blue didn't seem right. But I was tired, more than tired, and I didn't much care.

Rafferty dropped to his knees beside me. He was faintly blue himself, but in a second he was back to his normal color as he turned me over onto my back. He then laid his hand on my chest. There was already an anchor sitting on it. His hand didn't add much weight. When you couldn't breathe, it didn't matter whether it was an anchor or an elephant.

"I'd say hang in there, Cal, but it sounds goddamn stupid on every TV show I hear it on. Doubt it'll sound any better here." His hand was warm, warmer, and as my eyelids began to slide closed, it became fiery hot. That woke me up. My eyes widened as the heat passed through me. Every vein and artery carried liquid fire; ev-

ery cell burned like an incendiary round. If I'd had any
air left in my lungs, I would've screamed in agony. And
if I could've moved, I would've kicked Rafferty in the
balls while I was screaming. Multitasker—that was me.

But since I couldn't do either, I lay there and burned.
My vision went in and out as I went in and out. Eventually I was more there than not and the burning faded.
I blinked once, saw Rafferty's face, but I still couldn't
breathe—not until Rafferty lifted me and turned me
over as I hung uselessly, his arms wrapped around my
stomach to hold me off the floor. I would've been on
all fours if I could've borne any of my own weight. "I'm
sure you've puked a time or two in your day, Cal," he
said brusquely. "Think of this as your lungs vomiting instead of your stomach."

It was a good description. You didn't quite get the
range you did with vomiting, but the sensation of your
lungs turning almost inside out made up for the lack of
distance. It couldn't have been a gallon, but it felt like
it coming out and looked like it puddled on the carpet.
Green, yellow, and extremely repugnant. I coughed
harshly several times, before getting enough strength
back to wipe at my mouth with my jacket sleeve. That
was when I noticed I was breathing again, which, now
that I thought about it, was really underrated. Great
hobby. Couldn't get enough of it.

"That's . . . just . . . not right," I said, coughing again.
"Couldn't you just . . . have gotten rid of it?"

"I did," Rafferty responded with exasperation at my
ear.

"I meant, just make it disappear. Poof." He helped me
stand upright and steadied me when I staggered.

"I'm a healer, not Houdini," he grunted. "And that's
the second time I've saved your life. Show a little grati-
tude, you thankless jackass."

"Maybe I'd be more grateful if you, Mr. Super Healer,

had noticed all this shit sooner. You know, not been watching your cousin Sir Hump-a-Lot giving Delilah the eye and wanting to give her a whole lot more." I staggered back away from the pool of stinking fluids. Jesus, I could still taste it. I needed gum . . . toothpaste . . . anything.

"It was your Kibbles 'n' Tits that started that scene," he snorted.

My legs stabilized under me and I quirked my lips at the picture of Delilah's face if she'd heard that one. "It's good to be among my own kind."

"And what's that?" he asked suspiciously.

"Assholes." I grinned ruefully. I looked down at the ruined carpet at my feet. "I need to get rid of my DNA. Niko's been paranoid for a while about the government's accidentally finding a random mutant gene of mine floating around somewhere, starting a manhunt, and beginning to clone me to sell."

"For what? Soldiers?" He went behind the counter, rummaged around, and returned with half a bottle of vodka.

"Come on. Borderline psychotic. Do anything for the right price. Half-fiendish monster." I squatted down. "Supersoldiers, nope. More like an army of congressmen." Pulling out one of my knives, I cut a circle in the flat, worn carpet. By the time I was out the door, a matter of seconds, and tossing it on the asphalt of the parking lot, Niko was there to watch me use the vodka and my lighter to burn it.

"Considerate of you to not burn down the entire motel."

The fire was flaming nicely and I let Rafferty pull the bottle of vodka out of my hand to take the last remaining swallow. "It *was* nice of me. You're going to smack the back of my head anyway?" I asked Niko. "Because I'm beginning to worry about your causing a bald spot there, and I have enough going against me already in the dating department."

"No, I'm not. As far as I can tell, this, by some means completely beyond comprehension, is not your fault." His fingers were gripping my chin firmly, turning my face to one side, then the other. He was examining my skin color, the whites of my eyes, double-checking Rafferty's work. When it came to me, Niko trusted no one but himself for the last word.

"Want to look at my teeth too?" I asked. "Guess my age like a horse's?"

He decided to swat me after all. "Get your things and let's go." He stopped my first step with a hand on my shoulder. "You know, this may be one of the few times I was actually grateful you're half Auphe."

"You should be." Rafferty dropped the bottle onto the concrete. It didn't shatter, instead rolling from side to side with a musical tinkle. "Otherwise he would've never even made it to the door. He'd have been facedown in the parking lot right about where we're standing. Dead between one breath and the next. Suyolak's hypervirus had made it at least this far out. And if Cal had been human, all human, I'm not sure I could've brought him back." Reddish brown went to yellow, then to dark amber as he stared at us through ragged auburn hair. "The Plague of the World. They weren't shitting when they gave him that name. He's a harvester of death, all right, but I'll reap his ass."

"You can be sure of that?" Niko demanded.

"No," he answered, passing us on the way back to the car.

At least he was honest.

8

Catcher

My name is Catcher....

My name is Catcher. I was pretty sure about that, as I gave a sleepy blink—as sure as I was of anything. Sun and wind and smells; some were new, some not, and all of them confusing. There was also a hazy memory of a cat. My ears lay back and I decided I didn't care about my little way of checking if I was in my right mind, because then I sort of wished I weren't. Full consciousness had hit me, and I woke up to a massive case of unhappy. Despite the easygoing attitude I tried to hang on to all my life, I didn't think that was going to change anytime in the next day or so.

The day before Rafferty and I had gone to the Wind River Reservation in Wyoming to meet with an American Indian healer. He also happened to be about one-sixteenth trickster. One-sixteenth didn't sound like much, but when some tricksters counted themselves as gods, it could give you serious bragging rights and sometimes the ability to go with it. I didn't know if this guy had gotten anything extra from his trickster blood, but if he had, it hadn't superpowered his healing ability any. He couldn't undo what Rafferty had done and told us both, sympathetically but in no uncertain terms, that no one could. I'd been a dead man walking. Rafferty had traded my human half for more than five years of life, and only he could've pulled that off. No one else could do what he'd done to begin with and there was no way on Coyote's green earth that anyone could undo it either, the other healer had said.

My cousin didn't take it well.

He didn't say anything. He didn't throw anything either, and with his temper, that was saying something. I would've been less worried if he *had* thrown something. But he didn't. He just said calmly that we'd keep looking. He wasn't giving up, and he meant it. He actually meant it.

Raff didn't get it. He was never going to get it. He talked about Niko's knowing some Japanese healing entity and maybe ...

Maybe, maybe, maybe.

He couldn't let me go. He couldn't forgive himself when there was nothing to forgive. He had saved me, but as hard as I tried, I couldn't convince him of that. And now he was going to get himself killed on our one break from searching under every rock for my impossible, long-lost humanity. No Disney World. No Grand Canyon. No Hawaii, although they had strict quarantine rules there for my kind anyway. My cousin needed a vacation in the worst way. I liked him sane and the way he was going, he was going to be leaking lucidity as if his brain were a sieve. Disney World might not have cured that, but it was better than a psychotic antihealer who was turning the air itself into death. Rafferty had gone through more than enough these past years. He didn't need this burden too. Did I care if he was the only one who could stop this Suyolak? Not really.

I had cared before. I'd cared about the world and doing the right thing, but that was when I knew Raff could take down this Rom disease without breaking stride—because he was that good, my cousin. Then I'd heard Cal's voice as he went from perfectly healthy to death's door in seconds—a half Auphe taken out that quickly.

I cared about the world all right, but I cared about my cousin more. Besides, Niko and Cal just hadn't looked hard enough for another healer. I knew about looking. One day didn't count. Even if Rafferty was the only one who could take out Suyolak, that didn't make it fair. I'd always thought life should be fair, whether wearing fur or skin. I knew it wasn't—I wasn't naïve, but it didn't change my thinking it should be. Wolves didn't actually see in black and white; we saw in blues and greens. Yet *I* saw in black and white when it came to my view of the world. Things were either fair or they weren't, and this wasn't.

No, I wasn't happy about this whole thing, and my waking up with a dead cat curled on top of me didn't improve my mood at all. I liked to think I was a good guy. I was going to help stop global warming when I was a student; that and save the rain forest. These days I avoided watering people's prize rosebushes and put up with the humiliation of letting little old grannies pat me on the head while trying to shove dog biscuits down my throat. That was an effort, right? Considering the taste of dog biscuits, it was a big effort. But now . . . now this good guy bared his teeth at the cat before lifting his head to bare his teeth at everyone else around him. It was a good thing you could fit about fourteen people in an Eldorado—fourteen people or one human, a monster mix, a puck, two werewolves, and that damn dead cat. It was about equal comfortwise, but it was a tour I wished we hadn't signed up for.

I glared at my faithful cousin who'd put me to sleep when I'd been fighting with a female feline with male pattern baldness and an advanced case of dead. I wasn't sure if the battle had been an "episode" or just a general freak-out at the sight of a walking, grinning, tail-thrashing *zombie* cat. I'd seen a lot of things in my life; as a werewolf that's a given, but that was a first. Another first was its nearly kicking my furry butt. I should be glad Rafferty had sent me to naptime. That way I could pretend it was a draw and save some of my fuzzy dignity.

The cat felt me move, yawned, and leaped up front with Niko and Goodfellow to curl up on the dashboard. Her toothy, fanged grin was smug, and I couldn't help but bristle. I growled at her, then sat up to turn my head toward Rafferty and growled harder.

"She's already dead," he said in his defense. "I couldn't put her to sleep. Suck the life force out of her and rekill her, yeah, but not put her to sleep. And Goodfellow, with his usual bad taste, seems to like her."

I snorted and kept growling. That was no excuse and I let him know it. Niko was driving and I was between Cal and my cousin. We were on the road, the parking lot just a memory. That was odd. I gave up on the growling, and sneezed curiously. We'd left our car behind. I liked that car. I especially liked the catless atmosphere of it, and, sorry to say it about Cal, but he smelled of murder in the shadows. It wasn't his fault. I imagined he'd suffered more than I could imagine from being what he was, suffered from prejudice, suffered from instinct, suffered by knowing he had been created to be nothing but a living weapon. I felt bad for him, I did . . . but he still smelled like he smelled: Auphe—unkillable monster; five times worse than a demon from Hell. Granted, most couldn't smell him, but Wolves could. Couldn't they at the very least hang a deodorizer off his ear out of common courtesy? Pine-fresh maybe? I could handle that. I was the accommodating kind.

I poked Rafferty's shoulder once, then again urgently and almost instantly. "Okay. Christ. Give me a chance," he grumbled as he reached down to the floorboards for my laptop. He pulled it out of the computer bag, opened it up, and set it on his lap, swiveling it in my direction; then he fished back in the bag for my pencil. Once it was set up and ready to go, I typed in a question.

He turned to read it, but not before Cal peered around me and read it out loud. "*Where's our car, General Jack-off?* General Jack-off?"

Rafferty shook his head. "Don't ask. It's a theme. Although the cat thing apparently got me promoted. And I left the car, Catch. I stripped it of ID—the license plate was stolen anyway—in case it gets towed. I need to sleep. To rest up for Suyolak. I can't drive and do that. And the last time I let you drive, I got my license pulled. And you ended up in the pound because your rabies tag was expired. Some cops, they can't just let you go with a warning, huh?"

My cousin's sense of humor aside—the best place for it—leaving the car did make sense. Or . . . or maybe it meant he thought he wasn't going to walk away from his battle with Suyolak. Worse, maybe he didn't want to. The guilt, the burden of me; it was more than anyone should have to carry, but Rafferty wouldn't do that. He wouldn't give in. Anyone else would have. No Wolf alive would go on and on as he had, not even for family. They would've seen the sense long ago. Wolves prized family, prized pack, but we were also practical creatures.

Except for Rafferty. He hadn't given me life to throw his own away, but what if I was gone? Before Suyolak, what if I fell into my wolf half and didn't resurface? What happened if the next "episode" was the last episode? What would he do then? And how do you ask that? I hesitated, hit the CAPS LOCK for emphasis, then typed, *HUNT NO MORE?* And Cal, whose scent still had the hair along my spine bristling, faithfully repeated the three words. What was wrong with him anyway?

Couldn't he read without moving his lips? And Goodfellow, of course, jumped on the bandwagon. His mouth was faster than a speeding bullet, in all sorts of ways I didn't want to think about, like all pucks, but definitely when it came to talking.

"Hunt no more? That's dead for Wolves," he pounced. "If you can't take Suyolak, you'd better speak up so we can turn this parade around. I can think of better ways to die. Ten thousand at the very least."

Rafferty ignored him, but this was a puck we were talking about. You couldn't ignore one of them any more than you could a kindergarten class with each kid hyped up on five pounds of pure cane sugar. Goodfellow asked again . . . and again . . . and then again. That was when my cousin paralyzed the puck's vocal cords. When Goodfellow turned in the seat and started to swing a quick and what looked like a lethal fist, Rafferty leaned out of reach and, unimpressed, said, "Keep it up and your hair will fall out, your eyes cross, and I'll make you impotent for the rest of your long life." His eyes flickered back and forth between the colors of a noontime sun and a setting one. "There's immortal and there's immortally limp dicked. Think about it. You're asking me to kill a healer. 'Do no harm' has fallen by the wayside. Got it?"

He didn't wait for the puck to ponder the pros and cons of yapping endlessly like a newborn cub versus being the bald, double-visioned actor on the erectile dysfunction drug commercials for the rest of eternity. Instead, Raff handed the computer to Cal, slid down, leaned against me, and went to sleep, but not before murmuring too low for human hearing, "I'm not leaving your furry ass, Catch. Got that? Never."

I didn't complain at his weight against me as he began to snore. He needed it. He'd been up all night driving, and I'd heard Cal's call for help when Suyolak's little present got him. I might have been getting my tail half chewed off by that mutant cat, but I could still hear. I rested my muzzle on top of Rafferty's head, my fur mixing with his hair. He never had cared that much about getting haircuts in the old days . . . in high school or college. He was just that kind of guy who waited until his girlfriend dragged him to a barber. He didn't think about it at all now; he just chopped at it with scissors when it got too long and hit the Salvation Army when his clothes wore out. That was his life now with me. I wanted it to be better when I was gone. I hoped he meant what he said, because I didn't want him throwing that life away on Suyolak.

"Did healing you somehow infect him with your attitude?" Robin frowned at Cal, his vocal cords working again as one hand checked his hair and the other checked his crotch. He gave a long exhalation of relief when he was assured he was as puckable as he ever was. I rolled my eyes. Pucks. They were enough to make a Wolf change his mind about the whole Humane Society's neutering campaign.

"Half human, half monster, all attitude," Cal replied mockingly. He had attitude all right, but he came by it honestly. I had my problems, but I wasn't sure I would've exchanged them for his. Although his girlfriend . . . Kin or not, she was something. White fur—I'd always had a thing for white fur. It reminded me of snow, racing across it under the moon and stars, and having sex in the chill under a pine tree laden with icicles. Rafferty wasn't the only one who needed to get laid.

"I'm starving. And if I'm starving, I know Delilah is," Cal went on, idly searching my computer for games. I perked my ears up. Delilah, that was good; talk more about Delilah. "I can wait. Delilah probably could wait, but I doubt she will."

A Wolf with appetites; I liked that. Of course at this

point, any Wolf with a pulse was looking good. It had been a long, *long* time.

"That's what drive-throughs and bad diners are made for, not to mention what you live for. I'll stop at Omaha," Niko said, not that concerned with his brother's state of near starvation. "Did anyone—"

Cal interrupted him, "I was sick. I'm never sick. I could've died. I need to build my energy back up. At least—"

This time it was Niko's turn to interrupt. A box of Twinkies was tossed over the top of the front seat to hit Cal squarely in the chest. That was a good interruption. Straight to the point. Niko was a man of few words and flying sugary snacks. I liked that in a human. "There," he said sharply. "Happy? Convert your entire body to a Cal-shaped pile of sponge cake and crème. Now, may I continue?"

Cal immediately smelled contrite—more so than he would have for just annoying his brother. He'd said something to Niko that had sharply hit home, cut deeply to the bone. I didn't know what it was, but he must've felt genuinely bad, because he let the Twinkies drop carelessly to the floorboards, which was a crime. I loved Twinkies. "Yeah, sorry. I was being a fucking idiot as usual. I'm listening now," he responded quietly.

Okay, there was sorry and then there was stupid. He might not want a Twinkie, but I did. Before I could turn my head, though, and yip a protest, Niko exhaled and the scent of brooding worry faded to the more appropriate irritation. "Eat your Twinkies. You probably do need the energy." He watched in the rearview mirror and waited while Cal unwrapped the first one, which I promptly snatched from his hand without disturbing Rafferty's comfortable slump of sleep against me. Cal glared at me, which I ignored in crème-filled bliss, be-

fore he opened another. That was when Niko said, "Dr.
Jones called again last night. Seattle professor Daniel
Kirkland hasn't been by his wife's side for several days
now, according to friends on the faculty, which is not
just unusual. It's unbelievable to them. They were the
closest of couples. He has never given up hope and
has never left her side since she slipped into a coma.
They even said he typed on his computer with one hand
while holding her hand with his other." The computer
he could've done his research on, found out the most
likely location of Abelia-Roo's clan . . . and Suyolak.
"So there is a very good chance he is our man and our
driver all in one. He might have hired men to do the
stealing, but he didn't trust anyone but himself to do
the actual delivery."

"And those guys killed Abelia's men without thinking
twice. Now he's hauling Suyolak's ass back home. Love
can make you do some truly fucked-up shit." Cal shook
his head and looked like he was going to say something
else, but he didn't. He didn't have to. I had the feeling
everyone in this car, minus the cat, knew the last was
truer than any of us cared to admit.

Niko cleared his throat and asked, "Did anyone have
a Suyolak dream last night?"

Cal shook his head. "Like I said, I didn't sleep much.
I'm still waiting for one of you to have that fucking un-
paralleled joy."

That's right, I thought with a grumble to myself, rub
it in. He might smell like Auphe, but he smelled like
Delilah too under the soap of a morning shower. Goodfellow wasn't happy either, muttering, "I had a dream
or two, non-Suyolak related, and unfortunately for me,
just dreams."

"Yes, I and the long-suffering maid who will have to
wash your sheets are more than aware," Niko retorted.
"So none of us dreamed of him?"

"One doesn't have to sleep to dream. Life itself is only a dream, my brothers," the nightmare spoke.

Rafferty's head jerked up as he woke instantly. I growled and snapped, foam flying from my jaws. I couldn't help it even though I knew he wasn't really there. He had no scent. He wasn't real. Suyolak—the nightmare that Niko and Cal had talked about. He wasn't sitting cross-legged on the hood of the moving car, a skeleton covered with skin, pale moon eyes, and a gnarled mass of dusty dreadlocks that didn't move in the rush of air that swept over the convertible. He wasn't any of those things, although I saw him as he was. He made the dead cat look as normal and wholesome as our grandma Amelia's apple and squirrel pie we'd eaten when we were cubs.

For a healer to appear in dreams was one thing. For a healer to appear as a hallucination in the brains of the conscious, that was another. That took the kind of healing power I didn't want to think about. I remembered my thought that Rafferty was the best of this world and Suyolak the best of his. What if Suyolak was the best . . . period? What then?

"Don't shoot, Cal," Niko was saying. "He's not actually there."

"Yeah, I know." But I saw that Cal's trigger finger was having trouble catching up with his brain, same as my snapping jaws were with mine. "But wouldn't it be better to double-check?"

"I don't want to buy a new windshield because of this talking disease." Niko kept driving. Yes, a human was unfazed enough by the so-called Plague of the World sitting on his ancient boat of a car to keep it at an even seventy down the Lincoln. He was brave. His balls might not have been furry, but he most definitely had them. I had to give credit where it was due. He'd have made a good Wolf.

"That's what you are, Suyolak, a disease. You're not human; you're not a person; you never were. You were born a living disease, and as all diseases do, you have a cure," Niko continued.

The cracked and shriveled lips parted in a grin. "Do you think you're my cure, Vayash? Or do you think that mongrel behind you is? Is my equal? That a cur can face the man who reaped a continent? The Black Death himself?" The grin widened. "He is a jackal, only good for feeding on the dead that fall in my path."

I moved to leap over the seat. Nobody talked about my cousin like that—nobody. I felt hands on me, Cal and my cousin holding me back. Suyolak raised his hands to seemingly hook withered fingers over the top of the windshield, his bleached eyes staring dead on into mine. "Why, look at you, brave dog. Look at what has been done to you," he said with a gloating marvel. "Maybe I was wrong." The eyes moved left, to Rafferty. "Maybe you will entertain me. I kill, but you took his mind. Which is worse? Which is more thrilling?" A bone-pale tongue tip touched the upper lip. "The taste of that, you left his life and took half his soul . . . well done, my Wolf brother. We are two of a kind after all."

Then he was gone. The bastard was gone.

I settled back on my haunches. My teeth were still bared, as much at Niko and Cal as they were for Suyolak—for getting us into this. For getting Rafferty into this. Then I shook my head, fur flying, and turned to stick my nose directly in my cousin's ear. He was frozen. It was more in the face of the accusation than in the hideously dessicated one of Suyolak, I knew. Suyolak had hit my cousin directly in a wound five years in the festering. He hurt him, like no one else could. And now I was the only one who could reach him. I blew through my nose hard, sending an ice-cold spray against his eardrum. He jerked back to the here and now and away from my muzzle. He scowled before saying with a sigh, "Yeah, yeah. I know."

Not your fault. You did the best you could, the best any healer alive could. I said it silently and hoped he heard me, smelled it, that he really did know. It was the truth, but even if it weren't, I would've said the same thing.

It was what family did.

9

Cal

You shouldn't see things like that in daylight. You'd think it would be better . . . to see the yellowed spiral of a long nail scrape playfully down the windshield . . . in the sun. It would be less of a horror, less of an icicle stab to the heart. It wasn't. It was worse in the day. It didn't belong. Suyolak was wrong, but he was so much more wrong in the light than in the dark, because there was no way to deny it—to deny him. There was no way to say the nightmare was just that . . . only a nightmare. In our life, denial could get you killed, but a few seconds of it when the time was right could also keep you sane. Just like salt . . . A little made the bland taste a little better and a lot raised your blood pressure, dropped you with a massive stroke, and boom, you were dead. Denial and salt, not totally bad things on the surface of it, but in the end they both could equal death; who knew?

Lucky we had a healer with us.

Although from the heat of the unblinking glower searing the side of my face, someone wished we didn't. I'd gone back to poking around on the laptop after Suyolak disappeared. We didn't all sit around and discuss the meaning of it. What's to say? He knew we were coming—we already knew that. He wanted to kill us—still no news. He wasn't impressed by Rafferty. He was an egomaniacal genocidal killer; impressed or not, he wouldn't show it. Egomaniacal genocidal killers rarely did. If they did, they'd be sensible, modest genocidal killers, and those were fucking hard to come by.

So, no discussion needed. Niko drove on, leaving Illinois behind us as the Lincoln dipped south toward Omaha, Nebraska. Googled five dead there—same as what had hit me: viral pneumonia. I'd thought it before; I'd think it again, but, goddamnit, if he was doing all this now, what the hell would he do if he got out of that coffin? They were futile, poisonous thoughts and I gave up on them before they drove me nuts. Besides, I had a distraction to help me out there.

I had to make an effort not to raise a hand and feel the side of my face to make sure it wasn't melting from the acid gaze. Finally, I couldn't take it anymore. I turned to face the yellow eyes, radioactive twin suns of absolutely nuclear pissiness aimed at me—which was unusual for Catcher. He was the happiest damn Wolf I'd ever run across. Lassie had nothing on him. He was happy, cheerful, probably a Boy Scout as a kid—well, considering what he was, a Cub Scout. But with the current situation, I could understand the change in mood. "Look, I'm sorry, okay? If he were my cousin, I'd be mad as hell that anyone got him involved in this mess too." Rafferty was asleep again. He'd driven all night, healed me, and destroyed millions of hyperdeadly mutated germs floating in the parking lot and office. A helluva thing to see—that crimson explosion—but also a helluva drain on your resources, Wolf stamina or not.

But past all that, I could see he wasn't the same as he'd been when I'd last seen him, years ago. There were lines that weren't just weariness—permanent lines, years of disappointment. The last thing Rafferty and Catcher needed was us fucking up their already-fucked-up lives. That we didn't have a choice didn't make it any better. "I'm sorry," I repeated, "but this son of a bitch Suyolak can take down the whole goddamn world. Frankly, I don't give a shit about most of the world because it damn sure doesn't seem to give a shit about me, but there are a few people in it whom I do care about. Even if we hadn't called you, even if Rafferty hadn't answered Nik—hadn't felt that evil mojo tickle—once Suyolak got loose, eventually it would've become your problem too. A few hundred thousand dead people would have Rafferty after Suyolak sooner or later. He's single-minded, but sometimes you have to do what you have to do."

The dark brown lip that was peeled back to show Catcher's dinnerware didn't move at first, but after a few seconds it slowly lowered, but the eyes were no friendlier. They did look away, though, as he searched for his pencil on the floorboards. When he located it, he reached over with it to the laptop, switched to the window that held the Word document already up, and beneath the *HUNT NO MORE*, he typed, *PAYMENT*.

He had a point. We were getting fifty thousand for this. It wasn't fair to expect them to put their lives on the line for nothing. Robin never took our money. . . . He had more than we'd ever see in our lifetimes, but Rafferty and Catcher weren't Kin or immortal con men. They worked for a living or had. I'd seen the tired, old ranch house they'd lived in. They could use the money, especially to keep their search for a cure going. "Yeah, that's reasonable. How about half? Twenty-five thousand? Assuming you want a penny that Abelia-Roo has touched with her poisonous hands. Probably dusted it with arsenic powder, the bitch."

The Wolf gave a shrug so subtle it didn't move his cousin, again slouched against him, as if to say money was money, which was true enough. All money was touched by blood sometime or another—the way of the world. Clicking the caps lock off—assured I was paying proper attention—he typed again. *Half and more. I want real payment. Not Alpo money, not a down payment on a timeshare, bucko. Real payment.*

And I'd thought Suyolak was bizarre. Now here I was negotiating with a Wolf who typed at least twice as fast as I did and without having to use spell-check. If Lassie had had a laptop, Timmy could've cut his down-the-well time in half. "Okay," I said dubiously, "what do you want?"

Taptaptaptaptap. When he was finished, the screen may as well have been a bloody strip of his soul plastered in light and pixels. I gave it the respect it deserved and read it in silence this time. It was what he wanted. *Take care of him.* I looked up and saw true emotion, raw and desperate, in eyes that hadn't been human in a long time. I looked back at the computer. A strip of soul was better than the rest of the ragged wounded one revealed only inches away. I read on. *When I'm gone, take care of him. Make him your family. Make him your cousin, your brother. He gave you back to Niko. He gave your brother his family back. You do the same for Rafferty. Without family, there is no life. Give him life.*

Big order. Tall order. But he was right. Without Rafferty, I wouldn't be sitting here. He'd saved me twice now. Without him, Niko would be without a brother and I'd have died at least two damn unpleasant deaths. We owed him and even if we didn't, I knew what it was like to contemplate life without the only family you had. No one deserved that existence, definitely not the man who'd saved me and was now ready to try to save the world.

"All right," I said, grim at the memories and the ever-shitty nature of what-ifs. "Hey, why not? Adoption's the big thing in Hollywood right now. At least he's already potty trained." Up front, Robin started to open his mouth. Niko's hand firmly cut off the interruption. He would've guessed what I'd promised. Robin would've guessed too if his mouth weren't always a half second faster than his brain.

Catcher dipped his head, accepting my promise. I'd sounded like a smart-ass when I said it—I couldn't help it. Smart-ass was my native tongue, but I meant it and he knew it. The yellow eyes were on mine again, holding me to the assurance. He managed to hide his soul this time.

I added, "But he'll find a cure. Rafferty's the most stubborn bastard I've met, aside from Niko." The furry head nodded again, the eyes rolling in "Ain't that the truth" acknowledgment before they blinked and the muzzle wrinkled. That's when the wolf typed a PS:

BTW, could you get some cologne or Febreze or something? Sorry, Cal, but you're killing me here. He gave me a sheepish, sideways grin, then added, *Take it out of the twenty-five thousand. Fair's fair.*

"My smell? You're bitching about how I smell?" I slammed the laptop shut. "Oh, you son of a bitch. Do I complain about the fur? Another fifty miles and I'll be hacking up hairballs. Did I bitch when you ate half the Twinkies?" Actually I had, but they were *my* Twinkies. "And let's talk about Delilah, not my girlfriend, but we are doing it, but do I ask you to make it harder for her to hit on you? Hell, no." More like there was no point in asking. Delilah would do what Delilah would do, but damn it, I was pissed. And I'd never been one not to share my feelings, especially that one.

"I never would've thought I'd rather discuss a pestilence-spreading living corpse than listen any longer to this conversation," Robin groaned from the passenger seat before reaching into his linen blazer—he was all dressed up for the road trip—and pulling out a slim roll of cloth. He untied it and with one quick flip, unrolled it down the back of the front bench seat like a professional assassin from a James Bond movie. It held about ten glass vials. "Choose your poison. From Bulgaria, Aqua at the top; Bijan and several others far too good for you in the middle; and the neutralizer that blocks one from any and every nose, including werewolves', at the bottom. I sell that to Delilah by the gallon to keep her place Auphe-free and you a secret from the Kin. Up until recently, at least."

"Forget it," I snapped. "Einstein here can soak me up. I hope I get Auphe killer funk all over him. I hope . . ."

Niko bent his arm over the seat, took the last vial, and squirted me liberally, not once looking away from the road. Catcher grinned at me, tongue lolling, as a bead of the liquid rolled down the line of my nose, poised at the tip, then dropped off. Chuffing in amusement, the wolf fished around in the seat, finally raising his hindquarters to pull out one of my old T-shirts from beneath, and offered it to me with his muzzle.

At the volunteering of my shirt covered with his ass fur, I gave him a snarl every bit the equal of his earlier one. "Yeah, I'm wiping my face with that."

He grinned and tossed it into the wind. It was up over our heads and then gone. Just because I didn't want it then didn't mean I didn't want it at all. I could've washed it. "That's coming out of your twenty-five thousand too," I gritted. "That was worth at least three"— eyes slitted, I amended—"okay, two cans of Alpo, you mutt." He didn't seem to much care about my loss as he lifted his nose into that same wind and enjoyed the ride, all the while ignoring me. He was back to Catcher. Business taken care of and living in the moment, and that moment was flying in the wind—heaven for any canine-related creature.

By the time we reached Omaha, I'd given in to the

boredom, the ultimate forgive-and-forget incentive, and was back on the laptop, playing hangman with Catcher. Not a very exciting game, especially when he won every time. It was beginning to be a trend—losing in Go Fish to a chupacabra and hangman to a Wolf. What the hell was a *Paphiopedilum bellatulum* anyway? An endangered orchid, Niko informed me. "What is wrong with you?" I asked the Wolf. "That's what you learned in college? What about bonging beers? Banging sorority chicks? Road trips?" I caught myself. "Right. That's what we're on now. I can see why you skipped them."

"Spring breaks." Rafferty yawned, straightening from his nap. "The spring breaks were good, except this ass stole most of the girls." Catcher was grinning again, which I took to be a smug agreement.

"Speaking of women," Niko began, turning enough to flash a stern look at me. "Cal?"

He was right. Catcher and Rafferty were in this. They needed to know all of the dangers, not just about Suyolak. I put the computer back in their bag and rested my hands on my knees. "Delilah," I said matter-of-factly, "she's going to try to kill me. I think. Hell, I don't know. She might. She might not. But the Kin know about her and me. I have that from a reliable source—as reliable as a knife and an axe can make it anyway. She'll have to do something."

"What concerns me is not knowing what exactly that might be," my brother added as he took the first exit in search of food. "With the Kin, options are limited. We assume she was offered the choice of execution by her Alpha or by her pack and her Alpha. I don't underestimate her by any means in that regard. It would probably take them both. Her second option, the one I imagine she chose, would be killing Cal. They know he was involved in killing the Alpha Cerberus, and, amoral criminals that they are, they don't consider him worthy of life even outside of that." That was Niko's polite way of saying they considered me an unnatural freak and ridding New York of me would make it an all-around better place to eat, sleep, and lift a leg.

"Our good friend Caliban was of the opinion that it would be fine entertainment to let her come along so that we might play a game of 'Does Cal get screwed tonight or does Cal get *screwed* tonight?' " Goodfellow drawled. "The second 'screwed' being, of course, Delilah eating his liver with 'some fava beans and a nice Chianti.' I've never been a fan of fava beans myself; a little too spicy. I like a calm stomach when killing or having sex or doing both simultaneously. The last," he said pointedly to me, "is my bet on how Delilah will make her run at you. I recognize my own. She is a creature of very particular appetites."

"You're usually too lazy to kill unless you can't avoid it," I said. It was a way to escape the conversation for a few seconds, but it was also true. Robin had once done something similar to what he'd said to save a girl I'd known—and loved. He'd killed a succubus, and considering succubi were predators who killed with sex, I imagined he'd done it in the midst of the act. But I hadn't asked, and he hadn't told. He had done it for me and for the girl. There hadn't been much more to say.

The puck was an unbelievable fighter with thousands of years, maybe hundreds of thousands, to sharpen his skills, but he didn't much seek out battles anymore. He was satisfied with the good life unless, like now, we could use his help. Thanks to Niko and me, we'd brought him out of retirement, and while he was our friend—and as lonely as he'd been, had been desperate to be our friend, I still wasn't sure we'd done him any favors.

"I've mellowed over the years," Robin retorted. "And there were none that didn't deserve what I gave them. At least from my point of view at the time." His carelessly jaded smile reminded me of another puck who once had almost killed us all. It made me damn glad Robin *was* a friend—had fought so hard to make Niko and me accept him as one. And mellow was good. It didn't make me like his cat any better, though.

"Anyway"—I rolled up an empty Twinkie wrapper and tossed it at him—"long story not short enough, Delilah will probably try to kill me, but I wanted to give her a choice." That didn't make me soft. It made me a guy who'd been given a lot of chances in my life when I'd done bad things. . . . They could be blamed on a creature that had taken me over, blamed on genes that should never have existed, much less have been combined with human ones. It didn't matter who or what was behind the things I'd done. What did matter was I'd been given chances to prove I was better than that. I'd be one damn big hypocrite if I denied Delilah the same.

"Very noble. Very giving and understanding. Very much reeking of bullshit." Robin couldn't read minds, but he didn't have to. This was his field of expertise. "It's the sex, Hugh Hefner. Intercourse, coitus, carnal knowledge . . . especially the way Wolves do it, but one thing it is not is philanthropy."

"As if I could even touch the level of horndog you've reached in your life," I snorted. "I'm surprised you have a dick left at all. That it's not whittled down to a toothpick."

"If this is the way it's going to be the whole way, I'm going to get another car." Rafferty rubbed his eyes and yawned. "This is why you meditate, Niko? To keep from ripping them to small-enough pieces that even I couldn't put them back together? Not that I would bother to try without one helluva fee."

"Let's say it helps. Partially. At times. I'm looking into additional philosophies." Niko parked at the first restaurant we spotted. A truck stop. "We should eat on the road.

Except for the pneumonia in Omaha, there hasn't been any more news of outbreaks. Suyolak could be pulling far ahead of us or have left the Lincoln altogether."

"No. He's still ahead of us and no farther away. He's sucking energy from the driver, trying to get stronger, to break the seals entirely. That's why we're catching up to them despite their head start." Rafferty didn't make any move to get out of the car. "I've got the bastard's trail now. I feel him. Hell, I can taste him . . . like that sweet-sour stench of roadkill on the back of my tongue. There isn't a place on this earth that he could shake me. Not one goddamn place."

"You're positive?" Niko pulled off his sunglasses and slid them into a jacket that hid many other things, most far more lethal than eyeware.

"He's my kind. Twisted and sick as an asylum full of sociopaths, but still my kind." He brought out his own sunglasses and he slouched back. "Bring us four of the specials. We'll wait for the Rom caravan and Delilah." Catcher's ears perked up as they did every time he heard the name. Speaking of horndogs, the fact she might try to kill me didn't make much difference to him apparently. I let it go. The fact that he couldn't even go into the restaurant was one more reminder in years of them that he was different now. Let him lust. Delilah was worth lusting over, and in the end, whether she tried to kill me or not, she was *his* kind.

Wolves were for Wolves and, temporary encounters with me aside, that wasn't going to change.

"Four specials," I agreed. "Still coming out of your share, Chewbacca." He yipped an obvious "Like I haven't heard that one before," then focused on the entrance to the parking lot, waiting for Delilah.

Rafferty stayed in the car with him with the excuse of waiting for the Rom, but we knew better; all of us, even Catcher—especially Catcher, who hadn't had a bad spell yet, but it was only a matter of time. Robin was bitching as usual about the quality of food coming our way. "I've been craving Mayan food. If we were near any place civilized, like New York, we could perhaps have that." He then looked around, carefully noting any lack of what would pass for civility in his book. "But unless we rip the still-beating heart from our enemy and braise it over the engine block of Niko's car, I'm thinking not."

Niko was pinching the bridge of his nose. I fished a small bottle of Tylenol out of my jacket pocket and slid it into his. He was stubborn about taking medication . . . body, temple, and all that . . . but we'd had one hell of a ride so far. There was always room for exceptions.

The place wasn't that crowded. The gas station had a few truckers, along with postcards, shiny Mylar balloons, and fried or jerked meat, depending on how you liked it. But it was in the restaurant part where we found out how Robin liked his. We sat at the counter to give our orders when he moaned, "Temptation, thy name is truck-stop hash slinger."

It was a rusalka. I'd seen one only once before, but rusalki did give succubi a run for their money in the sexy department. Sunshine-bright hair with one pale streak of willow green that matched the eyes—pupilless eyes, not that any humans noticed. They might notice being shorted fifteen cents on their change or goggle her amazing breasts—and they were damn amazing—but a Russian water creature in Omaha . . . land of no water . . . that escaped them.

"*Zdrastvutay, solnyshko moyo*," Robin said, green eyes meeting green as his smile began and widened to the size of the Big Bad Wolf, only without Granny's best nightgown.

"Wasting your time, doll," she replied with a midwestern accent that said she'd never seen Russia, much less drowned unwary travelers in its lakes and rivers.

"Grandma was from the homeland. I was born in good old Omaha. But enough small talk. So . . . tell me now, what exactly can I get you?" She leaned toward us and her breasts leaned with her. The Russian might not have made an impression, but Robin himself did. Her smile was every bit as hungry as his. Niko and I might as well not have existed.

"I think that would be our cue." Niko took my arm and we were up and back in the parking lot before I had time to grab frantically at the door handle of the bathroom, which I needed desperately.

"What the hell?" I protested. "I'm starving and unlike you, I can't meditate my piss into good karma points."

"Let him make his choice and then we'll get you all the deep-fried everything you can swallow while still maintaining a continuous stream of constant complaint." He folded his arms and stood at the curb like a statue nobly gazing into the west. Onward, wagons ho! I, on the other hand, leaned against the wall beside the glass doors. It didn't turn out to be a wise decision. "I'll even give you the Heimlich if the two activities conflict," he continued.

Let him choose? I was not waiting for Robin to sort out his feelings about monogamy and hot rusalka waitresses that might drown you in a kitchen sink or a toilet if a dull moment or cultural nostalgia came along. My stomach and my bladder didn't have that kind of time. Then again, this was Goodfellow we were talking about. He might think with his dick, but that thing must've had at least two hundred PhDs in field experience alone. If he was going to make up his mind, he'd be quick about—

The door swung open and I barely kept it from slamming me in the face as the puck stomped through before I had time to complete my thought. "She's not my type. Order me the least offensive thing on the menu," Robin snapped, and kept going. Not his type? Everyone and everything were his type.

"Monogamy," Niko said, a hint of surprise in his voice . . . Niko who was never surprised. "He is actually considering it."

I was more than surprised. I was utterly blown away in addition to nearly being flattened by the door. I felt my nose carefully, but it seemed unsquashed. "Holy crap," I marveled, pushing the door back. "Goodfellow . . . Robin . . . just one person . . . monogamy?" Just one person in his life? He rarely screwed just one person in the same *moment*. He went through mattresses like most people went through Kleenex. "Even temporary monogamy? I think my brain just exploded."

"Doubtful. I think you need at least two brain cells to rub together for combustion." Nik gave me a light push. "And no matter which way he is leaning, it's his choice. Not ours to push on him. Now, food. Bathroom. Go."

By the time I got back to the car carrying eight or nine bags, I was in a better mood. They didn't have a Merry Monogamy balloon in the gas station, just in case he did do something so unpucklike, but that wouldn't stop me from having a little fun. Unfortunately, it ended up that the fun had to wait. Robin, Niko, who'd left me to do the food chore, and Salome were out of sight, which meant they were in Abelia-Roo's RV parked on the far side of the lot. She would naturally have parked it there to limit the contamination as much as possible.

Near me—near Catcher and Rafferty, more precisely—were three truck drivers. As I dumped the bags in the front seat, one of the truckers, a brawny guy who hadn't been on the road long enough to have made pear shape yet, said, "That ain't no damn dog. I've been to zoos. I've seen wolves. That's a wolf and that shit's not legal." The two guys with him were muttering agreement and about calling the cops and saving God's blessed little children, like they really didn't have anything better to do. They couldn't go inside and eat a gallon of grease, buy some porn, and live and let live. They were the kind who could find trouble anywhere they went and make it out of thin air if it was scarce.

I knew Rafferty and Catcher didn't need any help. Catcher could leap out of the backseat to tear out their throats in seconds. Raff wouldn't have to move at all. He could have them gushing fluids from every orifice in their bodies with a thought . . . if he was in a good mood. If he wasn't, hell, he might tie their balls in knots that no surgeon could untie. He wouldn't, though, not really. He wasn't Suyolak, as much as he threatened. But he was still a Wolf. Rafferty and Catcher could take care of themselves; I had no doubt. Or I could do them a favor because they were doing us a major one, what with the world saving and all.

I dropped the last bag and walked around to the back of the car as the lead sack of shit opened his mouth one more time. Maybe he was going to say he was calling the cops for sure or the dogcatcher. Maybe he was going to get his face in Catcher's and get it ripped off, potato-shaped nose and all. I didn't wait to see. I pulled my Desert Eagle from beneath my jacket and pressed the muzzle to his thigh where the car blocked it from sight of anyone in the restaurant. "Go away," I said without emotion. I'd been in this situation too many times to bother to emote in Shakespearean style all over it. To shoot or not to shoot. To kill or not to kill. Whatever. I wasn't Hamlet. I knew what I would do, and I wasn't wringing my hands over it. "Go away now."

Catcher's teeth were bared, but Rafferty didn't seem bothered, his arm stretched along the back of the seat. "Subtle's not your middle name, is it, Cal?"

I bared my teeth along with Catcher. "Not lately. If I leave people alone, I expect the same in return. I also expect the same for my friends." I focused on the trucker, his skin pale and sweating from the sight of the gun.

"You . . . you fellows from New York?" He must have seen the license plate.

"Bubba, you have no idea where we're from. No . . . fucking . . . idea." My grin twisted. "I wish I were carrying my Magnum. I love that flinch when I cock it. That's damn good stuff. But, what the hell, this is fun too." I couldn't chamber a round. I lived with one in the pipe. Always. I could pull the trigger to the halfway position and savor the soft click, though. The trucker tried to swallow, couldn't, then pissed himself. The wet patch was clear on his faded jeans and large, down to his knees at least. He must've had a Big Gulp not long ago. "Did I do that, Raff, or did you?" I asked lazily.

Rafferty leaned forward and took a few bags from the front seat. "Eh, does it matter?"

No, it didn't. "I repeat," I said softly, "one last time, and that's one more time than I usually give any other piece of shit nosy-ass bastard like yourself. Go away now or go away permanently. I'm fucking peachy with either option."

They left pretty damn quickly. Rafferty had unloaded his and Catcher's food while I was just opening mine, when my brother and Goodfellow returned. "Good, you're back," the healer said around a mouthful of chicken-fried steak. "Your brother almost shot a few truckers, I had to muddle a few memories by frying a few brain cells that, trust me, couldn't be spared, and Catcher doesn't like liver and onions, so somebody swap with him." He pointed the plastic fork at me. "Killing in broad daylight. Appreciate the sentiment, but would appreciate not being mobbed by the villagers more. Kill them in the dark."

I swapped my lunch with Catcher. "I didn't kill them."

"But would you have?" That was Niko, a pissed Niko, and there was no lying to Niko, no matter what mood he was in. That mood, I was forced to admit, had been annoyed since day one of the trip and it was ninety-nine point nine percent my fault.

I exhaled. "No, and before you add the 'but,' yeah, I wanted to shoot him . . . just in the leg, though, which hardly counts. He was an ass. He was looking for trouble. I'm a nice guy." And wasn't I, though? "I like to give people what they want."

I missed lunch.

Niko thought that if I had that much excess energy, not to mention excess stupidity, I needed a workout. Behind the truck stop we sparred hand to hand for about forty-five minutes until every part of me ached, sweat soaked my hair, and the only person I had a desire to shoot was myself to put myself out of my misery. Yet there was my brother, trying to ground me and giving the Plague of the World extra time up on us because he thought it was worth it—I was worth it. It was at times like this I almost wished he didn't think I was. I groaned, "Sadist."

Niko looked down at me as I lay on my back on the asphalt and gulped air. We'd had a ring of spectators for the first half-hour. More nosy bastards. Back in New York, no one would've given us a second look unless we were blocking the entrance to the Internet café or a bar. "A gun, a potential shooting, in broad daylight in a highly public area? You might pretend to be less intelligent than you really are, but this is not excusable. They were idiots and easily handled without a penknife, much less your gun du jour."

"I know." I pulled in more ragged breaths. It had been stupid and there'd been a hundred other ways to deal with the truckers than shooting them or even just threatening to shoot them. I *knew* that, but . . . "I was feeling on edge," I admitted, wiping stinging sweat from my eyes. "Bottled up. I wanted to do something. Anything, The truckers were just in the right place at the right time"—or would've been if I'd actually gotten to shoot one—"to let off some steam."

"In other words, you were feeling antsy," Niko said, studying me, before holding down a hand to help me up. But he didn't. He only gripped my hand and added, "It's been almost a whole day since you gated. Your need for it is growing and that means it's not harmless. It's not the equivalent of exercise endorphins. It is not a good thing in any way. Do I need to point out this is a problem?"

"No," I grunted as a boot rested in my gut, "but I have a feeling you will anyway."

He put a little more weight on me. "Brotherly love. Embrace the concept, little brother. No more gates. No more potential mutilation of the public at large. The entire adult concept comes with responsibilities. We have a job to do. If you get antsy again . . ."

"Suck it up?"

"I was going to say meditate, but you can do both. Or I can stuff you in the trunk of the car and set my mind at ease. I saw you. . . ." He stopped speaking and pulled me to my feet. But I knew how he would've finished it. *I saw you die once. I don't want to see it again.* I didn't think my traveling was near the threat he did, maybe because I didn't want to believe, but he was my brother. He was about three Nobel Prize–winning scientists smarter than I, and . . . shit, again, he was my brother. Everything he'd done in his life for me had been *for* me, not *to* me.

It was why he didn't speak Rom. Abelia-Roo could mock him all she wanted. I'd been there when we'd gone to our mother's clan for help when she was killed. I hadn't been in the best shape, but I remembered what had happened. It wasn't something you tended to forget, no matter what shape you were in.

I'd been sixteen, but still felt fourteen—the two missing years of memories a nightmarish whirlpool of black nothingness striped with chaotic red emotion. Not talking to anyone but Nik and then only one or two words at best. I'd never let go of the knife under my jacket . . . Nik's jacket. Mine didn't fit anymore. And Nik . . . Nik touched me at all times, now that I could bear to let myself be touched again, to let me know I wasn't alone. He had his hand resting on my shoulder, squeezing, and standing close enough that we cast one shadow. Fourteen, sixteen, sane, insane, human, monster; I hadn't known which of those things I was, but I'd known Niko was there. Even when I'd shut my eyes against a sun that still seemed far too bright after a month of escaping the Auphe, I'd felt the warmth of his hand burning through to my skin.

Cal.

My eyes had snapped open when he spoke, my knife already pulled.

"No, Cal," had come the reassuring reply. "No knife. We're here for help, remember? This is Sophia's clan. Our clan. Family." And because Niko was a good man even at eighteen, he'd believed that or wanted to believe it.

It was one of the few times he'd been wrong.

They'd known what I was. Sophia had left the clan, but the clan had never left her. She was Vayash. Vayash never left Vayash. They'd watched, kept track, and consequently knew about the deal she'd made with the Auphe to produce me. It didn't matter that I didn't have any say in the whole damn thing. The good people of the Vayash clan had spat on me, hid their children from the very sight of me, and they damn sure weren't going to take an abomination like me under their protection. Niko . . . Niko was all Vayash, all human. Niko was welcome. He had only to cast me aside.

Or preferably kill me. After all, I was a monster, a thing, a rabid dog.

A man-eater, just not quite grown to full potential. Niko blamed them. Honestly, I didn't.

Niko had turned his back on them, their life, their ways, their language, and hadn't once looked back. They were as dead to him as we were to them. How do you deny someone who does that for you? You don't. I pushed back sweat-soaked hair with an asphalt-scraped hand and gave his a tight squeeze with my other before I let go. "Sucking it up. Meditating. You got it." I brushed dirt from my jeans. "So, did I do good? Workoutwise? Going to grade me?"

"I hear failing grades only discourage students. You're progressing. Does that make you feel better?"

Considering Niko wouldn't be happy unless I could protect myself with the lethal skill of a sixteen-foot-long great white, it was praise enough.

"Puppies done playing now?" Delilah purred from where she sat in a small patch of weeds several feet away. The remnants of her own lunch rested on a plate beside her, the bloody bones of what must've been two or three very rare T-bone steaks. Not one drop of red stained her leathers. "So cute. Like a bone as a reward?"

Niko wasn't amused. He was a patient man, beyond patient, but that massive reserve was put aside for my smart-ass nature and our work in general. Right now he had little to spare for the Wolf who very probably was going to try to kill me. He didn't like it when people and monsters and all that fell between made attempts on my life. I made my own decisions on where to sleep and whom to sleep with, but he didn't have to like it and he didn't have to show my possible assassin any faked appreciation of her humor.

Delilah tilted her head as she stood smoothly to move close to me, inhaling the smell of my sweat. "Wish to play more? Plague of the World can wait fifteen minutes more, yes?"

"No," Niko said flatly. "The workout was delay enough." He pointed at the employees' bathrooms on the side of the building. "Clean up, Cal." Because, of course, he didn't have to. Sun, exertion, they were nothing. Me? I had to fucking man up, not melt into a puddle, walk away from a sure thing—sex or death—and go scrub down.

Delilah turned to look at Niko. I didn't know if he smelled of suspicion or not. Surely even my brother couldn't control his scent. But it didn't matter. Delilah already knew I had my doubts, that we all did; she was a smart Wolf. She also knew a doubt wasn't a sure thing. I was giving her a chance. Niko wasn't feeling as cooperative at the moment. "*You* want to play?"

Niko didn't pause to consider. Suspicion, distrust, it made her unworthy of sparring or conversation. And he was done with pretending. "Cal."

I went. He was right. The Plague of the World came first. Chances, for Delilah and me, came second.

When I made it back to the car, I had hair wet from water from a bathroom sink and smelled of industrial-strength soap good for ridding the restaurant workers of E. coli. It was good for sweat too. As I climbed into the back of the car, Catcher regarded me with a horror that had him nearly climbing into his cousin's lap. Auphe combined with the smell of twenty lemon groves mixed with bleach must've been worse than straight Auphe. Before Rafferty could complain about it, I put out a hand to Robin and said disgruntledly, "Give me the spray. I can't take the bitching."

"Speaking of bitching"—Rafferty elbowed his cousin off him and back between us—"your friend Delilah, if you can call any Kin a friend, is getting on my last goddamn nerve. Our families cut ties with our Kin relatives

before we were born. We don't deal with the criminal
trash we're related to. Having to listen to one we don't
even share blood with is more of a pain in the ass than
I'm willing to deal with. And I won't have anything to do
with her and her freak All Wolf."

It was rare I heard the name of the cult, the All Wolf,
the Wolves who bred for the recessive traits, hoping
someday to get their descendants back to the very beginning. All wolf all the time, even in thought—wanting
what Catcher was trying so desperately to get rid of. Up
until Catcher in fact, Delilah had been sort of the equivalent of a lapsed Catholic when it came to the All Wolf.
She might have had partial wolf vocal cords and who
knew what else inside, but she was pure human on the
outside. Her faith in the All Wolf was limited until she
met Catcher. Then she was born again, raise your paws
high, brothers and sisters.

"So get her to back off," Rafferty added curtly, "or
I'll put her ass in a coma until this is all over with. Got
it?" He was sounding more and more like Suyolak all
the time . . . and, hell, maybe that was the way it had to
be for him to win.

Catcher didn't seem to agree, giving a mournful-
sounding moan, but, yeah, I got it. Rafferty had enough
to deal with. So did I, but I'd created the problem by letting Delilah come along, and I'd deal with it. I watched
as Delilah rode out of the parking lot ahead of us. Later.
I'd deal with it later.

But later turned out to be a little inconvenient.

It was around seven when Rafferty came out of
another light doze. I was driving by now, spelling Nik.
Robin and Salome were still up front. Everybody
thought it best to avoid another Salome/Catcher throw
down. Goodfellow, on the other hand, was in the middle of what looked like a mental meltdown. "She was
comely," he'd been muttering over and over, so many

times I was tempted to slam my head against the steering wheel to knock myself unconscious. "Why did I deny her? Deny myself?" Then he would focus on me. "She was comely, wasn't she?"

"Yeah, her hair was nice, neat; she combed it a lot, but that wasn't what I was really looking at," I responded.

He'd regarded me with disbelief and turned his need for psychotherapy on Niko as I'd planned. I wasn't going to make any great breakthroughs in science or literature or even in the field of hangman obviously, but I'd been homeschooled by Niko. I knew what the word "comely" meant. I just didn't have to admit it. I was thinking how it was worth the revenge Nik was bound to visit upon me, when Rafferty woke up and said sharply, "The next exit. Take the next exit."

"What? Our Suyolak-napper go off the beaten path?" I asked.

"Yes, damn it. Now take the exit!"

It was getting more than a little weird not being the only foulmouthed, grouchy ass around. Maybe that was a reminder to me not to travel, to build no more gates— so I could retain my title as chief asshole on this cross-country trek. No more good moods for me if I wanted to retain my title. "Taking it already, Fluffy. Don't go frothing at the mouth. They shoot your type for that, you know."

The next exit happened to be yet another tiny town over the state line into Wyoming. It had a four-way stop, a post office, and a Dairy Queen coming soon—the big time. I didn't see a single reason for making a pit stop or detouring here unless your rent payment was massively overdue and you needed stamps. Or you were a vegan witch who wanted to salt the earth of the junk-food giant before it was built. Curse the land and save some cows.

But I didn't believe in magic or that Suyolak and his

driver were that desperate to mail anything. Neither did Niko. "Why here?" he said from the seat behind me. "It's early to stop for the night. Even if Suyolak is draining his kidnapper of life bit by bit, I can't see him stopping this soon."

"I don't know. All I do know is they came this way and I can smell the sickness ahead. Somewhere is Suyolak's taint, and people are either dead or dying. The son of a bitch is here."

He was the healer. "Which way?" I demanded.

It was left and through the four-way stop, the adrenaline of that world-drawing tourist attraction was killing me there. We then turned onto another road, another, and finally onto gravel followed by dirt. It had taken a good half hour, if not longer.

The rearview mirror was empty. Abelia and her buddies had stopped on the gravel at least a mile back, not that they couldn't have gotten farther. They could have, but after the zombie amoebas, they were giving us more space. Abelia might have the biggest baddest ovaries around—probably shot them at her enemies like cannon balls, but her clan members weren't as tough as she was, and if anyone died a gruesome death, she would most definitely prefer it was us. And Delilah was annoyed enough that she'd kept going when we'd gotten off the interstate. But that didn't bother me. Just as her possibly trying to kill me didn't bother me. She was Kin, doing what Kin did. I'd gone into this whole thing—sex, part-time relationship—with open eyes. I didn't have much right to bitch, and I didn't have to feel anything I didn't want to feel. I didn't. That was that. My story, write it down.

I parked the car in front of a house surrounded by trees in the middle of nowhere. The driveway was packed dirt and longer than two city blocks. The whole thing should've been run-down and creepy, with broken windows, holes in the roof, a rotting clapboard, Halloween-style haunted house with a skeletal body or two down an abandoned well out back. It wasn't. It was painted cheery yellow with pristine white shutters and some kind of flowers, blue and purple, surrounding the porch. There was even a rocking chair as immaculately painted as the shutters. I did not want to see Suyolak here, not in this impossibly cheerful house under an equally impossibly blue sky. I'd never be able to watch a Hallmark commercial again ... because I spent so much time doing that anyway, but still. Nobody should be sick here. They should be gardening or some such shit. Playing with their golden retriever. Baking cookies. Washing their car. Not dying among the scent of blue and purple flowers.

But as grim as that might be, it wasn't actually the point. "I don't see a truck and I don't see a coffin," I said. As harsh as it was, we couldn't stop every time Suyolak took a civilian down. If we did, we could lose him. If we did, he'd know, and he'd make sure we lost him by dropping everyone he could.

There was a rumbling growl behind me, throat vibrating and air ripping, and it wasn't Catcher. "He's here." Rafferty vaulted over the door with wolf speed, but still in human form. Catcher was right behind him. Both hit the door at the same time and it went down in a shattered mess of wood and safety glass.

Salome was moving too—out of the car and then under it. Considering the number of revenants she'd taken down, that was not a good sign. I ignored it, though, and, with Niko and Robin, was on the porch and inside the house in seconds.

There was a neat and clean living room to the right, stairs leading up in the middle, and a dining room to the left. At the back of the dining room was an arched doorway to a sunny kitchen. There was a man on the black and white tiled floor in plain view. He wasn't moving, and he wasn't Suyolak. Sad to say, that made him a low priority. Niko was ahead of me on the stairs, Robin beside me, and Rafferty and Catcher already out of sight above us. That's when I heard a howl loud enough you would've thought it would have blown off the roof. It wasn't terrified, but it wasn't a whoopee-here-comes-the-ice-cream-man yodel either. Catcher was not happy about something up there and a moment later I got to be unhappy about it too. We all did. There was enough unhappy about the situation to go around.

It was in the nursery—it and the mother, along with stuffed Pooh Bears and Tiggers here and there and more of them and their friends dancing in a mural painted on the wall behind the crib. It was just like the outside of the house—all too perfect; all too good to be true. That's what you get for being happy and having it all. That's what happens. Someone or something like Suyolak comes to take it away.

Or worse.

She sat in the rocking chair by the big, bright window. Her head was down, a long sweep of chestnut brown hair, gleaming and thick, hanging like a curtain over her face. I'd bet that the first thing her husband had noticed about her when they first met was that hair. It made you think of wild horses and beaches. Why? I don't know. It just did.

Her hands cradled a large mound of stomach and she was singing . . . in Rom. I knew only the curse words. Sophia had been free with those, even if I didn't know anything else, but I certainly recognized the language when I heard it or an archaic version of it.

It was a lullaby. Anyone, Rom or not, would've known that. The lilting harmony, the warm love and expectation . . . if only it hadn't had to gurgle its way through a throat full of blood. She lifted her head to smile at us with red-coated teeth. "It's a boy." The red fluid trickled out of both sides of her mouth as she said it. "A boy." One hand moved in a slow circle over her stomach. "Snips and snails and puppy dog tails."

"Oh shit," I muttered. I already had my gun out. She was sick, she was a victim, but she smelled so *wrong*, I didn't know how Catcher and Rafferty were still in the room with her. There was decay and death and a smell of . . . hell . . . a human gone off. Like bad milk. It was the only way to describe it.

She coughed and scarlet sprayed into a fine mist in the air, but she was beyond noticing or caring. "My precious baby boy." Her eyes were on us and the whites were pure blood. Proud. She looked so proud and so absolutely insane. "Here he comes."

She was right. He did come or he tried. Under the swell of her stomach I saw movement. It looked like tiny fists pressed against the flesh from the inside. Whatever was trying to be born, I didn't think was wanting to do it the old-fashioned way. I knew, *knew* that if it had its way, it would rip its way to freedom and blood would splatter on the highly polished wood floor that matched the too-good-to-be-true living room, the too-perfect-to-exist dining room one. The wood gleamed brilliantly enough, you could almost see your reflection. I would've rather looked at that than looked at her, which with my past mirror phobia was saying something. But I didn't. I kept my eyes up, because as much as I didn't want to look, I didn't want to die from carelessness either.

The woman in the rocker didn't move as her stomach rippled, didn't cry out in pain; she only kept smiling a beautiful, peaceful smile of joyful motherhood.

"Rafferty," Niko rapped as Robin crossed himself; Robin, who was not only not Christian but one of the original pagan tricksters—pre-Christian and then some. I didn't blame him. I wasn't Christian either—I wasn't anything, but if I'd known more than two lines of the Lord's Prayer, I'd have been zipping right through it. Because this . . . this was horror-movie stuff where the devil was real, heads spun around, and Hell was just a zip code away.

"Do we kill it or not?" my brother demanded. His mouth was tight. He knew killing the baby—or what had been a baby—meant killing her as well, and he didn't like it. But he would do it. Niko always did what he had to do, no matter the consequences to himself. He'd suffered enough consequences in his life for being a good man. If it came to that, I'd do it before I'd let him—but as it turned out, neither of us had to make the choice. Someone else did.

The healer shook his head and crouched a few feet away from her. His eyes unfocused and he shook his head again. "It's not viable outside the womb, and she's not viable for long either."

No, she didn't look it—twisted and warped, blood pouring out of her mouth, eyes, ears, dying from the poisonous thing inside her. And it was poisonous, as much as a truckload of cyanide. The Vayash had thought the same about me. If they hadn't feared the Auphe so much, I was positive they would've dragged a pregnant Sophia off and made sure I never became a walking, talking reality. And I could understand that, believe it or not. If this was what they'd pictured, fuck . . . I wouldn't have blamed them.

But I hadn't turned out that way, so I still blamed them plenty, not for me, but for turning their backs on Niko. "You can't heal her?" I asked, my gun still pointed. She was dying, a storybook mom in a fairy-tale house, and, damn, that sucked, but no way was I facing that thing inside her without a gun. I didn't care what Rafferty said about its expiration date. If it got out . . . the last thing I wanted to face without a gun was a Suyolak mini-me.

"I could keep her alive, but I can't heal her." He ran a hand over his face hard enough to redden the skin, then reached over to touch her knee. Her eyes immediately went blank and she slumped forward limply. The thing inside of her still moved for a moment or two, distorting her stomach, but then it stilled too. Call me a chicken-shit, but I was glad I hadn't had to see it. I couldn't imagine what it looked like now, but I was sure it was nothing like a newborn baby boy.

"What the hell kind of disease does this?" I dropped the muzzle of the gun to point at the blood splattered around her bare feet. There was a butterfly tattoo on her ankle, a color between red and pink. Rose—as rosy as her life had been before Suyolak had decided to play.

"Not a disease," Rafferty responded as Niko ripped the sheer white curtains from the window and draped it over the woman's still body. "Genes. Suyolak turned the fetus's genes into a mirror image of his own."

"Genetic tampering," Nik said, turning to him. "You said he could do only so much in the coffin and that wasn't much. Kill a few people with bacteria and viruses that already are available. Genetic manipulation is far beyond that."

"He's more than a thousand years old. How does he know about genes anyway?" I added, stepping back from the blood slowly pooling outward.

"First, genetic manipulation is assuming the patient lives. This . . . atrocity . . . never would've lived outside its mother and neither of them more than ten minutes. It was his mirror, to lure us here, and mirrors reflect, but mirrors don't live or have the talent of what they imitate."

"Easy to twist and destroy," Robin said quietly. "Not so easy to remake a living creature and keep it that way."

Catcher leaned against Rafferty's leg as the healer

said without emotion, "No. It's not. As for genes, healers have known about genes since there were healers. Even if they didn't know what to call them, they could still sense them, but there aren't many strong enough to manipulate them."

"Except for Suyolak?" Niko commented, leaving the "and you" silent. There was still another victim downstairs. Who the hell knew what he might do?

"Except for Suyolak . . . and right now all he can do is make a temporary mirror of himself to lure us off track and give his driver time to get farther away."

Rafferty's eyes were lamps of gold now, rage directed at Suyolak, and I was thinking probably for him too. "The husband is dead. We need to go."

"Is that your opinion, Hippocrates? Are you sure you wouldn't want to wait around for monsters-made-from-scratch waiting to pop out just for the fun and distraction?" Robin asked acidly. Despite the fact he'd lived longer than we had and seen more than we ever would, he was still shaken. Hell, we all were, but Goodfellow was always the most vocal of us all. He had the guts to show what the rest of us hid. "Because this first was so enjoyable."

"Shut up," Raffety ground out between his teeth.

It didn't stop Goodfellow. "The proud mother-to-be may have died a death from the most unsettling of horror movies, and the father is deceased on the kitchen floor, but that's no reason we can't stop, have an Irish coffee, and eat some cake on our way out. I'm quite sure she was a great cook. There's bound to be sugar-and-butter-filled goodness somewhere in the refrigerator. We should enjoy. Because that would be more useful than anything *you've* done so far in this place."

"Shut up." This time it was me, saying it under my breath as I moved casually between the puck and the healer. "Really. Shut the hell up before he . . ." Well, there were so many things I could think of at the moment: pieces rotting and falling off; pieces I liked and preferred to keep. It didn't pay to forget Rafferty was a healer, but he was a predator too—a carnivore; a massively pissed-off, guilting carnivore. Healer or predator, which came first? I preferred Suyolak found that out, not the rest of us.

"Shut up? You have the unmitigated gall to tell your elder and your superior in every way to *shut up*?" Robin was a predator too, only without the fur and fangs. We all were predators. But . . .

Niko finished my thought before I barely began it. "We are after Suyolak, not one another. I want civility, and I want it now. Do any disagree?" He didn't idly swing his katana toward his feet as he normally did. Instead, he buried more than two inches of the blade into the bloody floor and didn't look like he'd have a problem doing the same to flesh instead of wood. Rafferty and Goodfellow weren't the only ones who were pissed. We all were: mad and more than a little rattled, not that we'd admit it. I'd seen a lot of killers in my day, some sane, some insane. I'd always thought the insane were the worst and we'd thought Suyolak the same way, but right now . . . Suyolak was too sane. Sociopathic, genocidal, but with a focus so crystal clear, it was like a laser. Burning. Blinding.

"Let's go find this son of a bitch and do things to him that make this seem like a fucking baby shower," I said with savage bite.

Robin exhaled and let his dissatisfaction with Rafferty go. "Fine. I refuse to admit I was out of line. I am never out of line. In fact, I created the line, but I will graciously skip the kitchen when we leave."

That was the best we could hope for. Rafferty paid no attention to what was, for a puck, almost an apology, and headed for the stairs, Catcher at his heels. The rest of us turned to leave a nursery where Pooh had seen things no bear ever should. I grimaced and then gave Robin's shoulder a light shove. "Which line did you come up with? The one you don't cross or the one you jump over with both feet?" He glared back at me and his hand hovered near one of the daggers he kept tucked away.

"Naughty, naughty." I gave him a dark grin.

Niko, behind me, said abruptly, "It wasn't much of a distraction, however, was it? Horrifying, yes, but time-consuming? Not by as much as would be worth the trouble. Suyolak had us following his false shadow for an hour at the most. Why did he bother if he couldn't slow us down more than this?"

As answers went, the one we received was immediate and succinct.

First the detached garage out back blew up, and seconds later Niko's car followed it.

Timing, as with women, gambling, fighting, and massive fiery destruction, really is everything.

10

Cal

A car fire wasn't that much to see, whether it was in an already-engulfed garage or just out front in the open, not in comparison to other things I'd seen. An explosion was an entirely different animal from just a fire, but, hey, I'd been four seconds from ground zero of a nuclear one. Sort of. There was enough truth to that that a simple car explosion shouldn't faze me; not that or the flames visible through the house's shattered windows, front and back. And it didn't . . . until all the ammunition in the trunk of Niko's car started exploding with it. I carried a lot of guns and even more ammunition. Better safe than sorry; better lead than dead. There was enough in that trunk to start my own gun shop if we broke down in the Midwest with no way home, not that that was my plan, but it was good to be prepared. But now the stock was going up with the car and there wasn't much we could do about it as we dived to the living room floor as bullets randomly slammed into the outside of the house and some came through the walls themselves. Until now, I never met an explosive, incendiary, or armor-piercing round that I didn't like. That was the military for you. Six hundred bucks for a toilet while an armory sergeant was smuggling out whatever it would take to buy that big boat or pay for little Susie's med school. And if he was busy, there was always eBay.

One round punched through the front door and then the stairs, about ten inches from Robin's nose where he was flattened on the floor. He didn't notice. "My clothes. My suits. The Kiton, the Brioni, the Luigi. Gods, not the Caraceni. Someone is going to pay. Someone is going to *die*." He glared at me. "And if this is Delilah taking advantage of Suyolak's distraction, it will be you."

Delilah . . . I couldn't lie to myself there. It could be her. Let Suyolak do half the work while she finished a job he hadn't been smart enough to complete, that very well could be Delilah. It had her street smarts all over it. When I'd slept with her, before the Kin found out and after, I never knew if the moment would come . . . if she would genuinely try to kill me. I'd tried to anticipate how that would feel. It was impossible. If it was Delilah now, I wouldn't have to guess anymore.

Niko was already slithering on his stomach toward the back of the living room where another large window was supposed to let in the light of the sun. Now it was a framework to flames about thirty feet from the house— until a bullet shattered it too. Then it was a frame to flames and an entrance for wind stinking of gasoline. Nik went over the sill and disappeared. I followed him and heard Catcher, Rafferty, and Robin going through the kitchen.

"I will never let you pack your own gear again," Niko said as he moved through more of those blue-purple flowers. "You're a menace to anyone without his own bomb shelter."

I was right behind him, rounding the back corner of the house. "You can't honestly expect me to antici-pate your car's blowing up. If you don't get that thing

serviced, it's not my fault. And I'm a menace, period."
But I still had my Desert Eagle, not to mention my
backup—the Sig—and both were up and ready. Cars
rarely committed suicide or spontaneously combusted,
and especially not in groups like lemmings. They usually
had help. We came in sight of the front yard and of the
blackened frame of Nik's car caught in glimpses through
the flames. The trunk had been blown open thanks to
my explosive rounds.

No Delilah yet, and I couldn't detect her distinctive
scent over the scorched metal.

There was motion on the other side of the house,
Catcher and Rafferty . . . and Robin pulling up the rear
with a sword and an expression of cold rage. The man
took his clothes seriously, but he took attempts on his
and our lives as much so. After the quick look that
equaled ours, they and Niko and I pressed against the
respective sides of the house for a few minutes until the
bullets stopped splitting the air. The others did the same,
and when we finally moved out front, we all moved as
one. Raff and Catcher might not be Kin, but they were
Wolves and, whether in wolf or human form, they moved
like mercury sliding along glass. Quick. Quiet. Potentially deadly.

Now where was the bitch or son of one who'd done
this? Suyolak was an antihealer, not a pyromaniac. If this
wasn't Delilah, then someone had to have done this for
Suyolak. A lit twist of cloth in the gas tank would've accomplished it easily. It couldn't be his driver. He needed
him. It wasn't the others who'd helped steal the coffin—
they were all dead. And I didn't want it to be Delilah, no
matter how foolish that was. So who . . .

Fuck.

Branje. It was Branje. Dead. His body was sprawled
on its stomach in the dirt about fifteen feet from the

burning car with his face turned to the side, facing us, the chin tucked down. He had some burns on his jaw and on his arms, but I didn't think that's what had done him in.

Salome sat on the dead man's back, licking blood from her furless paw with a dried suede scrap of tongue. She spotted us, yawned, and curled up in a ball, basking with a sawmill purr in the heat of the burning Eldorado. The dirt had soaked up the blood around Branje's head and neck. I didn't have to lift up that head to know his throat had been ripped out.

I didn't think the spray-bottle punishment was working as well as Goodfellow thought it was, but with Branje being responsible for toasting our ride, I gave Robin's disciplinary methods and Salome's hunting a pass, although it was getting embarrassing that the one with the highest body count on this job was a mummified cat. I squatted beside them, giving Salome a gingerly pat on the wrinkled bald head. "Good kitty. Nice kitty." I scowled at the dead Rom. "I knew I should've cut your nose off when I had the chance."

"Branje must have run from where the Rom RV stopped half a mile back." We were doing the heavy lifting while Abelia was watching *Judge Judy* in air-conditioned comfort. Niko crouched beside me. "But why? If he were under Suyolak's control, he would've let him out of the coffin before it was ever stolen. And so far Suyolak has shown no ability to control anyone. Visit you with dreams or nightmares, but actually control? A healer . . . even an antihealer can't do that, can they, Jeftichew?"

Kneeling on the other side of the body, Rafferty shook his head. "No." Okay, that was simple and to the point. "But . . ." Damn. Life would be so much better if the human race had never come up with the concept of "but." It got you every damn time. Resting his hand on Branje's singed hair, the healer's face showed disgust in the twist of his lips and the lowering of his brows at what he felt. "This is the sickest bastard who ever roamed the face of the earth. Why they didn't find a volcano to drag his ass to and dump him, coffin and all, into it, I'll never goddamn know."

"Guess all the hobbits were getting the hair on their feet permed." I moved to the other side with him. The flames were superheating air that hadn't been that cool to begin with.

"What did the son of a bitch do now?" Robin demanded, staying several steps away from the blackened and bloody body, preserving the condition of the only clothes he had left. The world needed saving, but so did his wardrobe. A puck had to have his priorities.

"This one. He must've been one of Suyolak's regular guards." That made sense. Branje was one of Abelia-Roo's most trusted. "Long-term exposure. The seals didn't have to be that weak at all. Just a pinhole of an opening and years to work." Rafferty stood up and wiped his hand on his jeans. "Schizophrenia. Suyolak screwed with the chemistry of this guy's brain six damn ways to Sunday. He would've been hearing voices, hallucinating, easy to influence, for months, maybe years. Tough guy to hold it together and keep it secret. At the end Suyolak was just one more voice in a hundred, probably telling him if he did this, he'd make all the rest go away. And this poor dead bastard was far enough gone to believe it. Not far along enough to open the coffin. He had a lifetime of knowing what that would mean, but burning a few cars to get the voices to go away, that he could do."

"And Suyolak did keep his word, more or less. It all went away. Unfortunately, Branje went with it." Niko slid his katana into the sheath on his back and shucked off the lightweight duster that covered it. I knew it was hot when he was admitting it.

The man *had* been tough. I hadn't much liked him the

first time I met him; I liked him less the second time—on
this job, but he'd had a pair, and I wasn't going to deny
him that now that he was dead.

I pulled out my cell phone. No reception. Big surprise.
No communication in Satan's sweaty armpit. Niko had
mentioned on the drive that it was unseasonably hot by
at least thirty degrees. I never understood why people
said unseasonably. Hot is hot. Cold is cold. Screwed is
screwed. "Then we walk back to that bitch's RV. It's not
much more than a mile." Nik raised an eyebrow, and I
amended, "I mean we run back to the RV. No big loss of
time." It wasn't as if we could go back to the house and
use the landline. *Hey, could you send a cab, pickup truck,
tractor, mule, whatever. Just look for the house with the
multiple fires and dead couple inside. Can't miss it.*

We ran.

Naturally the RV was gone. There we were in the
middle of nowhere—a place where distance wasn't mea-
sured in blocks, but acres and sometimes miles. Fields
as far as the eye could see. Big Sky country. The death
house had been freshly painted, clean and neat, the in-
terior and exterior up-to-date, but that didn't mean it
hadn't been built on the bones of what had once been
a much older house. Some people, rich couples tired
of the city life, liked their privacy. They'd buy up old
ranches and either redo or build a new house. And the
thing about old ranches? They were fucking big. It had
been at least twenty miles since I'd seen the last house
before Suyolak's homestead of horrors.

"I suppose we have more running to do," Nik commented as he regarded the empty stretch of gravel,
the slightest twitch of annoyance at the corner of
his mouth. "We passed another house approximately
twenty miles on the way. We can borrow their phone
or transportation."

"Twenty-some odd miles. You're fucking with me,

right?" I bent over and rested my hands on my knees. Half a mile normally wasn't too bad; Niko typically had me run five miles every day. But it was scorching hot ... unseasonably, of course, not to forget ... and it wasn't air we were breathing but pure pollen. I didn't know what it was from—grass, weeds, occasional trees—I didn't care. It was all right when cruising along in the car even with the top down, but running more than twenty miles in blistering heat while trying to keep the heart pumping with pollen instead of oxygen did not seem to put a fun time in my future. The Auphe might have had a pumped-up immune system when it came to viruses, colds, diseases of all sorts, but simple pollen? Apparently they'd sneezed their murderous asses off the same as their good old human cattle. There was no way, though, that I was going to ask Rafferty for a quick laying of the Holy Claritin on me or whatever healing equivalent he'd come up with. Branje had suffered through frigging schizophrenia. I wasn't going to bring up snuffling, snot, and scratchy eyes after that.

"Would I do that to my only brother?" Niko asked, mock solemn. "Lie? Never."

"Oh hell," I replied morosely. "It's like a frying pan out here."

"You don't like the heat, I'm aware. You also don't like the cold or running or any other form of physical exercise that doesn't involve your penis, but Suyolak set us back with one mentally deranged man. One ... against the five of us. Pardon me, Salome—the six of us. Therefore we will run until we can find a car to buy, borrow, or steal, and then we will catch this monster and make him sorry he was once a cluster of cells in a woman's womb, much less born." He looked up at the sun. Nik wasn't one for watches. He didn't need one. "And we'll do it in two hours, arriving at that house around dark."

Two hours? A seasoned marathon runner could do it

in two hours. Niko could easily. Pucks could probably do it in two hours, though I sincerely doubted Robin would want to. Wolves could do it in less than two hours. Me? An everyday runner who hated it with a passion and who did not have Nik's Olympic potential—three hours. Three hours and that wasn't counting puke breaks. "If you want to keep me alive so much, I don't know why you're trying to kill me," I grumbled. "Why not let the furries run ahead and come back and pick us up?"

"I think the fact Rafferty would be nude while trying to negotiate for a car might be a drawback," Goodfellow said dryly, stroking Salome who was looped around his neck. "Or, considering his personality, it might actually be a plus."

"He could carry his clothes in his mouth," I pointed out, reasonably, I thought. "Dress behind a clump of whatever is turning the air piss yellow." I sneezed. "Problem solved. Or I could make a ga—" I stopped suddenly before the entire word "gate" made it out of my mouth. Niko was giving me a look and it wasn't a good one. It reminded me that while we didn't know where Abelia and the remaining four of her men were or what condition they were in, Suyolak was doing a nice ring around the rosy with us—the original version from the Black Death days with flowers to cover the smell of sickness, ashes from burning the corpses, and falling down because you were dead—reminding me that despite all of that, he didn't trust my traveling and its effect on me. Even if I thought he was wrong, I listened to my brother. The fact that he'd never been wrong before made things more difficult, but I was trying my hardest.

"Okay," I said, exhaling, "we run."

It took three hours and ten minutes. One vomiting episode . . . me. One stripping off all his clothes except underwear—don't ask; don't tell; don't look—and folding them over his arm so not to wrinkle or stain them with sweat. The half-nude Goodfellow wasn't what made me puke ... I'd seen more of him than that once, accidentally. It had mainly made me feel inadequate. It probably would've made a stallion at stud feel inadequate. No, this was the heat, the spores sprouting a new field of weeds in my respiratory system most likely equipped with grazing rabbits, and a run twice as long as I'd ever done.

When we reached the house and I pulled on my jacket to cover the holster and gun, I didn't mind the sniff Catcher gave me. I offended even myself and I couldn't smell the half Auphe that went with it. You can't smell your own genes.

I hadn't paid too much attention when we'd passed the house earlier. Tired and droopy, small, once painted chocolate brown but now the color of mud, one story, three windows and a door in front, two windows on each side, and a reddish-colored pit bull lying on its side on the porch. That was enough details as far as I was concerned—house, points of entry and exit, and a possible threat sleeping on the porch, but Niko could've told you if the dog was male or female, the classification of scrubby grass in the yard, how many shingles were missing from the roof, and if the wind chimes hanging from the one tree were made of wood, metal, or glass.

There was one spindly tree in the front yard—I didn't care what classification it was—and I leaned against it. Waves of sweat rolled down every inch of skin I had. The red dog had been still lying in the same position as when we passed it hours ago. It had lifted its cone-shaped head when we'd come down the road and grinned at us broadly. A happy dog, it liked Catcher and Rafferty instantly, cheerful almond eyes on them. Then it paid attention to me. A lazy, sleepy dog, too, or it would've caught a whiff of me long before I came into view. Dogs can smell that far and much farther. White bloomed around its eyes and its ears went back as it began to foam at the mouth, not in aggression, but in fear. It inched backward across the dirt and brown grass for several feet, then turned and ran, disappearing behind the house.

Dogs didn't like me. Never had. Never would. One drop of Auphe blood was one drop too much. Wolves were the same, with the occasional exception—Catcher, Rafferty . . . Delilah. It was not the time for thinking about that; it was time for breathing and not puking again. The second didn't do much for my rep as cranky monster-slayer.

"I hate to be the bearer of bad news, especially when it affects me, but I don't see a car or a garage," Goodfellow pointed out. "However, I suppose we could use their phone."

"It wouldn't hurt the situation if you put your clothes back on," I said as I wiped yellow-tinged sweat from my face.

"It depends. It might actually help to have the physical embodiment of a living sex god standing on their porch, revealed in all his magnificent glory," Robin retorted, but began dressing as Salome jumped down to investigate the scraggly yard with a tail twitch of curiosity. Niko was already at the door. He knocked once while I was still depending on the twig of a tree to hold me up. "You should've let me travel. Open a gate for us all. We could've been here in sec—" I shut up in midword as Niko turned a dark gaze on me. "But running is good. Cardio and all that. Glad we did it."

The look only became darker as my brother waited five seconds, knocked again, and then kicked in the door. It was too bad for the lazy son of a bitch who couldn't get his ass off the couch fast enough. He yelped as the door flew open, barely missing him. It was a lesson for the kiddies. No car didn't always equal no one at home, and if someone knocked at your door, you should answer it promptly.

"What the fuck?" the guy demanded. He was a tall man in a dirty white T-shirt and boxers that hung on what had probably once been a large frame. Now he was skinny, all bones, bad teeth, and hair that would've been blond, but now was so greasy and lank that it was brownish gray.

"Excuse me," Niko said smoothly as he walked over the remains of the flattened door. "You should be quicker about answering your door. We need to use your phone."

I concentrated on getting my ragged breathing under control and heaved myself upright to follow him into the gloom of the house. No bright and sunny windows here—just blinds and heavy drapes. There were shapes of furniture—a sagging couch, a fake leather recliner with a perfectly preserved ass imprint, and a shotgun propped up in one corner, which our proud home owner was lunging for. "Hey," I said with satisfaction as I jammed an elbow into his side to block him, sending him tumbling back onto the couch that had been his downfall. "A shotgun? For me? You shouldn't have." As I'd lost several of my old toys in the car fire, I thought I deserved it. I grabbed it as the guy nursed his ribs, then cracked it open to discover it was even loaded with slugs. Buckshot was okay, but slugs did the kind of damage I was into. I went searching for more ammunition.

Niko did a quick check of the place, sparing little sympathy for the man moaning on the decrepit couch. We spent most of our work chasing down or working with monsters, the criminal kind. It wasn't hard to spot a bent human as well. This guy didn't smell right and it had nothing to do with his hygiene. It didn't take long to find out why. Nik was quick with his search and the house was about a thousand square feet—a good size by your average New Yorker's standards, but small and cheap by the local ones. "Meth lab in the bathroom," he said as he headed for the phone.

"An entrepreneur," Goodfellow commented as Niko picked up the phone on a table by the recliner. "I'll wait outside. I have no desire to be involved in two explosions in one day, especially in a domicile I haven't seen the likes of since I lunched with some Neanderthals." He went back out the front door. Rafferty and Catcher hadn't bothered to come in.

"Bastards. What the fuck do you want? You keep away from my stuff, you got it? Stay the fuck away." His breath was far more nerve-racking than his threat, and as the threat wasn't nerve-racking at all, it didn't truly emphasize the rankness of his breath.

I tapped our friendly meth-head on the shoulder with the barrel of the shotgun when it looked as if he'd gathered enough courage together to get back up. "What do we want? You don't listen, do you? The phone. Just the phone . . . oh, and the gun. Or if you have a problem with that, we might also want to bang your head against the floor until it splits like a melon. Up to you. I'm flexible. You choose."

He picked not having his head treated like a basketball. Some guys are no fun. Seemingly. But he pleasantly surprised me by yanking a bowie knife, or an el cheapo knock-off version he'd picked up at a swap meet, from beneath the couch cushion. Niko had taught me many disciplines of thought when it came to knife fighting, and there were many, although they all seemed to come down to two options: "You're going to get cut, but suck it up and take the bastard down" versus "I will not be cut and dispose of my opponent like a child armed with a plastic picnic knife." The second option was mostly held by those living in a fantasy world where they whacked off to martial arts magazines and Chuck Norris movies.

But there were times your opponent was so pathetic that you could actually get away without a nick. Our meth buddy was one of those. He may as well have been a poodle with a switchblade—a hyped-up poodle, but still a poodle. He wasn't worth it. He definitely wouldn't provide any entertainment or further my education in knife fighting. Instead, I kept my distance from his desperately jagged slashes and smacked him with the barrel of the shotgun again, this time on top of his head. He went facedown into some truly nasty carpet or the flat nap that was left of it.

Over the next forty minutes he occasionally got to his hands and knees, felt around with a floppy, uncoordinated hand for the knife while dripping a good dose of drool. I'd wait until he got the knife in his hand—he looked so proud at the accomplishment, like a kid graduating from kindergarten—and then I'd whack him over the head again. After two times, Rafferty stuck his head inside the door and told me to stop playing with my food and either fish or cut bait.

I almost protested that's not what I was doing, but it would have been pointless. On the subject of food and playing with it, a Wolf would know.

Niko, while he wasn't cutting the phone line, didn't step up to defend me, which meant I probably *was* in the wrong and enjoying playing Whac-A-Mole a little too much. It was a boring forty minutes, the guy was stubborn, and I . . . I enjoyed my work. Just because he was human didn't mean he wasn't a monster that preyed on the weak. He deserved a whack or three, but to keep the peace with Niko and not annoy Rafferty, which more and more seemed like a bad idea, I hit the guy extra hard the last time. He'd stay down until long after we left.

We left behind us a nonfunctioning phone, not that that ass was in any position to call the cops. We also left that same ass unconscious on the floor. Maybe if we were lucky, his dog would come back and eat him. It was a happy dog, but happy dogs get hungry too. And an hour later we were back at the exit that had taken us on our side trip to Candy Land gone horribly wrong. We were all sprawled in Abelia-Roo's RV. Catcher, Rafferty, and I were sprawled anyway. Robin was sitting perfectly upright, touching as little of the cushions as he could for fear the eye-searing pink roses would jump from the upholstered bench seat to taint his clothing beyond redemption. "Is there no limit to what you will do to disarm your marks?" He sneered at Abelia who sat in the kitchen booth.

She sneered back. "This from a trickster. I take that as the finest of compliments, goat."

The old woman had answered Niko's call and come back to pick us up. Branje had suggested she and the others go back to the exit while he went to the house to make sure we were doing our job. Waiting on *gadje* was no task for a queen like Abelia. It was the perfect line for Abelia-Roo and the only one she would've bought. Maybe because she did buy it helped her to blame us for his death. Suyolak had done the damage, but we had a healer. We could've saved him. Hell, I didn't know. Maybe Rafferty could have, but Salome saw someone trying to kill us and she took care of the situation. Diplomacy and client relations weren't concepts in her pickled little brain—if she had a brain. Didn't they remove them during mummification?

It was not a subject I wanted to dwell on. One of the four men left was driving. He slowed at that same four-way stop I'd been so unimpressed with before. There was no way I'd be forgetting it now. "Should I stop, *Bara*?" he asked.

"Bah. Fool. Do you see any cars here to steal?" She tossed a bony finger at the window at the only building around: the post office. "Should they steal a mailman's truck? Such a fool. You shame me. Go to the next exit. Perhaps there will be better pickings there."

"And a computer," Rafferty added. "We need a laptop. As soon as possible." He looked down at Catcher who was sleeping. Unable to communicate on an in-depth level, there wasn't much else he could do—sleep or gnaw on those ugly cushions.

Brilliant white, store-bought teeth—those were new—bared in a smile of the haggling kind. "Perhaps this I can help you with, doctor dog. You could not do for Branje, but you can do something for me."

It wasn't at the next exit but the one after that that we found a car. We didn't steal it as Abelia suggested. We had more than enough of her money to pay for it, although with Robin, trickster and used car salesman, on our side in the negotiations, the guy we bought it from had to feel like he had been not only robbed, but mugged in an alley, then lost his retirement in a Ponzi scheme. We left him stunned with the key to the tiny car lot dangling from his hand, trying to get up the energy to close up. Goodfellow was smugly satisfied, Niko had another giant, ancient car, and I had air-conditioning. Genuine making-life-worth-living air-conditioning. It was almost worth the loss of my guns.

I closed my eyes and enjoyed the cool air in my face. Beside me was the clicking of a car lot ink pen against a keyboard—Catcher's new laptop. There hadn't been an exchange of money for it. From the looks of Rafferty and the car he'd left behind, he didn't have much to spend. But there was no way Abelia-Roo would give anyone anything for free. "What'd she want?" I asked. "For the computer?" I wasn't surprised she had one to trade in the RV. I'd bet the old witch had more stock than Kmart in there.

"She has a bad heart." I heard the rustle of cloth as Rafferty shifted position and I opened my eyes to see him lean and read Catcher's typing. He snorted in agreement, "Yeah, full of bitchiness too, but that I can't cure."

"So you could fix her heart?" I was surprised she had one at all.

"I improved the function some, but you can't cure old." Unless you were willing to do things only Suyolak would do. "Every heart has only so many beats in it. I gave her the maximum hers has. Another month more than she would've had—maybe. Not that I told her it was that little. We wolves can do creative bargaining ourselves; we just call it what it is: lying."

"Well, it's a month more than she deserves," I said under my breath as I used my cell to finally call Delilah and fill her in on what had happened, now that I knew she wasn't behind what had happened. She was still angry. I'd known that or she would've come looking for us. She would've sniffed us out, found us, made things considerably easier on our twenty-mile trek. But she hadn't. In some ways that was almost worse than her possibly considering killing me. Killing me was an intimate thing; it was personal. Being ignored . . . that was like not existing at all. That wasn't Delilah-like; it wasn't even Wolf-like. Ninety-nine point nine percent of Wolves regarded me with loathing, fear, and murderous fury. Rafferty and Catcher had given me the benefit of the doubt years ago, because one was a healer and one was different himself; at least that was my best guess. I could've been wrong. Who really knew? Rafferty might be a healer, but he wasn't handing out smiles and lollipops after exams in the surgery room of his house.

Delilah—I knew I didn't know her inside out either.

She was a different species. She was a killer, although she claimed not to kill humans because it wasn't enough of a challenge. She was a career criminal and enjoyed it. But she also liked me, gifted me with pretty fucking amazing sex, and treated me as nothing particularly special. When those in the preternatural world who could tell what fathered you were either terrified of you or wanted to kill you, and then someone came along who treated you as just a guy, nothing out of the ordinary, it was . . . good. It was damn good.

I closed the cell after she disconnected wordlessly after my explanation. This though—this wasn't good at all. If she was going to try to kill me, I wished she'd do it already. That I could handle. This sucked. This made *me* want to kill someone. Hell, this wasn't a new feeling for me—just a new feeling for me with Delilah. And the feeling lasted well into the next moment, although it shifted to someone specific, because he was back.

The goddamn Plague of the World.

"The sun has fallen; the moon will soon be a cradle for newborn babes rocked to gentle sleep."

He was sitting between Niko and Robin this time, up front, on the old bench seat. There was room enough for a hide-covered skeleton. I saw the line of the pointed jaw in the dark as the head turned to look from one side; then from the other; then the glimpse of a marbleized eye as Suyolak shifted his gaze back to Rafferty specifically. "But not all babes, my carnivorous friend, yes? Not all babes."

There was more than Catcher's snarl this time. There was his, his cousin's, the yowl of Salome, and my own incoherent growl. If only I knew where he was, if only I'd *seen* it, I'd have traveled there in a heartbeat despite what Niko thought about gates. But I hadn't, and I couldn't go where I didn't know the way. It didn't stop me from lunging at the image, my hands passing through where his neck would've been under all those tangled hanks of hair. The bone-gleam of a grin was there and gone as he disappeared, popping out of existence like a soap bubble . . . like a magic trick. When you wanted to strangle someone, magic tricks weren't what you wanted to see.

The snarling beside me continued, from human and wolf throats. I wasn't the only one feeling frustrated. "Monogamy, the Plague, and killer babies," Robin said blackly as Salome tried to crawl up the inside of his shirt. "This is officially the worst road trip in history."

"It's not your fault, Rafferty," Niko said, ignoring the puck and addressing what needed to be said. That's what he had always done for me. Now he did it for our ally. "It's far easier to destroy than rebuild. There's nothing you could've done and we know that. And Suyolak knows it as well. He's pushing your buttons. Don't let him."

The healer snapped his mouth shut on the next snarl and turned to look out the window at passing lights . . . the night . . . or nothing. Any of those would've been better than looking at the inside of his own head. I could see that blood-splattered nursery in IMAX fucking vibrancy on the inside of mine, and I could've done without it. And I wasn't the one whose specialty was doing something about things like that. I was more like Suyolak. Killing was about all I was good at; killing and being a smart-ass. Neither of those should've done any good in that baby's room, but the only good Rafferty had been able to do was the same, which had to make him feel like utter shit.

He wasn't alone. We had known there would be civilian deaths and accepted it. There was nothing else we could do about it and stopping to try to help would only make things worse and give Suyolak more power over us. We hadn't gone faster because we had to meet up with Rafferty. There was nothing we could do and nothing we had done—not one damn thing. We all felt like shit.

And there was still nothing we could do . . . except this time go faster.

11

Catcher

I was running. I loved to run. All my life, I'd loved it.

"Catcher, wake up."

Through the grass and into the trees, under a sky bluer than those of the best hundred summer vacations combined.

Running and running, trying to catch something, but I didn't know what. It felt like something already gone, but it didn't keep me from chasing behind it. Running and running . . .

"Catcher, you're having a dream." A hand thumped my ribs and I jerked awake with a snap and a snarl. A familiar scent was there, but it was surrounded by thousands of unfamiliar ones—unfamiliar smells, things, and shapes. Where? Who? My panic peaked sharply . . . what was . . . who was . . .

It had happened before. It had. I closed my eyes against the confusion and the unknown. I closed my eyes and concentrated hard. Hard. Hard? Right before the word lost its meaning, before *I* lost meaning, it all came back. It felt like a muscle cramp that unbunches and finally loosens, but in my brain. I'd stood on the edge, but this time I hadn't fallen.

My name is Catcher.

I hadn't fallen. No, not this time—but lots of times before.

My name is Catcher, and I am fine. Just fine.

I exhaled harshly in a hacking morning cough that sprayed saliva, opened my eyes, and smacked Rafferty in the head with a saucer-sized paw. Then I yawned elaborately to show I was still tired. There was nothing wrong with me, so let me dream already.

He knew better. I wished I could've fooled him, but I couldn't, not a healer and not my cousin. It wasn't like the good old days when I'd once swiped his wallet and his keys, taken his Mustang, and traded it in for one of those Volkswagen Rabbits from the eighties. We looked enough alike that I could pass for his license photo when I signed over the pink slip. He'd given serious thought to killing me and did kick my butt Wolf-to-Wolf, but to see a Wolf driving around in a Rabbit, it was worth it. Was it ever worth it. Our local pack laughed its collective furry butt off at the sight for weeks.

I pulled more than a few good ones on him back then. I'd thought he was too serious. I'd thought it was my job to lighten him up, to show him what a ride life could be. It turned out I had. Only he'd been the one who was right. Life was serious and not a ride anyone could count on. You could get a bullet train rush of speed and an amusement park picture at the end with your hair on end or you could get a rickety wooden roller coaster that crumbled, spilling you into the river far below. There was no way you knew what you'd get when you bought the ticket. It was the luck of the draw.

"You're moping. Stop moping and eat your damn fries." Rafferty shoved a bag of fresh, hot, salty-as-the-sea fries under my nose and I brightened. Okay, maybe the ride wasn't perfect and I was on the downhill slide into the end of it, but going up that roller coaster hill had been great. Family, friends, college, good movies, better food, lots of sex, and running under the skies of every season as human and wolf. I'd had a good life, and it still had high points: family, movies, my head out of the car window grinning in the wind, and fries. Who didn't love fries? I stuck my muzzle in the white paper bag and went to work on about half a pound of them.

So I had a little hiccup of the brain this morning, and it was morning—after ten if McDonald's was serving fries, which meant late morning but still morning. I could tell by the smell of the air, the color of the sky, the position of the sun when I peered out the window, and I could also read the digital clock of the bank across the street from where we were parked. I grinned to myself in satisfaction. Just a hiccup and I'd plenty of those. I was still here, all of me, and that's what counted.

When I did go . . . *if* I did go, Rafferty had firmly amended before telling me with a reluctance he'd never shown any other of his patients, it would be one big hiccup. I'd go wolf in thought, as I had many times before, but that time . . . the last time, I'd never come back to Catcher again. No *Flowers for Algernon* for me. No gradual loss of intellect or changing bit by bit until my mind wasn't mine anymore. No, the hiccups would get closer and closer together, as they had, and when it happened, it would be all at once. I'd never know I was going; never know I was gone. I tried to be philosophical about it. After all, chances were I'd be a happy wolf. I was a happy werewolf. I simply wouldn't be me anymore—not the Catcher me, but a simpler version of me, maybe. I hoped.

I dived back in the bag for more fries. I was lucky. I'd gotten to be me longer than I would have if Rafferty had let me die. I dropped a mouthful of soggy fries in his lap and gave him a more cheerful grin this time. My ride had been good, great even, just short. Rafferty's was

long and, if he didn't let go of his guilt, miserable. The
very least I could do for him was not add to that with
any gloom-and-doom brooding. And I really was done
with it. Resigned, no, not resigned . . . I was at peace with
my fate. If only Rafferty could be too and stop fighting
it like the stubborn bastard he was; stop looking for the
Cure, the impossible C. Fries couldn't fix that, though, as
much as I wished they could.

"Thanks." Picking up one fry to watch saliva drip
from it, he said what he always said. "You're a pal. We're
in Utah now. We stopped for gas, if you're curious."

I snorted, indicating I was more than capable of
smelling gasoline. Even a human could smell that. I
could smell something else too: Delilah, and she smelled
better than the fries by a long shot. She might be out to
kill him, but Cal was still one lucky son of a bitch in my
opinion. I gave my cousin a questioning woo and turned
to look out each back window for a glimpse of her.

"Jesus, just don't hump the seat, okay?" He sighed.
"I'll never live that one down."

"Cheerful one." Delilah slid into the empty front
seat. Niko, Robin, and that naked cat, Cal, they were all
off somewhere. "Litter mate? You all the fun, he with
none?" she went on, her smile bright and wicked.

She was stunning. Not beautiful, no, but something
beyond beautiful. Something wild and dangerous even
to another Wolf. Her eyes were naturally amber, not
wolf amber, with skin to match and that silver blond hair
that still mixed up snow and sex in one happy bundle in
my thoughts. I tossed my head to the side, pulling out of
range—either a refusal or a negative in wolf-talk. And I
definitely didn't mean it as a refusal.

She looked at us closer, studying—smelling. "Cousins. Tame cousins. Suburban Wolves," she said with not
a hint, but a good helping of scorn. In the Kin's eyes,
there were Kin and there was everybody else. If you

didn't rob, kill, run drugs, pimp succubi, and do other things not worth knowing, you weren't a predator. You weren't a Wolf. You were just a dog playing dress-up. But Delilah didn't seem to mind, just as she didn't mind Cal . . . aside from the possible killing-him prospect. Of course Delilah didn't mind us because of the All Wolf. If she could get Rafferty to do to them what he'd done to me, it was like standing on the mountaintop with your poisoned Kool-Aid and the alien mothership actually swooping in to pick you up: the ultimate reward to them, but an abomination to my cousin. He would never do it. She could talk forever.

I rested my head on the front seat and grinned at her, with the kind of grin that gave her the indication of where my brain, which I still had for the moment, was right now—definitely not in my head. Rafferty might not like her, but I didn't care what she said. She could've asked me to let little children ride me like a pony around the parking lot. She could've read the back of a cereal box. As long as I was able to be this close to her, smell her, stick a nose in those long strands of hair, I was good. Happy happy happy. If Algernon had gotten any, he might've lasted longer; that was my theory. Poor mouse. Poor janitor. Poor me.

I turned my head further and pawed delicately at Delilah's hair, radiating that "poor me" scent until I'd flooded the car with it. I don't know if she'd have fallen for it or not. Rafferty was too quick to grab me by the scruff and pull me back. "She's Kin," he snapped. "And she's a crazy All Wolf. You don't want that; I don't care how horny you are."

"So judgmental." She crossed her arms along the back of the seat I'd just been yanked from and rested her chin on that sunset skin. She'd left her motorcycle leather top elsewhere and was wearing only a tank top now. It showed a lot of skin, but, truthfully, skin or fur, I didn't care. It was nice—very nice. A strong hand untangled itself and she cupped my muzzle firmly. "But you . . . so beautiful. So all that is right. All that is true. We could be as you. Whole. Wolf as Wolf is meant to be."

This was America, land of religious freedom. She could've wanted to ascend to the higher being of a fire hydrant for all I cared. My only concern was about getting some. All right, I wasn't proud, but I wasn't ashamed either. It had been a long time. It could be a longer time and by then the Catcher part of me wouldn't be around to appreciate it. No, there was no shame as I vaulted the seat and landed on top of her. I might've howled in glee. I know she howled back. But before she could go wolf, we were interrupted—by my cousin and by Cal, who, to give him credit, didn't try to shoot me.

Rafferty pulled me back over the seat and Cal pulled Delilah out of the car altogether. He must've been furious, although again, nice enough not to shoot me. Then he avoided a punch from Delilah that would've broken his nose if it had connected—dodged quick, more than human-quick—and he looked at me. For a brief second, maybe I imagined it, but I thought I saw a red gleam in the gray of his eyes: Auphe red.

I decided I wasn't horny anymore. I further decided it might be a good time for a bathroom break, hooked my paw around the door handle, yanked and pushed the door open with my shoulder. If I hit the asphalt running, it was because I really had to piss—no other reason. I heard Rafferty following after me. I could've gone back for the laptop to ask if he'd seen it too or sensed it as a healer, but I didn't want to know, just as people didn't want to know years ago when I'd had to tell them I had leukemia, that I was going to die. You could see it in their faces. . . . Take it back. Rewind a few minutes. Make that conversation never have happened. Sometimes it was for me, the not wanting to know. They didn't want to lose me. They didn't want me to suffer. But sometimes it was for themselves, not me. Don't put that on me. Don't make me carry the burden of your being sick ... your dying. I don't want to know. I don't want to deal with it.

With Cal, I was even worse, because I felt them both. Sorrow and fear ... for an Auphe.

"Damn it, Catcher, wait. Your collar."

I stopped with an internal and external groan and glumly stood still as Rafferty slipped it over my head. It wasn't as if Raff wanted to put a collar on me, the most humiliating thing you could do to a werewolf, but it lessened the incidents like we'd had with the truckers the day before. That was why it was bright green with butterflies on it. *Butterflies.* I couldn't even have a butch collar with skulls and crossbones or just a plain-colored one. No, I had to have the girly collar to make me look as harmless as possible. He'd tried to put a pink one on me first and that had led to the destruction of a motel room. There was a lot I was willing to do to make things easier on my cousin, but I wasn't going pink.

I sat down on my haunches and took a look around, trying to ignore the sounds of my tags jangling against each other. One was shaped like a bone. Wasn't that cute? Wasn't that sweet? I moaned again and Raff said quietly, "I hear you, Cuz." He did. It was the only thing that made that thing around my neck bearable.

I leaned against his leg and took in our surroundings. This was a busier exit than the usual ones where we'd been stopping. Several fast-food restaurants, truck stops, gas stations, and the pervasive, big generic food-clothes-auto-electronics-banking-coffee-stand-photo-vision-salon-and-have-surgery-while-you-wait stores you saw everywhere now. "Goodfellow and Niko are in there buying clothes." He didn't smile often, my cousin, but he absolutely smirked when he said that, a smirk that dripped with pure evil.

I smirked back, my tongue lolling. Goodfellow buying clothes at the equivalent of Wal-Mart; it was worth the car getting blown up to see that. I wondered if polyester would actually burn his skin or simply jump off his body and scoot away. We'd walked to the McDonald's curb and Rafferty sat down on it. My eyes drifted back to the car where Cal and Delilah were arguing. It was too far for a human to hear, but for a Wolf, I might as well have been a foot from them.

"I don't give a damn who you sleep with," Cal was saying, his tone sharp but cold too. Ice-cold. I'd seen Cal only a few times in my life, but I knew what he was capable of. I wondered if Delilah did or only thought she did. "This isn't *Weres and Vamps 90210*. We're not going fucking *steady*. You can go bang the bag boy at the goddamn grocery store if you want, but leave Catcher and Rafferty alone. And when you do screw the bag boy, have the damn decency not to do it in the car where I can smell it all day long." Cal pretended he didn't care that Delilah might try to kill him, but he cared—too much. But it wasn't making him reckless; it was making him . . . less. Less of what he was and more of what he wasn't—or what he didn't want to be.

"Told you will do as I want," Delilah countered. "What I want is not to kill. Not you." I could smell it on her, the truth and the lie. She might not want to, but it didn't mean she wouldn't if it were her only resort. "The Kin can say, but I am Kin too. Better Kin. I do as I please," she said. Cal looked as if he wanted to believe it, and he didn't have any reason not to. Her words rang with truth. She was a good liar and when it was only half a lie, it was even easier to be convincing. Cal wasn't a Wolf. His sense of smell was Auphe, but they hadn't been able to smell the emotions of truth or honesty; only fear—the dark, sharp scent of a prey's terror. He had to trust his instincts. I was glad I wasn't human. It would be like being half blind, depending on only what you could see and hear, on the human oddity of subtext. How they managed to get anything accomplished amazed me.

Cal bowed his head. He had yanked Delilah out of the car either because she let him—human strength was less than werewolf strength—or because of that concept I didn't want to consider, that thing I didn't want to know—the other half of Cal that was growing, spreading. I shifted my weight on my paws and Rafferty murmured, "I know." But knowing and being able to do something about it weren't always the same.

Now Cal had her backed against the car, and Delilah, being who she'd shown herself to be, was enjoying it. He wasn't. His fists were clenched, knuckles white. "Then don't ignore me either. Change your mind and do your best to kill me, but don't fucking *ignore* me. I've been happy, except for that damn Suyolak, for the first time in my life. The Auphe are gone. I'm free. Don't ruin it, got it? Don't goddamn ruin it."

Cal was human, Cal was Auphe, but Cal might have the spirit of the wolf in him too. Being dead, being killed in battle, being *seen*; it was better than being nothing. It was better than nonexistence or the wrong kind of existence. Cal knew that.

"Happy," Rafferty murmured at my ear. "He has been less moody than the other times I'd seen him." Happy? Okay, everything is relative. What I paid attention to was that an upbeat Cal equaled a downbeat cousin, but Raff didn't elaborate on why it did. We both already knew. As I'd thought, as I'd seen, as I'd smelled, the Auphe in him was growing.

"Puppy!"

I turned my head just in time to have a McNugget shoved up my left nostril—or at least a good attempt at it. A toddler with a dandelion fluff of wispy blond hair was trying to pet me with one small hand and gift me with questionable chicken parts with the other. Puppy he knew; the difference between a nose and a mouth, not so much.

I loved little kids: manic balls of energy with four limbs waving like drunken windmills. They always were up for Frisbee, grabbing their bikes and going, running and shouting, racing, playing hide-and-seek. They were just like wolves, except at the end of hide-and-seek they didn't eat what they caught. They lived in the moment—not yesterday or tomorrow or even the next minute. It was a good philosophy, especially for my life now.

I opened my mouth and patiently let him stuff the food down around my tonsils while he giggled and his mother looked horrified, frozen, clutching several paper bags. I waited until the little boy withdrew his hand; then I swallowed the chicken and held out a polite paw to the mom. *See how harmless? Shake the doggy's paw. See what a good doggy?*

She didn't take it, but only grabbed the child and swept him up with one spare arm to bolt to her car. "You should have that thing on a leash," she told Rafferty in the most righteous of tones over her shoulder.

"Humans," he muttered, and looped an arm over the barrel of my body.

I chuffed in agreement to make him feel better, but actually I didn't mind humans. I'd dated enough of them in college. It *was* true that most of them started out fine, but some usually went wrong and lost their sense of play. Those you just ignored. I'd long since stopped taking it personally when I'd gotten locked in the fur coat. If I hadn't, I would've eaten someone and been in my right mind when I did it. I had to let it go, and I did. Bad emotions will eat you up as fast as any cancer. I saw that in Rafferty every day as another tiny piece of him was gobbled up by guilt and despair. But no matter what I said or did, I hadn't been able to change it. That was who he was, spending his life trying to stop the unstoppable, with me and every other patient he took on. In the end, he would always lose. For a Wolf and a healer, he was remarkably blind about death—stubborn to his lupine bones, denying nature itself, and he'd never be any different.

I would've given anything to hear him laugh.

Niko—another one who didn't do much laughing, not on the outside anyway, although I could often smell the silent humor on him—walked up to us across the Wal-Mart parking lot while carrying a bag in each hand. He looked down at us with a neutral gray gaze. "Have you seen—" Interrupted by the ring of his cell phone, he switched one bag to his other hand and answered it. "Yes, Ishiah?"

I'd never liked caller ID. It took the surprise out of life, and life could use all the surprises it could get as far as I was concerned—good ones at least. Of course, with the way things were going, this wasn't a good one. But I didn't know that yet.

A Wolf's hearing is more than exceptional and I had no ethical problems listening to Ishiah's side of the conversation. I wasn't entirely the goody-goody suburban Wolf Delilah labeled me. No Wolf alive was. And, hey, I was nosy. My life had been limited for a long time. Eavesdropping was a minor sin for a little entertainment value.

This Ishiah, the monogamy quandary—or victim, depending on your opinion of Goodfellow—didn't waste time on pleasantries. "Where's Robin?"

There was a thrum under the voice that vibrated the air in a way a human couldn't hear—in a very unique, deep, and musical way. A peri. A puck and a peri: That had my eyes crossing. The profane and the pure. It wasn't precisely a Match dot com dream come true.

"I was about to ask my traveling companions the

same thing. Still in the store, I was assuming." Niko looked over his shoulder back at the building. "Although considering the type of store it is, I would've thought he would have been in and out in five minutes."

"He just called me and he doesn't sound . . . himself. He sounds drunk and confused. You need to find him. *Now*." All right, a righteous and pure peri, but a pissed-off one. And worried too.

"Now," Niko confirmed, flipping the cell shut with a brisk snap that showed how concerned he was. "It has to be Suyolak. Robin certainly wouldn't drink any alcohol he could purchase from liter bottles in that store. Rafferty, Catcher, can you find him?"

I was already on my feet, nose in the air. Thousands upon thousands of scents, but a puck was easy to pick out, a piece of bright green yarn in a mass of bland tan ones. Rafferty was most likely feeling for him with his healing talent as well as following with his own nose, but four legs were faster than two, and I streaked through the parking lot with my cousin and Niko behind me. I had Goodfellow's scent off the bat. There were many scents actually: several kinds of cologne; silk; shampoo that cost more than the car we'd been riding in. He did like the finer things in life.

A few people shouted as I ran past them, but I was so quick that most were left gaping, mouths opening and closing like brain-damaged goldfish. I didn't care. I was running, I was tracking, and while I was apprehensive about Goodfellow, I was also doing what wolves did best . . . besides kill. I couldn't help but enjoy the adrenaline.

To run is to live and I was *living*.

I left the parking lot, ran through grass, passed Goodfellow's dropped phone, and vaulted a massive drainage ditch as if it were a puddle. He'd walked around it. I passed over it as if I had wings, and I caught him. I caught the puck a split second before he stepped into the first lane of four lanes of busy, extremely fast-moving traffic that ran in front of the shopping center. I snagged the back of his expensive if now-dusty and sweat-stained shirt and yanked him backward hard. He hit the grass and rolled several times back down into the graveled ditch. If it had been a cartoon, you would've heard the splat. In the real world it was more of a combination of a thunk and thud.

Whoops.

I jumped down beside him as he lay spread-eagle on the dried, cracked mud. His eyes were half open, but he wasn't seeing me. He was talking, but it was all Greek to me . . . literally. And I took Russian and Japanese in college, so I didn't have a clue. I licked a broad tongue across his face, figuring that would disgust him so much he would have to come around. He didn't.

Rafferty, Niko, and Cal came sliding down beside us, the latter wasn't going to let us go tearing off without following us. "What's wrong with him?" Cal demanded.

"He looks like he was sleepwalking. With Suyolak, that's certainly an option," Niko said.

"And into traffic to be run down—what a damn fun party trick that would be to him. The bastard," Cal muttered. "What's he saying?"

"You don't want to know," his brother answered dryly but disquieted as well. Worried. "Rafferty?"

Rafferty was kneeling beside Goodfellow, his hand resting on the puck's head with the brown curls springing between his fingers. "Huh. Never thought I'd actually get to diagnose the good old 'dead in a ditch' in my lifetime."

Cal snapped, "Rafferty, he's our friend, all right? So don't fuck around. Fix him." Fix him, because Cal didn't seem to have too many friends and he didn't want to lose those he did have. Being half Auphe wasn't going to make for the most popular kid on the playground. Poor guy. Although even if he hadn't been half Auphe, I still wasn't sure he'd win any congeniality contests. Like my cousin, he had a temper.

Snorting, unimpressed by his cranky counterpart, Rafferty took a more serious tone, "He's asleep, like Niko said, and thanks to Catcher's quick and heroic action, he also has a concussion."

I laid back my ears and growled. Rafferty used his free hand to shake my ruff. "Kidding, Cuz. A concussion is better than his ending up as roadkill." He closed his eyes. "Niko, Cal, go scare off the rubberneckers up there and I'll work on the concussion and then wake him up."

It didn't take long. The pale face regained a healthy color, the blood seeping out on the gravel beneath Goodfellow's head stopped flowing, and after five or so minutes, the puck's eyes cleared and he blinked dazedly for a second before his gaze sharpened. "Where am I and what is that I feel on the back of my shirt?"

That would be a little bit of good honest Wolf saliva, but I looked away and pretended an interest in a lethargic frog hopping down the ditch away from us. Just as I liked kids, I liked frogs too. A biologist couldn't not like frogs. They were fascinating. They came in all colors; some were poisonous; some could switch sexes. Amazing.

By the time it had hopped out of sight, Goodfellow was sitting up and talking to the peri on his phone either Niko or Cal had retrieved for him. "I'm fine, Ish. Lassie helped me out somewhat. What happened? Ahhh . . . some sleepwalking. Not anything to worry about. Didn't I say Lassie saved me? So how much danger could I have been in really? Other than falling down a well or getting trapped in the 'old mine'?" I bared my teeth and Goodfellow bared his back at me. Not only did he speak Greek, but he spoke Wolf fairly fluently as well. "No.

You don't need to come. Our doggy healer can handle it, he's quite sure. Oh, and anything I might have said while asleep that was of a sexual nature I promise to back up when I get home. No, back up was not a euphemism. I don't use euphemisms. If I meant that, then that's what I would've said. I *am* sitting in a filthy ditch at the moment, but if you want to discuss details right now, we can." Apparently Ishiah, thank Fenris and all that runs with fur, didn't. He was far more interested in the issue of Goodfellow's safety.

Ishiah didn't seem too reassured from his reply regarding the subject, but in the end, the puck convinced him, more to keep the peri out of harm's way than for our sake, I thought, and we were out of the ditch and headed back to the car and McDonald's. After all the excitement, I was hungry again. I was thinking strawberry sundae.

Goodfellow tried to wipe the dirt from his clothes and hair, glaring at me when he reached back to touch the wet patch on his shirt. Whatever the male version of a diva, he was it. I saved his life and he turned up his nose at a little spit. He kept walking back to the Wal-Mart after Cal tentatively slapped his shoulder, and Rafferty and I stopped at the McDonald's, claiming our same spot on the curb. Cal then headed back to Delilah, who was languidly leaning against the car, and started up their argument again while Niko kept the puck company. With Suyolak pulling even more tricks out of a bottomless hat, the buddy system did seem the way to go. Keep your buddy from drowning or falling asleep midstep. It was the same thing in this situation.

Fifteen minutes later Goodfellow was back, and I was wearing a now-empty plastic sundae container over my nose. I pawed it off and licked away my ice-cream mustache as Goodfellow stopped directly in front of us.

"I guessed you didn't want to leave your cousin long

enough to shop yourself, Doctor. I couldn't bring myself to dig you a nice pair of discarded jeans out of the
Dumpsters, but I estimated your size." The smile he gave
my cousin was more wolfish than any we real Wolves
had in us. "I'm very good at estimating sizes, although
I'm more than willing to confirm it by hand."

Five bags were dumped on the curb beside me.
I raised my eyes to see Salome, who'd hopped out of
the car to follow the puck into the store. She must've
thought she'd been lying down on the job earlier and
wasn't about to let that happen again. Curled around
Goodfellow's neck, she returned my gaze with an interest that made me feel much like that McNugget I'd
eaten earlier. As a werewolf, I wasn't used to feeling that
way. A two-hundred-pound machine of pure muscle
evolved to kill, facing off against a hairless, seven-pound
Mr. Bigglesworth stand-in. I put my head in one of the
bags and pretended to investigate the contents. If that
made me a chickenshit, so be it. A furry lover of peace;
that was me.

"That monogamy lasted, what, a whole day? But then
again a dick has no morals, yeah?" Rafferty said as I
sniffed denim and cotton.

"Clever. By dick I can choose whether you mean me
or the splendor that precedes me like Excalibur. Bravo."
He clapped in appreciation. If hands could be facetious,
these were.

I rolled my eyes back to see that unwavering Pan
smile turn more conceited. I almost lost my breakfast
into the plastic bag, but decided it would be a waste of
good fries and kept searching through the bags with
vague curiosity.

"Oh, help me." Rafferty dropped his head into his
hands.

"And I haven't made up my mind yet about monogamy." Although from hearing him talk to Ishiah on the

phone, I was beginning to doubt that. "If I had decided against it, I'd do you. I don't like you, despite your helping me with the concussion, you being the exceptional ass and all, but I'd do you. You're doable in a shaggy, natural man-wolf of the wild way." He folded his arms. "And if I had decided on monogamy, it wouldn't mean that I couldn't still look or fantasize or talk the talk. I simply couldn't walk the walk. Unfortunately for my decision-making process, I do truly love walking the walk. Besides, considering our current situation, I don't believe making choices about monogamy should be my primary concern. Staying alive long enough to ponder it at a later date while surrounded by naked flesh in a succession of strip clubs is slightly more important." The last words were so faint, even my wolf ears barely heard them. "Or naked flesh and feathers."

For someone who feared monogamy, he sure did like to talk about it, I snorted to myself. When a creature is forever like a puck, could monogamy be forever, though? I came to an instant conclusion. When one is forever, nothing can be forever. But something doesn't have to be forever to be good, and I knew that Goodfellow did have it good now, whether he'd completely come to realize it or not. I could smell it on him. I could see it around him like a halo . . . like an aura of I'm-getting-laid-and-you're-not. But not just laid; more than that—something extraordinary.

Right now I'd have settled for the just-laid part.

Lucky puck.

As I considered biting him just for the getting-laid part alone, his foot nudged one of the bags he'd dropped toward me in particular. When I found what he'd bought for me, I forgave him . . . just a little. I felt my tail wave back and forth in pleasant surprise and I dragged out the two calendars. One was swimsuit models, and one was *Wolves in the Wild*. "For you, for having some vague part in perhaps saving my life. Or so the others have told me. Despite soiling one of my best shirts with . . . never mind." Goodfellow cleared his throat. Pucks were so very good at fake emotions that real ones were something of an effort for them. It made the gesture all the more meaningful. "I tried to find one with the most female wolves on it," he added, "but a few shots were uncooperative in determining that, so you may have to lust after a male wolf too. The diversity will be good for you."

I held up my paw again as I had to the irate mother almost a half hour ago. This time there was no humiliation to it. I was reaching across a communication void to say, "You're welcome" and Goodfellow accepted it in exactly that spirit. He gripped my paw and said sympathetically, "I can't say I know personally what it's like to be in a consummately . . . ah . . . awkward situation. But even if I don't know, I've seen Cal's preoccupation with not passing on the Auphe genes. I also have an excellent imagination. I hope these help somewhat."

Pucks. They were rapacious in all they did—sex, money, trickery—but Goodfellow wasn't such a bad guy. I'd go as far as saying he was the king of good guys, for a puck. I was glad I saved his life; I just wished I'd left more saliva on his shirt. I picked up the calendars with my teeth and slapped them against Rafferty's chest. Open. *Open*. I didn't need my laptop to get that point across. He grumbled and ripped the clear plastic off them and I stuck a wet nose to each page to flip it for a look. Wow. I looked back and forth between firm asses and plumed tails and couldn't have been happier.

I stayed that way until we were all back in the car, Cal smelling more Auphe than usual, but I had booty and a great sense of denial, so I ignored it. Happy, happy. But unfortunately what I couldn't ignore was when Niko, now in the passenger seat while Robin drove, asked my cousin, "You are sure we're still on Suyolak's trail? Obviously he left another trap for us here that Robin fell into, but he's clever. I don't want to be doubtful, but . . ." He let the silence finish the sentence for him. He did doubt. A careful, meticulous man, if he had doubt, he was going to want it resolved. "You can still sense Suyolak?"

Rafferty wasn't offended. He wasn't anything except a mass of fury and determination at the mention of the antihealer's name—so overwhelmingly so that I couldn't believe even nose-blind humans couldn't smell it. "I have him," he said flatly. "He's ahead of us. Far ahead, but I'm not losing him and I'm not falling for any more mirrors of the bastard. As for the traps, they're small, harder to detect. Especially when all it does is make you sleepwalk. That does trip the healer radar. It's quiet, like a grenade, until it goes off, but I'll do what I can to sniff them out." He'd been looking out the window at nothing . . . again . . . but now he shifted his attention back to everyone in the car. "You don't get it. Do you think I took this job to save the world? I don't give a crap about the world right now. Catcher does." He locked a hand in the ruff at my neck. "He pushed me to take it, and I did . . . but for him. If I can take the life from Suyolak the way he's slowly sucking it from his driver, I can make Catcher as he was. His healing power and mine combined, I'll have enough to do it then. I'll be able to fix my cousin. So don't worry about my losing his trail. It won't fucking happen. Period."

Suddenly all the enjoyment of my calendar lust disappeared. He was right. They didn't get it. I hadn't gotten it either. I'd thought he'd done it for the right reason. He was a healer. Saving the world was what he did, one person at a time. I thought taking out Suyolak would put him closer to a balance again and help him see that curing me couldn't be the end all and be all of his existence.

He was a healer and that meant he belonged to everyone who needed him; not only to me. True, I'd come to regret the decision once I saw what Suyolak was capable of and wished we'd never come to be part of this. Family protecting family and the hell with the world; that's what I thought.

That was also Rafferty's point of view exactly. Hypocrite, me.

But it still wasn't right—stealing life force, no matter if it was tainted—not for a healer. I was turning my cousin into something that years ago he would've killed in a heartbeat. But there wasn't anything I could do about it. Nothing. I took the current calendar, swimsuit issue, grabbed it in my jaws, and tossed it aside in frustration. Cal caught it. "Whoa! Not enough tits for you? Need six more per model?"

He was in a better mood now, somewhat better; it was a subtle sniff of a difference, but I was Wolf enough to catch it. He and Delilah had come to a wary sort of trust, or so it seemed. I wasn't poking my nose into it. After all, I had *calendars* to occupy me, not the real thing like some half-Auphe bastards.

Not fair. No, that wasn't fair. Putting that on him, when I was really upset with myself. I pulled in a breath and released it, letting some of the anger go. It wasn't Cal's fault.

Although, I noticed, despite the mood change, he seemed twitchy too, which distracted me from my own problems. Tapping fingers on his knee. Unloading and reloading his gun. Playing with his knives. Changing positions often. Fingering the bracelet around his wrist. Except it wasn't a bracelet. They were mala beads for Buddhist meditation. I'd dated a Buddhist girl in college, not Wolf, but I hadn't planned on marrying her, and I wasn't prejudiced like most of my kind. I'd dated a lot of human girls. They were sweet and if they were jealous, they didn't threaten to castrate you with their teeth. You couldn't say the same about the she-Wolves you brought home to meet Mom and Dad.

This girl had been nice, with coppery hair, cheerful blue eyes, and penny-bright freckles across the top of her pale breasts. And clothes on or off, she always wore her mala beads. I knew Niko wore two or three of the bracelets as well, but unlike his brother, Cal definitely didn't come across as the Zen kind. But he was going through the motions, fingers moving from one bead to the next while his lips framed soundless words—his mantra, because I sure couldn't see him praying. He wasn't the praying type. Niko was watching him and, unlike his brother, he wasn't happy, eyes dark over his hawkish nose. I could sample it in his scent as well. He was watching Cal . . . closely . . . and when Cal caught that look, he settled down, dropping his hands into his lap and the calendar onto the floor. "It's okay, Cyrano," he said with an assurance I wasn't buying. *What* exactly was okay? Or not okay? I didn't think this was about what had happened to Robin. It smelled darker. Much darker.

I was about to get on the laptop and ask Rafferty what was up. If it was what we'd suspected, smelled—that Cal was more Auphe now than he had been last time we'd seen him. But that was pointless. What else could it be? I didn't need Rafferty to verify what both our noses had told us. But life decided we got a nice close shot of it anyway.

Something else showed us in brilliant, unforgettable detail that Cal might be less human than my werewolf cousin and I.

The Ördögs.

12

Cal

We hadn't been back on the Lincoln for even thirty measly miles when we saw it. A black truck. *The* black truck. I didn't need the ring of my cell phone from Abelia-Roo still following us in the pink RV of the queen of con artists to tell me that. I could smell the graveyard must creeping in despite the air-conditioning. So could Catcher. And Rafferty? I imagined he could smell *and* sense Suyolak. Half a mile behind him . . . it . . . and where were my explosive rounds when I needed them?

It wasn't a semi, but it was big enough to haul a coffin or two and more than several minions . . . ex-minions. Minions usually always ended up as ex, deceased, or late and not necessarily great. These guys had gotten their pink slip with a nice side order of cholera, and while that didn't taste as bad as hominy or the dreaded brussels sprout, it still couldn't have gone down too well. Read a fucking comic, for God's sake. Watch a superhero movie and you'd know that when your boss is powerful enough and motivated enough to destroy the world, you'd have to wonder: what good are you to him in the long run? Pensions are going to be scarce.

"It's him," Rafferty and I said, not exactly in harmony, but it was as close as echoes came.

"Pull up beside him," Niko ordered.

Robin gave him one of those incredulous glances that he was so good at. "On the Lincoln? Are you going to jump across and cling to the metal door like a ninja refrigerator magnet? Or is Cal going to shoot the driver? Neither of which, I'm sure, will draw any attention of the cars around us." He shook his head. "Blonds. They do try, but . . ." He tapped a finger against his temple.

Niko leaned closer to Robin, something the puck would've normally liked, and bit off one arctic word at a time. "Pull . . . up . . . beside . . . him." My brother wasn't happy about Suyolak and was worried about me—not that he should've been, and he was not in the mood for making things more difficult than they had to be. If shooting the truck driver on the Lincoln was our best opportunity, he'd take it.

"Fine, fine. Hold your no doubt pristinely organic urine." Robin moved into the fast lane and the car up next to the truck. The windows were tinted in the cab, not as black as the paint job, but enough that I couldn't make out who was driving or inside of the cab, especially as I was on the far side of a wolf and healer. While I would've liked to have seen the inside so I could've made a little hop in there, I didn't need to see the driver. It was a man, a stupid and desperate man, and it didn't matter what he looked like or what his name was or even why he was doing this. It only mattered we took him out before he let loose something that could potentially eradicate life on the planet and, worse yet, do it just for shits and giggles.

"I smell something else," Rafferty said as he studied the truck through his window.

"Me too," I responded. It was sharp and musky, mixed with old and new blood. It was the scent of an animal, only much stronger, and not one I'd ever come across. "But I don't have a damn clue what it is."

Catcher was growling softly, but that was his only comment, which meant he didn't know either. "All right then. Suyolak's picked up some new friends. He, like me, is a popular guy," Goodfellow said as he kept pace with the truck as it began to speed up. "Are we going to ride along until he invites us to a playdate with him and his entire tea party? Or are we going to do something productive?"

"All my plans are productive," Nik said, holding a hand over the seat. "Cal, your SIG Sauer."

That was the backup I'd been wearing when the other car had gotten torched. Niko was in the passenger seat. He had the better shot. "Why not the Desert Eagle?" I asked as I passed over the pistol—a 9mm SIG Sauer 226 X-Five tactical model—double action. I hadn't quite gotten a hard-on reading the description in the gun catalogue, but it'd been close. It was a great gun—accurate and good for those who shoot to kill, not just shoot to play.

"Because I didn't feel the need to spend a good chunk of my teen years measuring my penis. I prefer accuracy over size." He accepted the grip of the gun. "Although I do have both."

"Brag, brag, brag. Just shoot the son of a bitch." But he hadn't waited for my encouragement. He'd already aimed through the glass, not taking the time to roll down the window. But Suyolak's driver, the Seattle professor—I'd seen the license plate for verification— must've yanked the wheel and the truck was off on an exit that was too damn convenient to be true, so much so that not only the world had to be against us, but the universe as well.

Goodfellow veered across the lane, cutting off Abelia's RV, which spun in a quick one-eighty and ended up off the road. I saw a shaking fist out one window, so I wasn't too worried. Then again it could've rolled over and tossed her through the air like a hundred-year-old Frisbee and I wouldn't have been wasting an iota of concern. We made the exit and that was the important thing.

The town was something-ville, something-burg. I didn't catch the full name and that was fine. All these little towns were beginning to blur together into one big four-way stop-ville—like when we were kids. From town to town, school to school, liquor store to liquor store, and eventually jail to jail. Bribing a bum old enough to post bond on your mother was always a fun time. The stars, the clean air when we weren't driving through clouds of pollen, the green, the quiet . . . It was missed, but as for the rest, I appreciated New York with new eyes. There were no Sophia memories there. There were Auphe memories, but also ones of victory over the Auphe. It was home and I was more than ready to kick this guy's ass and get back there.

"Never send a samurai to do a street punk's job," I grumbled, slamming into the door as Robin treated the exit like a snowless slalom and he was shooting for the Olympics. "Don't lose them."

"Lose them? I was a charioteer in *Ben-Hur*. A car is nothing compared to four recently gelded and consequently highly pissy horses." He maneuvered around a slow-chugging Toyota and a slightly faster-moving, rusted-out pickup truck with a ruthless speed that would've had a New York cabbie bawling like a baby. The black truck missed them both as well. Maybe it wasn't a Seattle professor, but Charlton Heston behind the wheel.

It was not the best moment to pass the sheriff, but pass him we did. He was going in the opposite direction as we followed the truck at high speed. The department car slammed on its brakes, turned, and was after us for about fifteen seconds. Then it slowed, slowed further, and gradually veered off the road. He might not have shot the sheriff, but Suyolak had done something to him, and to the deputy too if he was with him—something probably permanent and considerably worse than what was in the song. And again I wondered—if he could do that with weak coffin seals, what would he be able to do if he did get out of that coffin?

I didn't want to put it to the test, with Rafferty on our side or not.

"Shoot the tires," I suggested.

"No." Nik had checked the SIG to make sure one was in the pipe. Where was the trust? "Let's see where he goes. Hopefully it will be someplace a little less conspicuous and less lethal to the local bystanders." It truly was another four-way stop-ville as I said, but there were two gas stations and a tiny pizza place, or what passed for pizza in Utah. There were people—only a handful, but it was a handful that didn't have to die because of Suyolak if we confronted him and whatever else was in that truck farther out.

"The salt of the earth, these people," Robin said with a cheer that made me wonder how many times in his long life he'd chased after death with a smile and an immaculate wardrobe. "Ever made love to a Utah woman? Or man? They actually do taste like salt. I don't know if it's the salt flats or the air, but they're like the very best potato chips. You can't eat just one."

"Does he ever shut up? Damn it, *ever*?" Rafferty looked close to desperate behind Niko's seat.

"Whatever. You've spent two days with him. Try the past three years of your life. Or is it four? It's too traumatizing to remember." I hit the door again as we turned right. "And maybe you should concentrate on why Suyolak isn't trying to do to us what he did to the cops back there."

"He is." Rafferty's face was drawn now that I bothered to take the time to notice, his knuckles white where he clenched the seat beneath him to stay upright during the rough ride. "Just consider me your force field of cold, flu, and goddamn plague repellant and try not to distract me." He closed his eyes, the better to concentrate, I hoped. I didn't have a desire to have my body try to drown itself again. "Particularly you, Goodfellow."

Robin had already opened his mouth for another comment. I didn't have to see him to know that. I only had to know him. He kept quiet, though. I didn't know what diseases pucks could catch, if any, and I knew they were resistant to poison, but he had a heart the same as the rest of us. And it could stop the same as the rest of ours. He could lose his life. The following silence was a sign of the high premium he put on that life. He might be a trickster, but he was up-front with his priorities and I respected that.

I respected his driving even more as we took another turn. I didn't think we took it on two wheels, but there was no way we took it on all four. I knew it the same as I knew Rafferty was keeping Suyolak from inserting invisible fingers into our brains, our blood, our bones, and contaminating them with his touch. I wouldn't call it faith; I'd call it fact, the fact that we were still alive. That made Goodfellow one helluva driver and Rafferty one helluva healer. It also made me tired of sitting on the sideline. That's not who I was, not what I did.

So instead I took a chance, one stupid, reckless chance. It was also one I was lucky to survive, but I didn't care. I didn't think "lucky" at the time, because it was what I was supposed to do, and who I was supposed to *be*, and it felt so damn good that I couldn't have not done it if I'd tried.

Being unable to not do something is a bad sign that should make you think, and think hard, but I didn't. Not then.

Because I was free.

I couldn't make a gate inside the car, but I could build it around myself, and I did. Between one breath and the next, I was on the hood of the truck. I snared one hand on the rim of the windshield wiper well and pulled the Eagle with the other. I felt exhilaration as the wind hit me, as I saw a glimpse of a pale face and silver hair behind the glass, and most of all as I started to pull the trigger. The feeling didn't disappear as the truck slid in a circle to leave the road, and I slid myself. I lost my grip and flew through the air. It could've been nasty, that fall.

Jack and Jill went up the hill. . . . Weren't things broken when they came back down?

But I wasn't Jack. I wasn't going to break. The truck had braked next to a creek bank, the creek rocky and ten feet down. I tumbled through the air toward it and into the second gate I'd made in three seconds. Passing through, I came out on the other side standing in knee-high water. I was about to go through the third gate and back up when the fight came to me.

There was a willow-type tree lining the banks of a creek, many of them, but they were wispy like feathers and didn't block much of my view. I saw the back of the truck burst open, but it wasn't Suyolak who came out. He must've been still trapped in the coffin—one for the home team. The driver, being sapped of life, was still enough of an expert in folklore to know Suyolak could have the cure for his wife, but he could also be the death of the husband if he escaped before the truck made it home. He hadn't opened the coffin. How he planned to negotiate with Suyolak and depend on the bastard to keep his word was his business. Or an impossible dream, because we weren't going to let it happen, no matter the flood of night that poured out of the truck when the doors opened.

I still didn't know what they were. They were as big as werewolves and somewhat similarly shaped, but sharper, leaner, with muzzles as pointed as the end of a sword. They were like foxes . . . if foxes were bigger than Great Danes, black as crows plucking at the eyes of a dead man, and their own eyes—gray. They were gray like mine and Niko's, only paler, but I wasn't in the mood to claim them as kissing cousins.

They slithered out of the truck in waves. I didn't know how many of them managed to fit in there, but they were emaciated, as if they'd run a long way. The truck started moving again while they were still coming out, its tires spinning, churning dirt and grass. It was out of sight in seconds, the same amount of time it took for the creatures, a tsunami of shadows, to cover Niko's replacement car. Several split off from the pack to come for me, vaulting through the trees and down the embankment with a speed that said they weren't only starved; they were ravenous.

Goddamn, this was going to be fun.

They were almost beautiful in their own way. A lot of things that could kill you were. It didn't stop me from shooting the first two in the head, then ripping space and appearing behind them to shoot two more. The four remaining ones hit the water, turned, and leaped back toward me. They weren't cowed by the deaths of three of their own or the one still thrashing in its death throes. They came for me so quickly that I didn't see the surface of the water ripple under their paws. Their bones showed under their black coats, but it didn't mean they were weak. Water didn't curve under them and my eyes could barely follow them—hardly frail; the opposite in fact. Did that make it less fun? Hell, no.

It made it better.

"Come and get me," I said, and traveled again, a fraction of a second before they would've reached me. This time when I appeared I was on the other side of Nik's new car, firing as soon as the world materialized out of silver light. I killed two and injured one, and it was easy. It was so easy that I couldn't believe I hadn't been doing this every time I came across a bad guy or a creature that wanted to eat me. I couldn't believe I hadn't been doing it every damn day just for the on-top-of-the-world, king-of-the-goddamn-universe feeling. It was good—so good, it was simple, and it was effective. It hadn't always been, but it was now and not using it would be practically criminal.

Two more ebony heads turned in unison away from the car and toward me, their eyes reflecting me . . . a distorted, twisted image of me, at least. Or maybe it was a true one . . . and that didn't bother me either. Both of them gave a yowl so high-pitched it could've been responsible for the shattering of the back window behind them, but it wasn't. Catcher got credit for that as he sailed through the glass. He landed on one of them, rode it to the ground, and snapped its neck with his massive jaws. He might have liked beach bunny calendars, playing hangman, and sticking a cold wet nose in your ear just as you fell asleep to see you jump out of your skin, but Catcher was also a Wolf—a born predator, and genes would tell. They always did.

Surprising how easy it was to forget that.

Another Wolf, red like Catcher but a shade lighter, followed him out the window and took down the other . . . whatever it was. It was the first time I'd seen Rafferty in wolf form. On the other side of the car, yet another Wolf, Delilah, had joined the party. I'd thought I'd heard her motorcycle. The driver's side of the car opened and Robin climbed out with sword in hand. "Ördögs. Usually found in Hungary." He ducked with alacrity, gutting the one that sailed over his head.

"But found occasionally these days in certain mountainous regions of the United States. Migration. Immigration. Whatever you wish to call it," Niko finished, at my side so swiftly that I wasn't sure if he'd come after Robin or around the car—probably around. There was already blood on his sword. He'd disdained my borrowed gun for close combat. "They have a kinship with the Rom, at least the Rom who walk the darker paths—like Suyolak. They definitely don't have a connection with healers. Suyolak must've called for them, gathered them up when they caught up to him." He swiveled and let gravity impale one on his katana. "And they came a long way, considering how malnourished they are."

"Run." The word was garbled, almost too mangled to understand. It came from atop the car where one Ördög crouched, teeth bared. It had only four of them, like the upper and lower fangs of a cobra—curving and longer than my hand. "He promised feast that never ends. Death that never stops. We run. No sleep. No eat." Its eyes focused on Niko and me. "Eat now."

In our world, it was sometimes hard to tell who was good and who was bad, and wasn't it a matter of perspective anyway? Either way, good or bad, right or wrong, it was always easy to tell who was hungry. Hungry was always the wrong side, and when they spoke up to yell you they were hungry and going to eat you, it made it even easier to spot them.

I could've dived to one side or tried for a shot before the chatty one jumped from the roof. The Ördög was less than six feet away . . . but where was the entertainment in that? Niko's hand locked on to my shoulder almost before I had a chance to finish the thought. "Cal," he said, his voice absolute. He didn't add "don't," because he knew I would listen to him. I always did. He was my brother. He'd protected me my whole life. He was one of the best fighters, if not the very best, that I'd ever seen and the best strategetician. He . . .

Shit. It didn't matter if he was the best. It didn't matter that he was my brother.

For the first time ever, I didn't listen.

Don't get me wrong. I'd on occasion deliberately not done what he thought, and strongly emphasized, was best, but I'd always weighed the pros and cons. In those cases I'd known I probably wasn't doing the safe thing but the necessary thing. And although I'd done those things, I'd listened to him first. Not this time. This time I wasn't listening to my gut either. I was listening to the need. It was talking louder than Nik and louder than the rest of me.

I brushed his hand off and traveled on top of the car, the gray light dappling the air around me, inches from the Ördög's muzzle. "Boo," I said with soft cheer. "Here's the gravy train." As much as I loved my guns, I didn't use the Eagle this time. I jumped it at the same time it jumped me. We rolled off the car and hit the ground hard, me on the bottom and the Ördög on top of me with its teeth snapping at my throat. I laughed. It only kept getting more and more entertaining . . . more like a game. "Bad dog," I whispered with a smile. Then I put my hand on its throat, called a gate around it, and passed my glowing hand through flesh and bone. Instantly dead, the light, almost silver eyes darkened to a gray the same as mine. I used my knee to fling the body off. The head, however, landed on my chest and that reflection I'd seen of myself earlier, I saw again in the mirror-shine that began to dull with every passing second. I saw my face, Auphe pale since birth with Sophia's eyes, except for a spark of red in them. I blinked and it was gone; only the fog of death remained in the Ördög's gaze.

I'd imagined it, because . . . because there was no other explanation. I didn't see it. It wasn't there and nothing was ruining the high I had going on. I jumped to my feet, my hand covered with Ördög blood. It was red, darker than human blood, but close. I'd seen enough of both or maybe I hadn't. The feel of it, slippery and warm against my skin... it was nice. It was more than nice. I looked for more Ördögs to kill. They were hungry, but so was I. It was a different kind of hunger—a hunger for more battle, more traveling, more killing, but justified killing. Self-defense. Defense of others. Whatever. Another wave of euphoria passed through me, and concepts like justification disintegrated beneath it. I only wanted more targets, more traveling, more of this sensation, and I didn't care how I got it.

But there were no more. Niko, Robin, the cousins, and Delilah had taken the rest of them. Black bodies littered the grass and dotted the water of the creek below, but it wasn't right; it wasn't enough. Then I saw her, frozen on the other side of the creek—a doe, wide black eyes surrounded by a ring of white. Mule deer, whitetail; I didn't know which was in Utah. Nik would know. Nik always . . .

That thought disappeared as the muscles under the tan hide bunched, and the deer swiveled to bound away. She shouldn't have done that. No. She shouldn't have tried to run. They should never run.

You chase what runs.

It was the rule, the law, the way life was.

You chase what runs. You catch what runs. You kill what runs.

Always.

It wasn't too clear after that. There were flashes of light, tears in reality, and there was food. Warm food that slid down my throat to heat my stomach. There was company: a red male wolf on one side of me, teeth ripping at a white and tan neck; a white female wolf on the other side, muzzle deep in a tan belly. She lifted her head and grinned at me, her white fur stained red up to her amber eyes. Good. All good. Friends and food, and maybe later those friends could become food. Why should there be a difference between the two?

Fun. It was all fun. Anything I wanted to do, *everything* I wanted to do, and no one could stop this feeling.

No one could stop me.

"Cal."

I turned to look over my shoulder at the more-than-familiar voice and reality smacked me in the face—that and a hard fist. It took it all away: the dark joy, the kick-ass fun, the utter invincibility. . .

Consciousness.

There was movement, a subtle rocking. Cool air. The smell of old plastic, old carpet, old foam. There were also wolves, a human, something green and fresh like a forest . . . a puck. All familiar; it was comforting, like all my naps, and I wallowed in it, which was also something I did with most of my naps.

"Hades damn us all. There's a five-car pileup ahead. It'll be hours before we make it past that. Suyolak's version of an orgy. Death and destruction. He's no doubt postcoital as we speak."

Goodfellow. No way that was anyone but Goodfellow . . . wishing he were postcoital, I was sure, in a hazy way, only in the more traditional sense. No death and destruction for him there. Not like Suyolak. It was the last that had me clenching my fingers into fists, shaking my head, and trying to open my eyes.

"He's waking up." And Rafferty. That was Rafferty. He didn't sound too happy.

"It's about time. It's been nearly an hour. I didn't hit him hard enough for that. You could've woken him." Nik . . . he sounded even less happy.

"I could've, but I damn well can guarantee you wouldn't have liked it. Cal trying to gut us like he did that deer. Trust me, the quiet time did him some good. Now he is Cal again . . . mostly. A half hour ago he'd have been an Auphe trying to chew through your face."

"Shut the fuck up." Every word was a separate dagger of ice. If Nik cut the air with those words, it wouldn't have surprised me.

It was hard, waking up. Harder than waking up from most naps, but what I was hearing kept me trying. Pushing. Not for me; for Nik. To be there for my brother. What Rafferty said about me didn't mean anything. I didn't feel it, but I felt my brother's anger, and if Niko was angry and allowing it to show, then the situation was bad—definitely bad enough to cut through the fuzziness that surrounded me.

I managed to crack my eyelids and saw a slice of dark blond hair. Niko. That was normal, seeing him when I opened my eyes. He was the one who usually kicked my butt out of bed when I was slacking, which was almost always. Most mornings he was the first thing I saw, or I would feel him firmly rapping the top of my head with my ringing alarm clock.

Then I noticed the hand on my shoulder and the one on my leg, just above my knee. The pressure on my shoulder I recognized—I'd felt it all my life. The weight on my leg I didn't. Or maybe I did—a distant memory of that same hand burning against a bleeding gash in my abdomen. Years ago. The hand wasn't burning now, but I could still feel the power in it. Rafferty.

"Cal, are you awake?"

I managed to open my eyes nearly all the way. "Nik?"

I saw his face then, not just a slash of hair. I saw the somber scrutiny, the tense line of his jaw. "It's me. You're safe, Cal. I swear it." I hadn't thought I wasn't, but if I had, I would've believed him. Nik never lied to me. But he didn't look himself: calm . . . in control. The anger I'd heard was gone, but the longer he met my eyes, the more bleak his own looked. He looked grim and a little lost, and that wasn't him. It simply wasn't and why would he . . .

What had Rafferty said again? About my waking up . . . Auphe?

Then I remembered—all of it. Remembered it and felt it. The truck, the traveling, the Ördögs, the poor goddamn deer. I'd killed it or helped kill it and I'd eaten part of it. I could still feel the heaviness of it in my stomach. I should've been nauseated, but I wasn't. I should've gagged and been sick, but my body wanted it—the raw meat—and it wasn't going to let it go. I swallowed hard. No wonder Niko looked like he did. No wonder he reassured me I was safe.

But was he? Was anyone around me?

"I fucked up," I said hoarsely.

"You fucked up," my brother confirmed, his own voice impassive—not accusing, but not letting me off the hook either. Trusting in my word earlier hadn't worked out for either of us, but his hand on my shoulder gripped harder. Whatever I'd done, we were family, and for Niko, that would never change.

I was leaning against his chest, my legs bent at the knees with my lower legs behind the driver's seat and in the floorboards. And the hand on my leg was Rafferty's. It wasn't moral support either. If I tried to leave—to travel—Rafferty would stop me, temporarily or permanently. I wouldn't want to guess which call he'd make, although, if he were smart, he'd pick the second choice, which I suppose told me the answer after all.

Because Rafferty was smart.

I tried to sit up. I could see now that I was in the backseat of the car with Niko and Rafferty. Goodfellow was still driving or, more accurately, sitting behind the wheel of a parked car. He'd been trying to catch up to the truck, but thanks to the wreck and Suyolak who had caused it, that wasn't going to happen. Catcher was curled up asleep in the passenger seat. He was knocked out, the same as I'd been knocked out, but a little more gently, by a healer, not a fist—or then again, maybe not. He might only be sleeping off a full belly. It didn't have to be one of his episodes. He could've smelled the blood when I hit the deer and joined in. The hunt and the kill was a natural thing to Wolves, the most natural of things.

Knocked-out or sleeping, he looked better than I felt. I rubbed my jaw. It didn't feel broken, but it definitely was bruised. "I'm sorry," Niko said. "Rafferty was occupied." Joining the deer buffet or putting out Catcher, one of the two. I didn't ask. "And I didn't have time to spare with your ability to disappear whenever you wish."

It was stated plainly; again, not an accusation, but I winced anyway. Salome, who hadn't shown up in the fight . . . coughing up a resin ball instead most likely . . . was on the dash, soaking up the sun. She lifted her head, stared at me, and hissed. A mummy cat that killed anything that moved didn't like the looks of me. That couldn't be the best of things.

I narrowed my eyes at her and she flashed under the passenger seat, fast as a water moccasin in muddy water. Then I caught sight of myself in the rearview mirror. No wonder Niko was so somber when looking into what should've been a reflection of his own eyes but wasn't. Instead, I saw red in the mirror—in the irises of my eyes, minute flecks of molten lava in the gray. Auphe eyes were that color red—had been that color.

And were still that color.

Because I was still here, wasn't I? I was still goddamn here. What Suyolak had threatened to do to me, I'd done to myself.

Niko's hand hadn't left my shoulder. "Can you turn it off, Rafferty? The traveling? It's what's done this." He didn't ask me, either because he didn't think I was in my right mind—and he could've been correct—or because I was so frozen that I couldn't ask for myself. The why of it didn't matter. He asked. He wasn't wrong either.

Before the traveling had gotten so easy, before it made me feel so damn good, I'd been myself. Being me had never been worth any prizes, but I hadn't been killing animals and eating their raw meat and considering rather happily doing the same to my fellow road-trippers.

I hadn't been in my right mind for a while now and never noticed. Or worse yet, I had noticed, but I'd liked it too much to wonder why life had gotten so much better, things so much easier.

I'd seen those people before, all my life, the jackasses. Everyone had seen them walking around, wearing those idiotic T-shirts—I'M WITH STUPID with an arrow pointed sideways. If life issued those routinely when needed, Rafferty and Niko would both be wearing I'M WITH SCREWED with the arrows pointed directly at me.

Really, really so damn screwed and it was my fault, all of it.

Rafferty didn't close his eyes as I'd seen him do once or twice when concentrating on a patient. He'd had plenty of time to examine my inner workings while I was out. "No."

"You're absolutely sure?" Niko persisted, his calm still seeping away bit by bit, and Suyolak wasn't responsible this time. I was.

"The only way to turn it off is to turn Cal off, and I

don't think you want that." Rafferty's hand was warm now, close to uncomfortably so.

Niko's grip tightened yet again, the joint creaking under it. "It's in his genes," the healer continued. "And the thing about Auphe genes? They're dominant over human genes. Hell, no matter what they'd managed to breed with, they would've been dominant. They were the first sentient creatures on this world. The *first*, and, in a way, the best—at least at what they did: kill. Up until now you said Cal had traveled rarely and with side effects: vomiting, dizziness, bleeding. But then it had gotten easier, right? That means the Auphe part of Cal's genes that had been dormant became active. And there's more Auphe in Cal than just traveling." He moved his gaze from Niko to me. "You might look human on the outside, Cal—mostly—but on the inside, that's not the case. In your blood, in your genes, you're something new and something old, and something completely unlike anything on this earth. Your traveling did that. It was a biological initiative . . . or for you, a trap. The more you traveled, the more serotonin your brain released, and the better you felt—a feel-good loop. A happy pill a hundred times better than any pharmacy could dole out. And now here you are." His hand wasn't letting me go.

Niko had said that back at the beginning of this . . . at Abelia's RV, when I'd opened a gate. When I'd said I could control it—control myself. When he'd also said I was an adult with adult consequences.

And here I was, Rafferty had said.

Here I was, all right, and it was a place way beyond meditation's ability to help, although Niko had done his best there. If I'd done it more often, been better at it, it might have worked. Then again, from the way Rafferty talked, it was all a matter of time. It had been since I'd been made. Each time I thought I was free of the Auphe, they came back closer than ever. Being one was as close as it came: not half, not part, but a card-carrying last member of a dead race. I wasn't going to go through this again. I wasn't going to agonize over it. I was through with bullshit. I knew what I was; I'd known all along despite a crapload of denial. It was time to pay the piper and no damn whining when I did.

Time to face those adult consequences.

I'd gotten upright with Nik's grip on my shoulder and the other hand helping me. I didn't try to move my legs. I didn't know how Rafferty would take that. My shoulder was now against my brother's and I felt him tense when I said it—without shame, without rejection, with nothing but acceptance of the alcoholic reaching rock bottom. "I'm Auphe. I'm not human. Not part-time. Not even on the fucking weekends. I'm Auphe."

"No," Nik refuted with instant sharpness, as he always had. He never gave up, but this time was different. He was going to have to, for both of us.

"No," Rafferty echoed, still focused on me. "You're not Auphe. But you're right, you're not human either and thinking you are while using powers that aren't is only going to get you dead or someone else dead. Maybe a lot of someones. All the wishing in the world isn't going to change that, and I can't turn off the Auphe part of your genes." He'd said earlier that he'd never manipulate genes again after what he'd done to Catcher. I didn't blame him. I could end up a lot worse than Catcher with the possibilities riding in my genetics. "I can't turn off the powers that go with them either," he went on, "but I can make it very unpleasant for you to use them. I can take the feel-good away, and you might, no promises, but you might stay where you are now. The Auphe in you won't progress. Or," he finished matter-of-factly, "I can end your life now. Your choice. But I won't let another possible Auphe, the last Auphe, loose on the world. Suyolak can't make you all Auphe like he threatened, but he doesn't have to. There's enough potential in you to be walking, talking murder incarnate without any of his help."

Rafferty was right and it absolutely did not matter. He might as well have been talking to the wind. Niko had kept my SIG while I was unconscious. The three of us in the back of the car, me between them, it made blades awkward, although not impossible for my brother. Nothing regarding a blade was impossible for him, but this statement was for me and he used my weapon for it. He had the muzzle of the automatic pressed hard against Rafferty's forehead with an inescapable speed. Caesar, Genghis, Attila, Alexander… I'd said it before: They all fell in Niko's shadow.

"The only life ending will be yours," he said flatly.

He had what looked like three pounds of pressure on a trigger that took a little less than four. Rafferty could kill him, stop his heart, explode a vessel in his brain, but the death spasm would take the healer along for the ride—all over an Auphe. A healer wasn't dying because of that. And there was no damn way my brother was dying because of me.

I put my hand on Nik's wrist and squeezed. He didn't look at me and I didn't expect him to. In battle, you kept your eyes on the enemy. I only had to get him to see that Rafferty wasn't the enemy. "It's okay, Cyrano. Adult consequences, remember? I'll let him fix me."

Fix me. . . .

He couldn't fix me, though, could he? He could only cripple me—the bastard who imagined I needed fixing at all. I'd accepted who I was, hadn't I?

Maybe I even liked who I was. I did like being able at work to scan the bar and make someone hate me or fear me with a single look. Wasn't that better than being ashamed as I had been in the past? Wasn't having others fear me better than fearing myself? Rafferty wanted to take the feel-good away. The feel-good was called that for a reason. It was the rush that made life better ... more than better. Made it what people wished for when they were kids: perfect, everything you wanted, everything you needed, and you were ruler of it all. King of the mountain. King of all the mountains and everything that lay between them. Nothing could touch that feeling. No one could take it away either—not if you didn't let them.

Not if you killed them first.

Ripped them apart. Eviscerated them and spread their guts for all to see.

Wouldn't that be something? Wouldn't that be better than the fanciest of paintings?

I could kill them all, saving my brother for last, to show him all the training in the world couldn't beat what you were born with. Even Niko couldn't kill me if he couldn't catch me, and no one could catch me when I started traveling. I could open a gate and come out behind him or above him and put a bullet in his head. It would be easy. I could see it: the head that had shared the same pillow with me when I was five; the bullet hitting, the blood staining his blond hair. I could see ... I could see....

The head that had shared my pillow then, to watch over me, because he knew before I did that monsters existed.

Monsters like me.

God. Rock bottom, I'd thought before.

This was rock bottom: thinking, *relishing* accomplishing what I'd die to prevent anyone else from doing to my brother. And if that anyone else also happened to be me, that was fine. I would die first. Fucking *die*.

"Now," I said in a voice not mine, not remotely close, "Nik, let him do it now." Or someone in this car would die. I only hoped it would be the right person. Rafferty would be reading my intent to vanish, because part of me was fighting hard to run, the part of me that had to be tamed so I could live. If it won, it would also lose. I hoped to God Rafferty made sure of that. But then Rafferty and Niko would follow me within a fraction of a second, Nik's finger still tense on the trigger.

"Now," I repeated, although it was so goddamn difficult to say.

Why was the sane option unbelievably hard to hold on to?

Then again, who wielded the almighty right to define sane?

Them? The weak? Why not me?

"Hurry the fuck up." Not only was it not my voice; it was not a human voice at all.

Niko slowly let the gun fall while Rafferty put that scorching hand on my head and I learned what brain surgery without anesthesia was all about. Later Nik told me the brain actually can't feel pain, only the nerves and muscles around it. I took it on faith that that was true for human brains, but for a part-Auphe brain, some Mayo Clinic geek needed to do some serious research in that area, because there was pain. There was more than pain. I could *feel* Rafferty in there, a thousand scalpels slicing every cell, a hundred, a thousand, a million times. It was pain beyond vision or breath, beyond hope of an end to it, beyond hope of anything but an eternal hell of agony. I wished that same million times that he'd killed me instead. It was never answered except that each time I made that wish, I felt another piece of me slashed open. It was minutes, in reality, I guessed, but it felt like years—thousands and thousands of years.

That made it easy to understand that when I could see again, I saw my hands around the healer's throat doing my best to strangle the life out of him. My best was good. If I hadn't been weak from that pain, I'd have succeeded. Rafferty wasn't doing anything to stop me. Niko reached past me to peel my fingers from the purpling flesh.

"Sorry," Rafferty apologized, massaging his throat. "You said hurry and I needed to. If I'd had more time, I wouldn't have let you feel that. But you were—" He coughed harshly and substituted a rough hand movement aiming toward the sky. He was right. I'd been more than halfway gone in intent and a second away from the deed.

My head still throbbed without mercy and I methodically pounded it against the front bench seat. It was that kind of pain, the sort that makes you want to knock yourself out to escape it. Hitting rock bottom, acceptance of your addiction; officially those two concepts sucked. Doing the right thing also sucked. I might think differently later, when this passed, but at the moment I wasn't counting on it. Niko's hand rested on my back and that should've made it better. He was Nik again, my brother—not just one more victim in the crosshairs.

I hit my head harder. This time I wanted the pain. I deserved it. Having that thought about the only family I had, the only one who'd given a damn about me for most of my life, I deserved pain. Being crazy was no excuse. Going Auphe was no excuse. There was no goddamn excuse for it. It was *Nik*.

Rafferty should've killed me.

But he hadn't, and I had to deal. Niko had done everything possible to save me. I'd let him down once—shit, more times than I could count. But right now, I was going to step up to the plate. Be a fucking man, even if genetically I didn't come close. I heard Robin move in the front seat to lay one on the back of my neck. It felt like ice through my sweat-soaked hair. My chest hurt too, my heart beating so fast I was surprised it hadn't torn its way through my chest. Yeah, good old rock bottom. Wasn't one of the twelve steps to recovery accepting a higher power? I didn't believe in a higher power. I wished I did so I could hope one day to kick its ass for this.

"It's all right, kid. It'll pass." He was probably guessing, but I appreciated Goodfellow's effort. He'd been my friend for a while now, as hard as it had been to admit I could have friends—that I could trust someone besides my brother. But Robin was a friend, and a friend would lie to you when the truth wasn't worth hearing.

"This is it," Rafferty said quietly, words raw from a throat he felt didn't deserve to be healed, else he would've done it. No bedside manner, but he'd been better off with a great bedside manner and a little less conscience. "It's called serotonin syndrome. A little serotonin makes you feel good—like you did before—but a whole lot of it will kill you. Every time you travel, this is what you get—a shitload of serotonin your body isn't meant to handle. The headache is from your blood pressure skyrocketing. A human might stroke out, but your human-Auphe brain can take it. The chest pain is from the tachycardia, your heart working triple time. Your body temperature will go up too, hundred two, hundred three. That's from one jump. You make another one, you get another serotonin dump, and the blood pressure goes even higher, which your brain may *not* be able to handle. Your heart beats faster; your temperature goes up to one oh four or six. All of that has a good chance of killing you. A third jump . . ." He stopped before completing that sentence. Complete it he did though, sounding anything but proud. "A third jump means no more Cal."

And that meant no more Auphe.

Okay then—problem solved. I couldn't travel enough again to remotely think black and bloody Auphe thoughts about killing my brother. I'd die first, and that was fucking peachy by me. I stopped beating my head against the seat, though, and suffered through the headache. Goodfellow's hand disappeared from my neck and I heard the gurgle of water. A moment later a bottle of water was slowly poured over my head and neck. It felt good, better than good, as my skin cooled beneath it. Taking a breath and shoving the pain down, I straightened, and what did I face?

The mirror again.

Things hadn't changed. No, that wasn't entirely true. The gray was still shot here and there with dark scarlet. The tiny flecks weren't the blazing fire glow of Auphe eyes, though, but they didn't belong in your ordinary human eyes either. Yeah, this was good. Before, there were some that could smell the monster on me. Now everyone in the supernatural world could *see* it. "What the hell," I muttered, wringing my hair out as I eased back against the seat behind me. I covered my eyes with my other hand. "Great opportunity to get a few pairs of dark sunglasses. Expensive. People will think I work for the government or the Sunglass Hut." I felt in my jacket pocket for my old pair. Nothing. Naturally. No sunglasses. No cheerful Cal. No anything. Auphe blood had made me a happy guy for a while, a short while, but it had felt nice. I should've known that was way too good to be true. No nice for Cal Leandros. It didn't mean I didn't miss the feeling—lie that it had been. But it didn't mean I was going to let myself dwell on it either.

Dwelling on what I'd thought about doing to Nik was a different story. Getting me to open another gate was going to take one goddamn compelling reason or an act of God, and since I didn't believe in the latter . . .

It wasn't worth the risk, a Rafferty-engineered bomb in my brain or not.

"No bother, Niko," Robin said. "I have several." Before my brother could pass me his, I felt a pair folded into my hand. "Not quite a thousand dollars, so bang them up all you wish. I probably have twenty in my glove compartment."

I slipped them on before opening my eyes. "I'm sorry." The apology was for Niko. He'd trusted me and I'd blown it. Massively. Or my genes had. It didn't matter where the blame fell. It served me right that now I could see what I'd done each time I looked in a mirror. I used to have a mirror phobia not that long ago—with good reason. I wasn't going to let myself get away with that this time. No, this time and from now on I faced all that potential Rafferty had labeled me with.

Something new, something old, and something entirely unlike anything on this earth, Rafferty had said.

That wasn't a lonely feeling. Not at all.

13

Cal

"You not talk to your brother."

The accident, the ambulances, the police cars, the fire trucks; it was all still keeping us from moving. Rafferty couldn't knock out fifty-some people, so we could drive around and follow the now-petless Suyolak. Or he could have if it hadn't been for the energy he'd expended on me—I didn't know and I wasn't going to ask. I'd contributed enough drama to the situation. I wasn't looking to add any more by making Rafferty feel guilty if he had run low on juice.

I was sitting on the edge of the highway among dirt and tufts of dusty grass here and there. I had my knees up, my arms folded across them, as I looked across the highway at nothing. Figuratively. Literally. Both applied. Although Utah wasn't the flat-ass empty state I'd imagined. It would've been more appropriate if it were, because I was feeling flat and empty myself.

Delilah sat beside me, careless of her white leathers. "You not talk to me either?" She could've gone around the mess, blocking both sides of the highway on her Harley, but cops would've chased her. They wouldn't have

caught her, but then if she caught up with Suyolak, there
wasn't much she could do but die.

It was that kind of day.

No, I wasn't talking to Delilah either. I wasn't talking to anyone. There wasn't much point. I was accepting. Accepting took quiet time. Quiet time let you avoid
thinking, if you were exceptional in that area, and I was.
It wasn't denial; it was layaway recognition. I'd think
about it about the same time I paid off Niko's Christmas
present. I was comfortable with that. Five months was
a good time frame . . . for presents and self-realization
and thoughts of blowing away a chunk of your brother's
head.

Delilah didn't cooperate with my plan and Christmas
went out the window. "Why the sulk?" She slid her fingers through my drying hair. "Things are no different
now. You are Cal as you've always been Cal." She in-
haled my scent before admitting, "Perhaps some different, but same ingredients." She smiled at her own joke
and tilted her head to kiss my neck.

The same ingredients. Yeah. Delilah was sharp and
she wasn't wrong. But someone had taken the cookbook
and rewritten a few amounts. A cup here, a cup there.
I'd always said I was monster; I'd always said I was half
human, half Auphe. But deep down I'd always wished
I were more human than Auphe. I'd known better, but
I'd wished anyway. All that dominant crap Rafferty had
been talking about; I hadn't known about that. I only
knew what I felt and what I hoped. It didn't matter,
though, the past, because it was the now that was important. Now I knew. I wasn't human with some Auphe.
I wasn't even a half-and-half hybrid. I was Auphe. If you
looked hard enough, you might find a trace of human, a
thin ribbon raveling through me, but when it came right
down to it, I was Auphe or one step away from it. Rafferty had said it. He hoped he'd stopped the progression.

I wasn't much on hope these days. Reality: It was the only way to fly.

I was Auphe now and I'd only be more Auphe as the years passed. Stick a party hat on me and celebrate the splendor of the homicidal in its larval stage. I turned to look at Delilah as her lips left my neck. I thought of how I'd considered eating her at the deer carcass when I'd been more outside my mind than in it. I wondered how long it would be before I had the same thought, but calmly, rationally? Not driven to it by running prey, the smell of blood, or the Auphe part of me fighting hard against Rafferty's building that internal wall. Thinking of eating her just . . . hell, just because.

She reached up and took off my sunglasses. "Ah, I was wrong. You are different. But different, it is not so bad."

"If I kill and eat you, you might think again," I said without emotion. "Or eat, then kill. Either or."

Her smile was both seductive and wistful as this time she kissed my neck again and then licked it. "Now you think like Kin. You should not fight it."

As she always had in the past, I guessed, and probably more so when the Kin found out about us. Another thing I'd known, but denied . . . or pretended to deny— before and after the Kin. I'd told myself that every night I'd spent with her was a carnivorous toss of the coin, but it was worth it. She wanted me, she liked me, and therefore it was worth it. Remarkably I still thought it was worth it, although it did make me respect myself a little less, which I would've thought hard to accomplish at that point. But life loved nothing better than proving my ass wrong. I took back the glasses and replaced them. Hell, she was a predator. I was a predator. Genes. Who knew how long it would be before I started tossing that bright and shiny coin soon, too, and one day . . .

Deer weren't the only ones who would run. How long

it would be before I could stop myself from the chase was anyone's guess.

"Go away." I resumed staring at nothing. She snorted at what she considered my brooding. Killers killed; predators ate; both played with their food. Why question that? Better to be who you were and not to look back. Kin, they were something all right, but I was hardly going to be a hypocrite and point fingers. I didn't have that right. As I sat unmoving, Delilah gave an exasperated sigh, then cupped my head and kissed me on the mouth this time. I tasted deer blood. I just didn't know if it was from her or from me.

It tasted good.

"Mopey cub, cheer up." She gained her feet in one graceful movement, trailed her fingers along my jaw, and disappeared in the milling people bitching about the delay and the sun and the dust. I was assuming it had to be hot. The lingering fever still left me feeling slightly chilled, enough so that when the fur-covered body leaned against my right side, I didn't mind the warmth.

I hadn't talked to Nik, Robin, or Rafferty after the change in me that had taken place had really hit me. I'd taken the sunglasses and gone quiet—the whole not-thinking thing that I was striving for. I'd only talked to Delilah to make her leave me alone, although I knew Niko would be back without a doubt. Catcher though— Catcher wouldn't talk. He wouldn't try to tell me everything would be fine, which would remind me that, nope, it wouldn't be. He wouldn't be supportive when he should be punching me in the face for becoming an addicted asshole. He wouldn't say I was still me—not that "me" had ever been that much to brag about to begin with. He would only sit there, a silent, wordless comfort.

The laptop dropped onto the ground in front of me.

Well, shit.

When I refused to drop my head and read the screen, teeth nipped me hard over the ribs. I hissed, glared at the wolf, and then read what was typed on the screen. He'd used the caps lock again, either to get his point across or because he didn't believe much in my reading skills.

SUCKS TO BE ONE OF A KIND.

He rested his chin on my shoulder, sneezed at the dust, and waited.

"Yeah," I commented after a long pause. "It does. Good Wolf or bad Auphe, it sucks to be the only one." Great. First Delilah, then him. They both had me pulling shit out of layaway early.

This time he nipped my shoulder before retrieving from the dirt the ink pen he'd dropped to bite me. He typed: *ALL AUPHE WERE BORN BAD. YOU ARE NOT ALL AUPHE. YOU HAVE A CHOICE. YOU CAN BE GOOD.* He considered, then backspaced, deleting the *GOOD* and changing it to *NOT SO BAD.* At least he was honest, the fur ball.

Then he punctuated the sentence. Joy. "I didn't know there was an emoticon for a dog humping another dog. Thanks for sharing." I took off the glasses and rubbed my eyes.

There was more typing. I glanced at the screen. At least now that he was sure that he had my attention, he'd stopped with the capitalization. Cal smart monster. Cal can read. Good for me.

Knock knock

"You've got to be kidding me," I groaned.

Knock knock, he persisted, growling around the pen.

"Okay, just to shut you up: Who's there?" I gave in. Why not? At this point, it was almost ludicrous. An Auphe being counseled by a butt-sniffing pound reject.

No one. The Auphe ate everyone in the house.

"You son of a bitch," I growled.

Knock knock. This time he didn't wait for the "Who's there?" *Twenty cocker spaniels the Auphe is going to skin to make a pimp coat.*

"Seriously, quit it or I will shoot your mangy ass."

Knock knock

God, he was as relentless as Niko. "Last one," I warned. "Last one or your ass is grass." The threat didn't hold much weight when it was followed with "Who's there?" I went on, resigned.

You, and what happens behind the door is up to you.

He was smart and he was right, but my decision making had never been among the very best. Not as disastrous as the sinking of the *Titanic* was what I was usually shooting for in final outcomes, but I could try to do better. If Catcher could deal with being stuck being half of what he once was, I could deal with being more than I wanted to be. For a while. As long as my genes would let me. Next to Catcher, I'd be a complete jackass if I didn't at least try to do that much.

"He's a wise person." Niko crouched on the other side of me. "You should listen to him. If you won't listen to me."

I closed the laptop and said to Catcher, "Scoot, Scooby." The wolf made a sound halfway between a growl and a grunt, seized the computer in his teeth, and trotted off. I brushed dust idly off my jeans. It was just something to do. I was sitting in the stuff. I wasn't coming clean. "I always listen to you, Cyrano," I said, still uselessly rubbing at the dirt—my brand-new hobby, "except when I ate Bambi's mom, and as I'd rather not mentally relive that, can we skip over it if I promise not to make any more exceptions in the future?"

He didn't look at me, and I didn't mind saying that scared the shit out of me more than the thought of being Auphe. Nik was always there for me. When I was a kid, if bullies picked on me, he was there . . . usually to pull me off the bullies' backs as I tried to strangle them with my backpack strap, but he was there. He was there to stand between me and a scotch-bottle-throwing Sophia; there when the Auphe took me—just too busy not burning to death to be able to do anything about it, but he was still there when I came back psychotic as hell—temporarily psychotic, but still no damn picnic. And when the Auphe took me again, that time he did get me back, and there was never a time in my life he wouldn't meet my eyes. But my eyes were different now, weren't they? They were the only physical feature we shared in common and now we didn't even have that.

He continued to look at the ground, braid of hair over his shoulder and lying on his chest, as he sketched a few letters in the gritty dirt. *Fratres*. "Do you know what that means?" He didn't wait for my answer, although I actually had one that time. "It means brothers. The plural of the Latin word for brother. It's part of that tattoo around your arm. At least they spelled that word correctly. We'll discuss sterility of instruments, hepatitis, and the ablative case of Latin later." Now he looked at me, amusement layered over something deeper and darker. "Yes, you have 'brothers-in-arm' tattooed around your biceps instead of 'brothers-in-arms,' but as always, it's the thought that counts."

Before I could groan at my . . . no, the tattoo parlor's stupidity . . . Nik gripped that same tattooed arm. "I'm kidding. *Fratres-in-armis* is correct. Although you should have me vet all future tattoos in foreign or dead languages. Just in case." His grip tightened as that deeper and darker became more so. "We're brothers, Cal. We always will be. I don't care if you grow fur like Catcher and hunt down and eat a deer every night. Six months ago I thought you died. This is nothing compared to that. I don't care about your Auphe genes, and no matter what you do, no matter *what*," he emphasized, "you will always be my brother."

That was a big promise to keep, especially in the face of so many things. "Mayhem, violence . . . murder?" I asked quietly. "If I try to do those things? If I try to do them to you?"

"You already know the answer to that."

I did. Real brothers, true brothers, stood by each other—even if it came to a Butch and Sundance moment. If there came a time that, like Catcher, I wasn't myself and never would be again, if Nik had to be my combination Butch and Bolivian army, there was no one I would rather be the one to do it. I hadn't wanted to talk to him earlier because I'd failed him. I often did and he more than often denied it. Sometimes I thought if I hadn't been born, I still would've found a way to let him down. Sounds impossible, but I would've found a way to do it. Been incarnated as a cranky Chihuahua and mauled his ankle. Who knows? But if I had faith in anything besides my brother, I had faith in that. Niko believed in karma and I had bad karma stamped on my ass from the day I was born; yet I'd gotten nothing but the good kind in the form of my brother. It was hardly fair to him or his life, but incredibly good luck for me and my fucked-up one. I would be an ungrateful bastard to spit on it, although it would be the right thing to do, the noble thing, the Niko thing. And yet Niko himself would never let me. He never had before.

And he thought I had survival issues.

"Brothers." I held out my hand and he gripped that instead of my arm. "But if you had any damn sense, you'd kick my butt off a ten-story building."

"Brothers," he reaffirmed. "And I know, but smothering you with your pillow would be less messy. You know I despise messy." Behind the joke, he'd answered me in all seriousness. For the first time I thought he did actually know and wasn't in denial about who or what I really was; yet that knowing still didn't make a difference to him.

Hell, Niko was as screwed up as I was.

It was a revelation, but it didn't change the fact that it was also a moving moment, doubly so when a foot slammed into my ribs, moving me over and against Nik. "This? This is why I give you the money that keeps starvation from our door? So you can sit in the dirt like a worthless beggar, the soulless monster and his clan traitor of a *bar*?" I'd picked up by now that *bar* was brother, and I also discovered an evil, vicious old woman could swing a mean old-lady shoe. Her foot was the size of a child's, but it had the feel of a three-hundred-pound football player's size thirteen . . . with a pointy heel.

An arm came over me and across my chest to hold me back. Niko knew before I did myself that I was going for Abelia-Roo and I couldn't blame it on the Auphe. I could've been human to the last cell, with ancestors who came over on the damn *Mayflower*, squatted on Plymouth Rock having tea and biscuits, and never saw a cute little fairy under a cabbage leaf, much less screwed a monster, and I would've felt the same: homicidal. She was calling Nik a traitor, when he'd almost died because of her? That took balls and if she'd been a man, I would've relieved her of them.

"We wait and we wait, because of you. Suyolak causes this." She waved an arm at what was left of the wreck down the interstate. "We hire you to work, and work means you find ways around Suyolak's machinations." Dusty black and purple skirts rustled as she aimed another kick.

Niko caught her foot with his spare hand, which was smart. If I had caught it, I would've turned it into a paperweight and she could've beat her next subcontractors with the stump that was left. "Attracting the attention of the authorities will only slow us down and give Suyolak more time to pull ahead of us. Also the fact that I won't let my brother take your foot home as a souvenir doesn't mean I won't pick up your eighty pounds of venom-spewing ancient body and stuff you back in that eye-searing RV from Easter Egg Hell. Now go." He released her foot. "And reexamine your knowledge of souls. Those without aren't equipped to make judgments about the status of others."

She hissed in a way that made any monster, including an Auphe, seem like an amateur. I was too hard on myself, because she gave me a run for my money and then some. Strangely enough, it made me feel a little better—all human and worse than ninety-nine percent of the monsters I'd run across. Skirts swirling, she turned, less than five feet tall, but that didn't make a difference. When she moved back down the highway, she was a miniature tornado of pure spite.

"Plague of the World and all," I said, getting to my feet, "is Suyolak honestly that bad?"

Niko was already up. "Next to her, maybe not, but we're not comparing apples and oranges. We're comparing black widows and black mambas. Both can make you wish you were dead. Now let's rid the world of at least half of that combination."

This time Rafferty drove. Any one of us would've had to fight him for the wheel. We were close, he said. As a wolf or Wolf on the scent, he would know. As a healer, he knew absolutely; he'd already told us. He wanted Suyolak and not for a fee or to save the world. He wanted him for Catcher and that was a thousand times more motivation than the rest of us had. I'd seen the same motivation and intensity in my brother a half hour ago that Rafferty was showing now in nailing the antihealer to save his cousin. Either kill Suyolak or drain him dry, whatever it took.

Best of luck to him.

appeared and reappeared. It was like a visual scream. The world was screaming.

I wasn't sure if that's what tipped me over into wolf and nothing but wolf. It could have been that or the battle. Sleek black shapes here, there, everywhere. There was flesh ripping under my teeth and the taste of blood. I wasn't Kin. I was proof that all Wolves weren't criminals and careless murderers. I'd been a biologist. My cousin was a healer. I didn't go looking for trouble. Sometimes you couldn't avoid it, no matter how hard you tried, not in our world where almost everyone was a predator—it was only a matter of big or little, slow or fast.

But me? I was a peaceful guy, laid back and fun loving. In the day, I could bong a beer and tutor you in anatomy. I'd pledged a *frat* . . . all the better to blend in, and, to my shame, get free beer. Once in a while in my past I'd run into those a little less nonviolent than I was. I'd tried to be reasonable, but there were those who wouldn't listen to reason. Then there were the times you just had to go to the woods, the forest, the jungle—whatever was available—to run and hunt. We were Wolves, first and foremost, above all other things. It was natural, and there was no denying we were at our most wolf in the hunt.

Either Cal or the blood; it didn't make a difference what had been the trigger. I remembered tearing into the Ördögs and then I remembered waking up in the car. In between were the dreams you forgot two seconds after waking up. You knew there'd been something and you had a sense of the emotion, even the happy, slow drift of colors, but anything tangible was gone. I woke up floating in blissful satisfaction and to a full stomach. Deer. I could still taste it. It was a familiar taste. It was what we "tame" suburban Wolves tended to hunt. The Kin would kill and usually eat their enemy. I couldn't do that. If it talked, I couldn't eat it. It could deserve to be eaten, but it didn't make a difference. If it could talk, I couldn't knosh down on it. I was a softy that way. I couldn't eat octopus either. I'd done a study on them in college. Those things could open jars to get at food. *Jars* . . . with screw-top lids. That was smart. I didn't remember how long it took me to figure out how to open jars when I was a kid. I knew it hadn't been anywhere near as fast as an octopus and I'd gotten all gold stars in kindergarten.

Rafferty had once said I was the closest thing to a wolf vegetarian he'd ever seen. A tree-hugging, vegetarian wolf—worse yet, Wolf, and he was embarrassed to be seen with me. This from the guy who healed broken wings on birds and tossed them back, free, into the sky. "What?" he'd gruff. "I just ordered pizza. I'll take pizza over blackbird any day."

It was why he fought the Ördögs as wolf instead of killing them with a brush of his fingers. It was to give them a chance. It was what was right and fair. He'd only ever killed as a healer to give mercy, the way he had the pregnant woman Suyolak had corrupted beyond all hope of curing. That he was going to change that when he took on Suyolak wasn't his fault. Only a healer could stop another healer as strong as Suyolak. Rafferty had to do it because that bastard had to die. I could live with that. Rafferty could too. I didn't know if either of us could live with his doing it by draining Suyolak of a life force that was as tainted as a well poisoned with cyanide.

Whether or not using it could bring me back to what I once was wasn't the issue. What was, was what would Rafferty be if he did. I'd give up my furry butt—no, I'd give up my life for my cousin, and I knew he'd do the same for me. While I didn't want it to come to that, it was part and parcel of family, the right kind of family. What I couldn't accept was his changing. Not the way I had changed, but like Cal had changed during the fight.

I didn't want to be whole and right again, only to look into my cousin's eyes and see a shadow of Suyolak staring back at me. If he could pull it off and make me like I once was without darkening himself, that would be great. I'd pay for the party . . . buffet and piñatas. We'd hit Mexico and the beaches and not come back for a year. Nothing but fun, sun, and knock-you-flat tequila. We more than deserved it.

But if he couldn't put me right and keep himself the same in the process, I'd rather live a clean if intellectually simplistic life. I'd rather be the Catcher who lived only in the moment, a Catcher without an identity beyond the most basic concept of "me." A Suyolak-contaminated Rafferty was not a clean life, for either of us. It was wrong, a polluted existence. And I couldn't do anything about it. I couldn't change his mind; I could only hope he was telling the truth: that he could handle it.

"Ah, but, dog, what if he cannot?"

I swiveled my head as I sat in the passenger seat of the moving car but saw nothing. It didn't stop Suyolak's oily voice from sniffing around the inside of my brain like a cat in heat, ravenous for any satisfaction he could get. I didn't know if anyone else could hear him, although no one looked as if goosed with an icy finger, which was how I felt. All that was missing was a doctor telling me to cough.

I closed my eyes and I could see him as he was a long time ago: human with wavy black hair to his shoulders, mischievous black eyes, and a smile that outshone a thousand commission-hungry salesmen. I didn't think they had such good teeth in those days, but he was a healer. Who needed fluoride if you could heal a dying person or turn him inside out, depending on your mental wiring? Suyolak had some very bad wiring. A conscience was only a word to him, without any real meaning. He had never healed a bird and let it fly away.

"You think that being born without a conscience is my fault, my friend?" The moon was orange as Cal had said it had been in his dream and Suyolak was sitting on a vine-covered log by a small fire with a pot of bubbling stew. In his lap he was casually bouncing a small boy. The child was three or four years old and dressed in an old-fashioned nightshirt with colorful embroidery around the neck. His head swung back and forth, lolling without any control. His legs and arms were limp and his eyes blank, but he breathed. He had dusky skin, a mop of black curls, and a face as flawless as Suyolak's.

"You're smart enough to follow the rules of society." There were only words in my head, but I heard them as if I were still able to say them aloud. It'd been so long since I'd heard my voice, even in my dreams, that I'd almost forgotten what I sounded like. "Smart enough to know they're there for a reason even if you can't understand or feel the reason behind them."

"You are the first sanctimonious Wolf I've crossed paths with. Curious. And, yes, I am smart, more than enough to know that rules don't apply to one such as me." Even as he said the words, the grin was as compelling and charismatic as before. The bait to pull in the unwary. Nature at its darkest and most chaotic. Biology. I was a biologist, but I didn't have to be to see it. I didn't have to be a psychiatrist either to know Suyolak was a creature beyond redemption. Nature was nature. The volcano didn't cry for Pompeii—it didn't care whom it killed and neither did Suyolak.

"I wanted a son," he added, the fleeting concept of conscience of no further interest to him. A sociopath before humans had come up with the label. He bounced the boy one more time and then let him roll carelessly onto the ground where he landed face-first. He hadn't cried or made an attempt to catch himself. "But that's a lie." The smile only became warmer. "I do like to lie.

Do not hold it against me, brother." Amiable; happy and amiable. Born in a human body, but one untouched by a soul.

"No, I did not want a son. I wanted another me, because, truly, what could be more entertaining than the Plague of the World? Would you guess? No? *Two* Plagues. We would devour the world and then one of us would devour the other. Now that would be a game genuinely worth playing; a challenge like no other. But instead, this is what I received." He pushed the unmoving boy farther away with a disgusted nudge of his foot. "Even in the womb of his useless cow of a mother, whom I took great pleasure in drowning in her own amniotic fluid during childbirth, he was like this. When he was smaller than my fist, I felt it. No brain. Oh, a spoonful perhaps, but not enough to be anything but an empty, breathing sack of nothing. No potential for consciousness. No chance to be the challenge I craved. And I could do nothing. You can change a brain; you can easily tear it down if you wish, but you cannot make one. I tried again and again, but it was only more of the same."

He followed my gaze still fixed on his son. I hadn't given nature the credit it deserved. It had tried to make up for its mistake. This was its answer to no more Suyolaks. I wished nature had found that answer before Suyolak himself had been born. "Do not worry about that one. I let him live although he's long dust now. I let them all live. Why kill what was never alive? Where is the pleasure in that?"

"But your cousin." That smile, that endlessly magnetic and intimate smile. "A challenge finally arises and at the same time that I arise. It is fate. Destiny."

"Why are you telling me this?" I demanded. "Because I do have better things to do than listen to the medieval version of Ted Bundy. Why are you yapping to me like a bored cub?"

"Because your cousin isn't listening right now. He isn't listening, and he is going *the wrong way*."

This Suyolak, the one suddenly in my face, the moon gone and the fire smelling of burning human flesh, was the skin-wrapped bones of before. Blind eyes not an inch from mine, snapping stained teeth far from the brilliant white of before, his breath carrying the stench of the Black Death itself.

I yelped, eyes opening, and jerking back quickly enough to bang my head on the inside roof of the car. "What the hell?" Rafferty said. "Did you have a bad ... shit, Suyolak."

I'd had a bad Suyolak, no way around it. But he'd said we were going the wrong way and there *was* a way around that. I clamped my jaws around the steering wheel and jerked it to the right. I believed Suyolak wholeheartedly. He wanted to fight my cousin. He wanted us there when he got out of that coffin. He was getting out too. We wouldn't be able to stop it. Destiny ... fate. I hadn't always believed in the theory, despite a different girlfriend than the Buddhist one. This one had played around with tarot cards. I'd thought she was a complete flake, although one with gorgeous legs and an amazing ... All right, that was beside the point. But that's what I'd believed in then, not fate. I believed now. This all felt designed: that I would be sick; that Rafferty would be this desperate; that Suyolak would choose this time to escape or that time had chosen it for him.

Whether you were a pawn or a king, everyone had a part to play in the world. It was time to play ours. I yanked at the wheel again, growling. "Will you quit it?" Rafferty said. "I'm pulling over already? See?" He pulled the car off the highway and slowed it to a crawl. "I smell Suyolak." Not a genuine smell, but a healer sense, although Rafferty wouldn't be caught dead saying the soppy, fake mystical "I sense. . . ." about anything. "He couldn't hurt you. I have us all shielded."

"He could speak to him, though," Niko said from behind me, "as he spoke to Cal."

"Through what I've got up?" Rafferty said dismissively. "No." My cousin had never lacked in self-confidence. Not being able to heal me was the sole exception to that. It made him a formidable fighter when he had to be, an incredibly talented healer, and sometimes a giant know-it-all ass.

I put my muzzle next to his ear and growled again, one very serious growl rarely heard from the nonoctopus-eating, almost-vegetarian, save-the-planet, mellow Wolf I was. Rafferty grimaced. "Okay, Christ. I can't believe I ever bought you pancakes and had the cojones to ask for whipped cream on them. Don't you forget that, because I'll never be able to live it down." He put on the brakes and brought the car to a complete stop. "Get your computer and tell me what is so damn important that . . ." He shut his mouth over the rest of the sentence before changing it to a quiet, "He's turned around. The son of a bitch has turned around."

"I thought you had him," Goodfellow accused. "No possible way you could lose him, I believe you said."

Sometimes you can concentrate too hard that you can't see the flock for the sheep. It was an easy mistake to make, especially when you were as emotionally invested in all of this as my cousin was—the same cousin no one could get away with talking badly about, especially fast-talking pucks. I turned the snarl on Robin in the backseat, for the first time ignoring the demonic King Tut cat sitting on his shoulder.

"That is what I said." Rafferty looked over his shoulder, then jerked the steering wheel and slammed his foot on the gas. The car tore through the dirt, across the asphalt of the road, and then more dirt that made up the median, and we were headed back the way we came. "When I thought I was better than he is."

The snarl became a startled gurgle as I again turned my head. The set profile of my cousin was enough to disillusion me that I'd heard wrong. Another gurgle, this time from Goodfellow, was a distant Grand Canyon reflection of mine. "What did you just say? I know you did not say he is better than you. As much as I agree that your ego is as enormously inflated as your social skills are nonexistent, but you told us you could take Suyolak. You were to do the heavy lifting on this little escapade, because apart from having our hearts explode and our brains dribble out our ears, there isn't much we can contribute to the campaign."

"We took this job before we knew Rafferty would be available, so that's not exactly fair," Niko said. "Behave."

The puck did not. I wasn't in any way surprised. I'd only met two other pucks in my life and they had been noise pollution on the hoof. Goodfellow was no different.

"Only if you're using 'we' with the broadest of definitions. He came aboard this ship of death before I did. I expected him to be our lifeboat, our coast guard rescuer in a tight uniform. I dislike having my expectations, especially of living, shattered." Goodfellow scowled, folded his arms, and slid down in the seat, but he didn't tell Rafferty to stop the car and let him out. That was huge for a puck. Besides making a good deal of noise, they were accomplished fighters when they had to be, but they were equally accomplished at keeping themselves in one piece. It should've been surprising that there were so few of them left. Still, if you thought about it, as I had before of Robin, if you lived forever . . . did you really want to? They had far too much time on their hands, and it was likely I had too little. The world was funny that way.

I thought I'd picked up enough about Goodfellow from our first meeting and this road trip to know that he was being brave, not suicidal, though, but what about Suyolak? He was going to be more than happy to make sure none of us saw the dawn of the next day, much less forever, and I didn't want my cousin giving up *his* life if he had no chance of stopping the bastard.

"Cuz."

I rolled my eyes back and forth again, but no one was speaking, not the others, not Rafferty. No mouths were moving and it wasn't my ears that had picked up the word. This was turning out to be the day of playing with my brain as if it were Play-Doh. Grumbling deep in my chest, I closed my eyes again. This time I didn't see Suyolak. I saw Rafferty. I saw the world around Rafferty. It was from our college senior ski trip. The air wasn't cold and the snow matted down in my ski boots wasn't freezing my feet as it had back then, but the vision of it . . . It was the same as the framed picture on Rafferty's guest room dresser. Rafferty could've stepped out of that picture himself. He was seven or eight years younger with hair that, while it still rivaled a well-worn janitor's mop, wasn't as unkempt as it was these days. I held out my hands, gloved and holding ski poles. *Hands.* I dropped the poles and stripped off the gloves. They were as I remembered: the scar across the back of my right one. Nails chewed short. I'd started gnawing at my paws when I was a cub and never stopped, as a wolf or a human. A plain ring of silver around my right ring finger . . . just because we Wolves loved to mock that whole silver legend.

"I'm me." I gave a wide and happy grin. "I'm me and I can talk. No stupid computer, which you skimped on, by the way. You couldn't fork out the big bucks for a Dell? This one takes an entire century to reboot. And don't get me started on Windows Vista. That's what demons pass when they get the Tijuana Trots. And—"

I was silenced as Rafferty tackled me and hugged me so tightly, my imaginary breath whooshed out of my imaginary lungs and I almost slipped and fell down in the equally imaginary snow. It was unexpected, although we Wolves were more touchy-feely than humans tended to be. But Rafferty had been born a grump, not that I didn't love the hell out of the guy. I did, but it didn't change the fact this was unexpected. It was even a little bit shocking and it was great. I was me and it was just . . . *great*.

"I wish I'd figured this out without copying it from Suyolak," Rafferty said gruffly at my ear. "We would never have needed a computer. We could've talked . . . even if you talk too much and carry on about the plight of the whales and shit. But we could've actually talked and you could've been the other part of yourself, if only in your head. I screwed up and I'm sorry."

I stepped back out of the hug. Since Rafferty was not the hugging type, that meant he felt guilty, he was scared, and he needed some good down-home counsel—pack style. He'd tackled me with the hug. I tackled him to the ground and rubbed snow in his face. "Awww, you're so sweet. You're like Lassie or Lady. Maybe we can find Tramp for you and you can share spaghetti and meet in the middle. Very cute."

Jumping up before he could kick me off, I continued. "We're here now. We're Wolves, Rafferty. We might fool ourselves by running around half the time looking like humans and buying houses, cars, going to college, but the bottom line is we're Wolves. And being only in the here and now is what we were in the beginning. I'm not saying let's go crazy and join the cult of All Wolf like Delilah, but we can't forget either that 'now' isn't so bad." I reached down and grabbed the hand he wasn't using to wipe snow from his face and pulled him to his feet. "And right here, right now"—I grinned again at the play on words—"is the best."

"It is pretty good," he admitted, and nailed me in the hair with the snow he'd scraped from his face and balled up in his other hand.

And it truly was the best. I hadn't had a better moment since before getting sick, but Rafferty was driving and how he was managing that and this at the same time was anyone's guess. Then there was Suyolak.

"You can't take him." I brushed nonexistent snow from my hair and went on with some trepidation. I didn't want to make things worse for Rafferty with doubt. "That's what you said. If that's true, then we should get out of here. Saving the world is never a bad thing, don't get me wrong—I had my car bumper covered with stickers that said the same thing—but if you can't take him, I don't want you dying for no reason. The world will have to find a different solution."

"I didn't say I couldn't take him." He scowled automatically at being told there was anything he couldn't do, the cocky SOB, but he sobered. "I said he was better than me. You've played blackjack with me. Football at Thanksgiving in your parents' yard back in high school. You've fought me roughhousing around during hunts. You know me. Being better than me doesn't mean someone can take me."

He was right. He . . . I . . . we all thought he was the king when it came to healing, but I was smart, in math and physics as well as biology. I could count cards; learned it second semester of college. That didn't stop him from beating me in games of drunken twenty-one in the dorm laundry room while we waited for our clothes to dry. I was a little bit bigger, faster, and stronger than he was as a wolf too, but he still kicked my tail more often than not.

Stubborn, ruthless, would cheat in a heartbeat, and was sneaky as hell; it usually gave him the advantage over me. It might do the same for him with Suyolak. In my heart, though, I was as tame as Delilah mocked me for being. Rafferty while in human form was a healer, first, last, and always, but as a wolf, he was Wolf. He hunted with no regret and killed enemies with a double helping of glee. He wasn't ashamed of it either. He was who he was . . . to the brink and beyond. He simply happened to be two widely different creatures.

As a healer, he healed and he didn't ask if you deserved to be made whole. As a wolf, he killed and whether you'd deserved it or not, *I* didn't ask. Because he was the normal Wolf, the predator. I was the one in the butterfly collar and if I hadn't been sick and stuck, I might have merited the ridiculous thing regardless.

"Not better than him, but you can take him." I nodded before having my last look at the trees, the snow, the blue sky that was a different blue to human eyes than wolf ones. I had already studied my hands; now I felt my face. Stubble, lean jaw, thick eyebrows. I'd missed this face. It was only half of the whole of me, but I'd missed it.

"I can take him."

"Okay, then. You can," I agreed with the same confidence Rafferty was putting out there, then smiled. It was the moment I never thought we'd get. If he took down that ancient Rom and cured me, it would be good. But if he took Suyolak and couldn't make me what I was, it would still be good, because I was able to say a real good-bye, one that, at the end of the road, had nothing to do with whether he could take Suyolak or not; one that was for him and me and our past wandering years.

Hope for the best; prepare for the worst.

"By the way, in college? I slept with that girl you were sleeping with junior year." Good-byes shouldn't be melancholy. They should be until we meet again. They also shouldn't include getting the crap knocked out of you on the memory of a snow slope, so I ran the last bit together a little hurriedly. "But you weren't actually dating, so it didn't count." I gave him a quick happy-go-lucky, life-is-good smile, the one my parents had said I'd had since the day I was born—a grinning golden retriever born of Wolves. "Be seeing you."

I opened my eyes quickly and was back in the car. There was no snow or the smell of pine. There *was* the smell of old vinyl, the faint scent of ancient baby food and dirty diapers, pot, cedar chips, and a long-gone hamster, and a puck and two humans or semihumans who hadn't had a chance to bathe in a while. The mummy cat smelled almost like gingerbread cookies, the kind Mom had made at Christmas, and I smelled like fries.

Rafferty just smelled pissed. "Goodfellow, where's the damn water bottle you spray your cat with? I have some serious behavior modification to do." To me, he accused, "You slept with Natalya? She was six feet tall, a model, and a Wolf. Orthodox. My mom, if she were alive, would've loved her. I might've dated her. I thought about dating her. You son of a bitch."

I grinned and panted in the fine spray aimed at my face. Ah, refreshing. Mummy cats were pussies, literally, if that slowed them down. I kept on grinning as we chased Suyolak until he went to ground like all prey. I could do that, because it was all about the here and now. My cousin cursing at the wheel. Left-over fries to munch. A tug-of-war as a sex-starved puck unsuccessfully tried to steal my racy calendars while desperately declaring monogamy and celibacy as the number one killer, miles ahead of heart disease. Then, when he lost the tug-of-war, pulling out a white and gold peri feather to slowly run through his fingers—a sensation he seemed to be memorizing. There was also the Auphe unconsciously humming under his breath along with Barry Manilow on the radio, the sunglasses beginning to slide down his nose as he seemed to find a meditation groove—no matter how evil and unnatural Manilow was. The ninja/samurai/assassin-could-be if didn't-wannabe glancing sideways at his brother as if slicing his throat to stop the non-melody was out of the question, but the fantasy of it not completely so.

It was good, all of it. The future was a myth, the past as lost as the innocence that falls away with a baby's first breath. The here and now ...

It was what made life worth living.

15

Cal

We ended up back in Wyoming at Yellowstone Park right before twilight. I'd never been there before. Rangers wouldn't let Sophia scam the tourists, so no parks for us as kids, but I damn sure knew a lot of red-light districts like the back of my hand. Then when Niko and I were on the run from the Auphe, hoping to hide as best as we could, wide-open spaces made up of thousands of acres weren't what we were looking for. That was a Where's Waldo? freebie right there.

Rafferty parked past the West Entrance just as most people were leaving, trickling out in carloads. We wouldn't have made it in if the park ranger at the station hadn't decided to keel over almost face-first into his beef stew. Luckily, he barely missed it and began snoring loudly enough that I hoped a passing lonely bear didn't molest him. With an irritable healer along for the ride, who needed Obi-Wan and his hoodoo protection for what I'd always strongly suspected were his love droids?

Yeah, I almost jumped in with Robin to fight for Catcher's calendars, but who could blame me? Delilah and I hadn't had a whole lot of alone time on the trip and that had nothing to do with her possibly having orders to kill me. When you weighed possible death against certain sex, I was the same as any other guy—I was willing to toss those dice. But time hadn't been kind to Cal junior. It wasn't the best road trip I could've imagined—in that or any respect. Surrounded by death and very little sex, I could've gotten the same if I were a hundred and stuck in a nursing home—if there were nursing homes for Auphe. What a way to spend the prime of my life: all but celibate, attacked daily, more Auphe than I'd ever been, and with all the porn hogged by a monster-sized wolf in a butterfly collar.

Life pissed me the fuck off.

We drove to the first parking area we could find. It was empty by the time we arrived ... except for a certain black truck. They said Death rode a pale horse. In fiction maybe, but in the real world, Death rode in a coffin in the back of a very plain, unnoticeable black truck. I was out of the car and at the back of that truck in seconds. Rafferty didn't say anything to stop my progress, which was a good-enough go-ahead for me. If Suyolak had been there, I'd have been on the asphalt with a healer footprint on my back. Rafferty wasn't letting anyone get ahead of him on this guy.

The doors were unlocked, which meant only one thing, but I opened them warily all the same. I'd seen what this guy could do. I'd *felt* what he could do. I'd nearly lost my life because of him and the twisted virus he'd turned loose at the hotel.

Dying was inevitable. You came into this world with an expiration date and there wasn't much you could do about that. Like Rafferty had said, your heart has only so many beats in it. There were the unexpected ones too, like milk going bad a week early. It came with the territory when you fought for a living. I didn't mind dying, the same way I didn't mind winter. Both were coming, one way or the other. However, if I curdled early, I wanted to go out fighting all the way. I didn't want to have some bubonic-plague-spreading asshole pointing a finger at me, and like that sour milk being poured down a drain, so I'd go—without landing a blow. Someday someone or something would kill me. Fact. But I wanted them to see the scars of that encounter every time they looked in a mirror.

Hugs and kisses from Cal Leandros, shithead.

The doors didn't creak spookily. No reality show ghost hunters/plumbers jumped out to wave idiotic electronic toys to either detect those passed on or snake your sink. As if when you died and there was life after death, which I highly doubted, you'd hang around the place where you took the big dirt nap. Get thee to a beach and haunt it if you have no place better to go. People—stupid when they lived; potentially stupid when they died.

But this was no illusion of a haunting. It wasn't the site of a vengeful mass murderer lying in wait either. It was only a truck . . . with a coffin in the back, a coffin made of metal and with the lid pushed to one side. "The seals are broken."

I could've jumped at the deeply somber voice right at my ear. Instead, I chose to give my balls a moment to descend and crabbed over my shoulder, "Do you want me to piss my pants, Nik? Seriously? Isn't the car a little fragrant enough at this point?"

"As entertaining a story as that would be to tell, you're correct. I apologize." He rested a hand on my shoulder and hoisted himself up into the truck, not that he needed the support. Then again, maybe we both needed it in the coming battle. Rafferty had said it himself: Suyolak was better than he was. If he went down, we would have to step up, very probably only to follow the healer right back down. Fighting a losing battle is one thing. Fighting

an absolutely hopeless battle is a different thing altogether. It certainly made catchy slogans harder to come
up with. "I'll be back." Well, no, I won't. "Yippe ki yay,
motherfucker." Too upbeat. "Hasta la vista, baby." Too
temporary and so idiotically clichéd. "I regret I have but
one life to give. . . ." Okay, that I could see. I did regret I
had but the one life and that it wasn't enough to kill the
bastard. When you were Auphe and that wasn't enough
to kill something, damn if you weren't having a seriously
bad day.

I followed my brother. There was grit under the soles
of my shoes, lots of it—probably what was left of those
seals Abelia-Roo hadn't kept up to OSHA standards,
thanks to that overblown ego of hers. I should've known
that from the first second she spoke to us. Abelia was
many things, bad ones, familiar ones from my childhood,
but she was also sharp as they came. Sometimes sharp
wasn't enough, though. She had a heart on its last legs,
but she wasn't anywhere close to senile. She did think a
lot of herself, however, a damn lot, more than Goodfellow did of himself, if possible. The seals had failed because, unlike Rafferty, she thought she was better than
Suyolak. If she'd thought less of herself, tried harder and
stayed on top of her duty, the seals, and the iron coffin
would've been sealed tight as it had been all those generations before.

But now we were left with an empty metal box filled
with dust and a smell like a cobwebbed attic that hung
in your nose and lingered on the back of your tongue.
"I've always enjoyed a challenge," Niko remarked, sift-
ing through the powder to lift something out. "I think
perhaps there are other things I could enjoy instead.
Bonsai trees, painting, forging my own weapons. The op-
portunities are endless." He opened his hand to show
me the small braid of several yellowed hairs. "Voodoo."

"Think it would work?" I perked up. Killing from

a distance wasn't usually my thing, but in this case, I'd make an exception.

"Unfortunately, no." He dropped the braid and dusted mote-sized bits of Suyolak off his hands. Horton wasn't hearing a Who on any of those—not unless it was a frothing rabid killer Who—and he wouldn't want to listen to one of those anyway if he was smart.

"The driver's dead," Robin said a few feet below us. He was catless. Salome was not only not with him; she wasn't in the car either. She'd jumped out of the window onto the top of another car that we'd passed at the ranger station going in the opposite direction. She must've decided, with whatever filled the empty space between her pierced ears, that not only was the station as far as she cared to go, but that, in fact, she would like to travel in a direction far from us. I thought her tail waved a cheerful good-bye, but it could've also been feline for *Screw you and your little werewolves too.* What did I know? It was a cat. Live ones were a mystery and dead ones . . . way out of the ball field.

"Great." Although truthfully, I didn't care one way or the other. Kirkland started this mess. Yes, to save his wife, and, yes, back me into a corner and I could say without a doubt I would've done it for Nik. But it wasn't me. This wasn't a hypothetical coulda woulda shoulda. Suyolak was gone and my empathy had gone with him, so the hell with the dead guy.

Niko jumped down and started toward the front of the truck, with me behind him. "Rafferty can't save him? Bring him back?"

Robin snorted. "Jesus fresh off his Lazarus Tour couldn't do a thing with this one."

Both Niko and I still took a look for ourselves. The driver's door was open, thanks to Rafferty or Robin. I was going with Rafferty, because I'd seen roadkill that was more photogenic than the late professor, and I couldn't see Robin panting in anticipation for a closer look. Kirkland could've been a corpse that had lain under the desert sun for months. Dried skin shrunken to frame the skeleton, coarse short hair drained of moisture and color that had fallen away from the scalp in patches. Eyes turned to raisins in the hollow of his skull. He was a long-dead spider found under your refrigerator. A husk.

He looked quite a bit like Suyolak had in my head.

"Mihai, Yoska," said Abelia, a still-scuttling spider chock-full of poison, standing behind us. "I might find a use for bits and pieces of him later. If nothing else, he'll be a good attraction for the marks. Mummy man, cursed to death by the hand of the Rom."

"You are a shame on any people, including the Rom," Niko retorted, but he stepped out of the path of the two men. It was simpler. An empty truck was easier for cops to overlook in their files than an empty truck with a dead man in it. The other two Rom stood to one side and respectfully behind Abelia while their brethren hauled the husk of Professor Kirkland over to the RV and stashed him away. The parking lot was empty by then. No one saw and if they had, they would've passed it off as a Halloween prop.

"Shame." She spat on the asphalt. She did have a thing for the liquid expression of her emotions. "It is you who are the shame and your own blood the monster. Now let us find the other monster and end this business."

"For the betterment of humanity and the improvement of the present company by your removal, I'm forced to agree with you." Nik did have a way with an insult—a way that sometimes required a dictionary, but a way all the same. He turned his back on Abelia, another insult but more pointed, and shut the door of the truck. "Rafferty?"

"He is gone. On the hunt. Following prey." Delilah

had pulled up on her motorcycle seconds ago and was now undoing her braid, the silver hair falling to her waist. She too was ready for the hunt. Despite the purple shadows of twilight, she was a brilliant flash of white. Her hair, the leathers; she was the moon come to Earth. "We follow." She stepped close to thread her hand in my hair and kiss me with a heat and familiarity that made it hard to forget that I'd had this so short a time. It seemed like years. I returned it with enthusiasm, refusing to wonder if I tasted different to her now. An extra dollop of Auphe in all likelihood would only make me spicier to Delilah. And there I was thinking about it after all, but before I could push it out of my mind, I heard a clearing of a throat. Niko. He was right; it had gone on for a few minutes, but I didn't have the ability to store up sexual pleasure like British rock stars with their freaky Tantric batteries. I had to take it when I could get it. There was a cough this time that would be promptly followed by a thwack of a sword to the back of my knees if I didn't step back.

I stepped back.

Delilah gave me a smile ripe with anticipation of the chase before us. "In case we hunt no more."

"Great for you two," Robin complained. "But what if Niko and I end up 'hunting no more'? Where's our kiss of potential death? Or quickie of potential death? I'm open to all options."

Both Delilah and Niko snorted and Robin did without. I knew he was serious about the kiss; I wasn't as sure about the rest as I saw him finger his cell phone before hitting a number. Speed dial. This relationship could be more serious than I thought. Monogamy *and* ranking on Robin's speed dial. He turned his back to us, but that didn't keep wolf or human ears from hearing. "It's me . . . of course. Who else would bother to call your cranky feathered ass?" He paused, listening.

"No, everything's fine. We're about to wipe this walking, talking, antibiotic-resistant son of a bitch out of existence, and I should be back soon." Goodfellow could lie like no one I'd seen in my life, except my mother, but this time, I wasn't so sure he pulled it off. "I only wanted you to know that you are wholly responsible for the vow of the priesthood I took on this trip. And if by some completely unlikely chance I don't survive, I fully expect you to pack your dick away in shipping foam and never use it again. Fair is fair." He paused again, then said briskly, "No, I'm not saying that or implying that. I just wanted . . . oh Hades." He flipped the phone shut. Good-bye was what I guessed that he refused to say and when the phone rang, he turned it off, sticking to his guns on the subject.

I didn't blame him. Saying good-bye was an impossible thing sometimes; no matter how long you had to prepare yourself. Niko and I'd learned that a few times more than I wanted to count. And when you didn't know in your heart precisely what you were saying good-bye to . . . that had to be worse.

Delilah turned out to be right about Rafferty. He was gone and Catcher had disappeared with him, but they weren't far away. We caught up with them in a short matter of time, all of us: Niko, Robin, Delilah, Abelia-Roo and her four men, and lucky me watching our flank. Fortunately, it was Delilah's flank I was watching and if I was going to die, that wasn't a bad last image to take with me.

We moved quietly along wooden walkways surrounded by trees, some kind of pine or fir. Big though, whatever they were. More than a hundred feet tall, easily. The wind played through the needles, a song you couldn't quite make out the words to, but a nice song. Peaceful—until the trees fell; hundreds of them, in slow motion, as roots gave way and they tore loose from the

ground. The first one would've landed right in front of
some of us and on top of the rest if we hadn't heard the
creak of wood and been hit with a cascade of now-silent
needles, brown and dead from above.

No one said run. The situation was self-explanatory
in that respect, and if it wasn't, then Darwin was ready
to take your hand and lead your oblivious ass to extinc-
tion. Delilah and I ran past Abelia and her men. I didn't
help little old ladies across the street. I should have, but
I didn't. And if I didn't do that, I wasn't going to play out
the tale of the Frog and the Scorpion with Abelia-Roo.
It was the scorpion's nature to sting the frog. It would
be Abelia's pleasure to stab me in the back if I hoisted
her up on it, only unlike the scorpion, she'd wait until I'd
hauled her to safety first. I let her men deal with scoop-
ing her up and fleeing with her.

We caught up with Niko and Robin as the first tree
crashed across the walkway behind us. It shook the
ground hard enough that I felt my feet leave it for a
split second. As the rest of the hundred or so fell, that
shaking became a good imitation of an earthquake.
We ran, we dodged, and in one spectacular, humanly
impossible leap, Delilah sailed over the huge trunk of
one already down. I started to look behind me once and
Niko grabbed my jacket and yanked me along faster.
Within minutes we raced out from the wooded area
and stopped to see . . . just to see. A massive stretch of
destruction lay behind us. The giant trees, dead but not
gone. They lay across the pathway, every one a stand-in
for a bullet through the head. Trunks piled upon trunks,
branches bare as needles had dropped away—the death
of nature itself.

With almost every step Suyolak had taken here before us, everything around was dying—or had already
died. The trees, the grass I bent and felt break under my
palm, the rabbit dessicated to nearly nothing by my foot.

Once Suyolak had started his engine, he'd stopped the same in everything else he passed, holding back only enough that the death throes were timed to crush us flat. I nudged the rabbit corpse off the wooden path and onto the dead grass. Not much improvement for it, but it was the best I could do.

"Let's keep going," Niko said, turning back to move on. As we did, I caught a glimpse of one of Abelia's men looking over his shoulder uneasily at the remains of what we'd barely escaped. Uneasy—holy hell, if he were smart, he would be fucking terrified. We were trailing after the actual embodiment of death; not the idea of it or the chance of it, but its purest distillation. Terminal cancer and every plague known to man crossed with a great white shark and we were chasing the bastard down. If that didn't make you think twice, then you had nothing to think with. Suyolak was loose, the Plague of the World, and he was already killing that world around him.

We found Rafferty and Catcher just off the walkway by a sign that heralded the Midway Geyser Basin. Sounded scenic and me without my camera. No way to capture the memories. What a pity. Or what a pity if I were alive next month to worry about it. As it was, even if I had a photo album, I think I had only the one picture for it—my sixteen-year-old yellowed and curled-at-the-edges Santa photo, and Niko wouldn't give that one back. My life didn't much lend itself to pictures I cared to revisit. If we got to live, maybe I'd do something about that.

Rafferty had stopped with Catcher standing stolidly at his side, waiting for us. "He's ahead," he said, "past the Grand Prismatic Spring. Too bad it's not daylight. Dark blue water, ringed by red bacterial mats. Colorful. Nice." That was a lot of words for Rafferty and none of them curse words. I was impressed. If he could do it, maybe there was hope for me yet. I raised my eyebrows and Rafferty shrugged. "Catcher's a tree hugger. We've been here before."

"Wonderful. You're an informative tour guide. Should we, by some slim chance, survive this, I'll be sure to tip you generously." Robin massaged his forehead as we ringed the healer and the wolf. "Are you absolutely positive this time? Because, honestly, he's led you by the nose up until now and rarely in the right direction, not to mention he did just try to swat us with several acres of trees. On the other hand, that rather bears mentioning. He tried to kill us with trees. Extremely tall Christmas trees and how diabolical is that? To ruin a gift-giving holiday and celebration of the pagan winter solstice all in one."

"Not kindly or succinctly put, but something we need to know. Rafferty?" Niko was carrying his sword and had discarded his coat when the wooden path had ended. There was no one and nothing to see us now; only the dead. "You do know where he is? If Suyolak is going to kill us, I'd prefer he do it from ahead and not behind. Granted deceased is deceased, but we'd have something more of a chance if we knew his position."

"He's ahead all right, more than ready and willing to play," the healer replied impassively. "He's in my head now. Talking, talking. Bastard won't shut up. This is what he wants. He doesn't think any of us is worth hiding from."

Always fun hearing that. The big badasses were like that. It had been so long since they'd had an actual challenge that they'd forgotten one could exist. But in the past, we'd taken down everyone we ran up against. Sometimes it took only you and the fear of what the son of a bitch might do trumping the fear of dying. Sometimes it took a shitload of backup and weapons. Sometimes it took your entire lifetime to date. Whichever it was, Niko and I had never failed to get them in the end.

We'd also never come up against someone like Suyo-lak. He could kill with a thought, and guns weren't much good if you were dead between aiming and pulling the trigger. True or not, I wasn't going to admit it. The bastard might get my life, but he wasn't going to get my fear. "Then let's go show him how wrong his mummified ass is," I said as I pulled my Eagle from the holster.

Moving again toward the spring Rafferty had—what did they call it?—"waxed poetic" about. I got the poetic part; where the wax came in had left me in the dark, and when Niko had explained it back in the homeschooling days, I would've zoned out immediately. How a language evolved throughout the centuries didn't much interest me then . . . or now. I knew what the phrase meant and that was enough for me, although I'd guarantee Nik had smacked me in the back of the head or flicked my ear painfully at my lack of interest at the time.

As he did now. "Jesus," I hissed in a low tone, and glared at him as he now walked silently beside me. "What was that for?" It was always for something. Niko had never outgrown the role of teacher—he never would. If we lived to be in our nineties, he'd still be force-feeding me yogurt, teaching me the new martial arts of our alien overlords, and jacking my brain directly into some long-winded documentary about the dung beetle and its place in history. On the day I was born, Nik became a big brother and until the day I died, he still would be.

"Don't gate," he warned me in the same near whisper, but no less authoritatively with the lack of volume, because that was Niko. Some, such as Goodfellow, radiated charisma rather like a supernova did light and deadly radiation, and some, like Nik, *were* that radiation. Whether it was a whisper or not, you listened. "Don't think you can travel next to Suyolak and empty your clip into his head before he can kill you, because you

can't. Rafferty is here for a reason. Let him do what he's
meant to—heal the world of a pestilence."

And if he can't, I wanted to ask, but whisper or not,
Rafferty would hear it. We were down to the wire now.
It was time to shut up about his qualifications. Besides,
if he couldn't put down Suyolak like the rabid dog he
was, traveling probably wouldn't be an issue. Trying to
shove the shredded lungs I'd coughed up into the dirt
back down my throat and into my chest where they belonged might be. However, in all likelihood, traveling
would be lower on the list. And weighing the risk of the
Auphe in my progressing because of it would be at the
very bottom.

"Cal."

Niko was serious most of the time, but there was serious and then there was now. I didn't push him on it.
"Okay. No traveling." This time I didn't bother to keep
my voice down. If Suyolak was in Rafferty's head, a
whisper wasn't going to be an effective stealth tool. I
was surprised the bastard hadn't dropped us all in the
parking lot the same as he'd taken down the mass of
giant trees.

"That's because I'm still protecting you," Rafferty
said as he stopped walking. Catcher's eyes glowed in the
purple light as he looked back at us.

"Great. I've had Suyolak in my brain," I complained.
"I don't want you sneaking a look too."

"It's no goddamn picnic for me either," he snapped,
but absently, his main focus elsewhere. "If your customers knew what you put in their beer." Before I could
protest that I only *thought* about it, hadn't actually done
it, he added, "There it goes."

By "it," he meant the spring . . . or now a geyser. We,
including Delilah, Abelia, and her men, were standing
on hardened, ridged dirt that rose slightly at a fair distance in front of us, and that's where the show was. I

smelled it before I heard it and heard it before I saw
it: sulfur, then the sound of boiling . . . as if something
as big as the ocean itself were churning, and finally the
explosion of water that hit the air and kept going up.
Up. Up, and holy shit. I felt like Moses at the parting
of the Red Sea. No, I felt more like an Egyptian soldier
just there for the paycheck, wondering where it all had
gone wrong as I drank the water down. "How the hell is
he doing that?" I craned my head to see the water high
above us shimmering with a light that was a pale purple
reflection of the sky above it.

"The bacteria in the water," Rafferty said. "He's agitated them to a thousand times their normal activity.
That light is them dying. He turned them into . . . hell,
stars. But microbial stars don't live long."

"Is he going to boil us alive, because, quite frankly,
that is the one near death I've avoided throughout the
millennia, and I've no particular interest in it now."
Robin had his sword out too, but for the first time it
looked useless and he, thanks to those millennia of experience, was Niko's equal in swordsmanship . . . if he
was sober. "Although at least these wretched clothes
from that equally wretched, low-fashion and inedible
food store are machine washable. If I do die, at least my
corpse won't reside in shrunken, wrinkled rags."

"No. We're not going to be boiled alive, but you just
made me wish we would be," Rafferty growled.

Rafferty was a lightweight when it came to surviving
the puck experience, but he was also right. We weren't
boiled alive. A good portion of the water splashed down
about two feet from us . . . a generous estimate. "Cutting
it a little close, isn't he?" I said it to Nik, because when
it came to healing, fine, Rafferty was our guy . . . Wolf . . .
both. But when it came to logistics in a battle, I trusted
my brother over anyone and everyone.

And when it came to the abrupt smell of copper and

calcium and the five piles of dust that appeared on the ground behind us, it looked like I didn't have to worry about trusting or not trusting a certain someone ever again. Abelia-Roo and her men were gone. The scent and the flicker out of the corner of my eye had me whirling around, Eagle pointed—except there was nothing for it to do. A dust buster was the only thing that would be any good now. Niko bent down and ran his fingers through one heap. The residue flew off his fingers, finer than flour dust.

"It's like Sodom and Gomorrah all over again," Robin said in a hushed tone, finally impressed enough to be almost quiet.

"Shit," I repeated, without the "holy" this time. There was nothing much holy about this. She'd been a bitch from Hell, Abelia, one so full of hate and loathing that every foot she put to the earth had most likely poisoned it . . . with just a slower poison than Suyolak's version. That she could be gone so quickly and quietly, without a screech or a curse, was shocking and almost unbelievable. Like someone's snapping the fingers at a town-destroying tornado and its simply disappearing. Poof. Gone.

"I couldn't protect everyone."

I looked back, but Rafferty hadn't bothered to turn around. "They were the ones that caused this clusterfuck. They're responsible for Suyolak's escaping that coffin. If someone had to go . . ." He shrugged again. He did that a lot. It was not my favorite thing, especially under deadly circumstances where I had no control. I had issues with control. We'd all seen that, but tricking myself into believing I had control was something that had saved my sanity more than once. Tricks and wire stitching us together sometimes was all you had, and I was missing it badly now.

"We all make difficult decisions in battle. You are

Solomonic in your wisdom," Goodfellow said to Rafferty smoothly, if hastily. There was nothing wrong with knowing which side of your bread was buttered, and as he'd been alive before bread or butter, Robin had mastered that maneuver.

"If you think your silver tongue will save you, goat, it will not." It was Suyolak's voice—a real voice this time, not manufactured in my brain. I heard it. I heard *him*. "To make it close to a fair contest, he will have to sacrifice more of you. All of you, and even then . . ." He stepped into sight.

It was darker now and I didn't have the eyes of the three Wolves, but between the lingering twilight, the rising moon, and the flickering glow of dying bacteria, I could see him as he came around the left curve of the spring. He was human again with flesh, dark eyes, and black hair that touched the ground and that cheerful Rom smile from my dream. It was that damn-are-we-going-to-have-some-fun smile; the isn't-the-world-one-big-party smile; a have-I-got-something-to-give-you grin. The last one was the one I believed. He had something to give us all right, a great big frigging present, and if it was what Abelia and her men had gotten, we'd be damn lucky piles of dust.

I hadn't believed in luck since I was five.

"He used them to reconstitute himself," Niko said. "Abelia and the others. He drained the life out of them to make himself whole."

"Not only them, Vayash cousin." He was closer, a little more than seventy-five feet away. Almost nude, he had only strips of faded cloth hanging from him. Hundreds of years in a coffin were rough on the wardrobe. He made a washing motion with his hands and the twisted, foot-long fingernails fell away. "I also took the trees, the grass, twenty-one elk, six bears, two mountain lions, several sheep, and numberless small vermin. Some creatures I didn't know existed in my time. It's always a pleasure to kill something new." He stopped and pointed at me. "You are new."

"And old and something the world had never seen before. Yeah, been there, heard that," I snapped, turning back, and this time I had something for the Eagle. I aimed and when the ground came up to smack me in the face, I was more than a little disappointed. Not surprised, no, that Suyolak had given me an invisible swat, but there was a complete lack of satisfaction, no doubt about it.

I heard Delilah's growl, but it wasn't her normal one . . . human or wolf. It was frightened—Delilah, who was never scared, who wasn't just borderline suicidal against an enemy, but flat-out ecstatic kamikaze all the way. She didn't fear pain or death. I thought she didn't fear anything, but I was wrong. I wasn't the only one. "He is *wrong*," she snarled. "Unnatural. Unclean."

I could smell it, what she smelled. Even on my stomach, facedown in the dirt, I could smell it. It had lingered around the coffin, but his odor this close . . . It could choke you. It was rotting flesh and disease and mass graves sweltering under a hot sun, but beyond that—beyond *who* he was to *what* he was, it was alien. Delilah was right. He was wrong and unnatural. Even the Auphe, twisted monsters that they were, had belonged here. They'd died elsewhere, but they'd risen from this earth. As much as you wanted to deny they were natural, they were actually nature at its most effective. Suyolak was outside nature; a mistake that could destroy what had accidentally spawned a creature it had no hold over. Nature had been an ant creating the foot that would crush it.

I had no idea what was in the dirt I was inhaling, but it must've been some potent stuff. Philosophical thoughts in a not-so-philosophical situation by the farthest thing from a philosopher as you could fucking find. Suyolak was one huge-ass mistake. Didn't need to say more than that. I got my hands under me and started to push up as I felt a hand tangle in the back of my jacket and pull me the rest of the way. Not to my feet, which was asking a little much right then, but to my knees. "What . . . the hell . . . was that?" I tasted blood in my mouth and I was hoping it was from a split lip or broken nose, because both of those were better than nearly anything Suyolak could dream up.

Niko decided that if I could talk, I could stand after all and finished the job by pulling me to my feet. He was right. I weaved, even with his hand still holding me up, but I did stay up. Niko was the rock that at times held me up and at other times could take me down as efficiently as Suyolak had—which reminded me. "What was that?" I repeated, wiping dirt and blood from my face.

"A distraction," Rafferty answered, his shaggy hair tangling in the wind.

A distraction could be good. If I'd distracted Suyolak enough that he'd swatted me with his antihealer mojo, then Rafferty might have been able to swat him right back—only harder. I looked past him. Shit. Suyolak was still standing, still grinning, looking so much the cheerful Rom, so like our mother, he could've been her slightly more sociopathic cousin. With hair grown long in the coffin and a face that was meant to attract the unwary, to anyone but us he would look like a god come to Earth. To me, he looked like a trap. One thing he didn't look was one bit distracted, which meant I was the one distracting Rafferty, not Suyolak—and that wasn't the best idea I'd ever had.

"Why the hell didn't you take him while he was doing the same to me?" I held on to my gun stubbornly. I might be the fly and Suyolak the swatter, but that didn't mean I was going to be flattened without getting off at least one round—not next time.

"Probably because if he had, you'd have done more than hit the ground. You wouldn't have gotten back up again," Niko said as he steadied me.

"I took only one or two beats of your heart." Suyolak raised his voice over the growling that was still coming from Delilah and had been joined by those of Catcher. "You do not miss them now, do you? One or two seconds of your life. Believe me, by the time I am finished here, you'll be glad to die those few seconds sooner than the rest."

Now Rafferty did split enough of his attention to the nearest warm body. It happened to be Goodfellow. He took his arm and pushed him toward Catcher. "Hang on to him. You might need some help, but do it. He's okay now, but that could change when it all starts. It could flip a switch and I don't want him any closer to Suyolak." He took Catcher's face, gripping the fur on both sides, focusing on him. "I've got one chance at this, Catch. I can do this, but not if you go Cujo on me, okay?" The growling and snarling had stopped and Catcher regarded him with an eerie silence before pressing his nose into his cousin's hair, snuffling, and then blowing out air in an aggrieved sigh. But he stayed put, aggrieved meaning agreeing if not particularly liking it.

"Good." Rafferty straightened. "The rest of you stay back and out of the way. That's the best thing you can do for me. I've got more power up between you and him. Hopefully he won't get through again if you don't give him reason to. He wants me first." With that, he moved toward Suyolak and away from us. Ill-tempered and bossy to the end, that's who he was. Cranky I could understand, but telling me what to do, that wasn't going to fly. Like him, I'd gone up against creatures better than I was, and I'd survived, but that was only because I'd always had help. Without the last, I still would've gotten the job done, but I wouldn't have walked away to tell the tale. We'd gotten Rafferty into this. It would be a piss-poor partnership if we didn't help him to live to pass through and see the other side of it.

The hand that had been holding me up now moved to my shoulder to hold me back. "Wait," Niko ordered.

I hadn't moved. There was a time to make your move. If you were good, you knew it when it came. There were many things I wasn't especially good at in life: handling customer relations, dealing with relations of any kind, keeping the smart-ass in check, not recognizing addiction when it bit me and everyone around me in the ass. But one thing I did know was the right time. The shot I'd tried to take at Suyolak hadn't been it. That had been the first punch in the first round. That wasn't the moment I was talking about. Our moment in this game now was the last ditch, now-or-never-again time that you had to take or you wouldn't live to take anything else. I knew it because Nik had taught me to know it . . . and being half predator—more than half, whichever—that didn't hurt either.

We were waiting for the end of the line, and we weren't there yet. "You're embarrassing me in front of the other kids, Mom," I grumbled.

"I feel for you," he commented wryly. But he let his hand drop away, because he trusted me. It was impossible to fathom how he kept that trust day after day when my subconscious was determined to do everything it could to deserve anything except that trust—or maybe it wasn't so much trust as acceptance, unconditional and never-ending. I'd been wrong earlier when I'd thought I hadn't felt lucky since I was five. I should've felt lucky every single day of my life.

"I wish someone felt for me," Robin complained with a sneeze. He was crouched beside Catcher with one arm hooked around the Wolf's neck. "Felt for me, felt *of* me. Anything at this time would be welcome, because I had much higher hopes of this ending with me not dead. So any fondling or groping would be welcome." Catcher turned and gave him one broad lick across the mouth and nose before going back to snarling and staring at the two healers approaching each other. "Not what I had in mind, but the effort is . . . ah . . . appreciated, thank you." Goodfellow scrubbed his face with his sleeve.

"You should've said more in your call to Ishiah," Niko said, moving to stand beside me now that I could actually stand on my own. "If you can actually consider monogamy, then you owed Ishiah more than a weak excuse for a good-bye." Niko, like me, did understand the impossible nature of a good-bye, but unlike me, had the balls and the spine to tell someone else to go above and beyond.

"Your brother might need a mommy, but I do not," Robin shot back stiffly, still hanging on to Catcher. He didn't need a mommy, but it looked as if he had one huge teddy bear. "When I tell Ishiah . . . Whatever I plan on telling him, it won't be only because I don't think I'll be around later for the consequences. He deserves better than that."

"Not soap opera. *Battle*. Be ready," Delilah contributed with an impatient toss of white hair and a deep rumble in her throat that outdid Catcher's. "Humans, pucks, even *Auphe*. Hopeless all." Delilah, who didn't trust anyone but herself and didn't want to; whole and complete within herself, that's what she thought. She was the unlucky one, but I didn't think she'd ever know it.

Catcher moaned. He knew what it was to be lucky, to have someone—family or otherwise—and that meant what he was now seeing had to be his worst nightmare: Rafferty and Suyolak coming together.

The moon had risen behind the antihealer. It was the same moon from my dream. Huge and orange, shedding the light of a forest fire down on us. It hardly ever looked like that in summer. I took it as a sign that fate was feeling particularly bitchy, giving a nightmare-perfect background to another nightmare, the one we were facing. Suyolak spread his arms under it. "So long has it been since I've seen the sky. So long has it been that I walked in a world that had never seen my like"—he lowered his arms and finished lazily—"and is now seeing it again, Wolf."

Rafferty staggered. I smelled the blood he spat on the ground in front of him, but he didn't fall. He wiped his mouth. I saw the dark stain on his hand. He spat again. More blood.

"It was called consumption in my day. Now you call it"—Suyolak tipped his head to one side as if listening, picking the term from a mind—"tuberculosis. It is an ugly word for such an elegant process that eats your lungs small bite by bite. A tiny predator ranging wild within. Marvel at the beauty of it."

Marvel. Jesus.

Straightening, Rafferty said, "We cured that a long time ago, asshole. And you talk too much." His voice was clear, not thick and choking, and the rest of us weren't dead on the ground. That meant he was holding his own. "Here's something new for you."

This time Suyolak was the one to stumble. It was only a few inches back and he stayed on his feet, but the blood that poured from his nose and mouth cheered me up some. He coughed, holding up a hand toward us, palm out. Whatever was behind that hand stopped Rafferty after a single step, one he'd been quick to take. He was a healer, but he was a Wolf too. He could kill with his mind and he could kill with his hands. With Suyolak he'd use whichever one would do the job.

"Ah, this . . . one." Suyolak lifted his head to grin with teeth now coated black in the moonlight. "This one is a thing of magnificence." The blood stopped. "What do you call this then? Ebola? Hemorrhagic fever? A fitting name for a glory I'd not even dreamed of." The grin widened. "I approve." This time Rafferty didn't just stagger; he almost fell, and I didn't want to even guess what kind of god-awful disease he was fighting. Leprosy. Smallpox. Suyolak's blue plate special, the plague.

"Goddamn it," I muttered. "Why doesn't he just go for the heart like he did to me?"

"I imagine that's quite thoroughly protected as Rafferty is protecting his and ours. They most likely have only the tiniest cracks that are weak enough to attack."

Niko's comment didn't satisfy Delilah. "No manner to fight." She paced the area behind us. "Throwing *germs*." There was a righteous disgust in her voice. "It is wrong. To stand aside. Wrong. Want to fight. Want to bite. Want to kill." Catcher was picking up on her bloodlust, his growls growing wilder.

I grabbed Delilah's arm as she passed to yank her to a stop. "Quit it. If you send Catcher off the deep end, you might distract Rafferty, and then we'll all be spreading the news about how festive Ebola is. If we survive this, you'll have plenty of other things to kill." One of them might be me, but there was a time and a place to worry about that. It wasn't now.

She threw my arm off. "It is not just the kill. It is the battle. The fight. I am Wolf, not sheep. I do not *stand*. I do not *wait*. I *fight*."

"Then look over your shoulder," Robin said, hanging on to Catcher for all he was worth. "You're about to get ten years of birthday wishes all in one. And thanks so very much by the way. It's just what we needed on top of the oh-so-entertaining parade of diseases throughout history."

Too agitated to pick up their scent or unable to detect it over Suyolak's own, Delilah hadn't smelled them coming—neither she nor Catcher. The Ördögs were

back. Or since we'd killed all of the others that had
come out of the truck the day before . . . hell, not the day
before . . . this morning. It had been this morning. Talk
about one long damn day. Time was so raveled in knots,
I honestly couldn't tell one day from the next, but it had
been this morning. It had been today—the day that I'd
argued with Delilah, eaten a Big Mac, then a deer, lost a
piece of what humanity I had left, and now it was time
to fight for my life . . . again. The army thought they did
more before nine a.m. than most do all day. Well, they
could get in line.

No, these Ördögs weren't from the truck or the creek
where we'd killed the others. There were more this time
and they looked . . . full . . . their sunken bellies now
bulging with food. From their appearance, they'd had at
least the entire day to hunt for prey and that would only
make them quicker and stronger than the last. Suyolak
hadn't chosen this place at random. Whether he'd gotten the location from the dead professor's mind or just
felt the huge area teeming with life, he had picked the
park; he had the Ördögs waiting. I thought he'd under-
estimated the seals, as Abelia had overestimated herself,
and had the truck pass it by until he could get out of the
coffin.

Or, out of the kindness of his heart, he'd waited to
wreak death and destruction until the noncamping areas of the park were empty. That, I sincerely doubted.
We used to have a neighbor when I was ten, for a few
months before we moved again as we always did. She
was pear shaped, her hair always in rollers, and she had
a mouth so small and pursed, she could've doubled as a
nickel slot machine. She'd once told me, as she crushed
a cigarette under one large rubber flip-flop, that I was
no better than I had to be. I hadn't gotten that as a kid,
and Niko for once hadn't felt the need to explain it to
me. No better than I had to be; seriously, what did that

mean? I'd long since learned what it meant, and I knew Suyolak was no better than he had to be either, certainly no kinder than he had to be.

And that wasn't kind at all. We were lucky we weren't hip deep in tourist corpses—instead of being hip deep in all-too-alive Ördögs. But better than all that, just too fucking good to be true, were the Wolves behind them. Ten of them: nine in lupine form and one still wearing his human suit in the midst of them all.

"Cabal," Delilah announced with a mixture of disdain and what sounded like reluctant pride. "Pack leader. Mine."

I understood the emotions then. Disdain because traditionally Alphas were male and that was not a tradition Delilah embraced. She wanted to be Alpha and, despite not being male or a high breed, and being a believer in the All Wolf on top of it all, I'd have put my money on her. That was before I'd come into the picture, and, it being a particular talent of mine, I was the straw that broke the camel's back. A female, maybe; an All Wolf, chances were slim. Screwed an Auphe—if that wasn't the sole reason the dictionary had the word anathema in it, you'd have to show me proof otherwise.

As for the pride part of her emotion, she might want to kill him and take his place, prove herself worthy, but if you were a Wolf, your pride also rested in your Alpha. He represented your pack. He *was* your pack. Every day was the day you hoped to end his reign and begin yours, but until then he was as the world saw you—the Wolf world. He was you.

"You called them here," Niko said to Delilah, not as an accusation but as a fact.

"Yeah, she did." I wasn't any more surprised than he was. I wasn't disappointed either. I wasn't hypocrite enough to let myself be. I'd known all along what she was, and I'd known this was more than likely coming.

But I thought it would be Delilah herself. Death was personal to her and a thrill she wouldn't care to share with anyone but her victim.

But I was wrong; right and wrong, but wrong in a way that didn't necessarily help me out.

"Yes. I call." She cupped my cheek. "I told them you too much for me." Her smile was bright and mocking. "They believed. They believe anyone too much for me, then they deserve to die. I call twice a day as Cabal orders. I call and they follow. I do this because I know, *you* are too much for them. My duty to my pack complete and you still live. It is a good plan."

It was a good one. If we fought off her pack and, more ideally, her Alpha, Delilah was free and clear. I felt a relief I didn't want to admit to, but admit it I did. I had too few people in my life. I didn't want to lose one. Delilah had done as her Alpha had asked: She had delivered me up, and if he and the pack couldn't manage to chew me up and swallow me down, then maybe they should start hunting little furry bunnies or the ferocious squirrel. She'd be happy to tell the survivors so—if she spared any. Werewolves, like ordinary wolves, were pack creatures. They were drawn to one another, the majority of them, but there were always exceptions—lone wolves. Delilah was a loner through and through. She was only pack as a career choice. She was Kin before she was Wolf; she was Kin before she was anything.

Yeah, it was a good plan, a perfectly Kin plan.

If it had been her only plan, things could've ended better.

Cabal didn't waste any words. Raising his hand, he motioned imperiously for Delilah to join them. He was in his mid-thirties with what was probably thick silver hair, wolf silver, shorn short. In the moonlight, it, like everything, had an orange tint. He had a thick build, with broad shoulders, and large hands that could strangle the life out of two people at once without changing form. I couldn't make out the color of his eyes, but as I didn't plan on staring into them soulfully and asking him on a date, that didn't much matter. In spite of his build, he looked as if he'd be quick—quick and lethal. That wasn't a guess. It was a fact. He wouldn't be Alpha if he weren't. But he wouldn't be the first Alpha I'd had a hand in killing and that Alpha, Cerberus, could've eaten this guy in three bites with one head while conducting Kin business with the other. You really hadn't seen anything until you'd seen a two-headed Wolf.

Delilah shook her head at her Alpha's beckoning. "I fight the cute foxes, Cabal. The Auphe, he is yours. A challenge. My gift."

Her words were phrased so Cabal couldn't refuse, for if he refused this "gift," he would lose his pack's respect. And if he lost that, then Delilah wouldn't be the only one jumping at the chance to replace him. Every member of the pack would look at him with different, dubious, opportunistic eyes. No Alpha could afford that. He bared human teeth and growled. It was a signal to his pack and they flowed forward, side by side among the Ördögs. It was a companionable joining. The Ördögs had their objective and it was the same as the Wolves. It was too bad for the Wolves that they didn't realize what might be waiting for them if they did kill us. While they had to smell Suyolak, they apparently had no idea how much worse he was than I could be.

For now.

Not that that would happen, a Wolf taking me down. Delilah was right. Suyolak might be too much for me, but I was too much for your average Wolf. Whether Cabal was above average or not, we'd see—if the Plague of the World didn't get me first.

I shifted my focus back to the healer battle. Both Rafferty and Suyolak were dripping with blood, but Raf-

ferty was wavering, weaving as if he were drunk. He was
fighting and having to protect us all at once . . . and he
wasn't as good as Suyolak. He'd told us so. Now he was
showing the toll of doing double duty. But he'd also said
he could stop the bastard. Right now we didn't have any
other choice but to believe him.

The Ördögs and the Wolves were seconds from
sweeping over us. I aimed the Eagle with one hand and
tugged Niko's braid with the other. He didn't need to
have his attention sidetracked by double duty the same
as Rafferty. "I'll be fine, Cyrano. Only adult, responsible
decisions." Allowing Delilah along had been adult—the
rated XXX kind of adult, and perhaps not the most responsible thing. I thought she'd wait until it was all over
to make her move, not in the midst of it. Although the
move had turned out to be for me instead of against me,
it was damn inconvenient all the same—and truthfully,
the move was more for her than for me. Whether her
pack died or I did, she still won.

"I know you will." The response was prompt and
confident; his sword was between him and the leaping
horde.

"Because you're my brother or because you'll kick
my ass if I don't?" I shot two Ördögs in the head, fifty
or so feet out. They fell so quickly, their eyes so instantly
empty, it was hard to picture them having been alive at
all.

"Both," he answered matter-of-factly before con-
tinuing. "Don't forget either option. Goodfellow, keep
Catcher out of this if possible."

Keeping a Wolf, especially one with only the loosest
hold on his mind, would've been a trick, but it was one
Robin didn't have to pull off. It was too late; the Catcher
we knew was temporarily on vacation ... gone... and the
body that had held him was gone as well—into the midst
of the Ördögs and the other Wolves, ripping and tearing

flesh right and left. It could've been worse. He could've gone after Suyolak. Delilah was a fraction of a moment behind him. She'd shed her leathers for fur in seconds and was as caught up in the fight as Catcher. Luckily he was the only red Wolf in the mix. That could've been awkward. Shooting your ally's cousin. Rafferty wouldn't be any more forgiving of that than I imagined I would be if someone took out Nik for being one of too many blonds in a crowd.

I hit the ground as two Ördögs sailed over me, missing me by inches. I heard them hiss and mutter in annoyance. "Food. Food gone. Food hide. Food like rabbit." That was fine. Insult me all you want in a fight. I did it too, but it was only worth doing if you were the one walking away afterward. As they turned, literally in midair before landing—bodies slithering into a serpentine U—I shot them both. Other than bleeding and dying in the next breath, they had no further comment. In that same moment I was hit from the side by a big gray Wolf. When you couldn't get your gun up in time, there was one move to save your throat from being ripped out. I'd done it before, but it didn't mean I looked forward to doing it again. It worked, but it hurt like hell.

I rammed my forearm into the Wolf's open jaws, back to the teeth that ground bone, not the ones up front made for tearing the meat. It kept my throat in one piece and let me put one bullet into its right eye. Werewolves were tough and could recover from most wounds, but the brain and the heart were as vulnerable as a human's. Lead also did the job fine and was a whole lot cheaper than silver.

I kicked the body off me and was back up a split second before going down under three Ördögs. You wouldn't think at the time, Christ, this was not my damn day. A murderous antihealer, a failing good healer, werewolves, Ördögs, and give a guy a break already. No, you might

think that later ... if you survived ... while lying in bed
nursing your wounds, because that was easier to swallow than what you actually thought at the time, which
would be more of a less manly "Shitshitshitshitshit." But
that didn't sound quite as macho, so you ran through the
things you would've thought, might've mentally said, if
you hadn't been A) fighting for your life and B) not to
be repetitive, but *fighting for your fucking life*.

My other hand already held my favorite revenant
slicing combat knife. I sliced one sleek black body from
jaw to tail and the fact it moaned, "No. Hurts. Hurts,"
made me hesitate for less than a second before shooting the other two. I made it to my feet again, wearing a
good deal of the Ördög I'd all but turned inside out, and
this time, instead of being a target, I saw another one.
A brown Wolf, a damn big one even by Wolf standards,
was in midleap toward Niko's back. Nik was taking care
of four more Ördögs facing him and two more to the
side. That didn't mean he wasn't aware of the Wolf and
it didn't mean he couldn't take care of the Wolf, but he
had a lot on his plate. I didn't like to take chances if I
didn't have to, not when I had so few to take. I hit the
Wolf from the side and rode it to the ground while pulling the trigger and putting one in its heart.

"Your charity, not that I need it, is appreciated."
Niko's back hit mine as I climbed, again, to my feet. We
were ringed by Ördögs and three more Wolves. We'd
faced worse ... not more times than I could count. I
could in fact count the times our asses hadn't been quite
so far up the creek, but there had been a few worse, and
I didn't doubt we could handle this ... until I heard the
gunshot. I looked in confusion at my finger on the trigger on a gun that abruptly felt heavy. My finger hadn't
moved. I hadn't fired the shot, and no one else was carrying a gun.

And how had I gotten on the ground? I hadn't lost

my gun. *Never lose your gun.* Over and over, Nik had told me that, because I wasn't like him. I wasn't Bruce Lee with an honorary license to kill from Her Majesty's Secret Service. I was . . . I coughed and tasted blood. I was a good fighter hand to . . . shit . . . hand? Tentacle? Paw? Whatever I was up against, I could give it a run for its money, unless it was human, and then I could kill it without much effort. I'd never killed a human with my bare hands . . . not yet. I could, though, but I'd never be as good as my brother and he knew it. Always hold on to your weapon, he told me, and there was that shitshit-shitshit again when I finally realized.

Someone had shot me.

"Traitor!" The howls began. "No Wolf is such a coward. No Wolf kills out of reach. No Wolf." The howls were everywhere now. "You are not a true Wolf. You are not our Alpha. You are *not* Wolf."

It wasn't Delilah's voice. It wasn't a single voice either. Three, maybe four. The rest of the pack, those left alive. They didn't sound happy with Cabal. No, not happy at all. A white Wolf leaped over me and was gone—on a mission, not from Buddha, but I heard the sounds of that mission being completed. Snarls and growl after growl that would send shivers down your spine at how it took up every molecule of air around us. They call them a pack of wolves. They should call them a storm. A storm of wolves rolling over an ex-Alpha to wash this place clean of him. I didn't shiver at the sound; I didn't have the energy. I swallowed blood, touched my chest to feel more of it, and resumed my standard shit . . . shit . . . shit—only slower and with less enthusiasm.

Besides the sounds of Wolves fighting one another and dying, I heard the slice of metal sizzling through the air to hit flesh with a meaty thud. "How is he?" The voice cracked. "Merciful Charon, turn away. Another time we need a thrice-damned healer and he's currently occupied dying himself." Robin ... Robin talking about Rafferty's dying, talking about my dying. Well, hell, give a guy the benefit of the doubt. But it was also Robin protecting me while I was down, giving Niko a chance to check me out. Because there was nothing else for Nik to do. Like Robin with Ish, Niko couldn't say good-bye. He'd done it once. I didn't think he could ever say that again.

The moon gone from orange to red radiated a light so bloody, I wouldn't have known where my own ended and the light began. Did I really want to see it pouring out of me that badly? Wasn't suffocating in it enough?

"Cal." Hands pulled me up so damn carefully until my head and upper shoulders were supported against him. Nik, on his knees, bent down the rest of the way to murmur in my ear. "It's all right. Cabal shot you, but it's all right. Rafferty will heal you." Because Niko could never admit to himself again that I could die on him. It took months to drag him back from the hallucination of it, back to himself. I refused to let him go back there again. I wouldn't let Cabal put him back there for real.

Cabal, a Wolf with a gun ... a Wolf with a gun and damn good aim. His pack was right. That wasn't the Wolf way. My reputation preceded me and that had caused a Wolf to do what a Wolf would not do, which in turn had a bullet proceeding into my chest ... into one of my lungs from the blood that kept rising in my throat. Preceding and proceeding and hadn't he bothered once to look past me to see the real monster? Rafferty was dying, Robin had said, and Niko refused to believe. If Rafferty did die, Suyolak would kill us all ... to a man and to a Wolf, and my keeping my brother sane, instead of the usual other way around, wouldn't be a problem.

Niko's hand rested on my chest. I saw the dark fluid that ran between his fingers, instantly covering his hand. With his other, he dug in my left jeans pocket. "Messy. I can always depend on you to be so damn messy . . . yes. Your sheer lazy ways save your life. Why am I not surprised?" He pulled out a Twinkie wrapper, uncovered the wound by pulling up my shirt with bloody fingers, and spread the plastic wrapper to cover the gunshot wound with it. The air that had been whistling in and out stopped. A Hostess wrapper wasn't the next best thing to sterile, especially with a bit of crème still left on it, but it did get the job done. I could breathe the tiniest bit better. One death by sucking chest wound slightly delayed. Go team.

Nik kept his hand pressed to the wound, keeping the plastic airtight. "Rafferty, now. Kill that bastard *now!*" The Ördögs were dying in droves around us, Robin no longer looking as if he didn't know what to do with his sword. He was an avenging angel, righteous with fury. An avenging, very horny angel. Ishiah was rubbing off on him, the avenging part at least. The metal flashes of the blade were so fast, so damn quick, I didn't know if I saw it at all or if it was the streaks of light that heralded the darkness of approaching unconsciousness.

"Nik?"

He looked down at me, grim and furious, at fate . . . at me. I didn't blame him either way.

Six months ago I had died . . . only I hadn't.

And I didn't plan on doing it for real this soon either. I wouldn't put him through that again. Not now. Not for as long as I could avoid it. I wouldn't do that to my brother. That was the easy way out, and while I liked easy, for Nik, I would and could do the impossible.

I wasn't going to die and neither was Rafferty.

I spoke again before he could, feeling the blood trickle down from the corners of my mouth, hearing the faint gurgle behind my words. "I fought with . . . my girlfriend today." I sucked in a breath and kept going. "Ate a Big Mac. Lost part . . . of me. A good part. Human part.

I fought . . . for my . . . life." I grinned at him, more blood in the back of my throat, rising higher. "Don't you . . . fucking dare . . . think I'm . . . done yet."

His hand, calloused from years of training, fighting, weapons sparring, rested on my forehead. "Promise, you bastard?" His mouth had always been home to the most fleeting of smiles, the wry quirk of lips, the angry line when someone crossed his, the twist of pain, the curve of belief. It was curved now. He believed. Of all the times I'd almost died, I wasn't going to let a simple bullet accomplish where far less mundane motherfuckers had failed.

"Promise." My grin became something else—not the grin of a little brother, but one of what Rafferty had labeled me: old and new; chaos and control. I let my head fall to one side to see Rafferty and Suyolak. Rafferty was on his knees. Good, ruthless, and maybe he could've taken Suyolak if it hadn't been for Catcher and the rest of us pulling him into the depths like an anchor. He was on his knees protecting us while he had one breath left in him, but protecting *and* fighting were too much against the Plague of the World.

Too bad I was the Plague of the World as well or what was left of them. Or better yet, something the world had never seen. Suyolak was wrong. It had seen him, a long time ago. It had only just seen me, the new me.

Something old, something new, something unlike anything on this earth. I would keep one promise to Nik, I thought, but I'd have to break another to do it. I'd thought I'd need a compelling reason or an act of God to open another gate.

Suyolak was the compelling reason.

I was the act of God.

I couldn't open one and appear next to Suyolak to shoot him before he stopped my heart. He would kill me before I pulled the trigger as much as I'd wanted to

believe differently. He'd kill me if I even aimed my gun.
But he couldn't kill me before a thought was sent flying
his way. After maybe, but there'd be no after for him.
There was something I could do all right . . . something
he wouldn't anticipate. Something no one would think
of. Something I'd only this moment thought of. Something *fun*.

I opened the gate.

I opened it in him . . . inside of him.

Ever see Fourth of July fireworks?

This was better. He glowed, bright as the scarlet
moon, then brighter, brilliant as the sun, if the sun were
an explosion of blinding silver light. Now there was a
silver lining to a dark day. The light shone through his
skin, his eyes, his open mouth as he screamed. And he
did scream, the Plague of the World. He screamed until
every Ördög and Wolf left screamed with him.

Me?

I laughed. It wasn't much of a laugh as it fought its
way through the tide of blood. Fun? Goddamn, yes, it
was fun. I meant it, too, and I felt it in every part of me.
He'd been a disease that had enjoyed every death he'd
caused. Rafferty was supposed to be his cure. I wasn't
anything close to a cure. I was the fire that made the
scorched-earth policy what it was. If you burned it, you
killed it. If you ripped a hole in reality that sucked the
majority of Suyolak's internal organs and torso into a
radioactive dimension that no one had the key to but
me, it was close enough.

He exploded. Fourth of July again. This time it
was one big-ass M-80, those brutes no self-respecting
adult would let a kid have. We hadn't known any self-
respecting adults when I was at the age when blowing up
things was damn cool. I was twenty-one now and it was
still damn cool. There was nothing left of Suyolak but
arms, one leg, and his head lying on the ground with the

amputation marks cauterized to a crunchy bacon crisp. I'd never been the freak—the Frankenstein's monster—who cared about the neatness of my kills, but this time I did a nice job. Good for me. A for effort.

My grin faded when I saw Rafferty drop to his knees, grab the head, and then lift Suyolak face-to-face. There was the moon, but moonlight can be deceiving. I saw it, but I didn't want to believe it. So I blamed it on the night and the shadows cast by the gory moon. I didn't see Suyolak blink . . . although he did. I didn't see Rafferty's fingers sink through hair, flesh, and bone up to his knuckles, but they did. He wasn't only mentally in Suyolak's brain—he was physically there too. And suddenly the good time of watching Suyolak go to pieces in the most literal way passed and I slurred, "That's so . . . not . . . right."

"No, it is not, but it might be necessary and that's good enough for me." Niko called sharply, "Rafferty! Now! We need you now!"

The healer turned and I could see red-amber eyes turn Rom black and then back. Suyolak's own eyes filmed a solid white and his head tumbled toward the ground, dust before it made it there. Rafferty was done with him. He had what he'd wanted all along: Suyolak. That was what made him tick—what made him creation and death all tangled into one immense tidal wave of power.

He moved to my side and knelt. "Great. What did you do? Shoot yourself?" His hand replaced Niko's.

"Yeah." The word was wet, as soaked as the oxygen in my lungs. Where he'd saved me from drowning in my own mucus before, now he had to stop me from drowning in my blood. No matter in what you drowned, the sensation sucked. "Watching . . . you pretend . . . to fight . . . made . . . me"—I gulped air—"suicidal."

"You did a good job of it," he grumped, enough like

his old self that I almost forgot the flash of Suyolak that had passed through his eyes. But monsters, we always knew one another. He was Rafferty, but he had something else in him now: a reaper. He was a healer harboring a grim reaper and he couldn't live like that. But right then I didn't feel like I could live at all. It might be better to concentrate on that. I'd told myself I wasn't letting Nik down and I meant it.

His other hand rested on the side of my head. "And you went and built another gate. After I practically rewired you. Now not only are you bleeding out, but your blood pressure is all but liquefying your brain and making you bleed out even faster while your temperature would blow up a thermometer."

"Like . . . Suyolak." I closed my eyes and curled my lips. "Boom."

"Boom all right." Robin was on my other side now. All the Ördögs were gone. When their master had died, they'd given one last shriek that shook the trees left standing and had poured away into the darkness. "Please endeavor not to get drunk and try that as a party trick. I don't wish to be a five-hundred-piece puzzle with four hundred ninety-seven pieces missing. I would greatly appreciate the restraint. But if you must, there is one piece I wish you to promise to leave in place. I believe you know the one I refer to. That would be the glory that is . . ."

"Mercy killing." I shaped the words to Rafferty, to Niko . . . anyone who could get the job done. My head hurt, I couldn't breathe, and I was racked with cold from the fever. And through all that, Robin's voice was still able to cut like a knife. It was comforting. Locations change, enemies change, even my wiring changed, but Goodfellow, his mouth would never change.

There was a snort in the darkness. "Like you deserve a mercy killing. Not today. Sorry about your luck," Rafferty sniped. Then the heat that flared in his hand on my chest arced through me to the one on my head. I didn't know if I was glowing like Suyolak had when my gate had gobbled him up, but I felt as if I was. I felt like the sun . . . hot, intense, and far up in the sky. Floating. Not that the sun floated, but I did. And the air that I floated in flowed in and out of my lungs. The pain was gone too, as were the headache and fever. Rafferty had given me that last gate for free.

I opened my eyes and saw the blackness of Suyolak shadowed behind Rafferty's eyes. "It's good, isn't it?" I said knowingly. "Being bad. Ironic, huh?" I coughed and was pushed up in time for the residual blood to spray on my jeans.

"He's in there. In you." Niko reached over and almost touched the healer's forehead, but at the last minute decided against it. "You were supposed to cure the world by killing him."

"Instead you ate him." There was blood all over my shirt and, black cotton or not, the color wasn't helping. I felt the warm stickiness of it everywhere. I peeled it off over my head, then wrapped my no-longer wolf-gnawed arm—Rafferty had healed that too—around Niko's shoulder and we were up. I got my "living legs" under me again. "Did he taste good?" I asked as if I genuinely wanted to know. And, darkly . . . dreadfully, I did.

"I can't imagine that he did. Death, any death, is not a taste anyone should want, crave, or have." Robin hadn't lowered his sword. "You were to be the cure, not the replacement."

"It's for Catcher. With what I took from that murderous bastard I can bring Catcher back. It's worth it, and when I'm done, I'll get rid of the rest of Suyolak. And that's the way it's going to fucking be, got it?" Rafferty snapped, a wolf snap—one with flashing teeth.

He started to stand until I caught him by the arm

and caught him quickly—a little too quickly. I'd noticed that. I kept getting quicker and quicker. "Could you—" I ducked my head to swallow the growl that wanted out, but the Auphe in me could growl all it wanted. On this, I ruled. I pulled Rafferty closer and asked my question close to his ear—where no one could hear if the answer was no. So no one could feel sorry for me, because that's the last damn thing I wanted.

He considered my request. "Yeah, maybe. I can't guarantee they'll stay that way, but I'll try." His hand came up to cover my eyes for a second. One second. He had Suyolak in him all right, a supernatural battery that could level this entire park if that's what Rafferty wanted.

Dropping his hand, he leaned in for a look and grunted. "Good as new, but, like I said, that could change." They were gray again then, no russet or scarlet marring them—but pure gray, the same gray Niko and I had shared all our lives. If someone looked at us, it was the only sign they would see that we were related. I wanted to keep that. I couldn't keep the happy, I couldn't keep the human, but I could keep part of my brother. In the end, that made this a win.

Rafferty had risen immediately after changing my eyes back. He was scanning the area for what it was that he wanted to keep. I hoped he was as lucky as I'd turned out to be. "Catcher? Catch?" He caught sight of the one red Wolf, flanked by a white one, in the middle of more dead Wolves. I'd had the feeling that Delilah wouldn't let there be any survivors. She and the others or just the others had killed Cabal, and Delilah had put down the rest of them. She was born a killer, born a queen, and now she had crowned herself both. I'd known, whichever way that it went, she wasn't going to lose. She never did.

Catcher lifted his head, although I didn't know if he

understood his name or not. He might have recognized the scent of his cousin; the call of the same whispering in his brain. He catapulted toward Rafferty, leaping over bodies, making a sound I couldn't identify except for "happy wolf" roo roo. His fur was even more red under the moon and Delilah moving leisurely in his wake was now a nude human statue carved from amber, her white hair now the color of fire.

Rafferty caught the boisterous Wolf that hit him, nearly bowling him over. "Catch. Concentrate. Come back, okay? I need you. I need you now."

Standing on his back legs with his front hooked over Rafferty's shoulders, Catcher snuffled, his eyes blinked, confused, and he bared his teeth. But then he butted his head against his cousin's chest and left it there for several minutes. The first time that Goodfellow or I tried to say something, Niko knowing better not to, the healer glared us into silence. Finally Catcher looked up, face-to-face, eye to eye. It didn't take a Wolf to see it or a healer. Anyone could see the intelligence in those eyes. Smart guy, he was a smart guy. He knew the scientific names of orchids, had a master's degree in biology, had gone to college, bought a car, had girlfriends, went on spring break, wanted to save the planet. Hogger of fries and Twinkies, he was blazing with intelligence and he was trapped. No one could fix me, but to see his cousin fix him, that would make things a little better, a little brighter.

Rafferty smiled. It wasn't much of one, the faintest movement of his lips, but it was the first I'd seen out of him. It counted. "Okay, Cuz. You're coming home." He rested a hand on each side of Catcher's head, his thumbs curving under the Wolf's eyes, the rest of his fingers cupping the round fur-covered head. I didn't see the energy that passed from Rafferty, but I felt it in the air. At first it was warm . . . the warmth I'd felt when he'd healed me.

I touched the bullet hole in my chest that looked as if it had been healed for years; warm, comforting, right.

But then it wasn't the same anymore. When Catcher didn't change, Rafferty did and what was left of Suyolak came out. This power wasn't the heat and the sun that had coursed through me. This was cold and black. You couldn't see it, but you could feel it. Catcher felt it too. He snarled, thrashed, and ripped his head out of Rafferty's grip. "*No*," Rafferty protested. "Catcher, I'm getting somewhere. I know it." He reached out again and Catcher snapped at him, fastened on to his arm, and drew blood. The right-in-his-head Catcher tore a chunk out of his cousin's arm and looked ready to do worse.

"Catcher." Rafferty clutched the bite and healed it instantly. Back on all fours, Catcher lowered his head, ears back, hackles raised, and showed every tooth he had. "No," the healer asserted, "it's not poisonous. If it can bring you back, it's not poison. It's a cure. Can't you understand that? It's the only cure there is. It's this or nothing. Don't you get that? After all these fucking years, don't you get that?"

Catcher stared at him. They were talking, somehow or another. . . . Hell, the Suyolak way, they were talking the Suyolak way. Rafferty was in Catcher's head as he shook his own. "Catch, no. No. Listen to me."

There was a growl. I'd heard many Wolf growls in my day. Wolves loved to fight, like Delilah, but if they could fight and live, they were satisfied with that. They didn't have the all-or-nothing attitude she did, unless they were taking on their Alpha and it was a kill or be killed situation. There were growls and then there were growls—and the last would be the one where a Wolf chose possible death over dishonor and life.

"Goddamnit, that's not true. I won't cure you by turning into him. We can both live. We can both be ourselves. I'm not trading myself for you," Rafferty said, the desperation he'd kept hidden since I'd known him finally showing.

Catcher stopped growling and simply stared at him. Unblinking. Unmoving.

Rafferty fell to his knees and denied one last time. "No, Catch. I'm not trading the world for you either. I'm not. I wouldn't be like him. I'd get rid of the rest of him before I turned like he turned. I would." The Wolf walked forward three steps and rested his chin on Rafferty's shoulder, his head against the other shaggy auburn head. Rafferty wrapped his arms around Catcher's neck and buried his face in the fur. "I know. I'm lying to you. I'm lying to myself."

I barely heard the words or the ones that came after them, but I did hear them. I didn't know if they made me feel better for the cousins or worse.

"You can't fix what isn't broken." Hoarse but accepting.

"The here and now, it's good. It's what's meant to be. I know—I do. The here and now." He sucked in a deep breath, then straightened before turning away from his cousin enough to plant both hands against the bare earth. Then he released it: Suyolak's power. I couldn't see it, ugly as it was and boiling with death and hunger— the same as before—but I felt it. It passed into earth where nothing grew anyway. In the old days they salted the earth after wars, Niko said, to keep crops from growing, to make the people leave. Not very neighborly. Then again, neither was war. This ground held enough sulfur to keep anything growing to several hundred feet back. It was already dead. What was left of Suyolak wasn't going to make a difference.

And then it was gone. He was gone. Even his arms and legs had turned to dust to be stomped on the next day by a random tourist. Suyolak was nothing but the medium for someone's footprint and I liked the poetry of that just fine. He'd thought he owned the earth and now he'd be nothing more than a footprint on it.

Off to one side, this time too far to hear, I saw Robin making a follow-up call, to say what he couldn't before—not that I could know precisely what he said to Ishiah. I could guess, but with Goodfellow, a guess was the absolute best and worst you could hope for. As I watched him talk, it began to snow—just on Robin . . . snow, in the middle of summer. No. It wasn't snow. It was feathers—white and gold feathers falling from the sky like a cascade of cherry blossom petals that I'd once seen in Central Park that had filled the air like a cloud come to Earth. Talk about when you care enough to send the very best.

Maybe there was a little magic in the world after all.

I looked away, the better to battle off any threat to my testosterone-manufactured stoicism to see Rafferty stand and say, "We're staying here. There are wolves in the park. Not our Wolves, but wolves. It's a good place to run and hunt; a good place to live."

"You're just going to . . ." I stopped. What could I say? *You're not going to give up everything for your family.* What kind of man or Wolf would he be if he didn't? Catcher seemed to know what I was thinking and he gave a lupine sigh. The promise I'd made him to make Rafferty one of us, to give him reason to live, to make him family, it wasn't going to happen. Rafferty had made his own choice. He already had a family and he was staying with it.

After Catcher's sigh of acceptance, the Wolf then perked up his ears and shook his head hard enough that I heard the jingle . . . metal tags ringing against each other. He wasn't going to need that when he answered the call of the wild. I moved forward and slipped the collar over his head. If it were daylight, it would've been fluorescent green with butterflies and dragonflies and about the most ridiculous thing I'd ever seen. "I'll save it for Salome, Catch."

He grinned, blew air out his nose, and held up his front leg, this time for a fist/paw bump instead of a shake. "You take care of your family, fur ball, and I'll take care of mine." We both knew it tended to be the other way around, but we both had our pride.

Rafferty was stripping off his clothes. He didn't say good-bye. He wasn't that kind of guy. "Take care of yourselves. There's no guarantee we'll stay here. We might move up to Canada. You guys play rough. Better sniff out a new healer. A good one. Especially for . . ." He jerked his head toward me. "An apple a day damn sure doesn't keep the Auphe away." He lifted a hand briefly, shimmered, and a wolf stood in his place. During the day you might have been able to tell them apart, but now they looked identical. I only knew Catcher from Rafferty because he stood on the left.

Catcher put his nose up in the air, sampling the wild smells of a wild place, and yipped happily. He grinned at us one last time, tongue lolling—facing the loss of identity, the loss of his whole, but he was at peace. You could see it. If I'd thought about it, I could see he always had been. He'd known how things would end up, but he couldn't take away his cousin's hope, so he'd hung in there as long as he could; as long as Rafferty had needed him to. Now he turned and started to lope toward a far ridge of still-standing trees. Rafferty studied us solemnly with yellow wolf eyes, dipped his muzzle, and swiveled to follow.

That's when Delilah lifted the gun she'd taken from the body of her Alpha—the others had scorned him for it, but she was more open-minded. She knew she couldn't take Catcher, Rafferty, and the rest of us as a Wolf alone. Catcher was running in the lead, and she aimed the semiautomatic at him. That's when I pressed the muzzle of my Eagle to the back of her head. From life, to the edge of death and back, but as trained, I'd never lost my gun along the way.

"No, Delilah."

"There is enough of All Wolf in the Kin to make our own pack bigger than any Kin pack," she said, the gun not wavering. "With Rafferty we could be free; we could be what we should be. Running. Hunting. Gone into the green to never be found again. If Catcher dies, Rafferty has no reason not to help."

Because that was how she would've thought if she'd been in his place. Friends came; friends went. Family came; family died. But she thought wrong. Rafferty wasn't like her, not that it made a difference. He wouldn't have changed her or the others regardless of Catcher's death. He would kill Delilah where she stood, but because he was a Wolf and a cousin, not because he was anything like the Kin. Or anything like Delilah.

I might be Auphe, but I knew good from bad, right from wrong. I might lose that ability as time passed, but at this moment I still knew.

I made my choice. Delilah had saved me . . . in a way. She hadn't tried to kill me. She'd given me a chance by arranging for her pack and her Alpha to die in my place—if I were good enough, benefiting us both, although benefiting her in more ways than one. But Rafferty had saved me more than once; he'd saved me three times—and on occasions of considerable inconvenience. Rafferty saved. Delilah killed. I liked Delilah, but I didn't love her and that was why.

She was too much like me.

"Drop the gun," I said.

She didn't look around, keeping her eye on her running target. "You not kill me, pretty boy," she said with complete confidence. "You not kill what we have, will you?" She thought she knew me, predator to predator.

She thought I would enjoy watching her kill, because Wolves did. There was no better sex for Wolves than sex over a kill.

I wasn't a Wolf. I wasn't Kin. I might be worse one day; I might be worse now. But not with Catcher and Rafferty. Not when it came to them.

I kept the gun against her head and leaned in to whisper at her ear, "You're asking the wrong question, Lilah. You shouldn't be asking me if I'll kill you. You should ask if I'll enjoy it." They say Wolves can smell truth. She knew mine.

Rafferty and Catcher ran on until they disappeared into the darkness. And not a single gunshot was heard.

Not this time.

But there could be a next time. Back home, before there or sometime after, our being alike would result in one of us being dead sooner or later. It was how the game was played, among her kind, Wolf, and among mine, last of the Auphe. For now, she didn't push me and for now, I didn't shoot. And if I wanted to—badly wanted to . . .

No one had to know that but me.

Epilogue

Catcher

My name is Catcher.

I'm running, my brother by my side. No, not really my brother, but he is of my pack and that's the same thing. He saved my life once, years ago. And I'd saved his soul today. He is Rafferty; I remember now, if I'd forgotten for a while during the fight. I remember more. I remember me. I remember my life. I remember how we came to be running toward the trees under a huge bloodred moon. I remember telling my cousin to go live his life and his saying I was his life; that not only had I saved his soul, but that I'd given him one to save; that I was his family, the best part of him.

He was right. Family should always be the best part of one another.

My name is Catcher and I think this is the last time I'll know that. Soon I won't remember that any more than I'll remember fries and birthday cakes. I won't remember a spray of freckles across a beautiful woman's breast and her lips soft under mine. I won't remember my mother's Christmas cookies, the brightly colored birds of the rain forest, card games, skiing a black diamond slope, drinking a six-pack and climbing to the dorm roof to howl at the stars. They are the best memories anyone can have. And I *had* had them. That counted; it did.

But that was then; this is now.

I feel night wind in my fur as I run, the smell of game in the trees, my pack by my side. There's a life to be made here, a good life for a Wolf . . . or only a wolf. There is a cliff up ahead; it's waiting for me.

My name is Catcher.

Finally I'm standing on the edge of that cliff. It's not a cliff beneath my paws, but it is a real one all the same. I don't see it with my eyes. It can't be felt by my flesh, but I can feel it in my mind. I can't see what's below. I'm not afraid, though. I'm not afraid, because I have family at my side. I have my cousin who is my brother. He is my pack. With all that beside me, how could I possibly be afraid?

It is now. It is always now.

Now is good. Now could be the best.

Is the best.

My name is Catcher.

My name was Catcher.

My name . . . my name . . .

I am . . .

I am lost, I am found, and then I am *free* and I am happy.

When I jump over that edge, someone leaps with me, shoulder to shoulder. I smell kinship on him. Kinship is all. I'm not alone.

Never alone.

I land, earth below me, moon above. I am wolf. We are pack.

And that is all I need.

> "*For the strength of the Pack is the Wolf, and the strength of the Wolf is the Pack.*"
> —Rudyard Kipling

ABOUT THE AUTHOR

Rob Thurman lives in Indiana, land of cows and ravenous wild turkeys. Rob is the author of the Cal Leandros Novels: *Nightlife*, *Moonshine*, *Madhouse*, and *Deathwish*; *Trick of the Light*, the first book in the Trickster series; a story in the anthology *Wolfsbane and Mistletoe*; and an upcoming stand-alone novel, *Chimera*.

Besides wild, ravenous turkeys, Rob has a dog (if you don't have a dog, how do you live?)—one hundred pounds of Siberian husky. He looks like a wolf, has paws the size of a person's hand, ice blue eyes, teeth out of a Godzilla movie, and the ferocious habit of hiding under the kitchen table and peeing on himself when strangers come by. By the way, he was adopted from a shelter. He was fully grown, already house-trained, and grateful as hell. Think about it next time you're looking for a Rover or Fluffy.

For updates, teasers, deleted scenes, social networking, and various other extras, visit the author at www.robthurman.net.

TRICK OF THE LIGHT

A Trickster Novel

by

ROB THURMAN

Las Vegas bar owner Trixa Iktomi deals in information. And in a city where unholy creatures roam the neon night, information can mean life or death. Not that she has anything personal against demons. They can be sexy as hell, and they're great for getting the latest gossip—but they also steal human souls and thrive on chaos. So occasionally Trixa has to teach them some manners.

When Trixa learns of a powerful artifact known as the Light of Life, she knows she's hit the jackpot. Both sides—angel and demon—would give anything for it. But first she has to find it. And as Heaven and Hell ready for an apocalyptic throwdown, Trixa must decide where her true loyalty lies—and what she's ready to fight for.

Available wherever books are sold or at penguin.com

NIGHTLIFE

by
ROB THURMAN

WHEN THE SUN GOES DOWN,
IT ALL GOES DOWN...

"There are monsters among us.
There always have been and there always will
be. I've known that ever since I can remember,
just like I've always known I was one...
Well, *half* of one, anyway."

**"A ROARING ROLLERCOASTER OF A READ...
[IT'LL] TAKE YOUR BREATH AWAY."**
—*New York Times* bestselling author
Simon R. Green

Available wherever books are sold or at
penguin.com

MOONSHINE

by
ROB THURMAN

After saving the world from his fiendish father's side
of the family, Cal Leandros and his stalwart half-brother
Niko have settled down with new digs and a new gig—
bodyguard and detective work. And in New York City,
where preternatural beings stalk the streets just like
normal folk, business is good. Their latest case has
them going undercover for the Kin—the werewolf Mafia.
A low-level Kin boss thinks a rival is setting him up for
a fall, and wants proof. The place to start is the back
room of Moonshine—a gambling club for non-humans.
Cal thinks it's a simple in-and-out job.
But Cal is very, very wrong...

Cal and Niko are being set up themselves—and the
people behind it have a bite much worse than
their bark...

**Available wherever books are sold or at
penguin.com**

MADHOUSE

by

ROB THURMAN

Half-human Cal Leandros and his brother Niko aren't exactly prospering with their preternatural detective agency. Who could have guessed that business could dry up in New York City, where vampires, trolls, and other creepy crawlies are all over the place?

But now there's a new arrival in the Big Apple. A malevolent evil with ancient powers is picking off humans like sheep, dead-set on making history with an orgy of blood and murder. And for Cal and Niko, this is one paycheck they're going to have to earn.

"Stunningly original."
—Green Man Review

Available wherever books are sold or at penguin.com

ALSO AVAILABLE

DEATHWISH

by
ROB THURMAN

*In a nightmarish New York City,
life is there for the taking...*

Half-human Cal Leandros and his brother Niko are
hired by the vampire Seamus to find out who has
been following him—until Seamus turns up dead
(or un-undead). Worse still is the return of Cal's
nightmarish family, the Auphe. The last time Cal
and Niko faced them, they were almost wiped out.
Now, the Auphe want revenge. But first, they'll
destroy everything Cal holds dear...

"A subtly warped world."
—Green Man Review

Available wherever books are sold or at
penguin.com